DEBTS OF FIRE

BOOKS BY INTISAR KHANANI

The Sunbolt Chronicles
Sunbolt
Memories of Ash
Debts of Fire

The Dauntless Path
Thorn
The Theft of Sunlight
A Darkness at the Door

THE SUNBOLT CHRONICLES BOOK THREE

DEBTS OF FIRE

INTISAR KHANANI

Snowy Wings PUBLISHING

Library of Congress Cataloging-in-Publication Data
Names: Khanani, Intisar, author.
Title: Debts of Fire / Intisar Khanani.
Series: The Sunbolt Chronicles
Description: Turner, OR: Snowy Wings Publishing, 2025 | Summary: Hitomi returns to the cursed lands located deep within the desert to pay her debts to the phoenix, reuniting with old friends and facing new challenges along the way.
Identifiers: Library of Congress Control Number 2025914950 | ISBN 978-1958051467 (Hardcover) | 978-1958051481 (Large Print) | 978-1958051474 (pbk.) | 978-1958051450 (e-book)
Subjects: LCSH Magic--Fiction. | Coming of age--Fiction. | Bildungsroman. | Fantasy fiction. | Young adult fiction. | BISAC YOUNG ADULT FICTION / Fantasy / General | YOUNG ADULT FICTION / Fantasy / Epic
Classification: LCC PZ7.K52654 Me 2024 | DDC [Fic]--dc23

CHAPTER 1

DAUGHTER OF THE VANISHED

"Vultures circling are a bad thing, right?" I ask, or mean to ask. My grasp of the desert tongue, while better than it has any right to be after I burnt my memories to a crisp a year ago, is still somewhat shaky. I might have called the birds locusts.

Huda and I halt our mounts at the top of a raised pass between desert valleys. Seated a good deal higher up on her camel than my little mare's saddle affords me, Huda shades her eyes and gazes out over the arid landscape. Like me, she wears a black thobe with bands of red and orange embroidery that match the scarf draped over her head. A diamond of tattooed circles shows on her brow and her chin is further inked with sharp, angled lines that mark her a member of the Bani Saqr, just as the embroidery on her thobe does. Mine, on the other hand, was a gift, the designs unknown to me, just as the inkings on my arms are hardly about family.

I turn my attention back to the land as she studies the sky. Here, the desert is all rocky valleys once flooded by ancient lava flows that have left behind a scape of soft-edged black rocks, worn down by centuries of sandstorms. Gaunt hills rise in long, scraggly rows. They sport bare brown faces, nooks and hollows scoured into the layered stone. Thorn bushes dot the valleys and hills alike, and in the lowest depressions, fragile winter grass has taken root. Good grazing, or it will be soon enough, as Huda has informed me.

"There's only one," she says finally. "I think it must be a hawk riding an updraft. Those that eat the dead—vultures—usually fly with their mates."

Whatever I said, it definitely wasn't vulture. I look back up to the bird, and a thread of fear wraps itself around my heart. "It isn't a..." I pause, not sure what a raven is called in the desert tongue. "A bird with black feathers?"

"A crow? No, this has a lighter-colored breast."

My tension dissolves. Crows are much smaller than ravens, but neither have a lighter breast. I'm still safe, the bird above nothing more than it seems. Definitely not the shape-shifting mage who tracks me. "Does it mean anything that it's circling?" I ask her.

In the three days since we left the small caravan stop where I found her after escaping Fidanya, Huda has taken to teaching me what she can while we travel. Our journey has been broken across the days and the nights, Huda happy to travel when I have the energy and rest when I don't, accepting without comment my need for a great deal more rest than when we traveled together less than a fortnight ago. She at least knows by now that I injured my arm, the wound still healing, though I have not spoken of the crossbow bolt that sliced it, or how I ended up in its path. While my injury, and exhaustion, is enough to require a slower pace, I push myself harder with every day.

Thankfully, Huda seems able to traverse these unmarked lands as easily by day with no sign to guide her as she is by night with the stars to light our way. I'm learning to read the stars from her—very badly, and only just. I have no idea how she can travel five or six hours across hills and valleys in broad daylight, never once achieving a straight line, and yet know precisely where she is in relation to our destination.

Huda shrugs, dropping her gaze from the single black dot circling lazily in the steely white sky. "It's hard to say. It may be resting its wings, or watching for goats to flush out smaller prey, or something else."

Just another unknown among many, then. Although, this I do know: if the High Council of Mages and their rogue hunters catch up with us, it will not go well for me.

I have the phoenix and a host of other allies to thank for my life and liberty—including Val, the breather to whom I'm bonded and who got me through my trial before the High Council unscathed, as well as the Lycan Guard who broke me out of the warded room that held me. Thus, my flight into the desert and my plan to meet the phoenix at the Barrier to the Burnt Lands. I owe him a debt three times over, and I intend to pay it. Helping him unravel the centuries-old curses that hold the Burnt Lands in their thrall seems about as bright a future as being caught by the High Council and being made a source slave. The critical difference being I've chosen the phoenix's curses while the High Council is hunting me down.

I cast a glance across the high ridges of the desert, but even with my mage sight, I can't make out the high white dome of the Barrier spells from here. Either we're too far away, or the sun-bleached paleness of the sky makes it too hard to differentiate.

"By evening we should reach the valleys my family may be grazing," Huda says, reading my gaze. "The Barrier will only be a half day's journey from there. We can rest in those valleys, or continue through, as you wish."

"I'd like to see your family," I remind Huda, as I did the last two times we had this conversation. I know I can't delay long, but a full night's rest would be a relief to my aching body. More than that, I want to ensure Huda is near family when I inevitably leave her for the Burnt Lands. I reach up to clasp the simple obsidian ring I wear on a cord around my neck, a gift from the Degaths, the noble family I once helped. It constitutes the single most powerful ward against tracking I've ever seen. Which means, surely, for this little while, all will be well.

At least there have been no signs of pursuit behind us, though I've been careful not to show I'm watching. As much as it chafes to keep secrets from Huda, I'd rather she didn't know the whole of my story. I can pretend it's for her own good—so she can plead ignorance of my crimes should we be caught. In truth, I'm using my friend and I don't want her to know it.

"Come, then," Huda says. She clicks her tongue, urging her camel forward once more. I let my little mare, Zahra, fall in behind, glancing back over the land we've traversed. There's no sign of movement, not even a hawk on the winds. When I turn to face forward, I find Huda watching me over her shoulder. I offer her a hesitant smile. She dips her head, dark eyes thoughtful, and returns her attention to the hillside.

Perhaps I'm not being quite as circumspect as I thought.

WE REACH our destination as the day slides toward evening, the sun hanging low over the rocky hills and sending long shadows across the desert scrub into the valley below. Here are only a scattering of the usual rocks atop dry dirt and a gentle layer of sand. The thorn bushes are more plentiful, as is lower-growing grassy scrub.

Huda sits forward on her camel and scans the valley before us, where the diminutive forms of some forty goats and a few camels rest around a gathering of thorn bushes.

"There," she murmurs just as I spot a pair of desert dwellers moving among the goats, touching backs and heads as they check in on each of their charges for the night.

"Your family?" I ask, frowning as I study the idyllic scene. When I last saw this herd—if it is indeed the same one—it numbered almost sixty.

"That is Sumeyya there, and one of our cousins with her, or perhaps our milk-brother. Come!" She urges her camel forward, grinning broadly, her headscarf flapping as the camel lurches into a run, entering the valley proper. I laugh and let Zahra race after her. I am by no means a practiced horsewoman, but after three days in a saddle, I've gained a great deal of sore muscles, bruises, and a general feel for keeping my seat. It's a good sort of skill.

Sumeyya shouts a greeting with reckless glee and leaves behind her charges to race toward us, leather sandals pattering over the ground, thobe hiked up to her knees and brown legs flashing. It is exactly how she greeted her sister the first time I met her. Huda and I whoop a return as we close the distance. With practiced ease, Huda swings down from her camel as it comes to a stop and embraces her little sister.

There cannot be a more beautiful place than this valley of scrub and sun, filled with the love of these two sisters.

"It is good to see you again, ukhti," Huda says as I clamber down awkwardly from my mount. Everything aches, from my injured arm to my knees to the turn of my ankle.

"I *missed* you," Sumeyya says, her voice muffled by her sister's thobe. "You were gone so long!"

Huda rubs her back. "I had an adventure! And I brought along a friend for you to greet."

Sumeyya twists to focus on me, eyes just a little overbright. "Oh, ahlan! You have come back to us!"

"I have, and I am very happy for it," I agree, as surprised in my way as she is. When I first crossed the desert to Fidanya, it was to rescue my imprisoned mentor and friend, Brigit Stormwind. I never expected to cross paths with Sumeyya again, even if I'd promised the phoenix I would return to try my hand at dismantling the draining spells that hold the Burnt Lands in their grip.

Sumeyya reaches to grasp my hand, preparing to shower me with the requisite kisses to my cheeks that are very much desert tradition.

"Oh, your hands!" she cries. "What lovely inkings!"

My fingers jerk in her grip, and she looks up in surprise.

"Thank you," I tell her, forcing my smile to stay on my lips. This is what I wanted: for people to see my markings merely as tattoos and nothing more. Certainly not as a visible sign of the spell that has made me a source slave. The dark lines of the magical markings spread over the backs of my hands. I've had the spaces between colored with indigo and amethyst and cobalt. The colors are my attempt to camouflage the magical binding that seals my magic within me, making me nothing more than a vessel to channel magic.

The color stops at my wrists—it was all I had time for—but the markings continue up my forearms to my elbows, looking like nothing so much as elegant, scrolled sleeves. On the underside of each arm are inked two red and gold firebirds. The markings were the first step in binding me as a source slave, which would have meant a slow and excruciating death, my power gradually drained by the mage who owned me. They are a tomb manifested upon my arms, with no door and no key. To call them lovely is to admire the claws of the lion as they sink into the gazelle. But Sumeyya doesn't know that, and I cannot show her how terrible they are. So, I simply continue to smile.

Sumeyya squeezes my fingers and stands on her toes to kiss my cheeks thrice. "I didn't mean to pry," she says as she steps back, sounding far more adult than her eleven years.

"Oh no," I reply, my voice light. Prying into a traveler's secrets would violate their guest right among the desert tribes, something even children know is taboo. "I am still just getting used to them. How are you?"

"All praise is due to God," she recites, which could mean she's doing wonderfully, or that she's faced hardships she has no wish to complain about.

Huda's eyes narrow with concern, but instead of inquiring further, she indicates the young man approaching from a distance. "Is that Kareem with you?"

He's tall and slim, no more than eighteen, with the brown skin of the desert folk and delightfully curly hair. A belt at his waist sports a hooked dagger, the lines of his thobe made more elegant by an open-fronted bisht worn over the top. He pauses as a baby goat bounds in front of him, then raises its hooves to bounce off of him.

"Yes," Sumeyya says. "Our brother chose to join me instead of —well, you see, there was a raid."

My attention snaps back to her. *That* is what she didn't wish to complain about?

"What happened?" Huda demands.

"The Bani Essam, of course. We weren't prepared, and they made off with four of our camels and a half-dozen goats."

Understanding flashes in Huda's eyes, a ripple of anger crossing her features before she tucks it all away. The Bani Essam share a border with Huda's people, and a history of bloodshed. Thankfully, when the two of us journeyed through their lands, their warriors treated us as guests and granted us an escort, as Huda demanded of them. Most likely, they are actually my tribe —or had been my father's before they disowned him and he left the desert. Which I suppose is neither here nor there, since they clearly have never cared to claim me.

I take heart from the fact that the raiders could not have included the men we traveled with. Laith and Faris and their companions could not have returned fast enough to have reached the desert and joined a raiding party before we ourselves reached Huda's lands.

"Any deaths?" Huda asks.

"No, and only one injury—our cousin Mahmoud twisted his ankle. He'll be fine soon enough."

Huda's relief is a palpable thing. She murmurs a word of thanksgiving, then says, "Baba has mounted a raid in return, hasn't he?"

Sumeyya shrugs. "They decided to go after a camp rather than follow the raiding party that struck us. The rest of us divided up the goats—if we cannot be safe in the more fertile valleys, then we must take fewer into these other valleys."

Huda nods. "Zainab's wedding will continue as planned, then?"

"Yes, but the goats—" Sumeyya stops herself with a glance at me. "It will be fine, I'm sure."

"Of course," Huda says as Kareem finally reaches us, the wiggly kid cradled in his arms.

"Salaam," Kareem says to us all, and then to me, "wa ahlan wa sahlan." The goat raises its head and bleats once before licking his chin.

Huda expels her breath in a laugh. "Goats instead of raids, akhi?"

He shrugs and sets down the kid. It immediately starts joyfully headbutting his legs. "The raid did not need me. Our sister did."

Huda hmms softly and turns to gesture to me. "This is Hikaru bint Al-Ghaib, guest of the phoenix."

I blink as Kareem inclines his head toward me, and the kid grabs his bisht in its teeth and tugs at him.

Bint Al-Ghaib. Daughter of the Unseen, or perhaps, the Vanished. I suppose it suits me even better than Hikaru, the name I chose with my old mentor, Brigit Stormwind, as a way to protect my identity. When I first met Huda and Sumeyya, it seemed wise to tell them as little as I could about myself. Now that the High Council of Mages has set their rogue hunters on me, it's a good thing my friends can't divulge my birth name, Hitomi.

But "Hikaru" still carries an echo of deceit in it. In truth, I thought I would have to get used to lying about who I was or risk being caught by the High Council once again. But "Bint Al-Ghaib"—that opens up a whole new world of possibility. It is a name that says, simply, that my father, though he might be of the desert, remains unseen—vanished from these lands. Among a people whose identity is rooted in paternal lineage, Huda has fashioned me a name that at once claims me as being of the desert while acknowledging that my lineage remains unseen, unclaimed by any family. It is both a gift and a sorrow I know well.

"This is our milk-brother, Kareem ibn Saleem," Huda tells me. I've heard of this relation before—children who become siblings because they nursed from the same mother, though they might have been born of different parents. Perhaps Kareem's mother didn't survive his birth, or simply couldn't nurse. Either way, he is assured a wider family now.

Sumeyya pipes up, reaching to collect my mare's reins. "I am so glad you've come! It will be so nice to have someone else to talk to!"

"How could you be lonely, with so many goats to share your campfire?" Kareem demands, eyes twinkling.

Sumeyya draws herself up, suppressing a grin. "You may sleep with the goats, since you speak the same language."

"I do, actually." He bleats at the baby goat by his feet, who immediately starts bouncing about once more and responds in kind. Kareem laughs then gestures to Sumeyya. "Let me care for the horse. You go warm some milk for our guest, and perhaps none of us will have to sleep with the goats."

"Are they messy?" I ask before I think better of it.

"Very," Sumeyya assures me. "Anyone who sleeps beside the kids wakes up stinky."

"It is not a fate I recommend," Kareem agrees amiably, taking Zahra's reins from Sumeyya. She immediately loops her arm through mine and tugs me toward their camp, a little skip in her step. Huda walks with Kareem, leading her own mount to where her family's camels rest.

At Sumeyya's urging I take a seat on one of the carpets. She bustles about building up the fire with a few small, thorny branches, and then readying the evening meal for us, chattering all the while about her family and her travels since last we met. After the quiet of my journey with Huda, sitting with Sumeyya is like resting beside a cheerfully burbling brook. I could stay here a hundred years.

Listening to her, I gaze out at the goats, and, during a rare pause, ask how it is that they have such young kids now, at the beginning of winter.

"Oh! That is the breeding season here," she assures me. "The winter is cool and forgiving, and there is more pasture for all. It is the summer that is hard. All of our goats have their kids once the summer's heat is past. I hear it is different in places where the winter is the hard season."

I nod, and a moment later, Huda and Kareem join us, having rubbed down our mounts. Sumeyya immediately transitions to talking about the changes in the weather, and how quickly their sister Zainab's wedding is approaching—to which, she reminds me, I am invited. I smile despite myself. I cannot quite imagine a future in which I might go to a wedding or anywhere, really, without the fear of hunters following. Of its own accord, my hand grasps the obsidian ring that protects me. But Huda's family will be fine—they will move on with their goats, and there will be nothing here for the hunters to examine but the remains of a fire and a scattering of goat dung.

Huda, recognizing the signs of Sumeyya's barely contained curiosity, offers to tell her sister about her travels. Sumeyya waves her hands about, nearly scattering the pile of dates on the plate she holds. "Oh, wait till I am sitting! It will only be a moment!"

Huda takes the plate from her, and Sumeyya hurries to check the spiced milk warming over the fire, still exclaiming. Huda exchanges an amused look with me, her expression gentle with love for her sister. I wonder if she can see the same in my face. Sumeyya is wonderfully sweet and innocent in a way I cannot quite fathom, and I want her to keep the essence of this all through her life.

"I would like a sister like yours," I say, surprised at the waver in my voice.

Huda regards me shrewdly. It is the first time I've mentioned family at all, and in keeping with desert courtesy, she has never asked. But I've already enjoyed the traditional three days as a guest, and on two separate occasions, no less. She could ask, but she doesn't.

"Sisters are special," Sumeyya announces, having caught my words.

"Brothers are better," Kareem says. His grin flickers white as he takes a seat to the side of Huda, leaving space for their little sister to join them.

Sumeyya snorts. "Brothers always think they know more than they do."

I match Huda's smile, and try to commit this to my memory: these siblings gathered together as the night sets in, the easy banter and deep care that binds them together, the gentle lick of the flames at the thorny branches set in the shallow fire pit. This is what family is meant to be. It is as precious to me as it is foreign—and impossible. I have no family like this. My father lies buried, and my mother—there is no use thinking of her. All that awaits me now are a treasury of debts and a past that would swallow me whole. Perhaps that's why I insisted on stopping here: that I might sit together with such love even if only for an evening.

Sumeyya serves us each a cup of warmed milk along with the plates of dates and goat cheese set before us. Huda adds a thick, flat loaf of barley bread from her saddlebags to complete the meal. As we eat, she shares her tale of our travels together.

Sumeyya dissolves into peals of laughter when she hears how Huda demanded an escort of her enemies, then grows serious as the journey continues to the city, where I left my friend. Huda describes her nights spent at the caravanserai and her days wandering the Festival of Guilds, the singers and storytellers she stopped to listen to, the brightly clothed dancers and the sweat-slick wrestlers and jugglers she watched. Woven into her story, she recounts the relatively unsuccessful conversations she had with the first of two different caravan owners, who demanded a full five silvers in return for the safety of traveling with them to the edge of the desert.

"It would serve them right if we raided them!" Sumeyya says, outraged.

"Sadly, our warriors are already off raiding the Bani Essam," Kareem says. "The caravan will have passed by our lands before our men return."

Huda nods. "Kareem is right, and it is just as well. I do not wish that any of them should die over such a thing."

Sumeyya considers this. "It's always the guards that die, anyhow," she says, showing a shrewdness I hadn't quite expected. "Not the owners."

Kareem sighs. "They still should have had more respect for you, ukhti, especially as a woman seeking to return to her home."

"They should have," Huda agrees. "But it seems unlikely that such a need will arise again anytime soon."

The desert tribes rarely stray far from their borders, the women even less so than the men. Still, it seems unfortunate that while Huda and her family have showered me—a perfect stranger—with hospitality and unpaid escorts, she could find no such return when she needed it as a guest herself in foreign lands.

"So then how *did* you return?" Sumeyya demands.

"The second caravan was more accommodating. And then our friend Hikaru met me a day's ride out from Fidanya, so I left it anyhow."

Both of Huda's siblings turn to smile on me.

"I have been grateful for your sister's company and guidance," I tell them, dropping my gaze to the remains of the fire. I tamp down on the guilt within me, the knowledge that I haven't told Huda who I'm running from, or even why I've come back, beyond the fact that I am traveling to meet the phoenix. Anything I tell her can be used against me, should the hunters on my heels catch up with her. But I had no hope of reaching the Burnt Lands without her aid. I *needed* her help.

Still, Blackflame wants me back—the prisoner who flouted his authority, broke free the woman he wanted imprisoned, and escaped after testifying against him before the High Council. Quite possibly, he will do whatever it takes to recover me, regardless of the High Council's usual rules. Just as they used blood magic to hold me in my infirmary room, despite having outlawed it. I suppress a shudder. I wanted Huda to have family near her when I departed with the phoenix, but maybe we really shouldn't have stopped here....

"We will only stay with you one night," Huda tells her siblings now. "Tomorrow, Hikaru and I will travel to the Barrier to meet the phoenix."

"Again!" Sumeyya exclaims, eyes bright. Even Kareem's eyes widen with awe. To them, the phoenix is a storied creature, steeped in myth, rarely glimpsed.

I take a slow breath, pressing down on my fears. Surely one

night is not too long to wait? "I made the phoenix a promise," I tell my companions, knowing I can at least share this much. "He aided me when I first came through the Burnt Lands, and twice more since. I owe him a debt three times over. It is time for me to pay it."

"A debt," Huda echoes, head tilted as she considers her empty cup. It isn't a question, just an invitation to say more.

"I suspect I will leave with him from the Barrier," I tell her. Her eyes flick up to me as she understands the real reason I was willing to adjust our route to look for her family: so that I would not leave her alone in the desert, something the desert folk know well to avoid. In this unforgiving landscape, with neither shelter nor water easily at hand, a single mishap can spell death. The least I can do is make sure my friend is safeguarded when I leave her side. Although I *had* hoped that there would be more than just two people here—any way we do it, one of them will end up alone in the desert for a time.

Kareem and Huda exchange a glance while Sumeyya fairly jiggles in place in excitement. She has clearly caught on to the question at play.

"Perhaps I can travel with you," she says to Huda. "I would like to see the phoenix again—and maybe even *talk* to him this time!"

Huda smiles fondly at her little sister. "But Kareem has not seen him at all."

"Oh, but the kids will miss him. He had better stay."

Kareem snorts with laughter. "Am I a mother to them now?"

Huda raises a hand to halt Sumeyya's reply. "The goats will only be grazing here. There's no need to move them tomorrow. I think you can mind them for the day while Kareem comes with us, and perhaps," she looks back at me, a line appearing between her brows, "perhaps you will remain with us longer? We had hoped you might stay for our sister's wedding."

"I know," I say. "I would like to as well, but I must pay my debt to the phoenix first. For that, I must travel with him."

I'm going to have to convince Huda that the herd should be

moved as well—but perhaps that's a conversation to be had when her siblings aren't listening.

"Where will you go from there?" Sumeyya asks baldly. "Surely not into the Burnt Lands?"

I hesitate, unsure how to avoid lying while telling them all they need to know. Even as Huda shushes her sister, telling her not to ask questions of their guest, I can sense their unspoken horror. To enter the Burnt Lands is to choose death. I know it as well as they do. The phoenix may have promised to guide me through their dangers, but even he cannot ensure my safety in such a place.

I do not want to die in the Burnt Lands, as the mage who pursued me through the portal did: unmourned, unburied, undone by the spell-creature that tore him to pieces while the phoenix tried to save him. But when I set off to save Stormwind, I made the decision to give up my choices. Now I must accept what I have wrought, the future I have made for myself. No amount of concern from those around me will change what I must do.

Tomorrow, we will travel to meet the phoenix. And perhaps, just perhaps, I will survive long enough to pay my debts before the consequences of my actions overtake me.

CHAPTER 2
THE NETTED FISH

I wake to the certain knowledge that I have run out of tomorrows.

My eyes snap open, my whole body tensing as a dome of magic bursts upward from the perimeter of our small desert encampment, coming together directly overhead. Beyond it, the moon-bright night sky shows almost grey, faded out by the dome.

I assess it for a heartbeat, note the slight wavering of the walls, how it does not hold as steady as the barrier High Mage Stonefall created and held with a thought when he caught up with me outside of Fidanya. Whoever has caught me now, they aren't the Council's best.

Not that the skill of the fisherman matters to the netted fish.

"Something's wrong." Kareem kneels beside his blanket across the burned-out fire from us, peering through the night. I glance toward him, surprised he could tell. Without mage sight, he can't see the spells holding us. "Huda? Wake up—I hear horses," he says urgently.

The thought of Huda—and Sumeyya—breaks me from my stupor. I had thought it safe to spend a night here in this valley. I should have known better. Now I've put them all at risk: Huda, Kareem, and Sumeyya.

I twist, grabbing my pack and scrabbling past the flap for my pouch of charms. My hand closes on it as Huda sits up beside the still-slumbering form of her sister, one hand automatically reaching to pick up her scarf while her eyes flit over the dark desert beyond the magic dome. She may not be able to see our prison, but she *can* see the two figures on horseback riding slowly toward us. Caught as we are, there's no reason for them to hurry. It's a reprieve I can't afford to waste.

I pull my string of wards from the pouch and hand the end to Huda. "Pass this around you both."

She hesitates, her gaze flicking from me to Kareem standing on the other side of the fire, his back to us and his sword in hand, providing the visual barrier I need to protect his sisters. "It's not a raid," she says softly. "They're here for you?"

"Yes! Huda, *please*," I beg. "It will keep Sumeyya safe. Hurry!"

Huda grabs the end of the string of wards, handing it back to me from the other side of Sumeyya as the younger girl sits up, her hair wisping out of its braid. She's only eleven years, the same age I was when I lost my parents and was left adrift in Karolene. Sumeyya's not going to lose *anything* because of me.

"But what about you?" Huda whispers. "And Kareem?"

I shove my pack between them. There's nothing I can use in it to protect myself anyhow. "I'll try to keep Kareem safe," I whisper back. "Close this," I press the two ends of the string into her hands. Huda clasps the string, and the ward springs into place, surrounding them. They're perfectly visible, but protected from both physical and magical attacks. The mages won't bother to break the wards if they've already got me. Nor should they bother with Kareem if he offers no threat first.

I grab my boots and give them the requisite shake to rid of them of scorpions, my mind racing. A single, tattered feather falls to the dirt. *The phoenix's feather.*

Perfect.

I grab it, looking to the fire, only it's out, and my firestarter is in my pack behind the ward string—there's no time to retrieve it, and without it I've no way to light the feather. The hunters are almost upon us. Swallowing a curse, I shove the feather into the fire pit, my fingers brushing the very bottom of the coals, still warm but by no means hot. Boots in hand, I race across the camp to Kareem as the mages reach the edge of their spell.

"They've come for me," I tell him, shoving my foot into the wrong boot. "You must give me up, or your tribe will—be hurt." There's probably a more elegant way to say that, had I more time to think.

He stares as I awkwardly shove on my other boot. "Give you up?" he echoes.

"Yes—and light the fire!"

"*What*?" he says, incredulous.

"The fire," I say urgently. "It will call the phoenix—you must light it. *Now.*"

Kareem's gaze darts past me to the dead fire, brow furrowed.

"Is that her?" one of the mages asks, a woman. My eyes snap to her just as she raises a hand, her smile glinting in the moonlight. Not Ravenflight. Power slams me off my feet, sending me skidding across the dirt on my back till I fetch up against a cluster of rocks. My mouth gapes, seeking air, but the magic offers me no reprieve, wrapping around me like a net and tightening until I cannot think, my breath wheezing out of me in small, pained cries. I grasp for the magic around me, but while I can feel it at my fingertips, I can't draw it in past my markings, can't fashion it—it slips past my fingers uselessly.

Vaguely, I can hear Huda shouting.

"It's her." A pair of large hands close on my wrists, and the magic eases just enough that my bones do not snap when my captor yanks my arms together before me. And then the magic melts away, leaving me trembling and weak-muscled, my breath shuddering in my chest. I blink, trying to clear my vision, but everything is a blur.

"What are you doing?" the woman's voice demands. I can't tell who she is addressing, but I'm not doing anything right now.

I stare down at my wrists, blinking hard, until they finally come into focus. A pair of fine silver cuffs binds them together. Silver. A metal so soft I might bend it, just as Val might have escaped his own imprisonment had his manacles not been carved with charms, warded so thoroughly that strength made no difference whatsoever. These are warded as well—as if I might have the physical strength to break them, or be able to cast a spell. It's almost laughable.

"Boy," the woman says, her voice cutting. "Get away from the fire."

I look up again, and focus on Kareem kneeling before the fire pit, a firestarter in his hand. A single flame licks at the handful of kindling he's dumped on the old ashes. He looks in confusion toward the woman mage, who stands opposite him, a saber in hand. Oh *no*.

"I said, get away from the fire, desert rat."

Kareem drops the firestarter and slowly lifts his hands, holding them at shoulder height, but he doesn't move. He shakes his head uncertainly, his eyes narrowed as he tries to parse her words. Saber starts around the fire, her expression cold.

"They don't know Tradespeak," I blurt.

Saber ignores me. As she bears down on Kareem with her sword drawn, he scrambles back, pushing himself to his feet and backing up until he's pressed against the wards encircling his sisters. With a flick of her free hand, Saber sends a lash of magic at Kareem. He gasps as it wraps around him, pinning his arms to his side and leaving him immobilized in the dirt before his sisters' feet.

"Who are you?" Huda demands in the desert tongue, one arm clutching Sumeyya. "By what right do you attack us on our own lands?"

"What's the goat girl saying?" the mage beside me drawls. He's tall and built like a mountain.

"Probably shouting about her lover here." Saber smacks Kareem's shoulder with the flat of her blade. He flinches, and Sumeyya lets out a small cry. "What shall we do with them?"

At that precise moment, the fire flowers with light, the phoenix's feather catching. It burns bright and steady, like a miniature sun nestled in the ashes. Around it, the remaining twigs and half-burned sticks flame to life.

"The *hell* was that?" Mountain demands as Saber pivots to stare at the fire.

Saber's gaze shifts to me. "What was in the fire, girl?"

Mountain's great, meaty hand closes on the back of my neck, hauling me to my knees. I teeter there, held upright by his hand, and fumble for an explanation they'll believe. "I don't know! It was probably a... a charm I dropped when you attacked!"

Saber kicks at the edge of the fire, and the phoenix feather, already nearly burnt out, falls to ash. "Fool," she spits.

Apparently, incompetence is an explanation she can well believe.

"We don't need any witnesses," Mountain tells her, jerking his chin toward my companions. "Best be done with them."

His words hit me like a gut punch. These aren't Council rogue hunters. Not if they're talking about killing witnesses when I'm supposed to be the criminal, not them. Fear shudders through me—because I hadn't thought of this: that *everyone* could be hunting for me, not just the Council. That the worst of the magical world might find me.

I need to stand up, say something before they do anything. I get a foot under me, try to heave myself up from my kneeling position, but I can barely move beneath the pressure from Mountain's grip. I have no spells at my fingertips, can weave no shadows, can't even call on the fire in my blood as it rages within me. Even without the cuffs binding me, I can't use my magic, not since I was marked, and my captors know it as well as I. They've barely bothered with me because there's nothing I can do against them.

But the phoenix *can* do something. I just have to play for time now—the phoenix will come quickly, just as he did the last time I burned the feather he gave me. I shove myself up again, and nearly pitch sideways as Mountain shifts his grip.

"Get up, then," he growls, hauling me to my feet by the back of my neck.

"These people are only guides," I tell him, bracing my legs to keep my balance. "They don't know who I am."

"Their mistake," Saber says. She has stepped around Kareem and bent to inspect my ward string. "This will take a good amount of power to break," she observes. "The boy is easy enough to dispatch. These girls, though...."

They're going to kill Kareem when he's already bound and helpless. And then they'll break down my wards and slaughter Huda and Sumeyya. Because these people are hunters for hire. And possibly—

"What kind of a reward is Blackflame offering you?" I ask, trying to draw them out.

Saber smiles coldly. "Do you think you can equal it? We're sworn to him, little rogue, and we'll bring you in because he asked it of us. We know what he can give us, now and in the future. Do you think you can offer us more than that, you with your puling desert friends and nothing else to your name?"

"Ignore her," Mountain tells Saber, dragging me forward. "Your shield is wavering, and I want this all done before we have to take it down."

Saber bristles, glancing toward the white walls of the dome encircling us. I follow her gaze—the shield is wavering even more than before, but it's hardly in danger of collapsing.

"How do you propose we break down this ward she's set, then?" Saber says, her voice sharp with annoyance.

Mountain brings us to a stop beside the still-smoking fire. "We've a rogue that's no different than a source slave. I say we use her."

Horror washes through me. Huda watches me, her eyes wide and worried—she has no idea what these mages intend. Kareem strains against his bonds, but he can't break free. And neither can I—not from the markings on my arms, and not from our captors.

"No," I say, my voice shaking.

Mountain shoves me to my knees, transferring his grip to my wrists as I struggle to remain upright. He wrenches my arms forward and holds out his other hand to Saber. "Key."

She produces a small silver key on a chain. A moment later, Mountain has the cuffs open. I twist my arm, yanking back in the hopes of breaking free, but he was expecting me to struggle. His grip turns brutal as he twists my arm the other way, my whole body turning until my arm is caught behind my back, my face inches from the dirt.

"So," he says, forcing me up again until I am standing, the edges of my vision bleached with pain. "Let's see how much power you can draw for us, shall we?"

I have half a hope he won't be able to manage anything. I'm supposed to be able to channel magic, but not once have I actually succeeded in the dozen times I've attempted it since my magic was bound within me.

His grip on my wrist aches, pulling at my blood, my bones, as he tries to harvest my magic. The markings burn, wound as tight as a spider's web around my arms, and my magic cannot pass through them no matter how the mage tries. Maybe he won't be able to use me just as I have not been able to channel my own magic—if he can't, that may buy me enough time to outwit them.

"Damn it," he mutters, and transfers his grip to my hand.

That makes all the difference.

A sickeningly cold twist of his magic snakes up my arm, sliding through my veins. My markings burst into fire, raging within my skin as he *pulls*. A scream lodges in my throat as he draws my magic out, slowly at first and then faster. I thrash out with my other hand, grasping for magic from the desert air, the slumbering sunshine in the earth, the stone dense with its own reality—drawing on what I can reach faster and faster in order to feed the pull of his demand. My arms blaze with pain, one hand drawing in magic while the other channels it to him. I am nothing more than a vessel, a bridge for magic to course through until my bones feel as brittle as glass.

Faintly, I can hear Huda shouting, Kareem's voice pattering in an attempt to reason with people who neither understand him nor care.

"There," Mountain says, his voice strangely distant to my ears.

I turn my head and see a mass of magic cupped in his other hand, swirling and turning in on itself, the beginning of a spell that will blast my wards to pieces, taking Huda and Sumeyya with it—and perhaps Kareem as well, as close as he is to it all.

No.

Still, the mage grips my hand, pulling on my magic as the spell he holds grows as bright as a small sun.

"Hikaru!" Huda cries from the trap she stands within, the trap I made for her and her sister. And she does not even know my true name to call me by it, because that is how good of a friend I am to her. She and her family will die because I brought these people down on her, because I did not warn her that I was being hunted, did not give her the chance to protect herself. She will die because Mountain has ripped this magic from me with which to destroy her.

No.

I am not a source slave. I will not grant this despicable excuse of a mage what he wishes. I will not be the tool that kills my friends. I squeeze my fingers tight around Mountain's and pull back, yanking with all my will on the flow of power, *my* power. The sunshine and stone, the fire in my veins. *Mine.* The pain of my markings intensifies, until my arm is cased in molten iron, but the flow of magic falters, slowing until, for a single heartbeat, it pulses in tandem between us.

"What—" he says, but I barely hear him.

If there is one thing I have learned from Stormwind, it is channeling. If I can channel one way, I can channel the other. I follow the weave of my magic through his to the very core of his power, wrap it tight in mine, imagining a fine-woven web spun of fire, and *pull.*

He screams, but I have no ear for his pain. I draw his power out of him wrapped tightly in my own, first as a mere trickle and then a cascade of magic that flows into me, filling me. This, I know, is dangerous. I should no more hold it within me than I should have housed my sunbolt.

"What the hell are you doing?" Saber shouts, grabbing my

free arm. She holds a blade—something smaller than her saber—a dagger, bright with runes. I hear a cry that is not my own as the enchanted blade slices toward me—and then the white dome above us splinters. I stagger back, the enchanted blade whispering past my cheek as Saber looks up in shock.

She doesn't have time for more than that one, horrified look, and then she is engulfed in a maelstrom of fire that carries her backward. The frightened bleat of goats fills the air, underscored by Sumeyya's scream. I stumble back from the wash of scorching heat, landing on my backside as the fire twists and consolidates to reveal a form within it: the phoenix.

There is no sign left of Saber.

He spreads his wings, still flaming, and alights upon the ground. He is roughly the size of a peacock, though his tail curls down in long, flowing feathers. He burns with crimson, yellow, and orange light, his deeper shadows flickering cobalt and indigo.

I blink, unable to focus, and realize I'm still holding tight to the magic I'm channeling from Mountain, that it's building within me, too strong to be held much longer.

I twist onto my knees and do as Stormwind once taught me— an emergency channeling of magic straight down through the earth. I wrap the stone within me around the fire, smothering it, so that what pours forth from me is dull and heavy and sinks into the ground without causing harm. The phoenix will handle Mountain. I just need to make sure I don't destroy myself or anything else while he does so.

I remain on all fours as the last of the excess magic sinks into the earth, my head hanging down. My heartbeat pounds in my ears, pulses through my arms. The pain of my markings rushes over me again, as if only waiting for me to notice. I press my eyes shut, breathing slowly, letting the pain ebb and flow until it begins to recede.

"Hikaru?"

I force myself to look up, the movement ponderous. Huda crosses the last few paces to me, the ward string lying open behind her. Sumeyya is nowhere in sight.

"Are you—are you hurt?" Huda's voice is strung tight but steady.

Then the phoenix is beside me, one wing flicking out to brush my arm. He tilts his head, dark eye intent, and his magic warms me from within, like the gentlest of fires by which I might sit. I'm not sure how magic is helping when that is what hurt me so much, but no doubt the phoenix can do things the average mage can't. At least my markings don't flare in protest at his gift.

"M'alright," I manage, in answer to Huda. She gently helps me sit back. "Sumeyya and Kareem—?" I ask shakily.

"They are fine. I've sent them to collect the goats—they scattered when the phoenix arrived. The camels ran too." Her voice has the forced calm of one dealing with a crisis because falling apart is not an option.

"And the... hunters?"

"There's nothing but ash left of the woman," Huda says. "The man is also dead." She gestures toward an unmoving shape less than a dozen paces away. Mountain lies on his side, his face sickly pale and his eyes open and unseeing. No breath stirs his great frame.

Good.

Wait. No. I don't want to be a killer—not again. I've been holding close the fact that I *didn't* kill Osman Bey, that the head of the Lycan Guard both took me prisoner and then freed me. But Mountain was nothing like Osman Bey. *Mountain* was the killer. I was only protecting my friends, and myself.

I take a slow breath, staring at Mountain's still form, and the truth is I'm glad he's dead, glad he can't get up and hurt my friends. Because if he were alive, if I had only incapacitated him, he would have come after me again—and he would have hunted down Huda and her family. All of them. Because that's the kind of people he and Saber were.

"But I didn't," I shake my head, trying to understand the fact of the body lying in front of me. "I stripped him of his magic, didn't I? That's what killed him."

"You did," the phoenix agrees, letting his wing drop. The

warmth of his magic still remains in my bloodstream. "Had you not, I would have finished the deed."

"You—r-right, yes," I stutter. The phoenix just turned Saber to ash. He would have killed Mountain as well, if I hadn't beaten him to it.

What I did though—it is precisely how Promises are stripped of their magic. I've heard of it, but it never crossed my mind as a thing one could simply *do*. Stripping a Promise—or a mage—of their magic breaks their health and minds, leaving them nothing but a husk of the person they used to be. Or it kills them outright, as it did Mountain. As *I* did.

I don't want to kill anyone. But I will if that's my only option to save my friends. I've done it before, and I'll do it again. I didn't want to kill Kol a year ago—didn't want to be responsible for his murder—but I would do it again in a heartbeat, just as I would defend my friends from Mountain and Saber again.

I take another slow breath.

Mountain is dead, my friends are safe, and I'm still free.

The relief of this moment, the horror of the previous one, the pain and physical toll, all come together in a wave that crashes over me. I turn, my whole body shuddering, and empty my stomach into the sand beside me. I retch and cough until there is nothing left, my insides hollowed out and my mind blank.

When I straighten, Huda passes me a cup of water. "Drink."

I take the cup in shaking hands. She rises and moves away, perhaps to help her siblings with the animals. I gargle twice and spit before taking a sip.

"It is not murder to stop one who intends murder themselves," the phoenix says, watching me. "You had no choice, and there was no time for anything else."

"Right," I agree. These mages were no different from Kol in their way, or Blackflame; unconcerned with the lives they destroyed, focused only on the advancement of their own wishes. More than happy to murder their way there.

"You understand?" the phoenix says sharply.

"I understand." I look back at Mountain, stripped of his

magic and so his life. It's one of the fates the High Council considered for me. I did that. Though how that is possible when I'm one step removed from a source slave, I don't understand.

Straightening, I push up a sleeve. The markings are darker than usual, angry-looking even in their delicacy. It's as if coals slumber beneath the elegant flourishes and unstudied designs; they burn even now. Staring at them, I remember the only other source slave I've ever seen: the boy in Blackflame's rooms, huddled against the wall and cradling his arms as I do mine, his marks like burns across his flesh. His vomit on the floor by the window—the reason I'd been called into the room at all.

Is this what it is to be a source slave then? Excruciating pain each time your magic is taken by your master? I squeeze my eyes shut. I can't think about this right now, not about all the young men and women who must live such a reality until the magic fully tears them apart and they die.

I focus instead on the fact that Mountain didn't succeed. He *should* have been able to take my magic without my stopping him. It doesn't make sense.

"Phoenix," I say. "I'm supposed to be helpless. How did I do that to him? How come I've never even *heard* of a source slave draining their master dry like I just did?"

"I imagine it is because you are not bound," the phoenix says. "The binding connects a source slave to their master and allows the master to draw on them at will. I suspect it also ensures that the magic can only be channeled in one direction. These mages certainly never imagined you could reverse the flow of magic." The phoenix huffs softly. "It is a fitting end for that one, I would say."

I look down at my hands, and then a pace away, to where I poured the magic I held into the ground. My handprints are pressed into the earth—or rather, sunk into stone that took form around them. How odd to see memorialized the shapes of my hands, small and slightly uneven, fingers splayed.

That never happened before with Stormwind, but I hadn't been marked with stone back then, and it had been much harder to dampen my fire. Usually, I left behind a circle of scorched earth instead—rather like the blackened circle where Saber once stood. I swallow hard, look back at my handprints. My lessons on channeling with Stormwind were back when I could cast spells, but to have done this now? It opens up a whole new world of possibility.

I can defend myself. I can channel magic where I like, how I like. I don't have to be at the mercy of whatever hunter corners me next, and I can stop myself from being used as a weapon against others. My breath catches on a shaky laugh. I can defend myself, and I just killed a man proving it.

"We should leave soon," the phoenix says, pulling my attention back to him. "I will help gather the animals for your friends. Perhaps you and Huda can go through the mage's belongings. Take what you need—especially from among the charms you find. What neither of you wants, leave beside him."

"You'll take care of it, I suppose," I say. He's at least four hundred years old and knows a thing or two about what he's doing. It's a little terrifying.

"If I leave behind evidence, these deaths will be blamed upon the Bani Saqr," the phoenix says, naming Huda's tribe whose lands these are. "There can be no sign left of these mages."

I shudder and nod.

"We need to move quickly, in case there are other hunters nearby."

I nod again, pushing myself to my feet. He's right. There was a *lot* of magic—and not just running through me. From the dome and its spectacular demise, to the phoenix's fiery arrival, nothing here has been subtle. If there's a mage nearby, they'll know exactly where to look for me. I can't be responsible for bringing more trouble down on Huda and her family.

The phoenix takes to the air, his fire dampened until he barely glows at all, on his way to round up the scattered livestock. He may say something to Huda, for a moment later she comes walking back to the camp, leading the mages' horses.

Together, we set about searching Mountain's body for charms and blades.

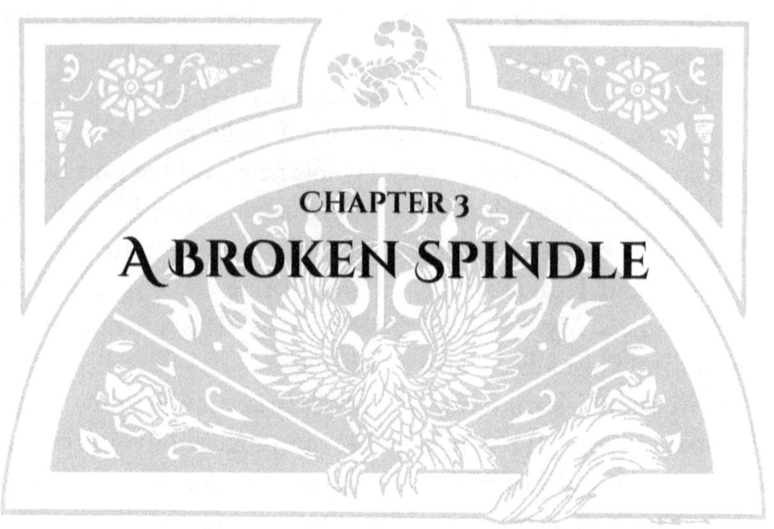

CHAPTER 3
A BROKEN SPINDLE

In the life I can't remember in Karolene, living as a street thief, it seems I must have handled dead bodies more than a few times. The feel of this body, cooling quickly, the flesh still soft to my touch but clammy and *wrong*, is familiar. Did I help wash the dead, perhaps? Or transport them? I cannot imagine I know these things from killing. That much, at least, I am sure about myself.

Huda takes a shaky breath and sets to work beside me, unbuckling his belt with its store of pouches and the two sheaths still holding their knives. Perhaps, with the harshness of life in the desert, she too has handled the dead before. I empty the charms and bits and bobs from Mountain's pockets, making a pile of them.

"You knew these mages were coming after you?" Huda asks without looking up.

"No," I say, shaking my head. "Not these ones, no."

"But you're being hunted. I've seen you looking over your shoulder. I knew there was trouble following you."

"I'm sorry," I say, my throat aching. I should have told her this from the first moment, at our meeting at the caravanserai. Sorry seems like such a paltry offering now. "I should have told you. But the ones I thought hunted me... they would not kill others." The

Council rogue hunters might incapacitate bystanders, but they have nothing to hide and are more than capable of disarming non-magical combatants. I can't imagine Stonefall attacking Kareem the way Saber did.

"Then who are these people?" she asks.

Mercenaries. Mages hired by Blackflame to bring me to him without the Council's knowledge. I lick my lips, meet Huda's gaze. "They hunt for money."

Huda studies me, then looks back to the weapon belt in her hand. "Will there be more?" she asks.

"Yes. I don't know when, but there will always be more. Until they catch me or I die."

"Till you *die?* Who are they?" Huda demands, eyes flashing. "What do they want with you?"

I take a deep breath and hold it, turning my gaze to the moon-thrown shadows darkening each ridge of sand, stretching out before us. I cannot put off this explanation any longer. Not if there are more of Blackflame's rogue hunters chasing me. Not even if it is only the Council's hunters, who likely won't attack or kill my friends—but who might still question the tribe's standing with the Council should it be found out they are harboring me. This isn't my companions' battle to fight, and I cannot use them any longer. I just have to find the courage to tell Huda the truth.

I unclasp the first of two necklaces Mountain wears, sliding the chain free. It's a ward of some sort. "When we first met, I was trying to reach Fidanya because my friend and teacher was... being tried before the High Council. She's an old enemy of Arch Mage Wilhelm Blackflame. I knew what happened would not be fair. The first thing I did after leaving you at the caravanserai was to find out exactly what had happened. She was innocent, even the Mekteb's Guardian thought so." I shrug. "I could not let her be sent to Gereza Saliti—the mages' prison."

Huda's frown is a fierce thing, made more so by her tattoos. "I heard of the mage's escape, and the rogue who aided her...."

Huda's gaze drops to my hands with sudden understanding, taking in the mix of markings and inkings on the backs of my hands. I push my sleeves up past my wrists. The markings are terribly visible, the lacelike pattern of black covering my arms still inflamed and angry.

"I was caught. The phoenix helped me. That's why I came back. I will stay here until I have done what he wishes, or the choice is taken from me."

Huda shakes her head, thinking over all I've revealed. In the silver-bright light of the moon, her expression is cool, sharp. Slowly, she says, "What you did to this mage—you would need training to overpower him so. But the stories I heard called you a rogue."

I turn my attention back to Mountain's second necklace. It's a cord strung around a small metal vial with a stopper. As I work it free, I say, "I have been trained, but never sworn to the Council. Jabir, the Mekteb's Guardian, called me a free mage."

"The Guardian did." Huda sits back, brow creased in thought. "He's of the desert." She casts me an opaque look and turns back to searching Mountain.

I pull the cord free and unstopper the vial. One sniff of the stuff leaves me lightheaded. Whatever it is, it's strong. I leave it by Mountain for the phoenix to dispose of.

"I'm sorry," I say again, wishing I knew what her look meant. "I didn't believe these hunters would find me so fast—not with the protections I have in place." Stonefall had even laid false trails for me, after tracking me down with the glowstone I used to save his life, and giving me the horse I now ride. I still don't understand how Mountain and Saber *did* find me, given the obsidian ward I'm still wearing.

"You should have said," Huda murmurs with no trace of accusation. It's a simple observation of what would have been better, and I feel all the more awful for it. I'd rather she be angry with me than disappointed, even though she has every right to feel both, all of it, none of it. I was so grateful to have her friendship, yet I didn't treat her as a friend myself.

"Let's see about the horses, then," Huda says.

I help her perform a quick search of the mages' saddlebags. We find little more in terms of magical items. I discover a mirror in a case which I immediately open and smash, remembering the linked mirrors Stormwind and I used to speak when she was first taken to Fidanya—and how her mirror was taken and used to attempt a trace on its mate.

"What's this?" Huda asks, holding up a wooden spindle with a cracked shaft.

I stare at it numbly.

"Hikaru?"

"It's a spindle."

She blinks, frowning slightly. "It's a strange one."

I had thought the same thing when I saw Sumeyya's spindle just this past evening. "You drop it, instead of holding it in your hand."

"And this one is special?"

"It's mine," I say, reaching out to take it from her as the answer to my question comes into focus. "It's how they found me."

A length of yarn is still attached to it, wound around the shaft as I'd set it down a lifetime ago, before Harith Stonefall came to Stormwind's valley carrying a summons from the High Council. I trace the crack down the shaft with my finger. These two mages must have been among those who raided our valley, blasting through Stormwind's protective wards on her house. They were searching for me—at that time, the unnamed and unknown compatriot of Stormwind—and they would have selected something small that I handled regularly and thus marked with my essence, my magical trace.

There were not many such items in our cottage—the pots and pans were large and cumbersome, and I took my most treasured belongings with me, such as they were: a few charms, and the crow statuette Val carved for me. But we had put out our spindles, along with the wool set aside for this winter's spinning, and grabbing them would have been an easy thing. If they took my spindle, then they would have taken Stormwind's as well. I can only hope she's had enough time to break free of the binding spells holding her, and so be better prepared to protect herself from attack than I am.

There's also no knowing if they found anything else of mine to trace me with. I am protected from general traces by the ward I wear around my neck—an obsidian ring, the inner surface carved with sigils, that was gifted to me by the Degath family. But even the strongest ward can only do so much when a mage has something of the person they are seeking—a lock of hair, a favorite mug, or—this time—a spindle I used all through the long winter nights of this past year.

It's no different from how Stonefall was able to track me as I fled Fidanya, using the glowstone I altered to burn away the poison that would have killed him. The glowstone brought him within a few blocks of Stormwind, Kenta, and me as we passed through an outlying town. This spindle must have brought these mages within a valley or two of our camp, close enough that they had little trouble finding us.

"Will other hunters have anything else of yours?" Huda asks, eying the spindle.

I grimace. "I don't know. I didn't think anyone would have this much."

I left nothing behind at the Mekteb that could have been used to track me, beyond the glowstone in Stonefall's keeping. I did not consider that they might have something of mine from Stormwind's valley. But this is the High Council and Blackflame on my trail, and neither likes to lose. I should have known someone would find *something* of mine. I should have been more wary from the moment I fled the Mekteb.

I slip the spindle into my pocket—it doesn't quite fit, but I'll move it to my pack once we're done here. As we finish, Kareem and Sumeyya return to the camp. I watch Sumeyya, the way her glance skitters past the dead mage lying on the ground, before centering on the mess of blankets where she and Huda slept. She walks straight to them, ignoring Mountain, and begins to fold them, her expression pinched. The phoenix sweeps down in a gentle arc, landing beside the dead fire.

Huda watches her sister worriedly, one hand on the horse's flank beside her. "Sumeyya? Are you all right?"

"I'm fine," her sister says, her back to us as she folds the blankets. Her voice is carefully neutral, as if she's struggling not to cry. My heart aches at the sound, at the bone-deep resonance of it. I have been where she stands, and I wish to God I had been able to keep her from the fear and danger of this night.

Kareem glances once at me before going to gather up his own blanket. "We found the animals that fled."

Huda starts forward, gesturing toward a trickle of blood seeping from a cut on his forehead. I don't even remember that happening. "You're still bleeding," she tells him.

"It's not deep. It will heal."

"Come," the phoenix tells him. "That I can help with."

I stand beside the dead mage's horse, my arms piled with belongings we don't want—clothes and personal effects that have nothing of the desert about them. I couldn't protect Sumeyya earlier tonight. And I can't seal Kareem's wound now—the thought *hurts*, a pang deep inside of me that I have no space for, no way to deal with. Such a simple thing, such an important thing, and I will never be able to do it again.

I push the thought away and focus on what I can do: deliver the pile of unwanted belongings to the dead fire. The Barrier spells glow in the distance, a few hours' ride away. Even without a camel, I should make it there easily.

I glance back at the phoenix and see his wingtip drop from Kareem's face. The blood there is dried and flaking away, the cut sealed together. It will take time to heal—there's no magic that can *actually* do that part for the body, but the phoenix will have burned away any contaminants and sealed it shut to protect against infection.

Huda has gone to join her brother, and now she watches the phoenix as he steps back, her eyes slightly narrowed, as if she's come to expect him to have his own motivations. Kareem, similarly, appears nowhere near as awed to meet the phoenix as he'd looked last evening when Huda shared her stories of the mythical bird—and our plans to meet him at the Barrier.

"Honored phoenix," Kareem says slowly, still ignoring me, "You knew my family might be attacked?"

The phoenix tilts his head. "Those of the desert know that there is uncertainty in all things. The mageling has enemies. I asked your tribe to protect her. But neither your guest nor I believed she would be endangered so soon."

Kareem dips his head, abashed. It's the height of dishonor to slight a guest, to refuse them guest right or balk at protecting them. Or to even imply such. He says only, "Had we known, my sister might have sought an escort as protection before this."

Sumeyya slips up behind her sister, peering around her back to look at the phoenix. Her eyes are wide and her face alight, despite the horror of what she's experienced in the last hour.

The phoenix casts a wry glance my way. "Mageling, tell your friends how well a band of warriors would have been able to defend you from a mage."

I hate him in that moment. Hate him for knowing the danger, knowing there was no protection to be had, and assuming that I at least would survive. "They wouldn't have," I say roughly. "But we both should have said something. We might have traveled faster," I say, glancing at Huda.

"Or we might have taken a different route, found a way to evade your trackers," Huda says coolly.

She's right. My silence only endangered her more.

Behind her back, Sumeyya looks at me, brow creased, all that delight drained away. Of course. Because I betrayed her sister's friendship—and that put them all at risk. However angry I am at the phoenix, I'm the one who did wrong.

I exhale slowly and say to the phoenix, "I need to get to the Burnt Lands. The safest place is somewhere I can't be traced— somewhere no one would dare to follow. You have a haven in there, don't you? Somewhere I can stay?"

He dips his head. "The draining spells make a dome over the

land. But as for the earth—the spells lie just below the surface, powering the spell-beasts, but not reaching very deep."

"You really do have a cave of riches?" Sumeyya breaks in, a hint of excitement in her voice.

"I would not say riches," he returns gently. "But there is water."

"That is a great wealth," Sumeyya agrees.

A cave isn't the most traditional place for a bird to nest. But then the phoenix seems a pretty good mix of traditional and flexibly practical.

He turns to me. "You are right to think a trace cannot follow you through the Barrier. However, I will not be able to fly you—I cannot sustain your weight for so long a distance without some way to draw on magic outside myself."

"That's fine. I'll walk." It's not like I have a great repository of magic left within myself to channel to him—if he doesn't have enough for it, then walking is my next best choice. Also, channeling *hurt*. I don't want to do it again any sooner than I have to.

"It will take you at least two hours from the Barrier."

"That's fine," I repeat. Chances are some awful spell-creature will come after me by then, but with the phoenix to help me, I have half a chance. At least this way I endanger no one else. Even if the Council mages manage to somehow track me that far, they'd be unspeakably foolish to follow me into the Burnt Lands themselves. More likely, they'll leave me to my fate—or wait to see if I emerge.

The phoenix bobs his head. "Then let us go." He turns his gaze on Huda. "I will mask your trail so that you cannot be connected to what happened here."

Huda nods. It's an acknowledgement without thanks, but then I suppose she wouldn't feel the need to thank him for protecting her people from the dangers he and I brought down on them. Ducking my head, I turn my attention back to our preparations. It takes barely ten minutes to make ready, my companions used to a lifetime of movement.

"Take the belts and daggers," I tell Huda as we gather up the items we took from Mountain.

"You won't need them?" she asks, glancing at me askance.

"The spell-creatures are formed of stone," I say easily, as if my words are no cause for alarm. "A dagger won't be of any use." Nor do I know how to use one. I scoop up the pile of seven or eight charms. "I'll keep these, you keep the rest."

"Hikaru—"

"Time to go," I say, pushing myself to my feet. Kareem and Sumeyya have brought the herd to the edge of the camp, the animals bunching together, still unsettled, the kids hidden within the ranks of the older goats. The camels are loaded and waiting beside them. My little mare waits patiently by the mages' horses.

"Hikaru," Huda repeats.

"That's not my name."

Everything about her stops.

"I'm sorry," I say, forcing the words out. "Most of what you know of me is a lie."

Her jaw takes on a stubborn cast. "You're wrong. I knew you had honor from the time we first met. And now you've told me that the phoenix and a desert dragon have both chosen your side over the High Council's. So, you travel under a different name? Very well. Stop wasting time. We need to go."

"What?" I say, taken aback. She doesn't care? She's coming *with* me?

"Let's go," she snaps, heading toward her camel. She then leads it over to me and makes it sit so I can clamber up.

"You can't come with me," I protest.

"I'm not entering the Burnt Lands," she scoffs. "But I *am* taking you to the Barrier instead of leaving you to stumble through the sands following a creature of the air. It's a half day's journey to the Barrier. You aren't walking it alone." She pauses, glaring at me as I cast about for a reasonable answer, and then adds, "We'll care for your mare until you return."

"An excellent plan," the phoenix announces. Clearly, he

intends to use Huda and her family again once I am ready to leave the Burnt Lands. Which he is absolutely *not* going to do.

"No," I say sharply, sending him a hard look before I turn back to Huda. At least this I know what to do about. "The mare is my gift to you. The mages' horses are yours as well—to share with your siblings. But Zahra is *yours*."

Huda's eyes widen, but she doesn't argue. I don't know much of desert culture, but I know that generosity is highly prized. In consequence, it is considered the height of bad manners to refuse a gift. "You are very kind," she says finally, though she seems even more grim.

"I agree," Kareem says, but apparently not about me. "Huda should go with you. Sumeyya and I will take the goats north, along the hollow valleys." He looks to the phoenix. "I don't like to separate—it's never wise for a person to travel alone through the desert. Can you assure us you'll see our sister back to us safely?"

"Yes," the phoenix says. "Once the young mage has reached my haven, I will light your sister's path to you."

Kareem dips his head. "I thank you."

"And I," Huda agrees. She glances back at Kareem, "Peace be upon you, my brother."

"And upon you both, peace," he returns, his glance flicking to me, hard as stone. He didn't hear my explanation to Huda, and I'm not sure it would have made a difference. I've lost any right to kindness or friendship here.

Sumeyya darts around her brother and wraps me in a tight hug. It takes me aback—the embrace, how tall she is when I am used to thinking of her as small, the feeling of love when I have betrayed my friends to danger. I only just manage to bring my arms around her, squeezing her back.

"Don't get hurt," she tells me, and then pulls away and throws herself at her sister.

"We'll be careful," Huda promises her, hugging her tightly.

I take a slow breath and go to gather what I need from my mare's saddlebags. Zahra was a gift from Stonefall, who filled these bags with supplies he thought I might need. I'm grateful for it, but there's no way a horse would survive the Burnt Lands—even if she got me safely to the phoenix's haven, there would be no food for her, and likely no path for her to enter the haven. I don't doubt it's well hidden and difficult to enter. No, she'll be safe and cared for with Huda's family, as well as a source of wealth for them—she has desert lineage, and is young enough to breed well. Huda has never spoken of her family's wealth, but I have the distinct feeling that her tribe has struggled while their enemies have only grown stronger.

I sort through Zahra's saddlebags quickly, transferring over only the most essential items to my pack while Huda completes her farewells to her family.

"My handprints," I say to the phoenix, glancing to where they are sunk into stone.

"I will call in a wind to disperse this ash," he says, his nod taking in Mountain as well as the scorched area where Saber once stood. "I will ensure the sand it brings covers the stone. Even if it is found, it is unlikely anyone will know what to make of it."

True enough.

"Come," Huda says, stepping up into her camel's saddle.

Kareem and Sumeyya call to their herd, slowly moving them out and taking Zahra and their mounts with them. I clamber up behind Huda, and a moment later we are on our way toward the Burnt Lands.

CHAPTER 4
THE HOLLOW VALLEYS

I keep a steady watch for signs of travelers—specifically, for mages going to investigate the valley we've left, but I discern nothing unusual. When I ask, Huda assures me that she has seen no fresh tracks from camels or horses. She takes a familiar string of prayer beads from her pocket, clicking through them slowly as she murmurs her remembrances. I send up my own silent thanks to God, including deep gratitude that my friends are all safe, and that Huda seems to somehow—inexplicably—have decided to only be mildly angry with me.

Huda glances over her shoulder at me, focusing on my hands resting half-curled on my thighs. "Do they hurt?" she asks.

I clench my fists and release them slowly, feeling the skin beneath my markings twinge. "Only a little now."

She dips her head and returns her focus to the valley we traverse.

I glance down at my markings again, feel that faint ripple of pain as I shift my hands. Source slaves die young. I've always known that, understood in the abstract the reason for it, but now I truly know it and it leaves me feeling sick and hollow. I wish I had some safety from a future where what was done to me last night cannot be done again—that I won't be used as a source for someone else's spells, a vessel to draw on for magic that will strip away my core with each brutal draw until, eventually, there is nothing left and I die.

But I'm not a source slave yet, nor am I defenseless. Though, if it will always hurt so much to channel magic, it will be a last defense against others. At least I can still sense magic without pain, whether it's the faint presence of a charm or the encapsulating walls of a mage's magical cage. There is relief in knowing I still have some of my old abilities, untouched.

I open myself to the breeze, letting my mage sense unfold—and nearly lose my balance. I grab Huda's waist to steady myself, gasping in an empty breath.

"Hikaru?" Huda reins in the camel, careful not to twist and dislodge me.

I reach out with my mage senses again, but the breeze here is thin with lack of magic, barely a hint of life in it. "Why is the air empty? There's hardly any magic," I say, bewildered. I've never sensed anything like this, beyond the absolute emptiness of the Burnt Lands. Which we are definitely not in. My brow furrows as I glance up and down the valley, but the Barrier to the Burnt Lands is nothing more than a pale smudge above the far hills.

"We're riding alongside the hollow valleys."

"The what?" I ask. Kareem had mentioned the term, but I hadn't thought much of it at the time.

"I will show you."

At the next pass, she branches into the valley to our left, where the air blows steadily and without a hint of magic in it. As we reach its center, the wind that whips through leeches at the faint wisps of magic clinging to our clothes and to the camel we ride. It's unnerving, and so very wrong.

"May I get down?" I ask.

Huda reins in her camel and makes it sit. I slide down and take a step, looking around, searching the staggeringly empty valley for any sign of magic. Then I kneel and press a hand to a stone, and then to the sand below it. Nothing.

Or rather, the faintest hint of magic that the wind whips away, spreading it so thin I can't sense it anymore.

"What's happening?" I ask, turning toward Huda. "This valley should be as full of—" I pause, looking around again. I was about to say *as full of magic as it is of life*, but as I spread my senses, I find that is exactly what it is, but in the worst of ways. It's not just magic that is missing, but that the land itself is dead—not a blade of grass grows, not one ant tunnels through the dirt. The only sign of life is a pair of vultures riding a current a valley or two over.

"The winds come out of the Burnt Lands. They are empty," Huda gestures, palm open, "and they hollow out the life of these valleys. By the time they reach the northern valleys, they have dissipated enough for the grass to grow, and the thorn bushes, so some grazing is possible with care. That lies in the territory of the Bani Jibaal."

I consider what she isn't saying. "Your territory ends at the hollow valleys?"

"They border us on one side, yes."

To the other lies the end of the desert, and the lands claimed by farmers and villages who hold the desert people in contempt. To the south lie the lands of the Bani Essam, who are stronger and more capable in warfare, and have a mage at their disposal. I did not appreciate until this moment how precarious her people's lives are—that they are dependent not only on the scarce offerings of the desert, but that they are surrounded on every side, pressed more and more tightly within a land that can offer them precious little succor.

"Do the Bani Essam raid you often?" I ask abruptly, thinking of the escort we had from among them, and of Laith ibn Hamza specifically, with his crooked smiles and kindness. A kindness that means little if he knows how dire the circumstances of the Bani Saqr are and yet follows his father's lead in the life of a warrior, finding glory in raiding Huda's people.

"Sometimes," Huda says, her voice neutral. It was upon their swords her brother died. And it is my uncle who serves as their mage—perhaps even Laith is related to me. After all, I know nothing of my father's family, other than that he and his brother were both mages, and he chose to marry my mother and leave the desert, leading his family to disown him. His brother stayed on and lives here yet.

Huda gestures to me. "We should keep riding. It is still some distance to the Barrier."

I clamber back up on the camel and grasp Huda's waist as it stands, but my attention stays with the hollow valleys even after we leave them behind. I can't do anything about the old enmities between the tribes. But the phoenix still believes I can do something to heal the Burnt Lands—to tease apart the spells that hold them in their thrall. If I can do that, these valleys may become fertile once again—and, no doubt, the neighboring valleys will improve as well. Huda's people will have easier grazing for their livestock, and so more food and a greater ability to buy what the desert does not provide. People cannot prosper when their land is dying.

I cannot end the violence, but perhaps I can lessen the need for it. It's worth trying for, at least.

THE PHOENIX SWOOPS down to us as we ride the length of yet another valley, bringing with him a low-blowing desert wind that sweeps away all signs of our tracks in the space of a breath.

Huda turns the camel to face the phoenix as he alights on a boulder on the hill at our eye level. A stray spark falls from his feathers and goes dark on the sands.

"There is a Council rogue hunter on your trail," he tells us without preamble. "High Mage Ravenflight."

I grimace as Huda casts an opaque glance over her shoulder at me. Ravenflight was the head mage in charge of my imprisonment, who oversaw the spells to mark me. She's also the same mage my mother convinced to petition the High Council to become master to me as a source slave. Both Blackflame and his greatest opponent on the Council, Arch Mage Nightfall, agreed to her petition. I swallow hard, pushing away all thoughts of my mother, her attempt to "help" me in her own terrible way, and her refusal to acknowledge me as her daughter even in the privacy of my infirmary room. No, I need to focus on Ravenflight, and how I will avoid her.

The phoenix continues, "She has not found the valley where you were camped, but she has taken to her raven form to search for you. I led her away, and I will attempt to do so again, but she is cunning."

I grimace. "What of Kareem and Sumeyya? Are they safe?"

"Yes. I masked their trail, and they are well past any danger of being accidentally found. It's unlikely any mages will bother them, now that you are no longer in their company."

Unlikely, but not impossible. At least the phoenix's words seem to have relieved Huda, the tension in her shoulders loosening.

It's a little bit terrifying to realize how close Ravenflight is, even without a way to directly trace me. The Council knew I owed the phoenix a favor, though. Ravenflight would have known to head for the desert, searching for reports of me along the way. If she catches me, she'll no doubt set the slave bond on me at once, and there will be no escaping her after that. The only defense I can think of is what I did to Mountain last night—but without the threat of someone else's life at stake, could I bring myself to do that again? Because Ravenflight wouldn't *intend* to kill me, even if serving as a source slave will.

"Mageling, are you listening?" the phoenix asks abruptly.

I realize belatedly that I've missed whatever he said. I shake my head. "Sorry. What's our plan, then?"

"The same as it was. I'll guide you through the Burnt Lands to my home, where you'll stay to study the spells. Then I'll come back to see your friend to her family before rejoining you."

Right. "I've about a week's worth of food, maybe less," I tell him.

"I can supply you," he says. "The critical thing is to get you past the Barrier now." He sighs. "All these years searching for a mage who might be able to bring down these spells, and now I suddenly have unwanted mages descending on the Burnt Lands from every possible direction."

Huda stiffens.

An unexpected smile tugs at my lips. "Who knows? Maybe they'll end up coming in handy. As long as I don't cross paths with them."

The phoenix gives a strange avian bark and takes off. It's only as he circles overhead that I place it as a laugh.

"Wait for me at the Barrier; rest if you can. I'll ascertain Ravenflight's position. We'll leave as soon as I return," he calls down to me, and wings away, keeping low over the hills once more.

Huda squints as she watches him disappear from sight. "It is a point of courtesy, among my people, not to ask questions of a guest and traveler," she says, careful not to turn toward me.

"I thought that was only for three days, though. Also, after what happened, I should be answering all your questions."

Her eyes flick to me, a smile hovering around her mouth. "True. Will you tell me what the phoenix meant just now, about bringing down the spells?"

I lick dry lips. "Yes. He—when I passed through the Burnt Lands the first time, I managed to unmake part of—one of the spell things."

"You destroyed one of the dead creatures?"

It takes me a moment to realize she means the spell-creatures. She's right, though; although the creatures beneath the spells once lived, now they are all just magical constructs built on a long-dead structure. "No—not altogether." I tell her. "Just part of it. Enough that it retreated. The phoenix helped me escape from there. He asked me to return and study the spells here, to see if I can unravel them. Make the Burnt Lands whole again." I give a breathy laugh. It sounds so unlikely, so impossible.

She clicks her tongue, setting the camel in motion again as she turns this over in her mind. Finally, she asks, "Do you believe you will succeed?"

"I don't know. I have my doubts. If I can stop the forces that have shaped your hollow valleys, that would be a good thing, would it not?"

For a long moment, she says nothing, and I find myself wishing I was riding beside her and could see her face. Regardless, I know she's thought of something else, something I should have considered. "How long will it take you?"

I hesitate. "I have no idea. I'm not even sure I can do it. Huda, what am I forgetting?"

She sighs. "It is nothing you can change. I will speak with the phoenix when he returns to escort me back to my family."

I grimace. I suppose I haven't earned her trust—or rather, I've done my best to lose it.

After a moment, she says, "The phoenix seems rather more willing to allow for the possibility of harm than you are."

"I think he's used to humans dying, or killing each other," I agree, watching the back of her head. "Though I believe he does not mean any of us any particular harm."

She looks over her shoulder at me, and I have a pang of jealousy for how she can twist her whole body while keeping her balance and not cue the camel to alter its path even a hair's breadth. "Even so, here is my concern: if you open the Burnt Lands, the desert tribes will be able to claim territory that has lain unclaimed for generations."

The ramifications hit me like a punch to the gut. "There'll be a war," I say numbly.

She nods, her eyes dark. "Indeed." She's already lost so much —and this thing, this supposedly good thing, could cost her so much more.

"What do I do?"

Huda looks away, to where the white of the Barrier shows above the hills—even if she cannot see it herself, her knowledge of the desert tells her precisely where the Burnt Lands lie. She settles once more into facing forward, her shoulders straight. "As I said, this is not for you to fix."

"Fine, what can the phoenix do?"

A pause. "He can demand alliances of every tribe."

I consider this uncertainly. "Would that work?"

She nods. "We do not fight family. The tribes will have to make alliances by marriage and agree on boundaries before the Burnt Lands open up. There might still be problems, but it could work."

I'm going to end up forcing people to marry? "That sounds… terrible."

She casts an amused glance back at me, a smile touching her lips for a heartbeat before slipping away. "This is good, Hikaru. If you succeed and the phoenix demands it, there will be peace. Just do not agree to finish your work until the tribes have sealed their alliances."

Well, if *that's* all. Unravel the spells *and* establish peace among warring tribes through unwanted marriage alliances, right when I'd convinced myself I only needed to worry about the spells. "But —I've seen how you hate the Bani Essam. You can't be the only one who has lost someone or something to the bloodshed and raids. How would such an alliance survive more than a few weeks?"

"It would survive if I knew I would not lose another brother to them. Our escort could not promise me that—nor did they wish to. That is why I would not eat their food. Don't assume that means I would not wish for the raids to stop. Our elders, and so our families, will all agree, especially if it meant greater prosperity for our people."

Oh.

Huda hesitates, then says lightly, "You don't need to worry about me, specifically, though. Those who will be called to marry will be the most eligible of our people, from our noblest families. I am neither."

"That's ridiculous," I say, outraged on Huda's behalf that she *isn't* considered a great catch.

She huffs a laugh. "And a boon, in this case."

I can't argue that.

She clicks her tongue and the camel picks up its pace, falling into a distance-eating lope. I grasp her waist to keep my balance. She adds, "The keeping of such peace lies in our hands. You need only worry about what lies in yours."

It's not a heartening thought.

CHAPTER 5
THE BARRIER

We reach the Barrier by midmorning, the sun warm on our shoulders and the desert eerily quiet. No breeze stirs here, no subtle movement of desert creatures disturbs the stillness. While there might be vultures or other birds behind us, there certainly aren't any past the Barrier.

We set up a small camp on the valley floor, some fifty paces from the Barrier. "There are markers erected along the edge," Huda tells me. "But we are between them here. It is just as well you can sense it."

"Yes," I agree, casting another glance at the Barrier with my mage sight. The land before me is encapsulated in a bubble of steady white magic, a mostly opaque bubble that sinks into the earth and arcs into the sky, enclosing everything within it, not unlike the dome that held us captive this morning, at least at first glance. But at four hundred years old and without any mage to steady it, it's also nothing like that. "I would like to study it, I think."

I *could* wait till the phoenix returns, but from his parting words, he likely intends for me to pass through the Barrier and head to his haven as soon as he rejoins us. If I want to study the spells here, this is the best chance I'll get.

"Shall I come with you?" Huda asks, setting down the camel

saddle at the edge of the blanket. With a wet snort, her camel flops down on its side in the sand a few paces away.

I consider her offer. The Barrier flows over the hills on either side of us and right through the center of the valley. From here, all appears clear. Still, it's never a bad idea to have an ally at one's back. Besides, I'm grateful for the somewhat easier feel of this conversation. I know a kindness when I see it. "If you don't mind," I say.

Huda follows me to the Barrier, keeping a pace or two back. At its edge, I ease myself down to sit on my heels, and put out a hand to touch the Barrier spells. They are immense and intricate, like nothing I've ever seen before. When I passed through them before, fleeing from the spell-creatures on my heels, I had primarily only noticed the existence of the Barrier spells. Now I give them my full attention.

Through my mage senses, I travel the spells. I examine how they are woven together, the seamless joining of one enchantment to another, the very depth of them, how they are layered. I assess how the Barrier spells renew their energy from the flow of magic through the natural world—the wind and sun-warmed earth. And I study those places where the enchantments have begun to wear thin, the draining magic within pressing hard against small, threadbare stretches of the containing spells. The Barrier is holding, but I cannot tell if it will continue to hold for weeks or months—it certainly does not have years left.

I sit back, letting my hand drop. My arm feels stiff, and I flex my hands a few times. By the slant of the sunlight, I would guess at least a half hour has passed.

Huda has been standing sentry as I've worked. Now, she casts me a curious look. "What did you find?"

"The Barrier is wearing thin in places."

"So soon? Your High Council sent a team of mages not two years ago to assess and maintain it."

I grimace. Perhaps the spells are just too old to maintain, fraying as soon as they're patched—or rubbing thin in new spots. I run my hands through my hair, lean back to look up at the spells arcing above me. The Council will have to send another team of mages very soon, or the Barrier will certainly fall. The results could well be catastrophic—the draining spells released to flow across the sands, devouring everything and everyone in their way. Unlike the Barrier, they appear as robust as ever. It's all sorts of ironic, when you consider they were created in a furor of attacks and counter-attacks, and have barely been touched since, while the Barrier spells have been adjusted and maintained for centuries.

Then again, the draining spells were built to push boundaries, to take more than what is right. Even now, they absorb any magic that makes it through the Barrier so that not a whisper of it lives in the land within. For the Barrier to maintain its balance, it *can't* absorb all the magic of the natural world—that would require it to be something more like the draining spells. Instead, magic passes through the Barrier and the draining spells continue to use and expend that. It's just not enough for them to actually *expand*, and the Barrier draws enough magic to maintain their containment, so we have a delicate stasis. You would think after four hundred years the draining spells would begin falling apart of their own accord, but here we are, with the Barrier weakening against their continuous onslaught.

"How often do the Council's mages come?" I ask Huda.

"Every five years."

So, three more years from now? That's definitely too long. Perhaps that's another reason the phoenix has worked so hard to bring me back to the Burnt Lands. "Do you mind if I take another look? I'll need to step inside. I want to assess the draining spells themselves."

She hesitates. "Will that draw the dead creatures?"

"It might," I allow. "I'll need you to watch for them and warn me if you see any."

"All right."

I edge forward, feeling the faint push of the Barrier against my knees, my legs, until I am sitting almost completely within the Barrier. I reach out once more, fingertips resting hesitantly in the air just beyond the Barrier, and open myself to the magic there.

If the Barrier might be described as a bubble, what roils beneath its steady facade is nothing short of a storm stretched wide and thin—no wider than my hand across, and yet continuously shifting and flowing, crackling with power. This layer of storm is purple to my mage sight, but there is nothing beautiful in it; it is the purple of bruises and old blood. It is thick and viscous and dangerous.

I hold my breath, taking small gasps when I must, as if I might drown amongst these enchantments, might lose my essence to these spells that drain the very air and earth of their magic. Perhaps I might.

I scoot forward, passing through the Barrier altogether, and moving quickly through the dark storm of spells plastered within them. I shudder at the oily touch of the spells on my skin—purple tendrils reaching for me as I push myself into the Burnt Lands. Once I am past them, though, they fall away, blending seamlessly back into the larger spells.

The sudden cessation of magic in the Burnt Lands is as shocking as a blow to my overwrought senses. Past the layer of dark storm lies nothing, the same nothing I found when I stumbled through a portal into this land two weeks ago. From hardly a pace within the Lands, I cannot sense the draining spells at all. Just as I could not sense them when I searched for magic in the dead city, trying to find some source to use—first against the mage who followed me, and then against the tentacled spell-beast. How do you break an enchantment that would suck the magic from you should you touch it too long, but that you cannot otherwise sense?

No wonder the phoenix said so many mages died trying to contain the enchantments that hold sway here.

I rise and turn back. I'll have plenty of time to investigate the draining spells with the phoenix, as well as how they power the spell-beasts—and perhaps he'll be able to tell me even more from his own experience with them. In the meantime, I don't want to draw any spell-beasts to me.

Huda's shoulders drop a notch in relief as I step through the Barrier once more to join her. "Did you learn anything?"

"The draining spells are strong. I don't see any apparent weaknesses in them. They're..." I shudder. "Dangerous. I'll need to study them further at some point, but I think it best to wait for the phoenix."

"You should rest, then," Huda says, starting toward our makeshift camp. "You will need your strength to cross the Burnt Lands."

"We should both rest," I say, following her.

"The phoenix will see me back to my family," Huda replies. "I can easily rest while he is guiding you to his haven."

True. I fold my legs beneath me to sit on the blanket, thinking of Kareem and Sumeyya, and the danger I put them and Huda in. We talked about it last night, and I apologized—but not properly. "I'm sorry for everything," I say baldly. "Especially for putting you and your family at risk without warning you."

Huda slides me a look I can't quite interpret. "Did you fear to tell me you were being hunted?"

I stare at the blanket, my eyes focusing on a thread that has come loose from the weave. I pick at it with my fingers as I work through the words I need in the desert tongue—aware that words are coming to me that I haven't heard used recently. They must be coming back from the part of my memory that didn't burn. I thought I'd already recovered everything I could, but maybe this is how things will be from now on: tiny bits of myself resurfacing from the ash as I go about my life. It's an amazing thought, and I hold on to it even as I make myself focus on our conversation.

"I didn't want to endanger you," I admit. "I was hopeful that no one would follow us so quickly. If they didn't have my spindle, they wouldn't have been able to find me at all."

She raises her brows.

I grimace. "And I thought the less you knew about me, the less danger my presence would pose you."

"Perhaps it was not for you to decide what dangers I might choose," Huda says coolly.

I open my mouth and close it again. She's angry, and she's also right. I've put myself in plenty of predicaments to protect my friends, no doubt more than I can actually remember. But from what I've found among the ashes and my conversations with Kenta, I had to fight my way into being a part of the Shadow League, making my own decisions about what dangers I would face. Just as I chose to risk my life and safety in Fidanya in order to free Stormwind. And then I had the audacity to make the decision to hide the dangers from Huda, so that she wouldn't have a choice in what she did.

"I'm sorry," I say lamely. "I'm used to—I wanted to protect you. But I should have told you."

She grunts. "Did you consider at all that we are friends?"

I blink at her. We are? I mean, I *have* thought of her as a friend, but I've also been terribly aware of the number of deceptions I've engaged in, about my name, about why I was going to Fidanya, and most certainly about the circumstances of my return to the desert. "I... haven't been honest. It is not a strong basis for friendship."

She clicks her tongue in irritation. "I have traveled with you through enemy territory, Hikaru—and no, I don't care what your real name is. I have gotten a measure of you, and you are honorable and caring. So, you have your secrets. Keep them. I will be ready to hear them when you can speak of them. Until then, you had *better* not forget you have my friendship. I will not be pleased with you if you betray that."

She regards me, her eyes sparking. With the diamond of tattooed circles on her brow, and the sharp, angled lines on her chin, she looks every bit a desert queen. "Are we clear?"

"Yes," I say meekly.

She gives me a firm nod, as if I had offered fealty, and looks up to scan the skies. I try to gather myself. Friendship apparently takes a good deal of work, and I haven't been doing it. But there's some little time and quiet now. All I have to do is start. Which, admittedly, is not the easiest thing. But surely if I've faced down the High Council, I can figure out how to talk to a friend.

Bolstering my courage, I say, "If you'd like to hear it, I can tell you more about me."

Huda flashes a smile, losing that austere, fierce mien in a heartbeat. "I would very much like that." She rummages through her pack, pulling out a band of half-embroidered fabric and a packet of threads. It's a good idea to have something to do with one's hands. I extract the charms I took from the mages this morning, and sort through them while I begin my story.

I've told this story so many times now—to Stonefall, and Kenta, and the High Council—that it falls from my mouth with ease. I don't even have to think too hard about the bits I don't want to share, like Val giving me a breath to save my life after I cast my sunbolt, and thereby creating a bond with me. I haven't told anyone that, and it is simple enough to gloss over it in the aftermath of our escape from Kol's fortress, and Kol's death at my hands.

I break off abruptly, staring unseeing at a small explosive charm as I realize what I hadn't had time or attention to notice earlier: at no time has Val spoken in my mind during or after the mages attacked last night.

"Hikaru?" Huda asks, her brow furrowing as she studies my face.

"Sorry, I—I just need a moment to think."

"Of course," Huda says, returning her attention to her sewing.

I close my eyes to focus. Every time I've been in danger in the last two weeks, Val has been there for me. He tried to help me evade the great tentacled spell-beast in the Burnt Lands; he took over my body to fight Osman Bey in the halls of the Mekteb; he spoke for me during the trial before the High Council when my own abilities were hampered by the truth spell; he even kept me silent company when I was marked. He's always been there.

Last night, he was not.

Maybe he was busy. Maybe, by the time he was able to respond, the fight was over—it happened very, very fast after all. But surely Val would have checked in on me since? And even as preoccupied as I was with what happened, surely I would have noticed his presence?

Unless he didn't come. His prince knows about our bond now, figured it out while Val was helping me through the hearing and then being marked. Val brushed off my concern when I asked, as if what happened to me was of more pressing importance. But it's been nearly a week, and his prince may have come to a decision regarding our bond, and Val himself. Now, Val has disappeared. If he can sense when I'm in danger, shouldn't I be able to do the same for him? Except that I still don't fully understand how our bond functions, how to use it.

I do know that I called him to the trial by calling his name in my mind. It seems as good a method as any.

Val?

I wait. I don't want to shout the name in my mind, don't want to give it everything I have, because I'm not actually in danger. I'll save screaming for help for when I need to; right now, I just want to make sure he's okay.

Val, I try again as a faint, dry desert breeze blows past. I close my eyes, listening for his voice, but Val is not here, and I don't know how to reach him. I can only hope he is all right. He has to be, though—surely, I would have felt if he was in danger?

Huda shifts. I open my eyes, watch her reach to change out her embroidery thread, though I can tell her attention is on me.

"I was telling you about how Val took me to Stormwind," I say, gathering up the threads of my narrative again. "I stayed with her all this past year."

"Isn't she the one you freed? Who'd been imprisoned in Fidanya?" Huda asks. "How did that happen?"

While I sort through the last of Mountain's charms, I tell her of Stonefall's arrival with a summons from the High Council, Stormwind's short and unjust trial, and how I'd awakened one night to the realization that mages were about to descend upon our valley. I describe my flight through the portal in Sonapur into the Burnt Lands with a mage on my heels—a mage who attempted to throw me to the great, tentacled spell-creature, and instead got eaten himself.

"The phoenix found me there and guided me out. You know of my journey from the Burnt Lands to Fidanya," I say.

Huda dips her head. "I do, and that you rescued your mentor, and somehow the Guardian of the Mekteb is involved. Though I should like to understand it better."

I tell her how Jabir let me into the Mekteb because of the token of the phoenix I carried—another feather, long since burned. I tell her of the assassination attempt on Stonefall, and the poison I called forth from his wound using a glowstone, and how he let me go in return. As I describe my adventures, from finding the key to Stormwind's shackles to reconnecting with the Degath children and my old friend Kenta, to breaking Stormwind out of her cell and immediately getting taken prisoner by Osman Bey, the captain of the Lycan Guard, I find myself more and more amazed that I managed to free Stormwind at all.

"I'm really quite bad at planning," I admit.

Huda coughs a laugh. "From what you've told me, and what I've seen, your plans seem to involve getting yourself to the right place and hoping everything works out from there."

"I do a bit more than *that*," I protest.

"You're very good at thinking on your feet," she says, unperturbed. "But you don't seem to think of *yourself* very much."

Someone else said that to me relatively recently, though I can't recall who. Probably Val. He doesn't appear to appreciate my tendency to go flying about trying to save people.

Val? I call out a third time, though I don't have much hope of hearing him. Wherever he is, he isn't at leisure to reach me. I'll have to try to reach him instead, and for that I'll have to figure out how to slip out of my body and find his. I think I've done it before, a handful of times when I was half-asleep and walking between dreams, but it was never intentional.

"So how did you escape after you were taken prisoner? Did Stormwind get away?"

"She did—the phoenix flew her to safety. I was tried before

the High Council, and marked," I lift a sleeve to bare my markings once more, and am relieved to see that they are already less angry looking. "But soon after, Osman Bey came back and broke me out. The Lycan Guard did not like the Council using them to unjust ends, and left their posts. He took me to a rooftop, and the phoenix flew me away to join my friends outside the city. We parted ways just a little while before I found you again."

Though not in a well-planned way. Rather, it was because Stonefall was following us. I feared he meant to corner me, and I didn't want him to find Stormwind and Kenta as well. I took myself off while Kenta was busy stealing the glowstone Stonefall was using to track me. Which... just goes to show I'm a terrible friend, deciding for Kenta what risks he could take as well. He had planned to stay with me, right up until I disappeared behind his back while he was protecting me.

I grimace. I still think the Shadow League will be better served with him in Fidanya, supporting the Degaths as they renew their claims against Blackflame, and generally keeping an eye on the High Council. But I shouldn't have made that decision for Kenta. No doubt he was furious with me.

"That is... quite a story," Huda says. "You underplayed yourself, you know. You are not just the chosen ally of the phoenix, but a friend of the Guardian of the Mekteb, and sister to the Lycan Guard."

"I... don't think any of the Guard considers me their sister." I barely even spoke with any of them, just Osman Bey. And sisterhood seems... something deeper. The bond between Huda and Sumeyya is the sort of thing my dreams are made of. Even friendship—I'm not sure Jabir would consider me a friend so much as a free mage whose ethics happened to coincide with his for a short time.

"They seem to hold you in high esteem regardless," Huda says.

Do they? I can't tell what the phoenix thinks of me, which leaves the Lycan Guard. I lift my head to the breeze, remembering how Osman Bey helped me escape the Mekteb, what he said as we waited for the phoenix to fly me out of the school. *Run far, run fast, keep the wind in your hair.*

There is something about that farewell that feels like a benediction. Run, not in order to flee something, as I do now; nor to run toward trouble, as I did with my eyes wide open, throwing myself fully into finding and freeing Stormwind. But to simply run for the joy of it. I wonder what that would feel like—to run because one could, and not from fear or desperation or fury or duty.

I'm going to find out, I promise myself. Just as soon as I take care of the Burnt Lands. The thought makes me huff with laughter—at the impossibility of it all.

"What is it?" Huda asks.

"Nothing," I tell her, sweeping the charms back together to put in their pouch.

Huda raises a brow. "In which case, you had better get some rest while you can."

It's such an older sister thing to say, I can't help grinning at her. "All right," I agree, and settle on the blanket to sleep.

CHAPTER 6

INTO THE BURNT LANDS

"Hikaru."

I blink my eyes open, tug the edge of my scarf away from my face. All lies quiet. The sun has moved only a little more across the sky. The winter season means the weather is more comfortable than not, the sun not too hot during the day, the nights just cold enough to require blankets. So, it's been quite pleasant sleeping with just my scarf draped over my face to block the sun.

"The phoenix comes," Huda says, tilting her chin toward the sky. I squint and spot his form arcing over the hill to our backs.

"Did you rest at all?" I ask, pushing myself up to a sitting position.

"I will rest once you have moved on," she tells me. "Anyway, I have an easy ride ahead of me."

While I'll be trying to keep ahead of the spell-creatures in the Burnt Lands.

"You should eat." She passes me a trio of dried figs as the phoenix circles down to us.

I grin and take a bite as the phoenix lands, flickers of orange and scarlet glimmering over cobalt shadows. "Are you ready?" he asks.

He's rarely this direct; he must still be worried. I swallow my bite and nod.

He turns to Huda. "If you remain nearby until your friend reaches my haven, I will return to fly with you." She dips her head in agreement.

Turning back to me, he says, "We should enter directly. I'll fly over once to look for any spell-creatures in our path and circle back for you. The longer you remain by the edge, the more likely a spell-creature will find you here."

"All right," I say, and the next moment he is airborne, his wingbeats reverberating through the air. I fetch my pack and double-check my water as he makes a turn over our valley, arcing back toward us.

Huda passes me a spare blanket woven in the brightly colored stripes the desert peoples favor. "Keep this. It will likely be cool in this underground haven of the phoenix. You may need it."

I take it, dipping my head in thanks, my heart full. Huda noticed that I'd forgotten to bring the blanket Stonefall had packed in Zahra's saddlebags.

She goes on, "I'll tell my family of your work, and we will look to the phoenix to demand peace."

"All right," I say uncertainly.

She laughs. "What was it I told you in Fidanya, before you raided the High Council itself?"

I raise my eyes to hers, grinning, "Walk your path with courage."

"Do that, and come back to us." She reaches out, drawing me into a quick hug. I drop my head onto her shoulder, and she tightens her arms, but none of that changes the impossibility of her words. I can't ever turn back now. Every step must be away, a flight from hunters who will not give me up—because to do so is for the Council to admit defeat. And they will never do that.

I step back and smile at this woman who is the closest thing to a sister I suspect I've ever had. "Maybe one day," I say with forced brightness.

"Sooner than that," she says firmly.

"I'm being hunted," I remind her, shouldering my pack. "I can only go forward from here." Or sideways, I suppose, though that sounds somewhat less dramatic. Still, I can't backtrack—that will only land me in Ravenflight's path.

Huda hmms softly and turns with me to walk to the Barrier. "We shall see. But this much is true, Hikaru: it has been one of the greatest honors of my life to know you."

I eye her askance. "You're only saying that because we got to demand an escort of your enemies."

She laughs as the phoenix soars by overhead. "That is certainly part of it."

"Follow me, mageling," he calls down to me. "Pace yourself. You may need to run at some point."

I raise my hand in acknowledgement and step into the Burnt Lands.

IT WAS TERRIFYING ENOUGH to travel through a dead city littered with the mummified remains of a long-gone people, having just stumbled into the Burnt Lands by accident. Journeying across a string of broken valleys with a scattering of empty houses—some carved into the hills with flat faces and gaping doorways, others of stone or brick that are tumbling to ruin—knowing full well that monsters may be hiding in plain sight, provides me with an expanded definition of the word "harrowing."

The terrain underfoot is rocky, filled with great cracks reaching through the parched earth. Despite my best intentions, I must either go slowly or risk turning an ankle. Only where the earth flattens do I dare pick up my pace, the hills falling away to a wide, sun-scorched plain, still riddled with deep cracks—though these are less wide. At least there's been no sign of the pack creatures as yet. Perhaps I'll manage to evade them.

As I walk, I continue to scan the lands around me with my mage sight, watching for the first signs of a spell-beast. The phoenix flies overhead, sometimes circling back again, sometimes landing ahead of me and waiting for me to reach him. Just as I'm beginning to wonder if we'll make our destination without any trouble at all, he swoops in to land a few paces away. I know he's seen something from the simple fact of how close he's landed.

"What's coming?" I ask.

"Scorpions. They're moving fast."

I spin on my heel, reaching out with my mage sight as I scan the land all around me. "How many?"

"Three."

Three? That doesn't seem like a great number for so small a creature. Given the phoenix's concern, I would have expected a carpet of the things, capable of destroying anything in their way. Still, if he's worried about three, then so am I. However big they are, the magic of this land will have made them deadly.

"How far are they?"

"Still a ways off, but coming quickly. From there." He gestures with a wing tip.

I can't see anything, but that means little. I start forward briskly, the phoenix following with a flap of his wings as I ask, "How far till your haven?"

"A half hour at that pace. It's at the heart of the next town."

I swallow hard, glancing in the direction the phoenix indicated. The scorpions are approaching at an angle, and if they're as fast as the phoenix has implied, they may well intercept me before I ever reach the town.

I lengthen my stride to a fast-paced jog, leaping over rocks and sidestepping the widest of the cracks. The phoenix takes off, soaring ahead.

My pack thumps against my back, and sweat beads on my brow. I glance over my shoulder as I reach an open stretch, and my mage sight shows me three blobs of knotted magic quickly growing larger in the distance. As big as their magical structure is, I have the distinct feeling that these scorpions are not of the palm-sized hide-beneath-a-rock variety. I can only hope that they won't equal the giant tentacled beast in size or speed. I have a bad feeling I'm wrong on at least one of those counts.

The town rises up as a series of bumps and ridges ahead of me, far enough away that their shapes rise and fall back again with each dip and furrow of the land. It's still too far for comfort, but I don't dare break into a sprint and expend all my energy too early. Now would be a good time to be able to run like a breather.

Val, I call, my mental voice uncertain.

No response.

My heart pounds as I run, sweat trickling into my eyes and drenching the back of my thobe. A quick glance over my shoulders shows me the gray bodies of the scorpions, now as large as horses, their legs blurring as they run. I nearly stumble at the sight of them. They've already halved the distance to me.

Valerius! Any time now!

I swear, if something has happened to him, I'm going to wring his neck. Right after I survive these monster scorpions.

"This way," the phoenix calls, passing above me and veering slightly to the left. I follow, sprinting hard toward the first of the town's outlying houses. If I can make it to cover, I might be able to survive.

I hope to God there aren't any other spell-creatures lurking among the buildings. Another glance over my shoulder shows the massive scorpions hardly more than two hundred paces behind me, their stingers already rising above their backs. I race down the ancient road the phoenix has chosen, fists pumping, my sides starting to cramp. At least there are houses here—some more broken than others, but walls still standing. As I pass the first houses, I can see that the farther in we go, the more whole the buildings stand.

"Behind you!"

I don't even look, just throw myself at the next window I reach, half rolling over the empty sill and dropping to the ground below. I scramble away from the window, clutching my side with one hand, terror sharpening my senses. A great pincer flies through the window, the wicked point slamming against the ground. The scorpion makes a strange whirring, clicking noise, scraping its pincer around as it tries to reach me. My breath shudders in my chest.

It can't make it through the window itself, but I'm not sure the wall will stand against it. The pincer, easily half as long as I am, bashes against the side of the window, sending chunks of brick flying. I flee, scrambling through the connecting doorway into a back room, where another window beckons. My pulse pounds so loudly in my ears I can barely hear the scorpion over it. I've won myself a minute at best. I've got to make it count.

Dropping down from the window into a back alley, I keep running, heading for the center of town. The phoenix swoops by overhead. "They're coming up to the next road!"

All of them? How am I going to evade all three? I climb through the next window, staggering into the room beyond. I can't keep this up much longer. But I also can't die like this, ripped apart in the Burnt Lands before I've even reached the phoenix's haven, let alone paid my debts. I *can't.*

I move to the center of the room and bend over, gulping down great lungfuls of breath. At least I have the walls to shelter me here. Perhaps if I move quietly enough, the scorpions may not find me so quickly. Stealth, not speed. Or rather, both.

I swipe my arm across my forehead, wiping away the sweat. As I start padding toward the door, I feel the faintest brush against my mind, as if I had caught a familiar scent.

Val? I ask, not quite daring to believe.

What is this place?

I almost stumble in relief at the sound of his voice. *You're all right!*

Of course I am. I'm not the one creeping through abandoned buildings.

I step through the doorway, listening for the telltale clicking of the scorpions. *Figured you'd gotten yourself locked in a tower,* I tell him, feeling lighter already.

Not this time. What's that on the floor?

A body. I keep my eyes averted and turn the other way down the hallway. This is one of the worst parts of the Burnt Lands: the mummified remains of the people who died here, paper-thin skin stretched over brittle bones, still lying where they fell four hundred years before. Fortunately, there are no other bodies between myself and the door at the end of the hall, leading back outside.

Where are *you?* Val demands, voice so sharp I flinch.

The Burnt Lands. There are a trio of scorpion monsters chasing me. The phoenix has a haven hidden at the center of town that I'm trying to get to.

Scorpion monsters?

Spell-cursed stinger bugs the size of elephants.

Ah.

I pause just within the entrance, listening for sounds of pursuit. *Any chance you can help me run like the wind?*

What did you do before we bonded? Val asks, amused. *Did you have someone else who helped you out of these predicaments?*

Not that I recall, though of course I don't remember much at all. But I have been depending on Val a great deal these last weeks. Too much. It's one thing to utilize allies, and another to automatically fall back on them every time you have a problem.

Warily, I step out of the door. The street lies empty. Perhaps five hundred paces down from me the houses open up to a darker space that must be the central square. If it isn't, I'm in worse shape than I want to admit.

Last time I'll ask, I promise.

I hope not. I'd like you to live long enough to get out of a few more scrapes.

As long as you get me out of this one, I respond, miffed.

I pause at the corner, peeking around the side of the building. A scorpion waits halfway down the side road, its pincers outstretched and its stinger at the ready, its armor shadow-gray in the midday sun.

That may be larger than an elephant, Val says. *With your permission?*

Yes.

This time when Val takes over my body, it's more like being nudged out of place than the disorienting sideways stumble I experienced the first time he did it. One moment I'm lodged happily within my body, and the next I'm a bit off to the side, still within my skull, still looking out of the same eyes, but no longer in control. My body shifts, holding itself differently now that a different mind directs it.

Val scans all the buildings and remaining roads one last time.

Just a warning, I say as he eases me back from the wall. *They move a lot faster than I do.*

Understood.

And they can't jump through windows.

I guessed. Good work on your part, that.

If I can't figure out windows, I deserve to be scorpion food.

Val shakes his head—or rather, it is my own head that shakes —and then we are running, crossing the street in a few silent steps and racing for the open square. Val moves with a lightness I could never manage, and a speed that is utterly inhuman. My body is going to *hurt* tomorrow.

I hear a scrape behind us, the clatter of armored bodies against stone as the scorpions brush against a building. The phoenix swoops past us, trailing fire and heading straight for the scorpions.

What's that? Val demands.

The phoenix.

No, up ahead.

A great gray mass fills the square. I can hardly make sense of it —though the top of it has the look of a thicket of brambles reaching broken fingers for the sky. *A... forest?*

A very dead one, Val says as we plunge in between the slender trunks. He slows within a pace or two, for the footing here is tricky, tree roots breaking through the ground in strangely shaped ripples, and broken bits of stone branches littering the dirt between. We glance back as a scorpion smashes into the trees behind us, raking its pincers in front of it. But the trees neither bend nor break, standing as solid as the bars of a cage.

The scorpion clicks angrily, another one skittering up beside it. The sunlight shines on their dark armor, gleaming on the rounded surfaces and glittering on the edges. Lashing their tails, they slam their pincers against the trees again and again, but the trees will not give, and spell-creatures are too large to pass between them.

We're safe.

The phoenix lands softly in the branches above us, his feathers gleaming in the dappled light.

You trust this bird?

He got me out of the Burnt Lands alive once.

So I recall. But that isn't an answer.

The phoenix tilts his head, and then says, so quietly, "Breather."

My muscles begin to flex slowly, slowly, as if Val were preparing me for flight, making sure I'm limber. *I'm sorry,* he murmurs. *I should have left you before he came this close.*

And then he slides back, until he is the one watching through my eyes, and I am once more in control of my body. Even with Val having braced my body for this, I jerk slightly, my body finally registering the toll his help has taken: my legs tremble beneath me, my chest ripples with pain, and the wound in my arm sets my teeth on edge. I have run too fast, breathed too quickly, my heart hammering too hard against the flesh around it.

But the phoenix is still balanced on his branch, watching me. I offer him a tight smile, strained at the corners. I have no answer for him, but then he hasn't asked a question.

"Come," the phoenix finally says, turning toward the center of the grove. "This tree cannot protect against all spell-creatures. We must get below quickly. And I think it is time you told me a little bit more about yourself."

That doesn't sound too bad, Val says.

He hasn't incinerated me, I agree, my mind flashing to Saber. I shake the thought away, trying not to shudder. *I think I'm still too useful to him, even if I am marked by mages and bonded to a breather.*

You had better stay useful then. Val sounds far too amused for my liking. *At least until you're sure you trust him.*

Sound advice.

The phoenix opens his wings to leap down and then pauses, head cocked as he looks through the branches overhead. I tilt my head back to follow his gaze. High up, a black-feathered bird hangs in the air above us, no more than a dark silhouette against the steel-white sky. My mage sight brings the dome of the Barrier into focus, washing out the sky even more with its pale color. The bird soars above it.

Too small to be a vulture, Val observes. *Is there a reason your phoenix would worry over a bird?*

Not just any bird, I tell him, dread threading through me. *That's the rogue hunter who's been tracking me. Ravenflight.*

"Come," the phoenix says, unaware of our conversation, and flutters down to lead the way between the trees. He hops quickly over the roots and threads his way through the vines that hang down to frame the open spaces between the trees. I force myself to shuffle after him, but I only make it five steps before I have to pause to catch my breath, my legs shaky.

I grab one of the finger-thick stone vines beside me to steady myself. There are thinner ones beside them, hanging down in clumps from the branches overhead. But they aren't actually vines. I look up, tracing the line of the huge branches overhead, branches that come from the center of the grove and continue, growing out and out and out.... All the slender trees we've passed already are not trees at all, but *roots*. Long, thick roots that grew down to support the branches overhead.

This tree, the phoenix had said.

"It's all one tree," I say, my voice barely more than croak. The tree stretches out over us like an ancient creature returned to the earth, greater in size than any I have seen, spreading itself out over the vast central square this town is built around.

"Yes," the phoenix says, pausing for me. "It was a banyan tree, and the center of all that happened in this town. Now hurry."

I push myself forward again, as fast as I can. The tree must have been amazing when it lived, its branches vibrant with bird-song, filled with leaves to shade the earth below. I can almost imagine the business of the town taking place here, in the wide spaces between the branches, the roots creating open-air walls to form makeshift rooms, all of it shaded by the canopy. There would have been merchants spreading out their wares, young chil-dren gathering in a circle to learn from their teacher, perhaps elders sitting together over cups of tea or spiced coffee. Nothing like this nightmare vision of stone and darkness at the center of a town that is its own mausoleum.

"I thought all the trees—anything that wasn't already stone—was drained of its essence and destroyed," I say as we near the central trunk, hoping despite myself that the phoenix will forget all about what he saw when he looked in my eyes. And that Ravenflight can't see where we are now.

The phoenix doesn't look back. "It's the only one that survived."

I stumble over a stone root underfoot, catch myself on another root that lends its pillar-like support to a branch above. "Doesn't look very alive."

"I meant that something of it was left behind. Unlike the others."

That's true. I haven't seen a single tree anywhere else. "Why this one?"

"Because there was a mage who lived just there." His beak jabs toward the south, though I can't tell if he means a building edging the town center, or somewhere farther off. "She died protecting it."

The phoenix's words, brisk though they are, are tinged with age-old regret. I follow, considering them. A mage had given her life to protect this tree, and all she had managed was to turn it to stone. Had she considered it a victory? Had she somehow managed to preserve its essence so that, even though it turned to stone, its magic was not stripped away by the curses cast by the mages?

"We're out of time," the phoenix says when we are still fifteen paces from the trunk. He stands, gaze fixed on the far edge of the tree's reach. "Get through the crack in the tree—anything that follows you down won't survive long. I'll try to hold them off."

He takes off with a great flap of his wings, bursting up through the branches overhead and speeding above the stone canopy toward the shadows entering beneath its shelter. Pack creatures with lithe black bodies weave between the tree's standing roots and reaching branches. Far above, higher than the draining spells and the Barrier itself, Ravenflight still hangs in the sky, watching. She'll know where I am; the only question is if she will follow or prefer to wait me out.

Move, Val orders, and I stumble forward again, my feet coming unglued. *Grab that branch there, quickly, and get inside the tree.*

I snatch up the branch by my feet. It's long, about as thick around as my wrist, with a slight turn at one end—which also makes it very heavy. I sincerely doubt I'll be able to club anything effectively enough to stop it with this, but I'm still glad to be holding it.

The phoenix dives through the branches, closing his talons around the spikes of the foremost beast and using their joined momentum to hurl the creature up and to the side, into the stone branches. It shrieks, writhing as if impaled, and does not fall back down again. The others flow right past it, speeding on padded feet toward us.

Let me, Val says, and I can feel him pressing against my awareness.

All right, I manage, and then I am shoved to the side. My legs falter once before I spring forward, crossing the remaining distance to the crack in the tree in the space of a breath. It reaches from the ground up into the heart of the tree, the opening long and narrow, though still wide enough to pass through. Holding the stick behind me, Val wedges my body into the crack.

My pack, I say as it catches tight behind me.

With a curse, Val pushes back, working my arms out of the straps.

Watch out!

A spell-creature leaps for the opening, its needlelike teeth bared, its eyes glowing red.

Val rips my arms free of the pack and shoves me deeper into the crevice, my skin scraping against the stone as we leave the pack behind. The spell-creature snarls, tearing past my pack, its claws reaching for me. The only thing between us is the stone stick—

The earth disappears beneath my feet. We fall through darkness. Val bends my knees and brings up my arms so that, as my feet finally hit the earth, he springs me forward into a roll, head over heels and back to my feet.

We swing around, ready. The room is dark but for a soft round of light filtering through from the ceiling. Then even that is blocked out, claws scraping on earth and stone as the pack-beast fills the hole. It hesitates there, hissing and clawing at the edge of the entrance.

We need light, Val says, scooping up the stone branch from where we dropped it. *And a better weapon.*

Glowstone in my pocket. And some kind of explosive charms too.

You had an explosive charm and you didn't tell me?

I forgot, I admit as Val checks my pockets. *I couldn't use it earlier because it would have drawn more spell-creatures to us. But it's not too powerful—it should be safe to use in here. Yes, that's the one.*

The room lights up just as the pack beast gathers itself and leaps. Val lets the glowstone drop and throws the explosive charm with unnerving accuracy—it slams into the beast just as its paws touch down, sending it catapulting backward with a screech. We squint against the flash of light, the strange, dry scent of scorched stone filling the room. The glowstone shines brightly at my feet.

Val throws the second exploding charm as the pack beast staggers to its feet. The blast sends it slamming back against the wall, and both of us stumbling back.

Gripping the branch with both hands, Val keeps me facing the pack creature. *Anytime your feathered friend wants to show up would be fine,* he says.

I don't want to think about why the phoenix hasn't managed to follow yet. He's much faster than the pack beasts. The only reason he wouldn't follow was if he hadn't seen this one come in after us, or if he's too busy fighting off the rest. Either way, we can't rely on him to come to our rescue.

We just have to keep the creature away for a little while, I say, remembering the phoenix's words.

There's something wrong with it, Val says.

Exactly, I say, glad to see the beast slowing. In the white light of the glowstone, it looks somehow paler, more gray than black. It heaves itself to its feet, shaking its head heavily. Then it shambles toward us.

With Val in control, I can't look at it with my mage sight, can't assess just what's happening, but... *It should be running out of magic.*

I'm not asking how that's possible, Val says, hefting the stick in readiness. *But that's something at least.*

I hope it's enough. I don't think a stick will keep us safe. Staring at the beast, with its nightmare fangs bared and its sharp spines rising up its back, and no magic at my fingertips—my own body given over to someone with quicker instincts and vastly superior fighting skills than my own—I feel strangely detached. Yet I'm also nauseously aware of the likelihood that I will die, witnessing my death from somewhere beside myself.

The beast crouches five paces away, the tips of its spines dulled and cracking, crumbling away. We hold completely still, facing it.

If I'm dead, can you still get out safely? I ask.

Shut up.

The beast launches itself at us. Val moves us, the branch swinging as if it were a natural extension of my arm. It slams against the beast's head, shattering on impact and sending the beast thudding to the ground a bare pace away. I hear myself grunt as Val jumps us back, shaking out my hand.

I'm not sure I want to know how badly my hand will hurt once I'm fully back in my body, if it's actually bothering Val.

The beast heaves itself to its feet, and then tenses... no, it's not tensing. It's turning to stone, the muscles and dark fur hardening and dulling until I'm staring at a gray statue, its surface rough with grit.

The light in the room brightens, edged with yellow. We look up to see the phoenix diving through the hole. He opens his wings, his head turning to take in the collapsed stone form of the pack beast, then whipping back to look at us.

Val closes my eyes, leaning back against the wall, and steps aside. Braced for the pain this time, I slide back into place and open my eyes to return the phoenix's gaze.

"He's helpful, at least, your breather," the phoenix says.

I laugh weakly, flexing a hand that feels like it's on fire. "Yeah."

I think he likes you, I tell Val.

I doubt it, Val says. *He just understands the importance of using the weapons at one's disposal.*

You're not a weapon. And neither am I.

Tell that to the phoenix.

I slide down the root-bound wall, my legs more jelly than flesh. "Are they gone?" I ask the phoenix, cradling my hand in my lap.

"I don't think any more will risk entering," he answers. "Even this one should have known better than to jump. They usually know not to leave behind the spells that feed them."

I didn't realize it was a choice.

"Mageling?" The phoenix watches me worriedly. "We should not linger here longer than necessary."

I give myself a moment to steady my breathing. "I lost my pack up there," I say, my voice hoarse. "I'll need the food I brought." And the crow statuette Val carved me, as well as the lapis wards made from Stormwind's necklace. Those, and I need a few moments to get my body to answer to me again. "It's in the crack," I clarify.

"I'll fetch it."

"If it's safe," I add. The last thing I want are more pack creatures throwing themselves down into this hole. Or for the phoenix to not return.

"It's safe enough," the phoenix replies, and launches himself toward the opening overhead. It's a sentiment I recognize. It seems the phoenix is as used to balancing risks as I've come to be these last few weeks.

It's a thought that offers little comfort.

CHAPTER 7
HAVEN

The opening at the top of this underground room is easily two armlengths past my own reach. It is small and dark against the earthen roof. Stone roots peek out and curl overhead, woven together to come down around us like an eerie underground cage.

As the phoenix drops back through the entrance, my slightly mangled pack gripped in one taloned foot, I finally bring my mage sight into focus.

"There's a hole," I breathe, stunned.

The phoenix sets my pack at my feet. "Of course there is. You came through it."

"No, I mean in the draining spells." They perfectly overlay each other, the sick purplish webbing looped around the entry beneath the banyan, held at bay by a darker rope of magic. It is not quite smooth, but holding it all the same.

"Yes," the phoenix agrees. "The mage who preserved the tree, that was her work."

So, she did succeed, creating a flaw in the draining spells here, at the heart of the tree. "Why didn't you tell me?"

He shifts from one foot to the other, still looking up. Then he turns and walks to the only break in the cage of roots around us: a low tunnel just large enough for a full-grown man to crawl through. "I did not think you would need to know in advance. Come, there is more for you to see."

I cast a glance upwards again. There's no ladder, no rope, no handholds that I will be able to grasp to get back up. I almost make a quip about breathers being able to jump, but catch myself.

Instead, I tell Val, *I think I'll be all right from here.*

You're sure?

I nod. At least for the time being. I ease myself to my knees, slip an arm through the remaining fully attached strap of my pack to drag it with me, and try crawling toward the tunnel where the phoenix has disappeared. His fire still provides me with enough light to find my way easily. And my arms and knees hold me, despite my aching muscles. At least the pain in my hand has reduced to a dull throb.

One thing, I say as I crawl along, pushing bits of stone roots away so that my knees don't come down on them. The unasked question I'm trying to form is awkward almost to embarrassment.

Yes?

Nothing for it but to try. *Last night, I got caught in a spot of trouble. I didn't call for you, but you've always shown up anyhow.* I hesitate. *I worried something was wrong.*

I was fine, Val replies. *I couldn't respond at once. By the time I got away, the phoenix was with you and you didn't consider yourself in danger any more. When you called earlier today, I could tell you were not in immediate danger. I was not in a place to answer, for which I apologize. By the time you called again, I was able to lock myself in my room to respond.*

It's kind of nice to know Val doesn't mind my reaching out when things aren't wrong, per se. But that's neither here nor there. *What of your prince?* I ask. *Has he decided what he thinks of our bond?*

Val doesn't respond at once. I crawl inside the tunnel, pushing my pack along in front of me. It's easier not to worry about his silence if my body is continuously complaining about each movement.

He has.

And?

Another pause. The tunnel descends gently. I can just glimpse the phoenix ahead of me, moving slowly so that I don't fall too far behind.

He wishes to meet you.

What?! I start in surprise, smacking my head against the tunnel roof. *Ow!* I press my good hand against my head and lean down, at which point my legs decide they are done with me, and the next moment I'm sprawled over my pack, still wedged within the tunnel.

Are you okay? Val asks, sounding strangely nervous. Maybe he's just worried I gave myself a concussion.

Fine. Just fine. After all, what else could I be? I'm alive, even if I owe a triple life-debt to a phoenix, am hiding out beneath a dead land filled with monster-sized scorpions and cunning, blood-thirsty pack creatures, have mages of all types chasing me, and now, apparently, am on the guest list of a breather prince. *Did you tell him I come with a complimentary set of rogue hunters?*

He's aware of your standing with the Council.

Still sprawled atop my pack, I let out a croak of laughter. *My "standing"?*

So to speak.

"Mageling?" the phoenix calls back to me. "Are you all right?"

Why does everyone keep asking that?

"Yes." I get my hands and knees under me once more and make a credible effort at crawling forward, shoving my pack along with each laborious pace I cover.

How about this, I say. *Once I've wrapped up fixing the Burnt Lands, I'll be happy to consider his invitation.*

That will work, Val says, as if we weren't speaking of the impossible. Because, really, how likely am I to survive this work *and* escape the hunters on my trail? Though I suppose, even with the impossible, one must keep planning. Maybe I can visit Val's prince after I've given Ravenflight the slip and attended Huda's sister's wedding. I manage to swallow my laugh before it breaks from my lips and makes Val worry even more.

I am unutterably grateful to find that the tunnel levels out and comes to an end a few paces ahead. The phoenix has already moved off to the side, his glow lighting up the edge of a vast darkness.

I had better send Val off before the phoenix decides to interrogate me. There's just one more thing I need to ask him.

What happens if you're ever in trouble? How will I know?

You'll feel a pull on your heart and mind together. If I were to call you, you would hear it and be able to follow.

You don't get in much trouble, do you?

I'm past that age.

I snort. It's a not-so-subtle reminder that he could easily be a grandfather to me, as slowly as breathers age. *I don't think so, old man. It wasn't that long ago you were locked up in a tower.*

Since then, I have kept a good distance from towers. I don't foresee any more in my future.

You don't foresee *towers. They creep up on you. Just like the future.*

That explains the Burnt Lands. And the Mekteb.

I shake my head, biting back a smile, all of which he can no doubt sense. *I don't suppose you have any news of the Mekteb, or the Council, do you?*

A pause.

I can see what I can find out for you, Val says, with just enough weight that I'm sure he knows something.

Is it bad?

I assume it isn't good, Val hedges. *I'll ask around and come back with more certain news soon.*

That seems reasonable. It's not like I could verify any news from down here, or do anything else about it, so letting Val make sure the news he's heard is accurate suits me just fine. I push my pack through the opening onto a wide earthen shelf. The phoenix stands to the side of the entrance, his light dimming to a faint glow.

Give your prince my greetings, I say, quite certain Val will catch my flippant tone.

I will, he returns easily. But still, he doesn't leave. I'm not sure if I should tell him more clearly, or if I should let him stay. Really, though, I'm too tired to worry about it.

I crawl out past my pack and move to sit beside the phoenix. A dark cavern stretches out before us. At its center something glitters.

"Open your mage's senses and tell me what you feel," he says.

I exhale slowly, make sure I'm not going to lose my balance, and reach out. Overhead, I can still sense a faint touch of the draining spells stretched out through the earth. And above that, a vast emptiness. But before me I feel... a faint vibration, like the flutter of a single leaf on a tree, or the hum of a lone bee drifting by in search of nectar.

"Yes," the phoenix says, watching my face. "This is the beginning. The Burnt Lands continue overhead, but here there is life."

And there is. He leads me down over the ledge which is, thankfully, no higher than my waist. My legs give me only one or two uncertain moments, but they hold me. We walk till we reach what had glittered in the dark: a small stream, its water running clear, and there, flicking past, swim small, pale fish. They weave among plants so dark they are almost black, their roots set deep in the streambed, leaves unfurled to wave back and forth in the water. On the opposite bank, moss grows, soft and lovely in the phoenix's light.

"Don't they need sunlight?" I whisper.

"That is why I come," the phoenix tells me. He gestures with his beak. "There is the nest I prefer."

Past the opposite bank, small trees grow, spread out over the remaining floor of the cavern like a handful of marbles dropped by a child. They are none of them great, sturdy things, but they *are* trees, delicate leaves unfurling on slender branches. In among them, cobbled together of their dead branches, rests a nest upon a waist-high stone pedestal—a stalagmite cropped short.

Food and water and wood. This, then, is the phoenix's haven.

Call me if you need me, Val says, his concerns about my immediate well-being finally appeased.

Thank you.

You are welcome.

"Come and take your rest," the phoenix says.

"What of Huda and her family?"

"I am not yet tired. Take your rest and I will go to see her safely to them."

"All right," I agree.

The phoenix pauses, one beady eye trained on me. "When you're ready, you will tell me about the breather who looked through your eyes at me."

"And you will tell me everything you know about these lands," I return. "I can't unmake the draining spells if you cannot trust me with what you know. Starting with just how that mage made a break in the spells below the tree."

The phoenix dips his head. "Agreed."

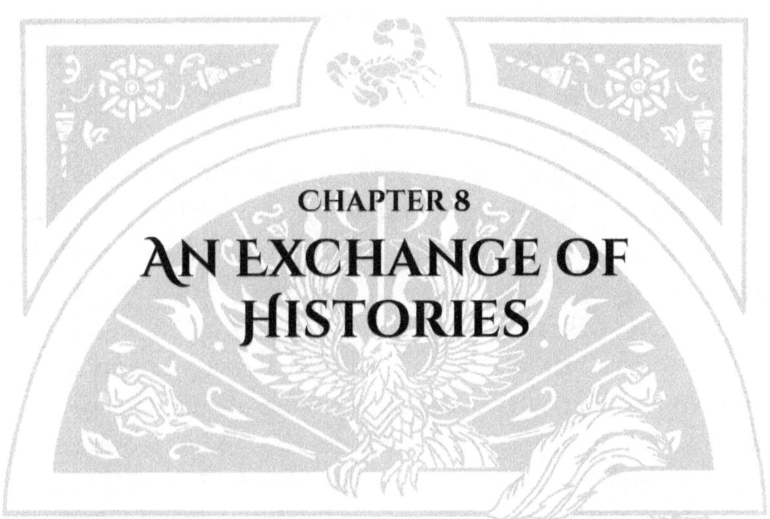

CHAPTER 8
AN EXCHANGE OF HISTORIES

I wake to the half-lit darkness of the underground cavern, the phoenix glowing gently in his sleep, and my legs cramping with pain.

I swallow a whimper, and slowly, slowly try to flex my muscles. I don't know how long I lie there, jaw clenched tight as my body informs me that I have been a very, very inconsiderate tenant. *It wasn't really me,* I tell my calves as the cramps finally ease. *And you would have been a great deal unhappier with what the scorpions intended.* My calves seize up one last time in reply.

That should teach me to argue with my body.

Eventually, though, I'm able to sit up, moving gingerly. Once I trust myself to be able to move without pitching over, I rise and make my way to the stream to refill my water bag.

As I pass the phoenix in his elevated nest, I pause to watch the rise and fall of the feathers at his breast, the warm glow of him. He sleeps with his head curled back, beak tucked beneath his wing. His nest, woven of sticks and bits of palm fronds and lined with feathers, speaks of both how hard he worked to build it, and how lonely he must now be. Male birds do not usually build themselves nests. Perhaps, when he first built it, he had a mate to share it with. Or perhaps this is all he can grant himself of companionship and comfort.

After visiting the stream, I return my water bag to my pack, easing myself down to sit on the blanket. A glance at the phoenix shows him to be still asleep. It's the perfect time to discreetly inspect my various aches and injuries.

The cut across my right bicep has a tight and shiny scar where the healer's spells sealed the wound together. There's no swelling or redness, and the skin already looks stronger. It still hurts like anything when I press it—which I refrain from doing—but overall seems to be healing well.

As for the rest of me—my forearms are scraped and bruised from my fall through the hole at the center of the tree. My hand aches as well, though it hasn't bruised—a grand improvement on the last time it encountered stone. There's a new bruise on my hip to replace an older one, and my knees are scraped up a bit, but nothing visibly worrying. I am, apparently, quite skilled at replacing older bruises with newer ones. But, as long as I give my muscles a chance to recover from their inhuman sprint—and all the horseback riding—I should be all right.

I spend a little while stretching out my body and thinking alternately about the phoenix's ability to sense Val when a roomful of arch mages missed his presence, the searing pain that accompanied the magic I channeled, and what precisely I'm going to do about the Burnt Lands now that I'm in the middle of them.

I haven't really gotten anywhere on any count by the time the phoenix wakes, other than to hope that channeling magic won't always hurt. But, remembering Blackflame's source slave as he sat shivering against the wall, I'm pretty sure it will.

The phoenix raises his head, blinking once at me over the side of his nest, and then flutters over to the stream for a drink. I pull out my rations and offer him a few dates when he joins me. He accepts one graciously, holding it with one foot and pecking off bites. I'd never considered how differently birds approach their meals than humans.

"What do you eat here?" I ask, glancing around.

"Dates." He sounds amused. "I carry them in and keep a store of them. I also enjoy insects and other fruits, but those are harder to come by."

He finishes his date, setting the pit next to him, and settles on the edge of my blanket, like my own personal bird-sized glow-stone. I find myself grinning at him.

"Yes?"

I shake my head. "If you'd told me a month ago that I'd be sharing breakfast with a phoenix, I wouldn't have believed it."

"A great deal has changed for you in a short time."

That it has, and it's not something I have any laughter for. I look down at the date in my hand, make myself eat it. "How is Huda?"

"She is safely returned to her family."

That's good, then.

The phoenix waits till I have finished my meal before saying, "Tell me the story of your breather. It is rare—rare past believing —for a breather to bond with a human anymore. I have not seen it in a very long time. And I have never heard of a breather bonding with a mage."

I don't suppose he has. "It's a long tale," I tell him. "And I would start with who my parents are."

"There is time enough to hear it," he replies.

So, I tell him of my father's death by a wasting illness that I know now was poison, vengeance wrought by Blackflame for opposing his appointment as arch mage. I tell of my journey with my mother to Karolene, and her disappearance and purported death after she went to seek help from Blackflame. Then I jump ahead to the Shadow League, and the Degaths, and let the story unfold from there—our capture by Blackflame's soldiers, Kol bartering to take me back to feed to the breather he held captive, and the Degath children's escape. I describe the making of the alliance between Val and me, our subsequent escape, the sunbolt that took my memories, and the breath Val gave me to ensure my survival.

It is the first time I've told anyone this part—how Val gave me his breath, some part of his own life, and then cared for me in the ensuing weeks as he escorted me to Stormwind and convinced her to take me on as an apprentice. Val knew what I only just learned this past week: that Stormwind had at one time been Blackflame's wife. Faced with a secret Promise whom her ex-husband had orphaned twice over, she accepted Val's demand to do what she could for me.

"You were nearly dead, then," the phoenix says, watching me keenly. "When the breather gave you his breath?"

"I was," I affirm. I had been horrified when I finally understood what he had done, thinking of the soldiers he had breathed from since we escaped Kol, how some part of them might live in me. I can still see the fallen form of James, the lycan in the tower room who attacked me and Val sucked dry, his wolf's muzzle bared in a rictus of pain, his body withering into old age in a matter of seconds.

Just as I drained Mountain dry. The thought, the truth of it, hits hard, stilling the breath in my lungs. I push away the image of Mountain lying slack-jawed and so very dead. What I drained from him wasn't life, per se, it was the magic at his core, and so I stole his life from him. Just as mages drain source slaves throughout the Eleven Kingdoms—perhaps not usually all in one go, but slowly, over time, the damage adding up until they die. But draining magic... in the end, it's not that different from breathing, is it?

I shudder, looking away from the phoenix. No, that's not true. Because generally mages *choose* to drain others of their magic, for their own ends, not because of survival. Breathers have to breathe in order to live, though they might choose to take a breath from animals rather than people. And what Val did in giving *me* a breath—he wasn't channeling someone else's life. He gave me *his* breath and joined his life with mine to create the bond we now share. That is what my life is built on now.

I exhale slowly, and something inside of me unknots just enough that I realize that I've been carrying it—a hurt, a fear, something dark and deep that I haven't let myself think about. I barely knew Val at the time, but he gave of himself to save me. I don't think I truly understood that before now. It makes me want to cry.

The phoenix shifts, drawing my attention back to him. "You did not know you were bonded when he left you with Mistress Stormwind?"

I rub my right eye with my sleeve, scrubbing away the tear welling there. "No," I tell the phoenix. "I only realized it a couple of weeks ago—when I first met you. He helped me when that great spell-beast was chasing us. He spoke to me, telling me what to do to keep from getting killed. I thought at first I was losing my mind, and then that the voice was yours. I didn't realize who he truly was until I was at the Mekteb, fleeing the Lycan Guard after Stormwind's escape, and he took over my body to fight Osman Bey."

"You must have had some sign before then," the phoenix presses. "A bond is not something that would go unnoticed a whole year."

"Moments only, when I found myself looking through his eyes," I admit. "I thought they were dreams, and they always ended quickly, as soon as he realized I had found him."

"He has never tried to control you outside of moments of danger? Perhaps control your magic working?"

"What? *No.* He's not interested in controlling me."

The phoenix shifts slightly. "It bears asking, and I am glad of the answer. What happens when he needs your help?"

Another question that really doesn't bear asking. "I'll help him. At least to survive."

"Even though he survives on the lives of others?"

"He prefers to take the breath he needs from animals, and he doesn't take all they have unless he must. There are a lot more humans out there who have eaten more animals and killed more people than he has. Blackflame, for one, and the High Council still elected him as their First Mage. I don't hear you questioning their choices." I don't mention Mountain and Saber, who were draining my magic to kill my friends. The phoenix doesn't need that reminder any more than I do.

The phoenix clicks his beak. "I think we have already established that I serve the land before I serve any self-appointed council of magic-users who cannot even keep their own in hand."

His answer surprises me into silence. What does it even mean to serve the land? That seems like it's so far open to interpretation, it might be just as dangerous as serving the High Council.

The phoenix dips his head. "I suspect we are more alike than at first we might appear."

Maybe. "I've told you about the breather. Now tell me about the Burnt Lands, starting here." I gesture to the cavern.

The phoenix bobs his head. "Before the Great Burning, the banyan tree had lived for a few hundred years. Even in that time there was a crack in its trunk and a space below, hollowed out from among its roots. It survived only because its branches were already supported by their own roots reaching to the ground. When the Burning came near this place, Mage Morningmist sought me out. I lived not far from here, and we had met before. She had joined with a group of mages who were trying to broker peace between the warring factions—until they themselves were attacked. She had only a little time; we could see that the draining spells would overtake her town within hours.

"It was her idea to create a haven from the draining spells. She sent as many of the town's residents down into the hollow beneath the tree as she could, and I flew down to join them. With me, she knew they would have a greater chance of survival. Together, we carved out the tunnel to the cavern, for we could sense the water flowing there, and then she went back up and cast her spells while her people escaped to the cavern. I aided her from below, steadying her magic working."

"You could have flown away," I say.

"The people could not have—not even the strongest of the young men, to say nothing of the elders, or children, or pregnant women. And we did not know how long we would have to remain underground. They would need me for my light and for what guidance and magical support I could give them."

I've had a great many doubts about the phoenix, and I'm still not sure I trust him completely with my future, but I find that I like him immensely more now. "And the mage?"

"She died. I believe she drew in the banyan's magic and concentrated it at its core, fashioning a loop of living magic that the draining spells wove themselves around. I worked to help her. Once the structure of her magic was set, the loop did not have to sustain itself for the hole to remain open. By then, she was gone."

I rub my arms, my skin breaking out in goosebumps. "So, the hole was created at the same time as the draining spells." Which makes it a different thing altogether from attempting to change the spells after the fact.

The phoenix nods. "She didn't try to stop the draining spells —they were as unstoppable as a tide by then. She simply made a point they would flow around, like a rock that parts a current."

It's brilliant in its way. "What happened to the people?"

"Most of them survived. When their food ran out, I brought them more, though it was never really enough. We lost some of our weakest to malnourishment and illness—children and the elderly." He turns his head away, looking out to the stream. "We remained here until the Burning was over, and then I led them out. We lost three more of our number on our way to the Barrier."

I reach out to touch his folded wing. "I'm sorry."

He swings his head back to me, his eyes dark. "Four hundred years, and the grief does not fade. I have never had children—or a people—of my own, but I came to love them as deeply as I think I would my own."

Grief doesn't ever completely disappear. My father died five years ago, and I can only just remember a few images of him. Yet I still recall him lying motionless on his bed, still feel the knife stab of pain that went through my chest at I looked down on him. And sometimes, at unexpected moments, I think of him, this man who spoke gently with me, and sang to me, and held my hand as we walked, and my heart aches with a grief that will not be assuaged.

"What happened to those who survived?" I ask.

"They were taken in by the desert dwellers. It is one reason why the desert tribes will now take in anyone I ask them to. They remember that I saved their ancestors."

That also explains the stories of an underground cavern of wonders associated with the phoenix.

"Are there other places like this?"

"Not that I know of. Nor are there other anomalies in the spells that I am aware of."

"Did any of the mages that have come since succeed in making any changes?" It seems utterly preposterous that no one should have accomplished what a bit of fear and a rudimentary knowledge of sewing allowed me to do by way of unraveling part of the great spell-beast at its seams.

"Of course. The Barrier itself was erected. The nature of these spells is to expand. It was no small undertaking to contain them. You also saw the mage light that burns above the bridge to the old city; that is powered by the draining spells themselves, a subversion of their intention."

Subversion. A tiny break in the order of the draining spells, taking magic out of the system rather than containing it within. "How did they do it?"

"It was woven into the draining spells themselves. The mage-fire burns within the Barrier, not on the outside. But it cost the mage who cast it their life."

I grimace. I would really like a story of a mage who did something here and survived. "And since then? Has no one changed anything?"

"There have been attempts. None of them have been fully successful."

"Tell me."

He does, going through each of a half-dozen concerted efforts to undo some part of the spells that hold the Burnt Lands in their thrall. As far as I can tell, only two met with any success. Of the two, one was a pair of mages who were able to slightly weaken the network of spells that weave through the ground, powering the spell-beasts, if only temporarily. The other was an attempt to destroy the greatest of the spell-beasts, and it is this group I have to thank for there being only one tentacled beast left in the Burnt Lands—the one I had the bad fortune to meet. Of the six teams of mages who came here, only one survived their visit without any losses, and it wasn't one of the "successful" ones.

I lean back, staring up at the dark expanse of the cavern roof, hidden from sight now that the phoenix glows as gently as a lamp. "What do you think I will be able to achieve?"

He sits for a long time, the only movement the slight lift and fall of his feathers as he breathes. "I do not know," he says finally. "You were the first in a long time to affect the spells here at all. But I envisioned this differently."

"You thought I'd have a lifetime, and that I would be able to call on other mages to help me."

He huffs softly. "I should have guessed it would not be so with you."

"How could you?"

He rises, shaking out his tail feathers. "There were signs. You came into the Burnt Lands through the portal, which no mage with any choice in the matter uses. You were with a mage whose death you regretted but didn't mourn. You needed me to break a prisoner out from under the High Council's collective nose."

I snort with laughter. "Their collective nose?"

He cants his head to the side, beady eye bright with amusement. "It is accurate, is it not?"

"You knew exactly what you were doing. You agreed."

"So I did. It also told me a great deal about you. And about what sort of help we might expect in this endeavor." He starts toward his nest. "Come, and bring your pack."

I heft it and follow along, wondering where we are going.

"Although," he muses as he continues, "I wasn't expecting your breather at all."

I'm glad he doesn't see me tense up. I make myself relax my shoulders and say as casually as I can, "Now that you know about him?"

"If he cares for your life, that may be helpful."

A tool to be used, just as Val posited. "You don't find it worrying?" I ask.

The phoenix lifts a folded wing in the avian equivalent of a half-shrug. "Short of one of you dying, there isn't much to be done about it."

"You don't consider breathers evil."

The phoenix continues past his nest, toward the near wall of the cavern. I wait for his answer, falling into step with him and adjusting my pace to match his.

"Breathers are what they are," he says finally. "Do deer consider wolves evil? I could not say."

"Breathers don't need to hunt us to survive," I remind him. Just as mages don't need a source slave to cast magic—it just offers them access to greater spells. Which makes me wonder if perhaps a human's breath offers more to a breather than an animal's...

"Perhaps," the phoenix says. "I have not made a study of breathers."

I nod. Neither have I, though I would like to learn more. One day.

The phoenix says nothing more until we arrive at the cave's wall, his light throwing the dark opening of a tunnel into sharp relief. It's taller than the one we entered from, and thankfully there is no ledge to climb up to reach it.

Turning to me, the phoenix says, "I cannot imagine a future in which humans and breathers live together in peace, but that does not mean I consider breathers evil. Their abilities are simply too dangerous for humans to accept. It is a matter of survival."

"We make pacts with fangs," I point out. "And fangs need our blood about as much as breathers need our breath. They can mesmerize us—"

"Breathers can control your actions and take away your memories."

I can do that last pretty well on my own. But he does have a point.

"All I am saying, mageling, is that I do not fear your breather, but you cannot hope for a future in which others will not. It is well that you keep your bond secret."

He doesn't know the half of it. I remember well Arch Mage Nightblade's interest in Val—how the otherworldly pari tried to torture the truth of my bond out of me while I crouched on the infirmary floor. He knew he was hurting me, but he believed the information I held too important—discovering it was a blood sigil he was using only deferred what he intended. He destroyed the sigil and walked away sure there was a bond to be discovered, a truth he would yet draw out of me, no doubt through other forms of torture. Had I remained, he would have kept me in his orbit, needling and cutting away at me until I gave him everything he wanted. It would have been devastating had Nightblade confirmed the truth and managed to hold on to me....

But Val's prince *does* know, and I don't know what that means for Val. He has acted as if the main question is what his prince wishes of me, how I will respond. But what of him? While Val knows so much about me, I realize now I know almost nothing about him, and what this means for his own safety and freedom. He has kept his life, his realities, completely separate from mine, even as he has literally walked in my footsteps. The realization that he might be protecting himself from me, that he doesn't trust me with his life, makes me feel unaccountably small. Even if it might be wise—after all, I'm constantly in danger, and the more I know, the more I can be forced to betray.

"Mageling?" the phoenix says, head tilted as he watches me. We're still standing before the tunnel entrance. Right.

"What's in there?" I ask roughly.

The phoenix steps forward into the narrow tunnel, his light illuminating the brown stone and earthen floor. "Forgotten things. Let us look and see."

CHAPTER 9
TREASURE TROVE

I am beginning to dislike tight spaces. Even though the tunnel is wide enough for me to pass through, it isn't quite tall enough for me to stand, and my whole body protests having to walk bent over. I keep a hand on the walls on either side of me, my pack protecting my spine from scraping the rock overhead, and force myself to breathe slowly as I follow the phoenix.

Thankfully, it isn't far. The tunnel opens into a small cavern, as big around as a good-sized bed. Against the far wall stand a few piles of carefully stacked items.

"These have been left behind over the centuries," the phoenix says, walking up to the nearest pile. "Many of them by mages, a few by the desert dwellers."

"The mages who died?" I ask, going forward to kneel beside him. I stifle a groan as I go from my knees to sitting.

The phoenix shifts, glancing toward me. "If I could return the mages' belongings to their loved ones beyond the Barrier, I would. But sometimes there was no one to be found. What remained unclaimed I brought here, to keep for those who might come after." He nods toward the pile. "Take a look."

It's a treasure trove of old charms and enchanted weapons. There are at least five glowstones, all of them long ago drained of power, but a quick inspection with my mage sight tells me that the formative spell still holds in two of them. Two is a great deal more than I can make for myself, although I am not sure how I will force myself to face the pain required to recharge them. Perhaps the phoenix can help—or perhaps he can't and that's why these enchantments have faded, rather than from neglect. I don't know enough of how the phoenix's magic works to say.

"There's more than glowstones there," the phoenix says, clearly unimpressed with my first priorities.

"Yes," I agree. "But these might be useful if I'm ever down here without you. What's this? A dagger?" I lift the handle and find it's a short sword. A rather rusty one, at that.

"It's more than it seems. Take a good look."

I do. The magic running through it remains steady and strong. "It can't be broken." I turn it as I study it. The hilt is bare, slim and unassuming, the hilt guard just curved enough to grant a hint of elegance. The blade itself is short wide, an unimpressively stubby specimen flaking off massive amounts of rust. Which makes the enchantment underlaying it unexpectedly amusing. "The blade will remain sharp," I tell him. You'd think whoever enchanted it would have charmed it from rusting. As it is, it looks more likely to kill people by lockjaw than any act of violence.

I set it down carefully, not wanting to risk nicking myself.

"You could use it," the phoenix tells me.

"Can't fight," I return cheerfully. "What happened to its scabbard, anyhow?"

"That didn't make it. Surely you at least know how to handle a dagger." He gestures to a jeweled hilt sticking out from beneath a pair of leather straps of some sort.

"Not really," I say, picking up the leather. "What are these?"

"Gauntlets."

I examine one carefully. The gauntlet itself is a wide strip of leather with a reinforced fingerless glove attached at the top. Three broad straps with buckles close the strip around the wearer's arms. It's of a simple, functional design, rather like the sword, with a faint geometric design embossed in the leather around the edges. Unlike the sword, though, whoever charmed these considered what it would need to stand the test of time: the leather is still supple, the buckles still smooth. The gauntlets are also charmed against blades and crushing forces, their faint shielding still glimmering in my mage sight.

"I like these," I say softly. Not only would they protect my hands and arms nearly to my elbows, but they'd hide my markings. I turn over the second gauntlet and find myself staring at a darker stain spread across the inside of the leather. I look up quickly. "How did their owner die?"

"They belonged to a woman mage," the phoenix says. "I was unable to protect her from the pack creatures that attacked you."

I shudder. The creatures must have torn her to pieces, even as these leather guards held.

"Keep them," the phoenix counsels me. "And keep looking."

I do, sifting through the remaining charms, the bits and pieces that have survived their owners. It makes me wonder what of mine the phoenix would bring back here. Probably not much—a glowstone or two, perhaps the wards I made of Stormwind's lapis necklace. Or if I'm really lucky, the wooden crow statuette Val carved, though that would be less hardy than stone. I don't really have much else worth saving.

I push myself to my feet, moving gingerly.

"Is there anything else you might use?"

I shake my head. All that really remains are weapons I have no use for and charms that have long since lost their magic, faded past recovering.

"What of the talisman there?" the phoenix says, dipping his beak to a velvet pouch worn thin and shiny with age. I had peeked in it once, but now I dump the contents into my palm. The talisman itself is a sapphire the size of my pinkie nail; it has been set in a simple, elegantly designed gold pendant still strung on an unbroken gold chain. It looks like a bit of pretty jewelry, which I suppose just makes it multifunctional. The spell set on the sapphire still holds, though the talisman itself is nearly drained of magic. Since it's meant to be a repository of power to aid a mage in casting spells, it is relatively useless as it is now. But perhaps it will still come in handy, somehow. I suppose if I survive, I could sell it to buy supplies, or passage on a caravan.

"All right," I say.

The phoenix turns to the tunnel. "Then let us go back to the surface and see what you can do."

I slip the talisman and aged glowstones into my pack and pause, my hand hovering over my old wooden spindle with its cracked shaft. I don't know why I kept it when we recovered it from Blackflame's cronies in the desert. I should have left it for the phoenix to destroy. Now, when I think of it, my fingers tighten on the shaft.

I have so little left of my year with Stormwind, of all the hopes I harbored, and the peace of that time in her mountain valley. I would rather lay those memories to rest than burn them. What better place than here, beneath a cursed land, in a secret haven, among the belongings of people and times long gone? No one will find it here. And this way, something will remain of me even if I don't survive the unmaking of the Burnt Lands.

I pull the spindle from my pack and lay it down among the emptied charms and forgotten weapons. Then I push myself to my feet and follow the phoenix to the main cavern. I drop my pack by my bedroll and strap on the gauntlets while the phoenix waits. They fit surprisingly well, the gloves only slightly big for me. I pull my thobe's sleeves down over the arm guards and flex my hands, my markings all but invisible. My fingers don't quite straighten fully, but it's still a pretty good range of motion.

Finally, though, I can't avoid the phoenix any longer, can't avoid what I have to say. "I tried," I begin, and come up short.

"Tried?" the phoenix queries.

I make myself go on. "Tried channeling. I couldn't do it with charms. Then, when the mages—when the one started drawing on my magic, he did it and it *hurt*." I rub one hand over the gauntleted fist of the other. "When I pulled his magic from him, it felt like my markings were burning through my flesh and bone."

I look up at the phoenix, wondering if he will care about my pain, if it will make any difference to him whatsoever. He watches me silently, and I cannot read anything from the darkness of his eyes or the stillness of his body.

"I'm not sure I'll be able to push myself to channel again if someone's life isn't at stake," I say into the quiet.

The phoenix doesn't respond. I wait, and the memory of Mountain's staring eyes fills my vision. I'm still glad he's dead, murderer that he was. I swallow hard and push the image away.

"I do not know very much about how such markings work," the phoenix says finally. "Perhaps the first time is the worst. Perhaps when force is used, the process is more painful. Perhaps it was the level of magic being channeled."

I nod slowly.

"Try again with your charms when you are ready," he suggests. "Go gently."

"All right."

"Now come. There is no need to worry about channeling today." The phoenix turns, heading once more across the cavern, this time toward the exit.

I fall into step behind him. "What are we doing up there?" I ask as we reach the stream. We cross over, he with a few sure wing strokes and I using the stepping stones set there who knows how many centuries earlier.

"I want you to have time to study the spells just above us." He pauses. "The spell-creatures know that the banyan serves as the entrance to my home. There are always a few of them nearby. We will have to be careful."

I've chosen the most-patrolled corner of the Burnt Lands as my base. That explains why so many spell-creatures converged so quickly on the town yesterday. Still, things could be worse. They could be able to get down here. Or Ravenflight could be coming for me. Which—I *really* should have remembered that sooner.

"When we were coming here, that was Ravenflight in the sky, wasn't it?"

"Yes. Once you were within the banyan, I flew up and demanded she leave. She cannot enter in her bird form—the draining spells would strip the enchantment from her, and she would fall to her death. Nor do I think her so foolhardy as to attempt to corner you in my stronghold. She will wait and watch for you to come out again."

"Do you have protections cast?" I ask, glancing about with my mage sight. Nothing presents itself as particularly obvious.

"A few wards you may notice in the tunnel, and," he shrugs a wing, "the whole of the Burnt Lands."

That surprises a chuckle from me. "Fair enough. I suppose most mages won't brave them." Even Ravenflight seems more likely to wait me out than to risk entering a land where her magic can't protect her. The spell-creatures are a much greater threat to her survival than any risk I pose. "What keeps the larger spell-creatures from attacking your haven, though?"

"Two things: their size, and the lack of a magical network to sustain them here."

"Couldn't the big one just level the whole banyan tree, smash its way through?"

"It has tried. The smaller branches break, and there is a section that it worked at for months where it has pared the tree down to its largest pieces—great branches, the thickest roots that support them. But it cannot break those."

"There isn't any magic holding them up, though."

The phoenix glances at me curiously before stepping into the tunnel. "But there is. Look again."

I follow him, wondering what I could have missed.

In the small hollow beneath the entrance, the stone pack creature still stands. I pause at the tunnel entrance, but the beast is stone, as still as death. There's nothing to fear.

"Here," the phoenix calls from across the room. He stands by a small niche, no more than a gap between wall and floor. I cross to him and retrieve the rope stored there, also charmed to stay strong. I've never come across so many items charmed to last before—but then, such enchantments are both difficult and exhausting to achieve, and potentially life-saving in a place like this. It would make sense for the mages who worked here to bring such items with them, however hard they might have been to make or procure.

The phoenix takes one end of the rope and flies up through the hole, dragging it behind him as he exits. He calls back to me once he has secured it. I grasp the rope, breathe a prayer, and start hauling myself up. I manage to make it two pulls up, not quite halfway there, when my wounded arm gives out. I drop back to the floor with a strangled gasp, hunching over to cradle my arm. The pain sets my teeth on edge, making the room three shades darker and the stone remains of the pack creature flicker and shift.

"Mageling?" The phoenix peers through the hole at me, the rope still swaying between us.

"I'm—" *Coming*, I'd been about to say. But I'm not. Looking up at him, my arm cradled weakly in my lap, I know I'm not. Perhaps I *could*, but my arm is getting weaker, not stronger. This may be one of the few opportunities I can take the time to care for it.

"I can't," I say. "I need another day. Maybe more."

The phoenix flutters down to perch on the pack creature's lumpy, misshapen head.

"What's wrong?" he asks.

"My arm is healing from a wound I received a week ago. I can't pull myself up right now. I'll be stronger tomorrow."

He shifts, then looks away. "I forget how frail humans are."

"I'll recover," I say, my voice unexpectedly sharp.

"I know," he says. "I sensed your wound when I checked on you after the mages attacked. It is healing, and there's nothing I can offer you that hasn't already been done. I just... forgot how great its effect might be on you."

"I'm all right generally," I tell him. "It's the climbing that's hard."

"Well," he says, sounding utterly unconvinced. "Do you have the energy to study what you can from down here?"

"Yes."

"Take a look at the tree first, then."

I scoot over and lean against the wall. Closing my eyes, I lay my hand against a knobby root that sticks out where the wall meets the ground. I can't sense anything at first, but the phoenix's words have me seeking deeper. Then I catch it: the faintest glimmer at the center of the root beneath my hand. I reach out, seeking with all my strength, and slowly, slowly the tree comes into focus, the roots glimmering all around me, the trunk rising above me in a great column of light that branches out to create a massive canopy protecting the earth above.

"The mage who you said made this casting…" She accomplished so much: created a hole in the draining spells, saved some of the people of her town, and then turned this tree into an undying protection for them, feeding off the draining spells and holding strong against any onslaught, so that the phoenix and his charges need not fear the spell-creatures she must have known were coming.

"Morningmist," the phoenix supplies, and I am so glad that after all these centuries there is still someone who knows her name.

"She was amazing."

"She was," he agrees softly, his voice tinged with sorrow.

I spend the next hour leaning against the roots of the wall, studying the spells around me. Then I tilt my head back, reaching through the roots, and concentrate my mage sight on the hole Morningmist created. I take my time, studying the flow of magic, similar and yet different from the network of wards and protections that I infiltrated at the Mekteb-e-Sihir in Fidanya.

Finally, I shift my attention to the draining spells. It's hard to study them—even reaching to them through the earth, I can feel their pull. Still, this place with the loop Morningmist created is possibly the safest spot I could imagine to make the attempt. The draining spells are more than the miasma I first sensed rising up along the edge of the Barrier. They would have to be, I suppose, to have survived so long. Here, underfoot, they are layered and yet fused together, a latticework of connections, sharp-edged lines of magic crossing over each other. I've never seen anything like it.

I can't imagine a team of mages could create this if they tried.

It's the mind-boggling, unplanned result of releasing a storm of spells on an unsuspecting populace; spells whose driving force was to absorb... and channel. They both leash magic and unleash it. But the strangest thing about what has formed from that is the hard structure of the spells. This is nothing like a fabric woven together—each so-called thread is sharp and straight, the spells overlapping and flowing in different directions to create a rigid, interconnected layer.

I sit forward, my hands in my lap. The phoenix tilts his head at me expectantly from his perch on the stone creature, as if I would have an answer for him already. As if I could possibly know how to unmake what a dozen other fully trained mages have lost their lives over.

"We need to talk about the magic here," I say finally. "And exactly how the previous mages accomplished anything."

CHAPTER 10
KINDLING

All the rest of the day and through the evening, the phoenix and I sit together deep in his haven and discuss the Burnt Lands. It's a cyclical conversation, returning again and again to the same problem as each possible solution proves itself nonviable. Although, each time, I learn a little more about how the magic itself works, diving deeper into the efforts of each mage team that has come to the Burnt Lands.

The most helpful of those, at least at first glance, was the one that created the magefire that burns above the bridge to the dead city, leading accidental travelers to the path out. The team managed to model the magefire after the spell-beasts, such that the draining spells recognize it and feed it, keeping it burning even now.

"Wouldn't the magefire have to have been built on a living base, then?" I ask, having already heard about and learned from the failures of all the other attempts. "Just as the spell-creatures were?"

The phoenix sighs. "It was."

"What... what did they do?" I ask. I'm shaking suddenly, remembering the blue-white form of a woman's soul pulling itself free of the blood magic that held it in the tower room of Kol's fortress. Is there a soul caught in the magefire now?

"Birds," the phoenix says. "They brought cages of birds, and sacrificed them one by one until they could get the spell to take."

Sacrificed—or slaughtered—their forms consumed by magic. Which means blood magic, no doubt. For all that the Council claims to uphold stringent laws against its use, they sure do engage in it a lot. "We're not killing anything," I say roughly.

"I did not like it either," the phoenix says, "but the magefire has served its purpose."

"We're not killing *anything*," I repeat, so that he can't misunderstand me. Unless I must weigh a sparrow's life against a human's—or any being of higher intelligence—I will protect them all. I've seen—and felt—blood magic at work. I want nothing to do with it.

"No," he agrees. "At any rate, their method resulted in one of their own number dying with the final bird, which is perhaps why the spell took at all."

"Then..." I pause, force myself to ask, "is their soul still caught here? And what of the souls of the lycans that were spelled into pack creatures?"

"I don't know. Perhaps their souls are still caught among the spells that encircle them. Perhaps they have escaped this world. I have no way to tell."

I rub my arms, my skin prickling. "You don't worry that your soul might one day be caught as well?"

"It already is," he murmurs. I look at him sharply, and he shrugs his wings. "I am a phoenix. My nature is to be reborn. If anyone can live in this place without such a fear, it would be me."

"Is that why you stay here? Because you know you'll survive it?"

"No. It is because this is my home, and I would like to see it reborn as well."

I dip my head, thinking of all the homes I recall having—Stormwind's cabin, a scattering of images of my life in Karolene, flickers of memories from before that, so fragmented they may as well be from a previous life. I cannot bring back Stormwind's cabin—it would be nothing but an empty cottage in an abandoned valley now, if its walls are even still standing. Nor do I know that Karolene needs me. It has the Shadow League; a rogue mage with hunters on her heels would hardly count as a help. And yet... I understand.

I wish that I could return to that time with Stormwind, when my life was full of hope and comfort. I wish that I could slip back into my life in Karolene, reclaim those memories and friendships, and live a life that I'm sure was full, even if it contained hardships. Those moments, those lives, are past and can't be reborn—and the phoenix knows that as well as I do. He isn't trying to bring back a time that is past, he is trying to afford the lands and the people who would live here a chance at a new future.

I have a new life now, here in this cavern beneath the Burnt Lands. Even if nothing is certain, I will try to protect it—to protect both my life and the hope of this cavern, and what the phoenix is striving to do.

"We'll figure out a way," I tell the phoenix. "It just might take some time."

"Ah, child," he says gently. "That I know."

Come morning, I do my stretches while the phoenix still rests. Then I take out my glowstone. For a long time, I just sit, turning it over and trying to ignore the leaden weight in my belly. I can do this. Surely, I can, without it hurting. Stormwind went to great lengths to ensure I knew how to channel because of my sunbolt. All a source slave *does*—all the markings are made to allow—is channeling.

Slowly, I try to gather a faint breath of magic from the cavern around me, draw it into me until my markings begin to itch. I take a deep breath, offer up a prayer, and *pull*. My markings awaken and a fine netting of pain tingles over my arm as magic pours into me. I drop the glowstone in shock.

From his nest, the phoenix's head pops up. "Mageling?"

"A moment," I say, and lifting the glowstone, I press the magic I've gathered into it. My markings flare enough to set my teeth on edge, but they don't *burn*, and I am able to pour the gathered magic into the glowstone. Shakily, I set it down and run my hand over the markings on my left arm. My skin feels warm to the touch, but already the pain is receding, my arm aching only a little.

"Did it hurt?" the phoenix asks, hopping over the edge of the nest, wings spread so that he flutters across the distance in a leap or two.

"Yes. No." I shake my head. "Not like before. Nothing like before."

"But it still hurt," the phoenix says, coming to a stop before me. He cocks his head to take in my arm, the faint red irritation showing beneath the markings.

I nod slowly, feeling a knot building in my throat. I am not sure if it's relief or sorrow. "I can manage it."

"That is good," he says finally. "I wonder if perhaps it hurts less now because you have chosen it, where before your magic was taken by force. Regardless, perhaps this means it will grow easier with time and practice."

I nod, turning away to rifle through my pack so that he won't see my face. I am not sure why it hurts so much to have even such a little hope. Or why it would hurt now when I was *so* grateful to know I could defend myself before. It only takes a moment to smooth out my expression, as if it were an old skill I need only brush off now to grow adept at again.

"Apricot?" I ask the phoenix gruffly, handing him a few rounds of dried fruit. He takes them graciously and we eat in silence.

"I want to experiment," I tell him as I wipe my hands, finished. "You told me about the pair of mages who temporarily weakened the network of spells that weave through the ground, powering the spell-beasts. I want to see if I can recreate that."

"To what end?" he asks.

I shrug. "Just to better understand how it works. And because," I pause, licking my lips, "it's a form of channeling."

"Which is all you think you can do now?" the phoenix asks. "Is that what you think? Because you can still work with spells, you just can't cast them."

"No—or yes, but that's not the thing. I've studied channeling because of my sunbolt. Stormwind said I am better at it than most mages ever become. So... maybe I can manage this. Maybe I'll learn something from it."

"Very well."

He leads me back up to the banyan tree. This time, I tie a series of knots toward the end of the rope before the phoenix takes the other end up through the hole to secure.

"Wait for me," he says before flapping off to check for spell-creatures. I wait alone in the glowstone-lit space, my only company the stone creature. It is hard to imagine it was once a lycan, no different than Osman Bey. It was mages who took the lycans that served them in these lands and transformed them into the mindless killers that are the pack creatures now, spells woven over a living base.

The phoenix drops back down into the room, spreading his wings to land lightly beside the end of the rope. "I'll help you up," he says.

I flex my arms, testing my wounded arm. There's a good chance I'll at least be able to hold myself steady with it. I grip the rope with both hands, trying not to use my right arm more than necessary, and swing my legs up over the first knot.

The phoenix's magic gathers around me, buoying me. I grin fiercely and work my way up quickly to the top, my body ascending as if I were riding on a gently rising bubble.

I scramble over the edge to kneel in the crack. "Thank you," I call down to the phoenix. He could have offered this yesterday as well, but instead he gave me a day of rest. I'm grateful for both of his kindnesses.

"Make your way out carefully," the phoenix says. "Stay close."

I push myself to my feet, hunched slightly to fit, and work my way to the opening of the crack, the phoenix right behind me. From here I can see the whole network of spells spread out just beneath the earth, a carpet of darkness interlocking beneath my feet that stretches across the land. Past the protection of the banyan's canopy, the town lies still.

I need to avoid working too close to the one aspect of the draining spells I don't want to change—the loop created at the heart of the tree. So, once we are sure there are no spell-beasts about, I walk out beneath the stone canopy, the phoenix keeping pace beside me.

I stop where there are still a few large roots bulging out of the bone-dry dirt, well within the sheltering canopy. Kneeling, I place a hand on the root and follow the magic of it down to where it touches the draining spells. Despite their rigid structure, the spells here are still dynamic in their way—it's as if they flow continuously through natural channels, as water might through a series of cracks. Should the need arise, the magic of these spells can well up from the cracks, channeling magic to the spell-beasts that roam above land. But here, in a resting state, the spells merely flow steadily in their accustomed routes.

The phoenix settles beside me, his long tail resting in the dust behind him. He makes no comment, his head held high that he might both watch my work and keep an eye out for spell-creatures.

I work quietly for the most part, attempting first one approach and then another, trying to put into practice the descriptions the phoenix gave me. I twist the finest of spell threads together, then larger strands when the small ones fail to hold, then pluck free a strand and reconnect it to another, channeling the magic that it might rebind itself—much as I did at the Mekteb, when I isolated the ward on the window of the building where Stormwind was held prisoner. But the moment I let the strands go, they slip apart again.

I sit back, massaging my arms, my markings uncomfortably

warm to the touch. They hurt, channeling hurts, and I know I'll have to stop soon. But at least I can manage this much. I glance around at the vacant buildings. "I thought you said the spell-creatures watched this tree."

The phoenix dips his head. "Look there and you will see a pair of scorpions waiting for us."

I frown, squinting past him to focus on the edge of the banyan's reach, and realize I am looking at the stone-still forms of two great scorpions, their tails lowered and their pincers resting against the ground. "Oh. I guess that's better than more pack creatures."

"Yes."

"What else lives out here?" I ask. "There are scorpions and pack creatures and the great tentacled... kraken. Anything else?"

"Every one of the spell-creatures here had a living base," he explains. "There were a few more at first, but the bird creatures were too fragile to last long, and were shattered by the larger creatures."

"Which leaves us with what, now?" I have no doubt there's more I haven't seen. It does not fill me with confidence that the phoenix is taking his time answering.

After a moment, he says, "There are giant worms that dwell where the land is hillier. The draining spells create pockets within the hills instead of spreading out flat as they do here. The sand strikers burrow into those underground pockets and leave only their mouths above ground. They have no eyes, but they can sense magic, feel a footstep through the earth, and sense shadows as well."

"Let me guess," I drawl. "They pop out and eat whoever happens by."

"They were created to hold back the movement of armies, I believe."

The movement of anything, really. I glance about. "There are no such pockets here?"

"No," the phoenix agrees. "If we should travel near those lands, I will warn you."

"I think I'd rather avoid them altogether," I say with forced cheer, because no way do I want to cross paths with monstrous killer worms. Even if I might learn something from the so-called pockets that house them.

The phoenix huffs softly. "As would I."

"Anything else to worry about?"

He looks out, past the hunched shape of the ruined buildings, to a desert I cannot see. "Scarab beetles."

"What? I thought those were—aren't they holy to some people?"

"Not these ones, any more than the pack creatures can be called lycans."

"Are they big then, like the scorpions?"

"No, they are small but swift and consuming."

I shudder. It's what I initially imagined of the scorpions, and it's no less disturbing to find that it is just a different insect that will swarm and kill.

"I have not seen them in a few decades though. There is a high likelihood their numbers have finally been worn away; they crush easily enough. And the other spell-creatures delighted in breaking them and absorbing their magic."

"Like candy," I blurt before I can rethink it.

The phoenix huffs. "Yes. A delicacy to be hunted when nothing else presented itself. So, there are few left, if any."

I try to take heart from that and turn back to my spellwork.

At midday, I return to the cavern for a small meal and lie down to rest through the afternoon heat. Above ground it is only a little extra warm rather than sweltering hot thanks to the winter weather, but it's a pattern the phoenix expects. It also gives me a chance to rest and think about my work while he flies out to patrol the Burnt Lands, as is his habit.

I doze for a little while, then lie on my back, my thoughts drifting to Val, wondering when I might hear from him again. Although... I've visited him a handful of times before. Never intentionally, and always halfway to dreaming, which I more or less am now. I reach out, thinking of him, testing my sense of him as if I might find—oh, yes, *that*—the faintest sense of him, like the draw of the north to a compass needle. I *know* his direction.

I close my eyes, turning toward the steady pull of his being, and press into it. My body falls away and just as suddenly I find myself in another body, taller and stronger and quicker than I am used to. I open my spirit eyes to find myself resting against Val's mind, watching through his eyes as he stands in the shadow of a wall, half-sheltered by the building beside him that sticks out a pace or two farther. The street is a busy one and has all the signs of a thriving town or even a minor city—except that it isn't busy in the usual way. Instead, people crowd the street, all of them facing whatever lies past the building that protects Val, and many of them looking angry.

Val shifts forward, peering around the building to what lies at the end of the street—

That's a portal, I think aloud.

Val startles, pulling back into his corner, but not before I got a good view of the portal, built as an overly grand arch enclosed within high brick walls that circumscribe it completely. The gates through the walls are shut and further guarded by two mages on horseback, their robes shouting their identity even if their arrogant demeanors didn't.

Hitomi! What are you doing here? Val demands.

What are you *doing here?* I counter. *And what is going on with that portal?*

You wanted news, Val says, turning to thread his way through the edges of the crowd, keeping as close to the wall as he can. *I came to verify it.*

He's here because of me? *What about your prince?* I ask. *Did you at least travel with someone?*

He pauses, and I can feel his amusement bubbling up. I hadn't realized how tense he was until this moment. *You're worried about me traveling alone?*

Val, there are mages down there!

I noticed, he says, and I can feel the curve of the smile on his lips. *But they won't notice me unless I draw their notice.* He reaches a tight alleyway running between the walled compound and the next building and turns down it. It's barely wider than the breadth of his shoulders. *Here's your first bit of news: the Head of the Mekteb— High Mage Jeweltongue, I believe?— disagreed with the school being locked down once again following your escape.*

During my trial, Jeweltongue had threatened to revoke the Council's welcome in response to their endangering the school and its students by housing prisoners like myself and Stormwind on the grounds. I'm not at all surprised she pushed back against the Council taking control of the students' movements. *What happened?*

Blackflame relieved her of her post and placed the Mekteb under the Council's jurisdiction.

What?! He can't just get rid of her!

Regardless, he did. The Council voted on it, I believe.

I hold back a curse—I don't even have a *good* curse to use, which is infuriating in itself.

Val pauses beside a window in the building opposite the wall we're following, then uses the windowsill to boost himself up and leap to the top of the wall opposite. We look down into what is clearly a pleasure garden within the little compound, with a carved wooden bench beside a miniature reflecting pond and a myriad flowering bushes surrounding them, a few still sporting some late blooms.

Why are we on top of this wall? I ask, distracted.

Val helpfully glances back to the road, where the unrest is growing, and then to the small alleyway now starting to fill with people hurrying away from the street.

It's safe, I supply, realizing he wanted a perch to watch from.

Safe enough, he agrees. *But that's not all the news I have for you. First Mage Blackflame declared a state of emergency upon your escape, which included a lockdown on all portal travel. Only approved mages may pass.*

Absolutely not! I would stand up in my fury, only I'm incorporeal, housed within Val, and have to stop myself from accidentally launching myself back to my own body. *He can't close* all *the portals like that!*

Val doesn't answer, but I can still hear him saying, *Regardless, he did.*

And I know it—not only is the proof right before us, but I know that Blackflame's done it once already without even the Council's backing, when his favored mages took control of the portal at Sonapur. That was the whole reason I ended up throwing myself through the portal and into the Burnt Lands, one of his mages on my heels. That was before he had the power to close them all. He certainly hasn't wasted any time about it now. He has always known that control is power. Controlling the portals—closing them—means controlling the flow of information through them, isolating each Kingdom from all the others in a way no one is prepared for.

What's he going to do? I ask. *Stormwind said—she said he wanted to raise up the Northlands. That he'll force the Eleven Kingdoms to bow to the Northland king of his choosing.* I just didn't expect he'd move this fast. Taking control of the communication lines between the Kingdoms as well as the fastest form of movement across borders puts him in prime position to cut off the Kingdoms, install puppet rulers as he has already done in Karolene... or just serve up each Kingdom one by one to the fate of his choosing.

Whatever he does, Val says, *it's not your concern.*

Of course it's my concern! He wouldn't be First Mage—he wouldn't have taken over the Mekteb or closed down the portals—if it weren't for me.

You give yourself too much credit. He would have done it anyway. You were just the first convenient excuse. You ought to know that.

Stormwind said something of the sort as well, but it doesn't change the fact that the reason it's happening now is because of the excuse *I* provided.

Hitomi, Val says. *Listen carefully. You cannot do anything about this from where you are, in a cavern beneath the Burnt*

Lands. Nor is it your responsibility. Every arch mage on that Council is responsible for their actions; every arch mage assigned to a Kingdom has their own choices to make. There's a whole world of mages who are connected to the Council and have a place of power and privilege from which they can choose to act. You have none of that.

I don't know how to answer him. I understand what he's saying: that I was the excuse, the spark that brought about the chaos that Blackflame took advantage of. Or rather, I was the kindling for him to light his own fire. But I can't shake this feeling of guilt, because without my actions, it wouldn't have happened in this moment. I don't know how to parse out my responsibility, or to let the overpowering sense of my guilt go when I know I wasn't the only actor, even as my actions had consequences.

But Val's right: I can't walk away from the Burnt Lands right now. There's no way Blackflame will ever bother to send a team of mages out to assess the Barrier early. And the Barrier is failing. It won't last the full five years. When it falls, the draining spells will expand across the desert and beyond, sucking the surrounding lands and all that inhabit it dry of magic and life.

It is mind-boggling to me that I never spared a thought for the Burnt Lands or their spells before I went tumbling through the portal into their midst. I suppose most mages, and the High Council itself, have simply acclimated to the danger they represent, and no longer consider them a real or present threat. There is only the phoenix to watch over them—and in four hundred years, he has not wavered.

Val's right about the High Council, and the threat Blackflame poses. There are people who will be fighting Blackflame's orders even now. Judging from my memories of the Shadow League, the arch mages who oppose him aren't the only ones who will try to stand against him.

Right now, I don't have the ability to help them. I'm not even fully a mage anymore. What I do have is the ability to help the phoenix try to mitigate the dangers the Burnt Lands pose.

From the street, a scream goes up. Val moves with lightning

speed—but he doesn't drop into the sheltered garden. Instead, he's up and running the top of the wall in a heartbeat, reaching the corner to pause there, looking out. The crowds dissolve into panic, people shouting and pushing, running away from the portal and its mages.

Val turns his head, leaning out. The mages at the gates sweep their hands out, knocking whole swathes of people back, as if they were ants being brushed from a table. Only there is no space behind them, and their hurtling bodies slam into the crowds behind them, people screaming in terror.

Goddamned bastards, Val snarls, and drops his gaze to the people below as screams rise up and the crowd begins to panic, people running and shoving their way past each other. *You need to go now, Hitomi. There's nothing you can do here.*

He's right—I can't even access my magic here. I can't help these people, can't help Val, can't do a *thing* about the horror playing out by the portal. *What about you—*

I'll be fine, he says tersely, still watching the road. A child of eight or nine years stumbles through the crowd, pushed and shoved as he tries to keep his feet. Val whistles sharply. A couple of people glance his way, and then the boy does, wailing—and his cries drop away.

Val's gaze, I realize, my thoughts freezing. I can't be sure, all I feel is a sudden sense of calm radiating from him, but then the child is alert and moving, stumbling around one man, avoiding another woman barreling past, and then he's below us. Val reaches down into the burgeoning stampede and catches his hand and hauls him up onto the wall. He doesn't say a word, just swings the child down to the other side and turns back to the street. The child hunkers down silently, waiting.

Val continues to scan the street.

Val, you're—you're—

I'm not a bleeding heart. Don't let this confuse you, he says sharply.

He's not; I've seen him kill before, ruthlessly. Still... *I've never been confused,* I tell him. *After all, you helped me.*

Val actually rolls his eyes, which is an unexpectedly strange experience to have from the inside.

You need to go. I'll be fine here, but I need to focus.

I pull back at once. *Tell me when you're safe,* I say.

I will, Val says, and with a gentle nudge sends me reeling back to my body.

CHAPTER II
RAVELRY

The following day begins a simple pattern, broken only by Val coming by to check on me in the morning. He brings no further news other than that he managed to help three people, and has now left them and the town behind. He departs after only a few minutes.

Beyond that, each day follows the template of the last: the phoenix and I wake in the morning, share our breakfast, go up to the banyan tree, and then I set to work on the draining spells, pausing now and then to discuss ideas and possibilities. We come down again by lunch, and then I lie down for a short nap while he flies out to make his patrol of the lands. He sees Ravenflight twice in raven form, but both times she turns away from him, and he lets her go. At least I know that means she isn't attempting to venture in on foot. In the late afternoon, I go back up to work again, and then it's dinner and bedtime from there.

The only variation is when the pack creatures come through the town. Then I stay below, exploring the cavern, or sitting in the root room and reaching up to the spells from there. The more I channel, the less my markings hurt, until I barely notice the faint tingle that accompanies my work. It is an unexpected grace I cannot be grateful enough for. The phoenix must have been right:

it is all about choice. I do not doubt that Blackflame's source slave ever had any.

The days are a strange sort of reprieve: nothing is too demanding, I have plenty of time to rest, and while I can't range out overland, the cavern is more than large enough for me to walk great loops that work out my nervous energy. If I get tired, it's from the mental strain of trying to do something that I still cannot quite grasp, even after so many hours trying.

The phoenix sometimes brings back food from his flights—more dates, but also, once a little sack of bread and a sachet of mint tea, which he then heats for me with his own magic. I speak with him about Huda's fears, and how, should we be successful, the tribes will need to swear themselves to peace before we complete our work. He listens thoughtfully, and is gone a little longer each afternoon after that, returning with rather more prepared food than before. I don't argue—not about the bread, not about the package of dried, spiced goat meat, and certainly not about the small ball of sweetened cheese he lays before me.

"You really think we'll manage this," I say, after the fourth such trip.

"I think you need to eat," he replies. "And I have only been reminding them that I am here, and that it is a great honor to speak with me."

I stifle a laugh. "You're appallingly arrogant, you know."

"It is a *great* honor to speak with me," he says, his eyes twinkling. Remembering Huda and Sumeyya's awe the first time he spoke with them, I know he's right. He goes on, "And I have not spoken to this many humans in *decades*. It is exhausting. They should certainly appreciate it."

"They know you're up to something, then."

"Of course," he says, and then admits, "Word has spread that you are here, working at my behest. The last two tribes I've visited both asked after you. They would have found out anyhow; I have merely helped move things along by showing up in each tribe's lands. It has been necessary to lay the groundwork of cooperation between them. They are not all amenable to peace—it will no doubt have to be as your friend said: marriages to seal the pacts. It is important that they know this and prepare."

"What if I can't manage anything?" I ask.

"It is never bad for a people to consider the possibility of peace."

There is a truth if ever I heard one. Unfortunately, it's not just the peace of the tribes that is needed, but for the Barrier to hold strong through our work, and for the effects of the Burnt Lands to be undone. I haven't forgotten the so-called hollow valleys Huda showed me.

I pack away our meal. "Let's go up then, if the way is clear."

I make a little headway working with the flow of the strands, but I still cannot get them to stay as I leave them—their capacity to regenerate, or self-heal, is incredibly frustrating. I shift, let my back rest against the stone root that supports the branch overhead, and let my mind wander for a few minutes, trying to find a question I haven't asked yet, and realize there's one right in front of me.

"Why stone?" I ask the phoenix. He perches on the next branch over, head raised watchfully. I wave at the tree, and the town beyond. "Why nothing else? Even the spell-creatures turn to stone when deprived of magic."

"Stone endures," he replies. "Fire burns out, water changes its form, air flows on, but the earth remains. Of the hard materials of the earth, stone is the most common and easiest to draw on." He pauses. "Perhaps that's why working with it seems to pose less danger to you than the mages that came before you."

Because not everyone is marked by both elements? I should hope not. "Even stone can be worn away, or broken."

"That is precisely what we are striving to do, is it not?"

Is it? I hadn't thought of the work I needed to do as wearing away at something or breaking it. If I thought of anything at all, it was of how I unraveled the magic of the great spell-beast as a seamstress might open up a seam, so that two of its tentacles came undone and were lost to it, turning to stone. The resulting backlash of magic washed through me, marking my magical core, just as my sunbolt marked me with fire. It's a consequence I have no interest in experiencing ever again. Still, the method itself was successful.

I shift, a nub in the stone root rubbing against my back. Perhaps, more than anything, we need a better way to think about what we are doing.

"We're not really trying to wear away the Burnt Lands, or break them, though," I say, watching the phoenix. He's a lot older than me, and a lot wiser. He's also been thinking about this a great deal longer than I. Maybe he'll have an idea I can use.

"No," he agrees. "We wish to unmake them, as you did the great kraken. Then we will need to contend with the consequences: as you discovered, doing so will release a vast amount of magic."

"Too much."

He nods. "If we succeed in unmaking the draining spells, we will need to capture that magic. We've discussed this."

We have, but I wasn't thinking of it in terms of *how* the unmaking would work, but rather protecting the desert tribes from any such backlash of magic. Although, even now, Huda's tribe deals with the ramifications of the draining spells—the backlash of a lack of magic. "Have you heard of what the tribes call the hollow valleys?"

"The lands that lie in the path of the winds that blow through the Burnt Lands?" the phoenix asks. "Yes. It takes some time for the balance to be restored."

I purse my lips, his words settling into me. "Balance," I repeat. "That's how the spells here have survived this long."

"Yes. You remember we also discussed if eliminating the spell-creatures might make a difference in that balance," the phoenix reminds me.

We had agreed it most likely wouldn't, given previous attempts. But that's not what I'm thinking about now. "It's a tenuous balance, though. They would be constantly expanding if the Barrier were not there."

The phoenix dips his head, watching me steadily. "They would," he agrees. "But slowly."

"Slowly? I thought if the Barrier failed, the draining spells would explode across the desert."

"They will at first," the phoenix agrees. "But that is only due to the rush of power the spells will gain from absorbing the Barrier itself. Once that power is spent, they should slow, creeping across the land. It takes immense power just to maintain these spells. The larger they grow, the more they require to sustain what they already are, and thus, the slower they grow."

"So, there might be time to raise a new Barrier," I say.

"Or escape. The people in the cities should be safe. But the desert will surely die when the Barrier falls and the draining spells explode across the land, as you so aptly put it."

"Is that why the High Council hasn't come out to assess the Barrier again? I assume you've petitioned them."

"They were here two years ago," the phoenix says, his voice deceptively mild.

"And they won't come back again before the standard five has passed."

"They have greater concerns than the desert."

I know it. I've seen the disdain for the people of the desert among the students of the Mekteb, had it flung in my face, when I was a prisoner there. And I know exactly what Blackflame will think: I've faced his contempt as well. No one will save the desert. That is why the phoenix tried to use debts to bring me back— because it was the only way he could think of to make sure I returned. I cannot fault him for it.

"What if we shift the flow from expanding outward to pulling inward? Create an internal focal point, something that could absorb the magic as it comes to it?" I ask.

"A talisman?" the phoenix suggests, though he doesn't sound like he's following me.

I'm not sure I follow me either. When I undid the tentacles of the spell-creature, I snipped a thread of magic at each end and then pulled it, as if I were opening up a seam. If I think of the spells that cover the Burnt Lands as woven together like a cloth, then I might snip a seam, if I could find one large enough and manage the work of it—but everything would go spilling out as it did with the great tentacled creature—the kraken.

I remember sitting in Stormwind's cottage, deep in the winter, learning how to knit, and then taking my ill-shaped squares and pulling out the yarn, unmaking my work stitch by stitch so that I might start over. Slowly, I sound the idea out loud. "We want to unravel the Burnt Lands by a single thread, gathering it into a ball wrapped tight, pulling in all the connected threads of magic together. We're not breaking apart the Burnt Lands, we're *unmaking* them." I look to the phoenix.

"A single thread," he echoes.

"The wrapping of a skein of yarn into a ball." I grin at him, the metaphor settling into me. "If we can create a single loose end to unwind the fabric of the Burnt Lands itself, we can wind that into your talisman, just like a knitter might unravel a bit of work and gather it up for another day."

"That is a *fascinating* way to think about it," the phoenix says.

It is, except... "This doesn't act like fabric, though," I say, looking back at the draining spells.

"It is stone," the phoenix says again, but a little more carefully, as if suddenly aware that I haven't caught on to what he really means. "Have you ever studied a crystal? Or a glowstone? Stone grows in rigid networks, building faceted edges and planes. That is what you see here."

It may be interlaced a little like cloth, but I can't wind it up like yarn. It's *hard*. But... "What if I soften the threads? Use fire to turn them into something I can treat like yarn?"

"A thread of liquid stone," the phoenix says, watching me. "You speak of lava."

I nod, repressing a shiver. Lava is not precisely a forgiving material to work with.

A thread of liquid stone being wrapped into a ball is certainly not a perfect metaphor, and I can just imagine Stormwind's consternation if I were to try to explain this to her. Still, I don't think any one image is quite right; this is just the one that makes sense to me. If the magic *can* be gathered somehow and then gently infused back into the land, that will return life to these lands much faster than the natural world would manage it on its own.

"It's worth a try, at least," I say. "But I'm going to need that talisman you gave me." It is an incredible thing to know that I may have lost my ability to cast spells, but I can still think of doing such work. "Be right back," I say, grinning.

Talisman in hand, I return to the same spot where I made my previous attempts, settling down to study the draining spells once more. Even if I have a new way of thinking of things, that doesn't mean I know precisely what I'm doing or that I'll meet with success on the first attempt, or even the twentieth. The one thing I have right now—precious as it is—is time. I'm happy to use it to keep working at this.

By evening, and likely well over a hundred tries, I meet with a minor success: when I concentrate on a single sharp-edged "thread" and draw on the fire in my bones, I'm able to feed it into the stone filament so that it heats and flows smoothly. I can even detach the fiery filament from the surrounding latticework and channel it in a smooth-flowing curve into the talisman. It is a single filament of a hundred million, and yet it is so much more than I've accomplished thus far.

Even the phoenix seems brighter than usual as we make our way down to the cavern for the night, and hums softly over his food. It's absolutely adorable.

I rub a hand over my markings as I think, the skin tender. I'll need to learn how to collapse this structure together to draw in more of the filaments of the surrounding spells. Somehow, though, that feels inexplicably more doable now, while before it felt like another weight I must carry. I reach up and wrap my hand around the ward I wear, the smooth obsidian ring warm against my palm. I can do this. Even if I don't know where I will go from here—how I will escape Ravenflight or if there will ever be another haven as safe as this one open to me, or a path that won't endanger those I care about—right now I have a focus. There is something I have a hope of achieving.

"You're smiling," the phoenix says, perched on the edge of his nest.

I glance over at him, my smile widening. "I am," I agree, and settle down to sleep.

CHAPTER 12
OF MAKING AND UNMAKING

Three days later, I've worked my way through all the layers of the latticework of spells, testing every sharp-edged filament I can find. I dream of the flickering flow of the draining spells, see them when I close my eyes whether I am connected to them or not. The pattern of them slowly takes shape in my mind. Not all the lines of magic, or filaments as I've been calling them, are the same, nor are their bonds to each other where they meet and interconnect. As in stone and minerals, some are stronger than others. Melt the strongest bonds and the weaker ones automatically fail, melding into the flow I'm creating.

Together, the phoenix and I try our hands (or talons) at melting the strongest bonds, drawing on our fire and guiding the searingly hot and viscous magic into the talisman.

"Did you *see* that?" I crow, jumping back and shaking out my hands. The filament I was working with has disappeared into the talisman, taking with it a few of the weaker connected filaments whose bonds melt as well. The layers *they* were bound to then proceed to dissolve at the edges, resulting in the small, stinging backlash of magic that hit the backs of my hands before being reabsorbed into the draining spells. What is left now is a small empty space within the latticework of the spells.

"Brilliant," the phoenix says, even as the draining spells press against the empty space, filaments slowly reaching out to snap together, new connections forming.

The space I've cleared is no larger than the size of my admittedly small boot sole, but it's a start, and that's an incredible success. I can't help grinning like a fool.

The phoenix bobs his head, eyes bright. "Excellent. Show me, and I will try as well."

I cast a quick look around for spell-creatures; thankfully, today it's quiet above ground. Still, we both remain on our guard while I walk him through each step of the process. This time, I keep my hands a little farther back, and the backlash barely touches me.

The phoenix, fairly glimmering with excitement, attempts it himself, and manages an even larger section—nearly a pace across.

I laugh. "You're already better than me."

"I have more fire to draw on." He pauses, his light dimming slightly as he glances toward me. "I worry you are already drawing on your core too much—even in my haven, there is not very much magic to replenish it."

Maybe that's the reason I'm so deeply fatigued every night. It never occurred to me that I needed to replenish my magic. Then again, I've never spent so much time in a place that wouldn't naturally do that for me.

"I'm going to take that talisman with me this afternoon," he says, "and see what I can do to add to it. It will be better for you to draw on that instead, and use it to replenish yourself as needed."

"Sounds good."

The phoenix turns his gaze back to the draining spells. "Now comes the question of doing this on an expanded scale."

It's a good question. We spend the next few days refining my process. Our experiments are much less tiring once the talisman holds some magic within it that I can channel, rather than relying on my own reserves. Together, we learn to guide the flow of magic down the strongest connectors of the latticework. As each bond melts, drawing the filament it connects in with it, the flow increases. The more we do it—with progressively larger test patches—the faster and easier the filaments and connectors melt and flow, success breeding success. But also, the more uncontrolled magic is released from the melted edges of the spells we don't manage to channel to the talisman.

"That backlash will pose a challenge," the phoenix says on the third day when I jerk back from the talisman, shaking my hand to ease the sting from yet another such backlash. He has been experimenting as well, and has lost a few feathers to his own backlashes.

"Yes," I agree. "The way this effect builds, I think we could dissolve these spells on a larger scale. But there will be a backlash from what is left behind any way we do it, no matter if there is a talisman there to absorb the magic or not."

"The Barrier should contain a certain amount of backlash," the phoenix says.

"I hadn't thought of that."

I look up at the faint white dome far above us. We've already discussed how the Barrier can't handle a full backlash—if the spells were to collapse altogether and release their full power into the desert, the Barrier is too weak to contain so much power. It already has all the source power it needs from the outside world; its debility is one of structure, not sustenance. A backlash would blast it to pieces. But a *partial* release might be held back by the Barrier. We'd still have to figure out how to handle that magic on this side of the Barrier, but it wouldn't cause any damage outside at the moment of release, which is the critical consideration.

"What if we try clearing a larger section within a contained space, to mimic the Barrier," the phoenix says, "and then we try funneling the backlash into the talisman as well?"

"We don't have anything to protect ourselves, though," I say. "I have no interest in being hit by another such surge, even if I am already marked by stone."

The phoenix huffs in amusement. "I imagine not. However, I can use what the talisman contains to create a small shield. We'll have to work quickly, because the draining spells will absorb it as well, but it should hold long enough for a trial."

I flex my fingers, looking down at the talisman, and my chest tightens. A shield is something I *can't* make. I can channel magic into the talisman and back out again, and I can absorb a little to replenish my reserves when needed. I can even work with the spells already created around me. But I *can't* weave anything of my own again—my castings are pure power now, channeled out or through. Brute force with no ability to shape what leaps from my fingers. I hate it. Hate what I have lost, hate that I can no longer do this, that nearly three weeks ago Huda's brother bled before my eyes and there was never a question of my helping him.

"Mageling?" the phoenix asks softly.

I take a slow breath, holding on to the fury. It is so much easier to carry than the helplessness it disguises and the sorrow of what I've lost. "My name's Hitomi," I tell him, because this is one thing that is still mine and I want to claim it, share it with whom I can. "I'm sorry I didn't tell you sooner."

"Hitomi," he repeats, a faint breeze ruffling his feathers.

"My friends call me Tomi," I add, thinking of Kenta.

The phoenix tilts his head, and in the shape of his neck I see his grief, age-old and unspoken. "I thank you. I am afraid I have no name that I remember, and few friends to call me anything other than 'phoenix'."

"Well," I say doubtfully, "you can still call me mageling if it makes you feel better."

He gives a short barking laugh and shakes his head. "I would be honored to call you Tomi."

"It's all right. I'll find a nickname for you, too. How about..." I pause, considering, and say with utmost seriousness, "Foofoo?"

"I think *not*," he huffs, all righteous indignation, but his eyes still sparkle with laughter.

"Yeah, it's about as bad as Kiki," I acknowledge, remembering the name Val gave me before the High Council.

"Kiki is a very excellent name," the phoenix argues. "Foofoo is...." He shudders, his wings fluttering in distaste.

"Whatever you say, Foofoo."

"*Tomi!*" he protests in helpless outrage. I laugh as I haven't laughed in a long time, first a giggle and then a rush of great, deep laughter that pours out of me until my eyes run with tears. The phoenix's wings shake with his own amusement.

"You deserve it, anyhow," I tell him. "Acting all high and mighty with the tribespeople. Someone's got to make sure you stay humble."

"Mmm," he responds, not arguing. "Well, let's try this, shall we?"

I wipe away my tears, shift over to kneel beside him, and together we work on healing the Burnt Lands.

Each of our next three attempts ends just short of disaster. Watching the phoenix cast the shield is vastly educational regarding just how fast the draining spells can *drain*. Each time, I have only a handful of seconds to melt the bonds of the connected filaments I've chosen, sending their magic flowing in a single thread toward the talisman, and then pull back. The superheated flow dissolves the connections attaching to it even as the shield wavers and begins to fail, barely absorbing the resultant backlash. The unexpected help in the situation is the draining spells themselves: what the shield bounces back before failing, the spells reabsorb before the backlash can escape out to us.

"That... could actually be helpful," I say, studying the new configuration of the spells underfoot.

"How so?" the phoenix asks.

"We could do this in stages, one after the other. The spells heal quickly, so we can't wait too long, but we don't have to clear all the draining spells in one fell swoop. We could do two or three. Each time, the latticework will be thinner, the backlash smaller, and more magic will be absorbed into the talisman. We'll just need one heck of a talisman. Or a dozen of them."

The phoenix nods, considering all the angles. "If we can achieve that larger flow, we would need to set the talismans at the center of the Burnt Lands to draw *in* the magic. That way, any backlash would have to travel back out over the remaining draining spells before reaching the Barrier."

It's a good point, and a safeguard against overstraining the Barrier. "It will take some practice—to direct the flow from the outer edges of the Burnt Lands all the way to the center."

The phoenix clicks his beak. "It will. To truly work, it must be started at multiple points along the edge—all together, dissolving the latticework from the outside in."

He's right. As we've already learned, if we only work in patches, they'll heal. "We'll need help," I point out. The phoenix and I, even working from opposite ends of the Burnt Lands, will only be able to do so much from our two points. It doesn't seem like enough, but where we'll get more mages...

"Yes," the phoenix agrees. "And while you might have an affinity for stone, I doubt anyone else I can call on will."

It's rare for a mage to be marked by an element, let alone two as I have. With stone at my core, I can send my mage sense skating out over the draining spells underfoot and they don't seem to affect me too badly. It's tiring, but not exhaustingly so. Even having been marked by stone, though, I haven't tried to send my senses out as far as the phoenix is suggesting, halfway across the Burnt Lands. One more thing to test, then.

"The other critical piece will be the placement of the talismans." The phoenix is as adept as I am at studying the threads, if not more so. He has been watching them for centuries, even if he did not think of them the way I did. If I can figure out how to do this, he can easily place the talismans on the specific threads where we need them. "But I think we can manage it," I say, scooping up the talisman. "Let's give this another go."

The phoenix opens his beak to answer, then pauses, his head turning once more. "Pack creatures. Run."

I push to my feet, scrambling over the great rippling roots. I catch a flash of darkness from the corner of my eye, and *run*. Behind me, I hear the heavy flap of the phoenix's wings, followed by a snarl and a burst of light. I twist as I reach the crack, glancing back to see the phoenix in all his fiery glory, one taloned foot wrapped around the largest spike of the foremost pack creature's spine.

The other pack creatures surge forward, toward the phoenix. He twists, his fire flaring out—and my mage sight shows how it envelopes the creatures and pulls away, dragging at their own magic. He lets go of the spine he held, now a crackly grey, and launches himself up into the branches as the pack creatures fall back, snarling—and limping. They're not turning to stone, nothing like the tentacle of the kraken I unmade, but he's taken some part of their magic and they need the draining spells to aid them as they regroup.

"Child, *go!*"

Right. I dive into the crack, banging my knee as I scramble the few steps to the opening. I slide over its edge, grabbing the rope with both hands and clamping my legs around it as I swing down.

Faintly, I hear a snarl from above. They've regrouped already. I let go, dropping down through the darkness to land on my feet. Backing away from the center of the room, I keep my eyes trained on the rough-edged circle above. *Come on*, I tell the phoenix as the circle remains empty, dim light filtering through. *Come on*.

I know he can manage himself—I just saw him do it. But I still want him down here and safe.

Finally, the phoenix's glow fills the hole, shining down into the root-bound room, and a moment later he wings down to join me, his fire muted. "Take the tunnel down," he says, barely sparing me a glance as I swallow my relief. He perches on the stone pack creature as if it has become his favored landing spot, his head craned to keep watch on the entry above our heads. "They may yet try to follow."

The faint scratch of claws on stone echoes down to us. I fumble my glowstone from my pocket. "What about you?"

"They cannot kill me. Not here. You, on the other hand...." He shoots me a worried glance. It warms me like the gentlest of flames.

"Be careful anyway. You can still get hurt," I say, dropping down to crawl into the tunnel to the cavern.

He makes no response, his head crooked to look at me.

It's only when I'm halfway through the tunnel that I finally place his expression. It is the avian equivalent of Stormwind's stiff uncertainty the first time I hugged her, all unexpected vulnerability.

CHAPTER 13
DEPARTURE

We manage to spend only an hour experimenting the next day, the pack creatures lurking too close for comfort. By late the following morning, we can empty a section as long as I am tall, working three times in rapid succession to clear the various layers of spells, and leaving the land completely bare and unexpectedly warm to the touch.

I shake out my hands, my arms only slightly achy. "What do you think?" I ask the phoenix, nodding toward the bare section of earth.

He watches the slow pulse of the edges of the hole we've created as the draining spells once again attempt to self-heal, crystal-like filaments pressing out and snapping together. It will take them a little while at least to recover such a space. He returns his attention to me, his gaze pausing on my hands before returning to my face. "I think we should depart for the desert today."

I start. "What? Shouldn't we work at this a little more? I know we've managed a bit, but..." I gesture to the town square, and everything that lies beyond. "There's still so much to try."

"We need a better shield, and the only place we'll find that is the Barrier."

He's right. He can't make a shield stronger than he already has —the draining spells break everything down too fast, and the talisman has only so much for us to use, given that we draw on it every time we add to it. The Barrier will offer better protection against the middling sort of backlash caused by attempting to clear a larger section; we will just have to be smart about not straining it.

I just don't want to go. I know that leaving the phoenix's haven will be as final in its way as fleeing Stormwind's cabin was. The safety here has been closer to what I had in her valley than anything I might hope for in the future, bloodthirsty spell-creatures and hovering rogue hunter notwithstanding.

I sigh. I'm just putting off the inevitable. When I left Stormwind's valley, I knew that I was choosing a hard future—that Stormwind's arrest gave me only two options: to hide forever or try to help her. Really, though, it was only one choice: I was going to have to hide regardless. So, my choices are as bare now as they were then: I cannot stay. Therefore, I must go—and survive however I can, as long as I may.

"All right," I tell the phoenix. "What's our plan?"

"We will attempt this on a slightly larger scale at the Barrier, though we'll have to avoid your Ravenflight's notice."

"She's not mine," I grumble.

Ignoring me, he goes on, "Then we'll continue on to meet the healer-mage of the Bani Essam, unless he manages to join us there."

I study the phoenix. What are the chances he knows—or suspects—that the mage he speaks of is most likely my uncle? "Why him?" I ask.

"He'll be the easiest for us to reach from here. I... may have spoken with him yesterday on my afternoon flight."

I grunt. Of course, the phoenix has been consulting and laying plans; I just thought he'd discuss them with me first. Still, the convenience of reaching the Bani Essam is hard to argue against, especially when the alternative is a longer journey through spell-creature infested lands.

The phoenix clears his throat. "I want you to teach him your method, so that he and I can then train the other mages I am working to gather.”

“Is he marked with both stone and fire, too?” I ask innocently. “Or just fire, as you are?”

The phoenix snorts. “Unlikely. However, we will need multiple mages acting in concert for this to work. He will be our first test outside of the two of us.”

Fair enough. “Do you trust him, though?” I press. At the phoenix’s look, I add uncertainly, “I mean, not to betray me to Ravenflight first.” After all, I may suspect the man of being my uncle, but he has no reason to believe me any relation of his. I’m not even using my father’s name. Even if I was, he is part of the family that disowned my father. I can’t expect he’d have greater loyalty to a niece he’s never met than he had to his own brother.

The phoenix unfolds a wing to brush my arm with the fine, stiff feathers of his wingtip. “I do not believe he will—as much as he holds allegiance to the High Council, the loyalties closest to his heart will be that of his tribe and people. Further, he and his people hold me in high regard, and you are my guest. But, regardless, I will put myself between you and any who would offer you harm. This I promise you.”

He *cares*. It takes me by surprise, even though I knew he could care, knew he still mourns the folk he lost here and crossing the Burnt Lands. I just didn’t expect him to care about *me*. I’m a tool for him to use, a chance to figure out a problem that has haunted these lands for centuries. Only, apparently, I’m more than that.

It makes me want to scoop up his feathered body and bury my face in his gleaming plumage. I don’t, of course. Instead, I ask, “When do we leave?”

The phoenix glances once more at our work. “This afternoon, after you’ve had a little time to rest, I think.”

I take a slow breath. “What of the pack creatures? Are they still nearby?”

“They’ve moved out some distance, but it would be best to draw them further afield.”

“They’re drawn to magic, right?”

The phoenix's eyes gleam with amusement. "I had the same thought, although a charm will only draw them away for so long. It may also attract other creatures to it, and so potentially bring them closer to you."

"Well," I say, pushing myself to my feet, "we'll just have to plan where exactly you'll leave it, then."

We go below and eat a quick meal while discussing the logistics of the journey. Then I lie down for my afternoon rest while the phoenix flies out to check on my uncle's location and take stock of the nearby spell-creatures. I can't help wondering what sort of person my uncle is, if he will act as the phoenix expects and protect my identity until this work is done, or not. I want to meet him, to see what the family I have left is like. Is he like what I remember of my father, strong but gentle and caring?

Except my uncle disowned my father along with their parents. Just as my mother disowned me. I pull Huda's blanket around my shoulders, suddenly cold. Best not think of this mage as my uncle if I can help it. It's not as if he will claim me back.

I close my eyes and somehow manage to push away my worries and fall into a light doze. By the time the phoenix returns, I'm ready to go; the last of my belongings are packed, and the sapphire talisman hangs by its chain from my neck.

For our decoy, I give the phoenix one of the glowstones I rescued from his treasure trove, now charged up with magic from the talisman. He departs once more, promising to return as soon as possible. I begin stretching out my muscles, trying to calm my nerves. I haven't yet made it through the Burnt Lands without encountering some danger that very nearly took my life. For all the phoenix's confidence, I'm not at all sure I'll make it through this time.

Valerius, I call quietly. I only say his name once, knowing he'll hear me. That he'll know this is a warning that I'm about to do something ineffably stupid, and may require his help to get out alive. This time I also know to use his full name.

It isn't long before he joins me. *You're stretching. I assume that means you're about to start running again.*

I laugh, the sound small in the cavern, but still warm and light. *Running is what I do.*

Have you ever considered making a home for yourself? They can be quite comfortable.

Can't quite seem to hold on to any of the homes I've had, I respond, trying to keep my tone light. *But I do like the idea.* The truth is I will always be running—toward something, or away. I can no longer quite imagine a life in which I'm not running. The only way I won't have to run is if the rogue hunters who track me think I'm dead... and I can't really imagine a way to trick them into truly believing that.

Where are we running today? Val asks, thankfully letting all talk of homes go.

Back out of the Burnt Lands.

I surmised as much, Val says patiently. *You have a destination in mind as well, though, don't you?*

The phoenix wants to recruit another mage to help us.

Val considers this. *Does that mean you've repaid your debt to the phoenix?*

I frown. *I don't think so? It didn't occur to me. I really haven't done that much yet.*

Certainly, Val says, amusement warming his voice. *You've just done something worth teaching other mages, that's all.*

I cough a laugh. *It was just the right moment, and the right amount of playing with things.*

I'm sure.

Anyhow, I have to make sure the desert will be all right.

I would expect no less, he says wryly.

Any news? I ask.

I have a little, though most of it may be rumor. It's hard to tell what's truth and what's changed in the telling.

What's happened?

The portals remain under guard, although the Kingdoms have registered a complaint. Blackflame has assured them it's temporary, but there's also no sign of their reopening. Word is he's called in allies from the Northland Council to back up the High Council's needs.

Allies? I repeat, my mind racing. Stormwind was planning to travel to the Northland Council to seek out her own allies there when we parted ways. Somehow, I doubt that the mages Blackflame called in are actually here for the good of the Eleven Kingdoms.

I could be wrong, Val cautions me. *It is difficult to verify anything now with the portals closed.*

I frown. Val is supposed to be in the stronghold of his people, in company with his breather prince. How is he getting even this much news? *Where are you now?* I ask. *How did you find out even this much?*

I am traveling again, Val says.

Why?

I often do, he replies, which is vague but true. The last dream I had of him before I left Stormwind's valley was of him and another breather sailing by ship, leaving a magically hidden city built into a cove. Not to mention, he told me of many of his past travels in the weeks we journeyed together to reach Stormwind's valley in the first place. I suppose if he doesn't want to share his reasons for traveling now, it's hardly my right to pry into them. Although his prince knows about me, asked to meet me... and now Val has left his home. Did he have a choice—or was it the kind of choice I keep facing?

Val, I ask hesitantly. *Why did you leave your home* this *time?*

To travel, obviously, he says, which is *such* a rubbish reply.

The far side of the cavern brightens with golden light as the phoenix steps from the tunnel. I wave to him, thread my arms through my pack, and scoop up my glowstone from the ground.

I will be back shortly, Val says as I cross the stream. *Then I'll be able to stay as long as you require.*

Thanks, I say, wondering if his departure is because he needs to situate himself somewhere safe for the next couple of hours, or if it he's just that desperate to change the subject. Possibly both.

"The pack creatures are following the charm I left behind,"

the phoenix says as I reach him. "As long as its magic holds, it will create a beacon for everything that moves out there."

I nod, and we make our way back up to the root-bound room. Then, for what may be the last time, the phoenix helps me up the rope, his magic falling just short of the beginning of the loop in the draining spells, as always. I scramble the rest of the way up and make my way out, unfastening the rope and tossing it back into the cavern. The banyan, surrounding buildings, and streets lie empty.

We pause at the edge of the canopy.

"Will you be able to run if needed?" the phoenix asks, casting me an anxious glance.

"Yes."

He hesitates. "Your breather bond?"

"He knows."

The phoenix dips his head and looks out at the silent buildings, the only sound that of the breeze whistling through the stone branches overhead. "We'll move quickly. Keep your strength for running, should you need to."

I nod and step out into the open, the phoenix beside me.

WE TAKE A SLIGHTLY different route from the one I came by. It is shorter by only a few minutes, but experience tells me a few minutes may make all the difference.

As we leave behind the buildings of the dead town, the phoenix wheeling just overhead, Val rejoins me.

Do you trust this healer-mage the phoenix intends for you to see? he asks as we start across the empty land, the sunbaked earth cracked and crumbling.

I take a slow breath.

You don't, Val says.

It's complicated, I hedge. *The phoenix swears the healer-mage will have allegiances to both his tribe and the High Council. Our goal is to get him to hold off on reporting me until we finish our work here—which would benefit all the desert tribes. If he only reports me at the end, that gives the phoenix and me time to plan an escape.*

You had better have an escape planned at all times, Val says.

I try to, I agree cheerily. *Some things are easier to escape than others.*

Val doesn't answer at once. When he does, though, it's not what I expect. *What are you not telling me?*

I let out my breath with a sigh, wishing that the phoenix would swoop in at just this moment so I won't have to answer. As one might expect, he doesn't. *The mage the phoenix has chosen—I believe he's my uncle.*

Of course he is, Val says, as if this were just another inevitable calamity of my life.

What if he recognizes me? I ask, my thoughts tumbling out. *What if he betrays me?*

Ahh. I can sense Val's tension, at odds with the gentle way he says, *Only one way to find out, I suppose.*

Comforting, I say, but it's not all sarcasm. He's right—and I do want to find out.

I'll stay with you. Val says, and while I'm still absorbing the truth of the relief I feel, the absolute kindness of his words, he adds, *You'll want to escape the bloodbath that will follow all this regardless.*

You mean the tribes going to war over the land we've opened up, right? I cast my glance upward to where the phoenix glides overhead. He's staying low so as not to attract Ravenflight's attention, but still high enough to spot any spell-creatures in the distance.

The prospect of wealth usually brings out the worst in people.

"Yeah," I admit aloud. I drop my gaze and keep moving. *The phoenix is working to make sure that doesn't happen.*

You think he can do it?

They revere him, and if he makes it a stipulation for the opening of the lands themselves, then they might agree. Huda said it would take marriages to seal their pacts. She thought it would be possible, though. At any rate, I'm not healing the Burnt Lands just to bring about a war.

You sound much more confident about your ability to fix things here.

Yes, I say, unable to keep the hint of pride from my tone, and tell him what we've achieved so far. *We need to carry out a larger test, but for that we need the Barrier to shield us,* I finish.

Hmm. It seems possible. But if the reaction cascades, or if the backlash can't be absorbed fast enough by the draining spells, you don't want to be caught in that.

No, I agree. *I definitely don't.* It's curious he called the melting of the filaments a reaction—though I suppose that is what's happening. The greater the heat and strength of the melted bonds and filaments, the more they then draw after them. *We're working on the details still,* I tell Val. *We won't do anything foolish if we can help it.*

You never do, Val says. *But some things can't be helped.*

Someday I'm going to find out about all the unwise things you've done, and then you'll be sorry.

Unwise thing number one, Val provides helpfully, *getting locked in a tower for a year by a sadistic fang.*

That's true, I agree, grinning. *I haven't done anything that bad. At least not yet.*

Oh? Getting caught freeing a prisoner of the High Council and being put on trial as a rogue mage doesn't qualify?

Well, when you put it like that... I shrug, readjust the straps of my pack. *Perhaps we could both be a bit more strategic.*

I can feel Val's amusement, though he makes no answer. I continue on, both of us on alert as we pass a tiny, abandoned town of a half-dozen yellow-brick buildings. Nothing stirs, and I make no attempt to look inside the distant windows. Instead, I walk on, keeping my thoughts to myself.

A half hour later, the phoenix swoops down to land before me.

"What is it?" I ask, my voice sharp.

"A spell-creature comes. Give me a charm from your pouch and I will try to lead it away."

I nod, slinging my pack around and pulling out the pouch. "Another glowstone?" I ask. They have the benefit of remaining active even when left behind, creating a small but steady beacon.

"Yes."

I grab the second one I took from his trove, pass it to him. "What kind of creature?"

"The great one," the phoenix says and takes to the skies.

The great one, Val echoes dryly. *I suppose that's the one with the massive tentacles that end in talons and a huge, beak-like mouth that can snap a person in two.*

I prefer to think of it as a kraken, I say, haphazardly stuffing a few more charms in my pockets.

Oh, certainly. Gigantic stone desert kraken with a taste for human blood. Absolutely less frightening when you say it like that.

I snort a laugh and shove my pouch back in my pack, hoping Val can't tell my fingers are shaking. I set off walking briskly. The phoenix drummed a series of landmarks into my head when we planned this trip, and I know that within a few minutes another town should come into view. From there, I'll be able to see the hills of the distant desert ranges and use their shape to find the nearest edge of the Barrier. Which is likely still an hour's walk away.

How can you take a word like 'kraken' seriously? I ask Val to distract myself. *It's like Kiki—what's there to worry about?*

Kiki is not meant to cause worry, Val says. *Depending on how it is written, it can mean anything from hope to happiness. Kraken, however, is a Northland word that was adopted into Tradespeak. I believe it means 'sea monster.'*

I dunno, I say, trying to keep myself steady. Val must have made a point to find out what Kiki meant; he didn't know the last time I asked him. *Kiki and the Kraken sounds like a tale to delight young children.*

It does not, Val says flatly.

I glance over my shoulder in the direction the phoenix flew.

He's already disappeared from the skies, and I cannot make out anything in the distance. I force myself to keep to a walk, my palms sweaty from nerves.

Get to that town, Val counsels me. *We'll see if any of the buildings are still sturdy. If your phoenix can't draw the kraken off, that will be where you want to meet it.*

I don't want *to meet it,* I say, just to be clear.

But if you must anyway? He's pushing me to think, to plan, as if I will surely survive this if I just put my mind to it. Maybe I will—there's half a chance I can survive the kraken behind me. But everything else—meeting a mage, taking down the Burnt Lands, evading Ravenflight and all the other hunters on my trail? Not likely. I'm walking away from the one safe place I had. There isn't anywhere else to go.

Still, I'm not going to offer myself up to the kraken just because it presents the easiest death. Especially not with Val keeping me company.

My hands close on the charms in my pockets. Most of them will be no use at all. But... I raise my hand to touch the smooth planes and beveled edges of the near-empty talisman hanging from my neck.

I guess I'd better scare it off the way I did last time, I tell Val.

For that, I'll need a few minutes to plan.

I break into a jog, headed for the town, as Val says, wearily, *I thought you might say that.*

Kiki and the
Kraken

CHAPTER 14
SPLINTERED

The buildings here are broken shells of their former selves. Of the two dozen or so structures that compose the town, only a handful retain their full height, and of those, only one still has a roof. Staring up at it, I decide I'll keep my feet on the ground, and the open sky above me.

Easier to run that way anyway.

Any sign of it? Val asks as I pause in the center of the main street.

I pivot, looking down the wide empty road to where we'd come from.

Yep, I say, for there is the bright speck of the phoenix, swooping and dancing above a great mass of writhing tentacles, already as big as a horse despite its great distance.

I turn back to the town and scan the streets. There are only three: the main drag on which we stand, roughly cobbled; a single cross street of dirt; and an additional little alley on one side. Not that the buildings are built so close together that I couldn't run through the space between them. Still, I want to consider where the beast will most likely come from and most prefer to move. It might not mind dragging itself over the buildings—that may be why they're already as broken as they are—but the streets will still be easier for it to move about.

It's cunning, if I recall correctly, Val says.

Yes. But so am I. I move to the center of the cross street, take the sapphire talisman from about my neck, and wedge it into the crack between two ancient cobbles.

The buildings that stand at the corners of the cross street are in various states of destruction. Both of the buildings to my left have been all but leveled. But to my right stands one whose walls are still complete, and on the other side of the road rises the single building with a roof. The perfect place for a stupid human to take shelter.

I slip inside, resolutely ignoring the bones scattered across the floor, the human skull half-shattered beside the wall. Spell-creatures must have run through here before, uncaring of what lay underfoot. I leave my last glowstone brightening an inner room, hidden from the front windows and entrance.

A decoy, Val says. *Are you sure it will fall for it?*

It will sense the magic, I reply, heading for the building on the opposite side of the street. This one is half broken, its walls still standing but its roof long since fallen in.

What are you planning to do? Sneak up on it?

Pretty much.

Hitomi—

I'll need you to wait till I ask for help, I say, a reminder of what he promised me in Fidanya. From the main road I can make out the massive form of the kraken. It has already halved the distance to the town. Ducking low, I race across the street to the buildings whose walls still stand intact. Whatever tenants it once held, I can only hope that they escaped before the roof fell on them and the draining spells took hold. There is no sign of any remains now.

I take a shuddering breath and move to shelter behind a window that affords me a glimpse of the road. From this angle, I can see down the road in the opposite direction from the one the creature will come from. Which means that, while I can't see it, it won't be able to see me either.

The phoenix flies overhead, a streak of golden fire. He slows, circling once over the intersection, coming into sight for a few moments as he passes overhead. I wave up at him, pointing to the other building. He descends to its roof, smart bird that he is, before taking off once more.

I love that bird, I tell Val.

I don't. He's the only reason you're here right now.

That's true, I agree, leaning against the wall, my pack pressing into my back. It's light enough I'd rather wear it—and perhaps it will protect my back from injury. *If it weren't for the phoenix, I might have died a long time ago in the Burnt Lands. Or never escaped the High Council. He's* definitely *to blame.*

You give him too much credit.

You just don't like that he's calling in my debts. Now hush, it's almost here.

I don't particularly want to watch you die right now, Hitomi.

Then close your eyes. Or have a little more faith in me.

I have great faith in you, Val mutters. *I also remember that spell-creature.*

I do too, and I know that facing it is nothing short of a death wish, but it's all the choice I have. *It doesn't like losing its legs.* I remind him. *I'll be fine.*

Let's hope so.

We sit in silence, listening for the spell-creature's approach. We don't have long to wait. I feel it first, the earth vibrating from its movements.

Then, so faintly I could mistake it for the breeze whistling and humming through the abandoned buildings, comes a scrape.

Then another, and another, and I know for sure it is the kraken, its great scaled tentacles reaching out, talons cutting into the earth as it pulls itself forward.

You're planning on touching it, aren't you? Val asks, making me jump.

I can't reach its magic otherwise, I admit. *If I still had the talis-man, I might be able to use a thread of magic from it to reach the kraken, but that's not an option now.*

Val makes no further comment. I hunch down, breathing as slowly and evenly as I can. If it attacks here first—if it senses not just the glowstone across the road but my body, the magic within me—I'm *dead*.

Don't. Val's voice jerks me to a stop, halfway to my feet. *Don't panic now.*

It'll sense me as easily as it will the—

The spell-beast screeches, a ghastly shriek that reverberates through the air, rattling the bits of gravel and stone on the floor.

I take a shaky breath and turn my head toward the window. Two great tentacles come into view, one sliding through the doorway of the opposite building, the other hooking over its rooftop.

See, Val begins and then a half-dozen massive tentacles come flying over the wall overhead.

I swallow a scream and throw myself sideways, just avoiding being pierced through by an enormous metal-gray talon.

Touch it, Val says as I twist to keep from slamming into the tentacle that lands on the other side of me, its talon gouging the bricks. *Work your magic.*

Right.

I press both hands against the tentacle, bringing the spell-creature's magic into focus, and catch hold of the central thread that glows beneath my fingers.

The creature shrieks again, making my head pound, but I can see the center, the same internal structure of magic that I remember from before. The thinner strands I had used before are gone, fused together into a knot at the creature's bulbous center. These aren't the sharp-edged filaments of magic that form the draining spells. This creature was created on a living base, and while I've been thinking of its magic as threads, it could as easily be characterized as veins and arteries. However I think of it, though, it's still stone and I know what to do with that.

Move! Val shouts.

I take a stumbling step forward against the wall, my hands outstretched as if to keep contact with the shifting tentacle, but my hold on the magic, now established, doesn't give. I twist away, my eyes registering a rushing shadow, and a talon slices through my pack, tearing it from my back. Above me, the magic-bright structure of the creature comes into sight over the wall, its great eyes round and disc-like, the huge, beak-like mouth gaping from the central body, and its tentacles descending from around it in a writhing mass.

I still grip that thread of magic. Holding tight, I stumble to the window and leap out, pushing away from the wall as the bricks collapse beneath the creature's weight. Next to me rest more tentacles braced against the ground to support the monster as it struggles to pull back over the wall and find me. I lay a hand on the nearest one, finding the magic at its core.

Then, I reach up through the two thinning strands of magic I hold to the thick core of magic at the center of the beast. I barely see two more tentacles descending toward me, the brilliant light of the phoenix weaving through them and drawing them off, for there is the knot, and around it, the magic, snarled and twisted. If I can force the flow of magic up the tentacles, emptying them, they will turn as inert as the pack creature did below the banyan tree, deprived of magic. That should be enough to send the kraken into retreat, its stone appendages torn away, and save me from the backlash that hit me the last time I faced the creature.

Drawing on the already dwindling reserve of magic I hold within me, I feed a few drops of fire into each strand I hold, heating the stone and urging the resulting liquid heat upwards.

The tentacle beneath my hand lifts, twisting toward me. I stumble away, lose my footing, but none of that matters, for the creature is there, above me. *Flow*, I shout, pushing the fire-hot flow of the creature's magic up through the tentacles, toward its body—straight to the snarl.

Get back, Val orders.

I scoot back, using my legs without looking, unable to see out of my own eyes now, my mage sight consumed with urging the flow of magic toward the kraken's center. With a satisfying *crack* the magic leaves behind the tentacle beside me, rendering it inert stone. I could end this creature here and now, I realize. Keep it from killing again if I do this right.

Reaching up, I draw on the magic coursing through the beast, the fiery flow dissolving the threads connecting each and every tentacle, drawing their magic in. My eyes catch a glimpse of an arrow of gold arcing down, disappearing from sight behind me. Something sinks into my shoulders, a grip hard and ungiving, but it is not my death and I cannot pay it any mind.

The kraken is shrieking now. It cannot flee, its tentacles hardening to stone as the magic flows out of them. But the beast cannot hold all of its magic in its center, so I must do the only thing I can, the one thing I truly did plan.

Down, I command, channeling the magic in a tightening spiral until it slams straight through the knot, bursting through the bulbous body in a blue-white blast of pure power.

Down. Down to the talisman waiting in the road beneath the creature—only the magic slams down around the talisman as well, cutting through the earth and piercing the draining spells.

No. I refuse to be hit by another backlash of magic. I *refuse.*

I clench my hands, focusing the flow of magic, my mage sight catching the brightening spot of the talisman itself. I tilt my head, as if that would help the magic itself flow, and then I have it right, the spell-creature emptying directly into the sapphire talisman waiting below, funneling its magic down to be swallowed by the waiting gem. I hold the flow of magic, my markings slightly itchy, my back pressed against rough stone, my eyes blind but to the bright glow of magic, until the last of the magic trickles down into the talisman.

There.

I let my mage sight go. The afternoon sunlight is dim and shadowed by comparison. The spell-creature hovers before me, stone still and terrifying, its beak still open and its tentacles spread across the cobbled road, hooked over the walls of the buildings on either side, two frozen in midair just above me and another turned to stone just past my feet.

If I needed a reminder not to get on your bad side, that would be it, Val says.

I choke on a laugh, the sound dry and rasping. Squeezing my

eyes shut, I take stock of my body. I'm sitting on the ground, my back against a stone tentacle. All limbs still there. No new injuries other than a host of new bruises and a soreness about my shoulders. My shoulders.

I twist to find the phoenix beside me, watching me steadily.

"You pulled me back?" I ask.

"It seemed the least I could do." He turns to inspect the building, the tentacles reaching over the wall. "Let me see if anything from your pack survived."

I nod, turn my attention back to the stone creature.

Hitomi? Can you stand? Val asks.

I frown and decide to try. In one tottering attempt, I make it to my feet. *Yeah,* I say proudly.

It seems like I should be proud of the dead thing before me, that I should feel a thrill of excitement, but all I feel as I look at the kraken is a vague sense of relief. It's been undone, and now I can go on.

Could you see it all? I ask Val. I lean against the tentacle before me, peer over it toward the monster itself and, more specifically, the space directly beneath the creature, which is thankfully empty of tentacles.

I couldn't see everything you were doing, Val says. *Not the way I think you could. I did see the blast of pure magic coming out of that beast.*

So, he can't sense everything with my mage sight, even when I'm using it.

I consider trying to clamber over the tentacles before me, but they're huge. Their metallic sheen and snake-skin texture are already roughening to the dull gray of crumbling stone, which will make for difficult footing.

"Are you looking for something?" the phoenix asks as he swoops back down to me. He drops my charm pouch and the remains of my pack beside me. My stomach gives a lurch. My pack is torn to pieces, which isn't a surprise. Except that I hadn't considered what that meant.

"Yes," I tell the phoenix, forcing myself to focus. "The talisman. It should be somewhere toward the center of the crossroad, beneath those tentacles. I blasted through anything in the way, so you should be able to reach it."

"I'll find it."

I return my attention to the shredded remains of my pack. It contains my small water flask, my spare tunic with a hole gouged through it, and nothing else. The charm pouch is ripped open on one side and contains only a seeker and a firestarter. That is all.

My fingers tighten on the pouch convulsively. They're not shaking, of course they aren't, nor are my eyes blurring. That wouldn't make any sense. I'm alive, isn't that what matters? Only it isn't—not really, or at least, it's not all that matters.

Hitomi? Val sounds even more nervous now.

I take a shaky breath, try to calm myself. *Yes.*

Are you all right?

Just lovely. Much better than that oversized stone squid.

Then why...?

Val trails off as I stand up and move to the window. *Gotta check for something else,* I say, and heave myself into the wreckage of the room. Two massive tentacles still fill the space. I walk around one, scramble over the next where it coils around the earth.

The bright, woven edge of the blanket Huda gave me peeks out from beneath the other side of the coil. Beside it is a scattering of shredded leather from my pack. I take a step forward, my eyes flickering over the mess of strewn beads from my string of wards, the crushed charms, the pouches of herbs emptied of their contents.

"Oh," I breathe, and go down on my knees to work at a bit of wood trapped beneath the stone. My fingers catch on it, and it comes away in a splintered memory of the statuette it used to be. I stare at it, aware my eyes are tearing, the taste of healing herbs bitter on my tongue. "Oh, no."

Hitomi, Val says again, and now he sounds worried, so worried, though I don't know why.

I twist and begin gathering up the blue beads of the ward,

lapis lazuli from a necklace that once belonged to Stormwind. It's hard to see them, for my vision keeps blurring.

Hitomi, they are only things. It will be all right.

Shut up, I think fiercely, stuffing the broken crow into my pocket so I can reach for more beads. *They aren't* things. *They're... they're* memories.

You already have these memories, Val says gently.

Those kind don't stay, I nearly shout in my mind. *Not for me. I just—these were things I could hold, okay? It doesn't matter anyway. They're gone just the same.*

A sob breaks from my lips, a great ugly wheezing sob that I don't have time for, because I need to keep moving. There will be more spell-creatures coming. That blast of magic will have called to every cursed resident of this dead land.

I inhale the next sob, choke on the knot it makes in my throat, my chest. There's nothing left here. No sign of the look-away ring that Stormwind left with me, or the silver cuff glamor I wore on our escape from Fidanya, or of anything else.

I don't care. None of it matters, none of it lasts.

Turning, I scramble back over the stone tentacle, making my way to the window. Each breath is a battle against whatever it is that wants to swallow me, to pull me down and keep me here.

Hitomi.

Not. Now. I grip the windowsill with both hands, then clamber through, grateful I can still get through it, that it wasn't blocked as the doorway now is, that I didn't have to find a way to scramble over the half-fallen walls where the tentacles smashed them down. That my body still answers my demands.

"I have it," the phoenix says, winging out from beneath the shadow of the stone kraken, the talisman hanging by its chain from his neck.

I nod, swipe at my face with my sleeve. "We should go," I say, my voice choked.

The phoenix watches as I pocket the two charms he managed to save and carefully wrap the remains of my tunic around the water flask, making a compact bundle to carry. I look up at him when I'm done, my breathing much steadier. My cheeks are probably still smudged with tears, but they'll dry soon enough.

He seems about to ask a question, then exhales heavily and says instead, "I'll fly overhead. Keep the fastest pace you can maintain. With the talisman's aid, I may be able to fly you out, but it is better to escape before the need arises."

"Right," I say, and turn my back on the town.

"You did very well," the phoenix says from behind me.

I nod and start walking.

CHAPTER 15
THE COMPANY OF FRIENDS

Someone has pitched a low, simple tent a short distance beyond the Barrier. Two camels stand disconsolately in the barren valley beyond, the late afternoon sun stretching their shadows far across the sand. If I had any breath left, I would call a question to the phoenix. Really, though, it's all I can do to trudge the final stretch to the Barrier. I'm drenched in sweat, my legs weak beneath me. At least we have not met with any more spell-creatures since we left the great stone kraken behind.

Can you tell who it is? Val asks.

Dunno. I squint as I step through, the draining spells pinching at me before the Barrier cuts them off. The air on the other side is dry and hot and wonderfully alive with magic. I take great heaving breaths, so very proud that, now that my legs are no longer moving, they are still holding me up. I hadn't realized, either, how parched I'd been for a breath of living air. It's as if my blood can suddenly flow more smoothly, my heart beat more easily.

Friend or foe? Val tries again as two figures duck out from the tent.

Friend, I say, since the phoenix has swooped down to land beside them. One wears a long, plain men's thobe, the other in an embroidered thobe featuring, I'm quite certain, the particular patterns favored by the women of the Bani Saqr. The only two

155

people of that tribe who would come to meet us here are Huda and her brother.

I blink again as Huda raises her hand to wave at me, and a grin breaks across my face as I wave back—and I then realize exactly what this means.

I thought I was too tired for any more emotion, but clearly, I did not consider the potential for rage to sweep through me. The phoenix brought her here—ordered her here, more like, as if she were doing herself a great honor. I don't want Huda and her family here where they might get caught up again in the trouble dogging my heels. I twist, casting an eye up at the skies behind me, but there's no sign of Ravenflight. Which means precisely nothing, now that I've stepped through the Barrier.

How could the phoenix *do* this? I'm shaking, and if I'm not careful I will stalk over there and lambast that little Foofoo into next week for not consulting me on this.

Val, I say, *I think I'm going to sit down now.*

That might be wise, Val says, sounding as worried as he has been the last hour within the Burnt Lands. Which is just irritating.

I'm not dying, you know, I snap as I attempt to bend my knees. That doesn't quite work out the way I planned, and I end up half-sprawled in the dirt, my hands out to catch me. I take a moment, then carefully rearrange my limbs so that I'm properly sitting. It's only as I brush the grit off my palms that I realize Val hasn't answered. *I'm angry right now, all right? Really, really angry.*

"Mageling," the phoenix says, approaching me. It's the first time since I told him my name that he hasn't used it—probably to preserve its secrecy. Huda and Kareem remain behind, perhaps at his request.

"Phoenix," I return in Tradespeak, just in case my voice carries farther than I intend. "Would it have been too much to ask that you not demand anything further of the Bani Saqr?"

"It is their honor—"

"*Their* honor? What about yours? What about mine, what

little I have left? I don't want them killed, and I don't want to lie to them, and *you need to leave them alone.*"

"You," the phoenix pronounces, "are tired."

"You are about to lose the one person you don't want to lose." I push myself to my feet, even though I sat down to control my anger. I'm too angry—I know I am, know I should stop talking, know this isn't *that* bad. But I can't stop myself. "Of course I'm tired, you flea-bitten bird-brain! That doesn't affect my reasoning to the extent that I want to abuse the rights of others. Send them away."

"Now that they are here, sending them away would greatly dishonor them."

He's right. Of course he's right, and it enrages me all the more. "Then you'll find an excuse to send them away in the next day. I'm *not* traveling with them. I'm *not* risking their lives again. I sure as *hell* am not letting you decide to do so for me."

"Mageling—" the phoenix begins.

"Stop calling me that."

"Would you have me use your name now?"

Hitomi, this anger isn't like you, Val interrupts, making me want to scream.

"I would prefer if you didn't talk to me at all," I bite out. "At least until you learn to leave my friends alone."

The phoenix ducks his head, but then comes right back at me. "If they are your friends, then they would not want you to be alone."

I let out my breath in a growl of frustration and raise my eyes to the heavens. "I really, really want to kick you right now."

Not the wisest thing you could have said, Val observes. *Though accurate.*

I close my eyes, press my lips together so that he doesn't surprise a smile from me. *Shut up. I'm not trying to be* wise. *I'm trying not to kick him.*

I noticed. You never really seemed the sort to go around kicking people, though. That seems more like the evil arch mage sort of thing to do.

I let my breath out in something between a sob and laugh. *You're not helping, Val. You're really, really not helping.*

Aren't I? I'm just trying to break you out of your anger. It really isn't you.

Then what is it? I demand. He's right, but I'm not sure why my anger is so outsized, why I couldn't stop myself.

I suspect it's the hurt you're carrying, Val says. *Maybe rest and then you can talk with the phoenix again about your friends being here. He's right that you shouldn't send them away this moment.*

"All right," I say, opening my eyes to meet the phoenix's gaze. He blinks at me uncertainly. "I'm resting, and then we'll talk about this again. No giving them orders about what to do in the meantime, though."

The phoenix hesitates. He actually hesitates, which makes me want to kick him again. My foot twitches in response.

In my head, Val clears his throat, which ought to be physically impossible.

While I'm hung up on that, the phoenix finally dips his head in acquiescence. "As you say."

I let out a slow breath, trying to release my anger, and raise my gaze to Huda and Kareem. They watch me carefully, their faces perfectly neutral.

"Peace be upon you," I say in the desert tongue, taking a step toward them, only my knee gives out and I end up sprawled full-length in the dirt. I lie there, my cheek pressed into the sand, staring at the far side of the valley and wishing I could start this season over again. Wishing that the sky overhead was that same sky I looked at some two months ago, over the lake in Stormwind's valley. Wishing that I was anywhere but here, sprawled like a fool on the ground in front of my friends, having just had a shouting match with a mythical bird.

Val? Any chance you can just make me disappear right now?

Not a mage, he answers. *If you have the energy to sit up, it might work out better.*

Maybe I could just go to sleep instead.

The phoenix pokes his head into my field of vision, his head tilted in a particularly anxious way.

Pretty sure they know you're awake.

You're really not much help at all.

"I'm fine," I tell the phoenix. "My legs aren't working. That's all." I push myself upright to find Huda kneeling beside me and Kareem hovering a step behind her.

"Let me help you to the tent," Huda says, her brow furrowed with concern. "Your argument with the phoenix can wait."

"Already had it," I tell her, accepting her proffered hand. "Thank you for coming."

"Of course," she says, helping me up. "Did you think I wouldn't want to see you again?"

I bite my lip, recalling Huda's words from earlier. I suppose I *am* always trying to protect my friends from trouble, making decisions for them instead of with them. "Would you have chosen to come, even if the phoenix had not asked it of you?"

"Am I not your friend?" she returns as she helps me shuffle to the tent. "I asked him to tell me when you would be leaving his haven, and if I could travel to meet you or not."

The phoenix casts me a pointed glance, which I pointedly ignore.

"I've been grateful for the updates he's brought me," she adds.

"Updates?" I echo, throwing another glare at the phoenix. How unfair that he's been telling Huda about me, but not bringing her news to me!

"Just twice," he mumbles. "Once to ask your friend to meet you here."

"And the time before to collect supplies for your women's flow," Huda says, grinning while the phoenix attempts to look unruffled and succeeds only slightly.

"I *wondered* who he went to! I would have liked to hear your news then." I'm pretty sure I've mangled the verb tense in the sentence, but Huda pays no mind to my poor grammar.

"I'll tell you myself, but not before you rest."

I can't argue with that. The tent is comfortably set up with a rug and a trio of cushions. I settle on the rug, pull up a cushion for my head, and ask only if Sumeyya is well before I let myself sink into the flow of magic around me.

After the Burnt Lands, the desert feels as if it were bursting with magic. The earth beneath me thrums with life, the breeze whispering in the tent flap laden with it. I slip my palm beneath the edge of the rug and press it against the sand. The magic of stone and earth presses back at me, the residual warmth of sunlight curling against my skin. It flows gently up my arm, past the tingling of my markings to fill my chest, and then spreads through the rest of me, slow and strong and true.

I let go of consciousness only after the rightness of the world has sunk back into my bones.

WHEN I WAKE a few hours later, the tent is dark. A glance through the open entryway shows a faint lightness to the horizon, telling me it isn't yet full night. I stretch out my arms and legs as I lie on my back, then sit up slowly, inordinately proud of myself. I'm a bit sore and achy, but remarkably well. And I didn't have to give my body over to Val to survive.

Not only is that a vast improvement in my survival skills, but I don't have to recover from a shared-body experience now, either. On the flip side, though, I made it through the Barrier with just enough energy to fall over. Repeatedly.

Well, I suppose one can't have it all.

I rub my face, then glance around. My torn spare tunic lies folded nearby, my small water bag refilled and resting beside it. My most precious belongings, though, were in my pockets. I check them now, fingering the splintered bit of the crow statuette Val made me, the few lapis ward beads left from Stormwind's necklace. Mixed among them are the two charms I managed to salvage: a seeker, that will help me find missing items or people, and a firestarter. I'm still wearing the gauntlets as well—I loosen the buckles and slide my hands out, laying the gauntlets carefully next to me. It's not a lot to call my own. Certainly not enough to get me through the desert.

I stretch my back, cracking my spine, and push myself to my feet. Outside, my companions sit around the glowing embers of a tiny fire, the sky already bright with stars overhead. Kareem sits quietly on the other side of Huda, and opposite them, to my left, sits the phoenix, his fire muted so that not even the faintest glow escapes his feathers.

"Qahwe?" Huda offers as I join them.

"Thank you." I gladly accept the miniature cup of cardamom-brewed green coffee. It will give me a good dose of energy, and I suspect we will want to start traveling as soon as the phoenix and I have completed our experiments.

Now that I am outside the Barrier, my obsidian ward should protect me against trackers. But there's still some chance Raven-flight will simply catch sight of our camp and wing her way down to investigate. Which means we need to move on quickly. But first, I need to make amends for my tantrum.

"It is good to wake in the company of friends," I say. "Thank you for coming."

The phoenix brightens, literally and figuratively. "Are you feeling recovered?"

"I am," I say stiffly, and take a sip from my cup. The qahwe is strong and bitter on my tongue, and I automatically reach for a date to add some sweetness.

And then, remembering my manners, I ask after my friends' family and confirm again that Sumeyya as well as the goats made it back to their family's camp safely. I listen between sips of qahwe that warm me from the inside out and bites of date that sweeten each sip. I could sit here forever with my companions, pretending nothing is wrong, the stars shining overhead, and a slender pot of qahwe to share among us.

As I set my cup down, Huda lifts something from the carpet

beside her. It is no more than two small rectangles of blanket fabric with an improvised shoulder strap, hastily sewn together. "I thought you might like a bag," she says, passing it to me.

I take it reverently. "You made this for me?"

Huda shrugs. "It is not very well made, but it will hold for now. I can make you something better given a little more time."

"Oh no, it's perfect," I say quickly, passing the strap over my head so that it lies cross-wise over my chest. I clutch it tightly, as if it were a new memory I can't be parted with, when I already know that nothing is forever. "Thank you."

The phoenix rises to his feet. "Shall we inspect the Barrier, then? The talisman you used earlier can still absorb a little more for us, for a final experiment."

I nod, glancing to where it hangs from his neck. I'd forgotten it beyond telling the phoenix to fetch it after I drained the kraken.

He turns and starts for the Barrier. Huda glances from him to where I still sit watching him, and shoos me after him. I push myself to my feet.

"Wait up, Foofoo," I call after him, and flash him a sharp smile when he blinks over his shoulder at me.

Together, we cross the sands to come to a halt before the pale glowing wall of the Barrier, the Burnt Lands stretching out before us, bleak and shadowed in the weak light of the crescent moon.

"You're upset that I asked your companions to return here to wait for you," the phoenix says as carefully as if he were navigating a thorn bush. Or five.

"I wasn't happy about it," I agree.

He cocks his head. "You trust them, do you not? Outside of the Burnt Lands, it's best if you have a desert guide, and a camel to carry you more quickly. These lands are only slightly more forgiving than what lies within the Barrier."

I rub my face and glance back toward the camp. "I understand the need, but why them? Why not ask that a warrior from their tribe come?"

"Because these two feel responsible for you. They care for you."

"Did you have to use that against them?" I ask. Even as I say the words, I know the phoenix was wise in bringing someone to meet me. And not just anyone, but friends I can trust, especially since I'm riding into a meeting with a mage who might betray me. It was wise and thoughtful, and my anger seems even more misplaced now.

Perhaps it was just the dam breaking—the emotions I didn't feel when I vanquished the kraken, joined with the broken grief at losing the last few things I treasure. I think of Val's assessment, that it's the hurt I'm carrying. Perhaps I'm as broken on the inside as the things I once loved are. Not that there's anything I can do about that now.

"You need to develop allies," the phoenix says earnestly. "Or you won't survive this."

I stare at him and then, despite myself, I start to laugh. The sound bubbles up, breaking from my lips, and I can't stop it, can barely speak around it.

"Oh," I manage. "Oh, you think—you think I'm," I shake my head, wipe a tear from my eyes. Another breath, and the laughter fades to a smile. "Phoenix," I say gently, my voice still warm. "I'm not going to survive this."

He goes still, frozen in the act of resettling his wings. Then his head cocks, one dark eye fixing on me. "You don't believe that."

"I don't *want* to believe it, but it's true all the same. And you know it, just as I do. Perhaps you're trying to trick yourself into believing I can survive this, but it's too much, isn't it? Fixing the whole of the Burnt Lands while evading the Council's rogue hunters...." I shrug. "Two impossibilities at the same time is a bit of a stretch. Either one has finished far more skilled mages than I."

"No," the phoenix says tightly.

I meet his gaze, perplexed. Surely, he understands these realities?

"Things happen in threes," he says finally. "You will survive. That will be the third impossibility, and you will achieve it."

I hold his words in my mind and in my heart, as if that might make them come true. But if there's one thing I've learned in my short life, it's that actions have consequences. The path I've chosen is littered with them. I am only going to be able to avoid them for so long.

"You're a good friend," I tell the phoenix. "I'm sorry I was so angry with you. Now, let's see what we can do here."

CHAPTER 16
TALISMAN

I step into the Barrier, the phoenix beside me. The draining spells press against the inner edges of the Barrier a hair's breadth away from us.

This is where I'll need to find my starting point, here where the spells press up against the Barrier—choosing a jagged line of filaments and bonds that travel down and away, into the Burnt Lands. From here, I can reach the draining spells, and yet still be protected by the Barrier within which I stand.

"Oh," I say, my stomach sinking. "I forgot."

"Forgot what?" the phoenix asks sharply.

"The draining spells pressed against the Barrier—they're always shifting and roiling. They're not as stable as the ones underfoot."

"Because they're trying to expand," the phoenix agrees, his gaze on the spells.

Now that I better understand the stone underlying these spells, I can see the crystalline layers shifting, cracking and reforming and reaching, whereas when I looked at it earlier, I thought of it as fabric. However I look at it, though, the spells are too dynamic here. "I think I'm going to have to use the spells underfoot again."

Casting my gaze down to my feet, I follow the mass of spells into the earth with my mage sight. Unfortunately, the more stable network of spells doesn't begin right here against the Barrier, but a little farther into the Burnt Lands. No more than a pace or so, but enough that it becomes tricky to reach it through the constantly shifting spells at my fingertips. I'll have to step through to reach the filaments I need, which might pose an issue in keeping safe from a backlash.

"Should have known it wasn't going to be easy," I grouse.

The phoenix barks a laugh. "It never is. We'll have to go in, won't we?"

I nod and pass through the maelstrom of draining spells to step into the lands beyond. The emptiness hits me like a blow to the face. I shake my head, the air searingly empty in my lungs. Taking a steadying breath, I drop to one knee to study the latticework here. It comes into focus easily, appearing no different than what underlies the land around the phoenix's haven.

"How big do you want to go?" I ask the phoenix.

"Enough to test our process without risking your safety."

"All right then." I look up, that comfortably sharp smile back on my lips. "I'm going to go have another cup of qahwe. You take that talisman back to the big spell-beast."

"So far?" the phoenix asks, casting his gaze over the darkling plain.

"It will pull the magic away from the Barrier," I point out. "And if it fails, the draining spells will protect the Barrier."

He huffs. "That was always the plan."

"Yep," I agree, and pop to my feet. "Let me know when it's ready."

"Don't get arrogant, mageling," the phoenix says, amusement warming his voice.

"I'm not," I assure him. "I'm getting qahwe."

Barely a half hour later, another cup of qahwe coursing

through my veins, I step back through the Barrier with the phoenix.

Opening up my mage sense, I place my hands on the dirt and watch as the latticework of draining spells comes into focus. When I raise my eyes, I can see the network spreading out until it fades into a haze.

"Gonna borrow a thread," I murmur. I reach out a hand to pluck a single strand of magic free from the sapphire talisman looped about the phoenix's neck. Then I press my fingers into the dirt, channeling it to the spells underfoot. I follow the connected lines of the filaments, skimming over them in as straight a path as I can go, seeking.

It takes me only a few minutes, for I know what direction I traveled to reach the Barrier, and it is not so hard a thing to go back again. I've gotten used to following the latticework of spells, and skim over them with ease. There, where I undid the spell-creature, the spells underfoot are thickened, melded together by the power that blasted through them before I managed to control the flow into the sapphire talisman. Somewhere just above them lies the new talisman.

I start by searching out the filaments and stronger bonds that I need. The phoenix would have placed the talisman above the line he thought best suited to our purpose. A careful study brings into focus two that might serve, one slightly larger and stronger than the other. I tease a hair of magic free from it and cast upwards, sweeping across the earth with it even as it begins to thin and slide back down to the draining spells—and then it catches on the talisman.

Perfect.

I retrace my way to where the phoenix waits beside my immobile body.

"Time to go," I say through stiff lips, and drop my consciousness back into the latticework. Drawing on the fire in my bones, I merge with the magic I'm still drawing from the talisman and press it into the filaments. The bonds heat, the filaments between them glowing with fire, and then they all begin to flow. I keep pouring more fire into it, channeling magic as I never have before, until it's coursing forward, pouring through the land and dragging the connected filaments with it. Whole sections dissolve and follow as the channel I've created courses through the earth. Fire and stone arc through the land, following the thread of fire I laid to the talisman.

I pull away as the reaction I've created spreads, the magic growing into a torrent. I race to reach my body, rousing to the sound of the phoenix shouting for me to *get back*.

I shove myself backwards, limbs akimbo, and stumble through the Barrier, the phoenix's foot smacking my knee. He lands beside me in a flurry of feathers and turns at once to look through the Barrier. I sit up, chest heaving, and stare at the Barrier.

It shines bright and steady, even with its thin patches. I can't tell anything from here of the lands beyond. I clamber to my feet and step within it again, straining with my mage sight. The draining spells along its height shift and settle into a slower storm, as if stabilizing after being stirred up.

Across the plains, there's a rift in the draining spells. A long, curving empty space, widening before thinning into a slim line that disappears into the distance.

"Phoenix," I whisper.

"Well *done*," he says, his voice thrumming. "Well done, indeed."

IN LARGE PART thanks to the qahwe, I manage to stay upright behind Huda on her camel until well past midnight. We break our journey to make camp in yet another shadowed valley. It is strange to realize I am already growing familiar with the broader patterns of making camp and journeying through the desert. There are still a thousand things I do not know, but I know enough to be able to help now, to recognize the steps of making camp: caring for the animals first, then setting up our camp, and finally eating and drinking as needed.

It is unexpectedly comforting to be a part of these things, for this is what home is to my friends, at least in part. They have their families and traditions, of course, but home is also wherever they make their camp, and for just this moment, I am a part of that. I can't help hoping we'll travel together at least a little more.

I help Huda care for her camel, then spread a pair of carpets for us to sleep on. We won't bother with the tent tonight, given how short we expect our rest to be. Huda and Kareem set out a light meal of dates, cheese, and, wonder of wonders, a dense, hearty barley bread. I haven't had bread in a week, at least. I try very hard not to dive for the loaf, waiting like a well-mannered guest until they are settled as well.

As we eat, I glance at the star-studded sky, but there's still no sign of the phoenix. He has gone to inspect our work and collect the talisman, and instructed us to start the journey to meet the mage of the Bani Essam. I thought he would rejoin us within a half hour at most, but there is yet no sign of him. I'm not sure if he's simply flown on to seek out the other desert mages, scattered as they are in the areas that surround the Burnt Lands, or if his delay is due to something else altogether.

It should be fine, regardless. We still have a fair way to travel to reach the well where Huda and I camped once before, located at the edge of the lands of the Bani Essam. That time, I exited the Burnt Lands through the ruined city, and it took about a day and a half of riding. This time, we're coming from the north, which actually puts us a little closer to the well. If we start riding again at dawn, we should reach our destination in time to take our rest there through the hottest part of the day.

The mage of the Bani Essam should also meet us there, or so we hope. I don't like traveling without the phoenix, nor do I like that my uncle has been delayed as well. He should have met us at the Barrier instead of still being so far away... though perhaps there was some trouble he needed to see to, an injury or illness among his people. He is a healer mage after all. No doubt the phoenix has flown around to check on him as well.

Huda passes me a bowl of figs and asks, as if she shared my own thoughts, "Why do we seek the mage of the Bani Essam? It seems you are able to do much of what the phoenix has asked."

I shrug. "We've come up with a method we can use, but to actually apply it, we will need as many mages as we can gather, all doing the same thing together." Which means they'll also need to be able to channel a bit of fire; a problem I have yet to discuss with the phoenix. Perhaps my uncle will have some ideas. I glance toward the hills that mask our destination. "Do you know much about him?"

"The mage?" Kareem queries.

I nod.

"He is trained as a healer, though he seems more than capable as a warrior-mage as well. He does not ride with the warriors of the Bani Essam against us, but he charms their weapons and strengthens their borders."

I grimace. He clearly makes a formidable enemy, even if they never see him on the battlefield.

Huda nods. "It is why we are often driven so far back from all but the smallest watering holes and least fertile of valleys."

I look down, fidgeting with the buckles of my right gauntlet. It's not my fault, so it's absurd that I should feel guilty. Even if he is, in all likelihood, my uncle. "What's his name?" I ask, focusing on unbuckling the gauntlet.

"Abbas ibn Shakir, called High Mage Abbas Miragecleft." She says the final word awkwardly, for it is in Tradespeak.

"Miragecleft," I repeat, trying to make sense of it. What kind of higher order spell could that be—did he cleave through reality with a mirage? Isn't that what a mirage does anyway?

"These mage names do not always make sense to us," Huda says, as if not a lot can be expected of mages.

Which, fair, but the naming conventions are meant to signal a higher order working, and this one seems unusually opaque. "Miragecleft," I repeat quietly, pulling my hand from my gauntlet as I turn over what sort of spell it might point to. There's a pressure line running along the inside of my arm, overlapping with the markings where they curl around to meet the phoenix with its wings outspread. I look up to find Huda eyeing me thoughtfully, and realize I've said the mage's name again. Kareem glances at her, taking care to avoid looking at me.

"It's an odd name for a mage," I explain. "More so than usual. Is he considered honorable?"

"As honorable as any mage," Huda replies. I cannot tell if this is a jaded sort of realism or meant to be comforting.

I don't find it reassuring in the least. I strip off my other gauntlet. "Does he have any children?"

"His eldest daughter has left to be trained at the Mekteb in Fidanya," Huda tells me.

I look up in surprise. She must have been there the same time I was—must have heard the slurs thrown at me for having desert blood when I was escorted through the grounds on my way to my trial. Did she hate me for it, or pity me? Not that it matters.

Huda goes on, "He also has two younger children, but we do not know yet if they carry the Promise of magic."

"I see."

"Let us rest," Huda suggests. "The phoenix should return soon with news for us."

And, with Ravenflight's location unknown, we'll need to move again soon.

I lie on my side on the blanket and fall asleep repeating my uncle's name to myself.

THE PHOENIX ARRIVES SOMETIME during our night's rest. When I open my eyes in the brightest part of dawn before the sun rises, I find him nestled on the blanket, his head tucked beneath his wing, the faintest of golden glows warming the air around him. Huda lies on her side, watching him pensively. She smiles at me when I turn over and catch her observing him, a quick flash of amusement, and sits up. Kareem sleeps on the second blanket a short distance away, allowing for the demands of propriety. He lies on his back, snoring toward the sky.

By the time Huda unpacks a light breakfast for us, the phoenix has roused, lifting his head to regard us sleepily. Kareem has rolled to his side with a muffled grumble, his snores subsiding to a faint rumble.

"Wake up, brother of mine," Huda calls, pelting him with a date pit. He yelps and sits up, offering her a dark look before rubbing the sleep from his eyes. He comes to join us, his head of curls smashed flat in the back. He throws a kufiyah over his head, no doubt to look somewhat more acceptable in company.

Once we are all seated in a circle on the blanket, our breakfast before us, the phoenix shares his news. "I have spoken again with the mage of the Bani Essam," he tells us. "He is farther away than I had hoped. He will meet you at the border of their lands, at the camp with the well just west of the Howling Caves."

"We know it," Huda assures him. "It is where Hikaru and I camped before we crossed into their lands last time."

"Good." Dipping his head, he uses one foot to catch the cord of the sapphire talisman, and slides his neck free of it. "Wear this," he tells me. "It will grant you my protection in his eyes."

I take the talisman from him, the sapphire dark as night yet lit with glints of magic like the pinpricks of stars. They are visible even now, when I'm not using my mage sight. I cradle the stone in my palm. It weighs no more than it did yesterday, and yet it feels heavy in my hand. "Is that wise? This has a good deal of power. If it should be taken from me...."

"It won't," the phoenix says. "Or the mage who takes it will answer to me."

Huda glances away, but not before I see the sly quirk of her lips. I suspect she rather enjoys the idea of the phoenix taking a mage to task. Especially when that mage is of an enemy tribe.

"Where are you going now?" I ask the phoenix, since he clearly doesn't intend to stay with us.

"To do this work, we will need a much greater talisman than that to hold it. As you said, perhaps even a few of them."

"You have an idea of where to look?"

"Not for a talisman, no. What we need are the stones themselves—stones with a structure strong enough that, once formed into a talisman, can hold the amount of magic we intend to pour into them."

"You don't think sapphires can do it."

"No. The sapphire talisman could not hold all of what you sent toward it; the spells beyond it were already self-healing their edges from the surplus of magic it could not hold. A new, unused sapphire would fare better, but not, I think, enough."

"A diamond, then?" I ask.

"Precisely," the phoenix says.

I shake my head. Large diamonds are not just rare but impossibly expensive. "How are you going to manage that?" I don't get the feeling he's usually a thief, but I can't think what else he can do.

The phoenix puffs his chest feathers out smugly. "I have a few debts to call in. I doubt it will be a problem."

"Of course," I say wryly. "There are always debts to call in, aren't there?"

The phoenix goes still.

"I'm glad of it," I add hurriedly. "I certainly don't have any spare gemstones to offer."

"No," he agrees, subdued.

"When will you return?" I ask the phoenix as he steps off the blanket.

"I cannot be sure, but I hope as soon as tomorrow. I wish the mage of the Bani Essam had already reached us, but it is perhaps better to meet him elsewhere to discuss your work. We will travel together to the Barrier via a different route once I return, so that we might teach him your methods. It is best to keep you moving in new directions and in unexpected company in order to stay clear of Ravenflight."

"And then?" I ask. "Once I've shown him, what do you plan after that?"

The phoenix hesitates. "Much depends on whether he can learn to do what you and I can. If he cannot, we'll have to form a new plan."

I nod—because if my uncle can't learn this, it will likely be because he is not marked by either fire or stone. There are precious few ways around that. After all, most mages won't agree to be exposed to an overwhelming wash of elemental magic so they can then help with a potentially suicidal mission.

"If he can," the phoenix continues, "I will call a meeting of the tribes as we've discussed, and bring the other mages together."

"When do you plan to do that?" I ask, wondering if the phoenix will release me of my debt then, once he has all the mages he could want—and if so, where I might run from here. Raven-flight will certainly follow the rumors to me; no doubt at least one desert mage will inform her of the phoenix's call. If I somehow survive this work, she'll be waiting for me. It's all impossible, any way I look at it. There's almost a relief in knowing that.

"It will take time," the phoenix says finally in answer to my question.

"Time," I echo with a wry helplessness. I look away from the phoenix to the distant ridge of hills, counting out all the ways I cannot escape my fate. "I suppose that's one thing I don't have."

"Time is something none of us ever has," the phoenix says quietly. "We get used to feeling as though it is something we control, but it is beyond us, our control an illusion. It will pass all of us by one day. Even me."

I cross my arms, holding myself in. "How much time to gather the desert mages, though? Surely you have some idea."

"A fortnight, I would guess. Perhaps less. I will begin gathering them once we've tested your methods with High Mage Miragecleft."

Huda and Kareem exchange a glance.

"You are sure of Hikaru's safety with him?" Huda presses.

The phoenix glances from her to me. "I do not think he will

betray you," he says. "If you suspect him, then take shelter in the Howling Caves."

Huda begins to speak, then cuts herself off. Kareem frowns, his gaze on his hands.

"If we can get that far," I agree, not at all heartened by this thought.

"If you can't, you have that new feather of mine. Burn it and I will come to you at speed."

I nod. He had made a point of replacing the last one I burned, and I now have a new feather plastered to the inside of my boot.

"Farewell," the phoenix says. He spreads his wings as he starts forward, and then he is airborne, soaring away over the hills.

"I may not be a great judge of such things," Kareem says, shifting to pick up one last date, "but it is a little worrying that our plan, should we meet with betrayal, is to run to the one place that no traveler has ever survived entering."

Huda coughs on a laugh. "Let us hope it doesn't come to that."

"No traveler?" I repeat, glancing between them. "You mean no one, *ever*?"

"There is a reason the Caves have such a reputation in the desert," Huda says. "But the Bani Essam have honor, and you are the phoenix's guest. It should not come to that. Come, let us pack up. We should reach the camp by afternoon if we set off now."

Between the three of us, we pack up the food and blankets in a matter of minutes. Kareem steps away to saddle up his camel while I hover by Huda as she finishes packing her saddlebags.

"You will need a name," Huda says to me, sliding her blanket into the saddlebags. "Mage Miragecleft will expect one."

I set down the final blanket roll beside her. "I cannot give my birth name. There is a power in names, and I cannot afford for those who hunt me to learn mine."

Huda regards me thoughtfully. "I see."

"You named me Hikaru bint Al-Ghaib to your brother. Can I not use that?"

"We will have to call you Hikaru if any of the men we met

before from among the Bani Essam are there. But if they are not, I assume you would not want Miragecleft to realize that was you. Would you?"

I shake my head. At some point, I will have no idea who I am, from one name to the next. I remember my things lying strewn across the stone floor like so much detritus after the kraken attacked—the scattered beads and shredded leather and splintered crow. I wonder if I am becoming as fragmented as those memories I used to hold, shedding bits and pieces of myself with every name I cannot keep.

Huda is still waiting for my reply, so I ask, as if we were making a trade, "If I change my name, will you eat their food?"

"We meet on the phoenix's business, even as our tribes have begun to discuss peace. It's... a different place from where we were when you and I first traveled through the lands of the Bani Essam. If they offer us food, it's a promise of peace now more than ever, and I will accept it."

I nod, relieved, as Huda straps the final blanket onto the back of the saddle.

"If I need another name," I say finally, "it had better be the name I gave the High Council. High Mage Miragecleft already knows that was me; if I use that name, he'll think I'm being honest. Perhaps he'll be willing to trust the phoenix and wait until I've done my work before calling in the Council."

"But it is not your true name either," Huda says, amusement creeping back into her voice. "How many names do you even have?"

"Too many," I admit. "And apparently also not enough."

"There is still a risk in using it. You know that?"

"I know."

She studies me a long moment. "What is the name they are looking for you with, then?"

"Kiki Hibachi."

Her brow furrows. "What does it mean?"

"I, um, it is from my mother's people," I stumble. I *could* admit the meaning Val shared with me. But considering hibachi means firebowl, that means I'm—what? A happy little firebowl? For all his seriousness on the subject, Val probably laughs up his sleeve thinking about it. I still can't believe that was the best he could come up with at the time.

She grunts. "It will do, though it would be better to claim a desert name. Once this is all done, what will you do?"

I glance toward her, surprised.

She regards me steadily, this friend who has stood by me even when her family was at risk, and offered me only kindness and trust, again and again. She believes I will survive, and I love her for it.

I smile even though my heart hurts. "I'll do what I always do: run."

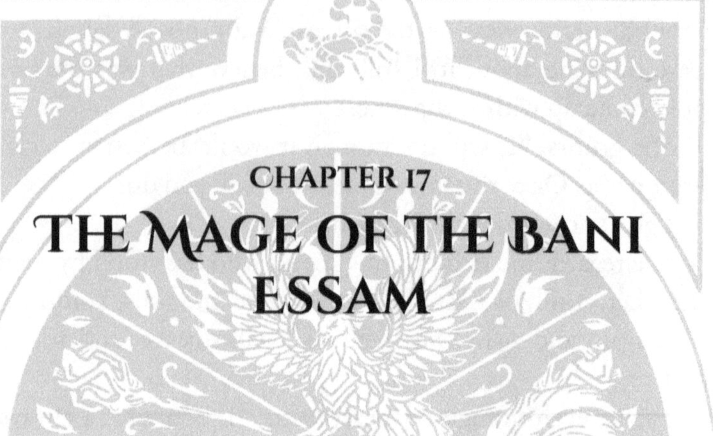

CHAPTER 17

THE MAGE OF THE BANI ESSAM

We reach our destination late that afternoon. The camp is precisely as I recall: the well with its round stone cover, a square of smaller stones carefully laid out to house a fire, and not much else to remark upon but for the faint, eerie keening of the Howling Caves.

Together, we fetch water from the well, heaving off the stone cover and drawing up the water with the leather bucket for the camels, just as I did with Huda a month or so past. Only this time, we put off setting up camp. Huda and I wait beside the well while Kareem walks up to the dip between two hills to check the valley beyond.

He pauses for a moment, silhouetted against the bright blue sky, then raises his hand in greeting to someone on the other side.

Huda sighs. "It seems they are here."

I swallow a laugh at her chagrin. "It was our hope."

She shrugs. "It gets complicated from here. You cannot blame me for wishing for a longer reprieve."

"No," I agree. I wish it too—a reprieve from everything hurtling forward, from Ravenflight finding her way to me.

"They've set up camp below," Kareem tells us as he reaches us. "I expect we should offer them water from the well."

Huda grimaces. "In the name of peace, yes. They cannot camp below very long without a water source."

The siblings look at each other and then Kareem shakes his head. "Let us meet them first. The camp is larger than I expected, and I—I would like to think well of this mage, but I do not like being surprised."

"You mean," Huda says darkly, "he does not need as many warriors as he has brought."

Kareem glances back toward the unseen valley. "I cannot tell if they are warriors—only their camels are visible. Most everyone must be resting. If it is mostly his family, that would also be strange, but not as concerning."

"He doesn't need warriors to fight us or take me captive," I point out. "He is a mage." A bigger group, though, is more visible—which means it's more likely to attract Ravenflight's attention.

"No," Kareem agrees, dropping his gaze to the sandy ground. "They have not taken possession of this well, though they could have. So perhaps there is no need to worry."

"At least nothing has gone wrong yet," Huda says philosophically.

Kareem nods and moves to the well. Together, we heave the stone cover back into place—water is too precious a resource to leave exposed for so long in the desert.

Any news? Val asks as I dust off my hands. He had promised to keep me company as I met my uncle, and apparently he hasn't forgotten.

We're about to meet my uncle, I tell him, warmed by his care. *I'm all right, though. Huda is here. You don't need to stay.*

I think I'd like to take his measure, if you don't mind, Val says.

You think he'll attack outright?

No, Val assures me. *But it would be helpful to have a sense of how safe you'll be in his company.*

Fair. I follow Huda to her camel, basking in this sudden unexpected warmth: to be surrounded by friends who are here *for me.* I never realized this was something I didn't have, or perhaps I've just never allowed myself to appreciate that I had it before. Kenta was there for me in Fidanya, and Val has been too. Stormwind came back around for me, just as I had come for her. Huda, even in the process of getting to know me before, still offered her support and kindness.

It makes me want to wrap Huda in a hug, which would probably only worry her at this point.

Kareem pauses on his way to his camel and says, "If we go down there, they may invite us to stay with them."

Huda and I exchange a look. I definitely don't want to sleep among those who might betray me... but I also don't want to mortally offend them for refusing their hospitality.

"We cannot refuse if they do," Huda says, confirming my worries. "The best we can counter such an offer with is to invite them to make camp here."

Kareem grimaces. "Let us hope the phoenix rejoins us soon."

That makes four of us, Val mutters, and I have to look away to hide my grin.

We mount our camels once more and ride over the ridge in time to see a small group exit the largest tent and start toward us. The campsite consists of three good-sized tents pitched around a central cooking fire. The welcoming party walks up to meet us as we descend the trail, High Mage Miragecleft at the front of the group.

My hands close on Huda's thobe, fisting as I stare at him. I know this man, know his tall, slim figure, recognize the elegant sway of his thobe with an open-fronted bisht over it, the front richly embroidered in subtle colors. But more than that, it is his face in my memories—the high cheekbones and sightly hooked nose and perfectly trimmed beard and mustache. His gaze meets mine, his brows rising slightly at the sight of me staring over Huda's shoulder. I tear my eyes away, ducking my head behind her form.

What is wrong with me? Surely, I'm not this foolish. I knew Miragecleft would be my uncle. To find that his features bear an uncanny resemblance to the few memories I still have of my father is no more than expected.

"*All right?*" Val asks, his voice gentle.

Fine, I say, steeling myself to act more normally. I look out once more, glancing past my uncle, allowing myself just long enough to observe that this man's face is a little wider, and his nose just slightly straighter than my father's. Beside him walks a woman in an embroidered thobe. She is equally as tall, her build as strong as the planes of her face, her expression gentle but firm. She smiles at me without an inkling of recognition, which eases my nerves significantly. Not that my uncle should recognize me either—we have never met, after all.

"Unfortunately," Huda says, "I believe that is Laith ibn Hamza behind Abbas Miragecleft. Both your names will likely be known."

She nods toward the trio of young men bringing up the rear, all of them wearing kufiyahs, their leather slippers kicking up dust. Laith, with his perpetually crooked kufiyeh and smiling eyes, is familiar to my sight in a much more comfortable way. I nod to him.

"Then I will go by Hikaru," I say just loudly enough for Kareem to hear. It will be easier to answer to that than any of my other alter-names, and easier for my friends to remember as well.

Tread carefully, Val tells me as we draw closer.

I know.

"Peace be upon you," Miragecleft calls, his voice easily crossing the distance remaining between us. His companions chorus the same greeting even as we return it.

We come to a stop with just a few paces between our parties. Kareem swings down from his camel while Huda orders ours to sit. I clamber off, aware that it doesn't make a difference if I'm mounted, and still wishing I was.

As we turn to face the welcoming party, my uncle dips his head. "We are honored to welcome you to our lands. My name is Abbas ibn Shakir, called Mage Miragecleft. We have been expecting you, the honored guests of the phoenix. Allow me to introduce my wife, Amina bint Hassan, as well as our young relations." He gestures to the boys behind them and rattles off a trio of names including Laith's. I glance over at them, and note the slight furrow in Laith's brow as he focuses on my thobe. But then he drops his gaze again, his expression clearing.

"We are honored to join you," I say awkwardly when my uncle looks back at me. "I am called Hikaru bint Al-Ghaib." It's only as the words leave my tongue that I realize how telling they are—Daughter of the Vanished is all very well and good, but it is *his* brother who vanished. I can only hope he doesn't think on it too carefully.

Don't panic now, Val says, which is just annoying. It's not like there's a kraken bearing down on us.

I'm not panicking, I tell Val. *I'm just regretting using that appellation.*

Miragecleft's gaze flickers, but he makes no other sign.

Would it be such a bad thing if your uncle recognized you? Val asks.

I don't know, I snap back, though it's not quite true. If he betrays me without actually knowing who I am, that will be a great deal easier to bear than if he knows who I am.

Mmm, Val returns.

My uncle shifts uncertainly. He's waiting for me to complete the introductions of our party. I clear my throat in embarrassment and quickly say, "These are my friends and companions, Huda bint Ahmer and her milk-brother, Kareem ibn Saleem, both of the Bani Saqr."

Miragecleft dips his head in welcome.

"Please, come and refresh yourselves," Amina says, gesturing toward the tents. "You have traveled far and should take your ease now."

Huda and Kareem murmur their thanks, and I quickly add my own. We walk to the camp together, our hosts leading the way down the rocky path.

You don't have to stay, I remind Val. *Unless you think I'm in deep waters.*

You're always in deep waters, Val returns, amused. *But no deeper than usual, I think.*

That is unexpectedly comforting to hear.

Call if you're worried, Val says. *I should be able to come as needed. Even if only to discuss any worries you might have.*

It is even more unexpected to realize what a comfort it is to have an adult at hand whose knowledge and experience I can call on.

I stay with Huda and Kareem as we care for their mounts. This tradition seems so known and expected that our hosts keep us company and, while they offer to take care of the camels, seem neither surprised nor insulted when their offers are politely refused. Perhaps it has to do with how a person's camel is their connection to survival in the desert. It is their honor to care for it before even themselves, and not to pass this task on to anyone else.

I remember with some chagrin how happily I'd passed my mare's reins on to Sumeyya and Kareem when I first arrived at their camp with Huda. I had meant to honor their kindness, but I hope I did not make myself look bad in the process. For all my apparent connections to the desert, I do not know these traditions at all.

Laith brings a bucket of water to offer the camels, but they've already drunk their fill. Kareem takes the opportunity to casually suggest that he might walk up to the well with Laith to refill any buckets they may need. Laith visibly brightens at this, and immediately plunges into a conversation on the bloodlines of Kareem's camel, if it has won any races, and whether Kareem has raised any calves himself.

I glance askance at Huda, wondering if this is male bonding talk. She watches the two of them with a slight line between her brows, which draws attention to the four small circles tattooed on her forehead in a diamond. I have grown so used to her tattoos— the diamond on her forehead, the sharp angled lines on her chin —that I barely notice them anymore. But now, as she watches Kareem and Laith with keen attention, they grant her a quietly fierce demeanor.

She gives herself a slight shake and slips her arms through mine. "Come, let us rejoin Amina bint Hassan."

Amina accompanies us to the cooking fire, inviting us to sit on a carpet spread before it. She pours a portion of green coffee beans into a wide pan for roasting, beginning the slow but wonderful process of brewing us fresh qahwe. There is also a pitcher of water, another of spiced milk, and a platter of food set out for us. Miragecleft glances once toward the camels—barely visible past the tents—and smiles, eyes crinkling. I know enough of desert culture to know that he won't serve us until Kareem has arrived, which he does a few minutes later, still deep in conversation with Laith.

Miragecleft fills our cups with spiced milk and enjoins us to eat. I smile and take a little of the food, as Huda likewise helps herself to a small serving of olives and white cheese.

Laith looks up from where he sits, straight at Huda, his eyes lighting. The last time we shared a camp, she refused to accept the food he offered, knowing it was only offered out of guest right, and did not actually promise peace. He grins in delight as she pops an olive in her mouth.

Huda notices him with a slight start and immediately looks away, discomfited. I glare at him on her behalf and he drops his gaze, his lips still quirked as he attempts to appear abashed. It was a breach of desert etiquette for him to be staring at a woman he had no relation to. Admittedly, if I weren't defending Huda, I would probably be laughing. I'm not sure Huda realizes she has an admirer from among her enemies.

Time to start a conversation about something unrelated, I decide.

Turning to Miragecleft, I say with profound awkwardness, "Honored mage, I believe you have spoken with the phoenix." I do not have the hang of formal address in the desert tongue *at all*.

"I have had that honor," Miragecleft agrees, his eyes crinkling again. "He speaks highly of you, and of the work you are doing."

My heart warms at that, even if I didn't really expect any less. After all, it's not like the phoenix would badmouth me to our hopeful allies. I lift up a bright red succulent date from the plate before me. "He has set me a task in the Burnt Lands. A task which we cannot complete alone."

"It is a great work to which you aspire," Miragecleft says, or at least I think he says. My grasp of the desert tongue is good enough to give me most of the sentence and I fill in the rest. The sentence might have actually ended with "you will die attempting" or "you were dumb enough to take on." All three being accurate, I nod.

Huda, at least, does not look affronted.

"I have promised the phoenix what aid I can provide," Miragecleft continues, dipping his head toward me. "First, though, let us enjoy this food, and share what news we have."

I swallow a curse, which reminds me that I *really* need better curse words. Perhaps I can start swearing by cursed creatures. At any rate, it seems I've forgotten my desert etiquette. We may not have mutual acquaintances to ask after (at least not that my uncle might realize), but we ought to be sharing news and building relations before getting down to business. Although, really, sharing news when his tribe just raided Huda's—and her father just returned from a semi-victorious counterraid—seems fraught at best.

I smile and nod, leaving the next conversational gambit to him, and pick up another red date. These dates are not dried as the rest are, but fresh and crunchy and juicy, with a white flesh that reminds me distantly of apples and a sweet-tart flavor I cannot quite place. They are *delectable*.

As I chew, my mind flicks to the great tentacled spell-creature, it's magic streaming down from its core. Kraken on a skewer? No, that's not right. Hmm. Kraken spit? Actually, that should work quite well.

Miragecleft clears his throat, drawing my attention back to him. He proceeds to prove his skill as a host by sharing news of the other tribe whose territory borders their lands to the south somewhere, their lands curling around the southern border of the Burnt Lands. Huda mentions what her people know of the Bani Hakam's doings—a tribe whose name it takes me a moment to place: that is High Mage Stonefall's people, and it is their embroidery that graces the thobe he gifted me and that I now wear. That no doubt explains Laith's curious look when he first saw me.

"We have had a little news from Fidanya," Amina says, stirring the beans as they roast. "You have heard, perhaps, that the Council of Mages has closed the portals across all the Kingdoms?"

Huda and Kareem nod while I help myself to a dried fig, as if I had no concern at all in this. I set aside the matter of better curses for the time being.

"It is unfortunate," Huda says mildly. "Surely, they won't stay closed forever? The Kingdoms cannot be happy with such a change."

"They are not," Miragecleft agrees heavily. "We will see how the Council navigates it, but for now, the portals remain closed to all but those mages approved by First Mage Blackflame."

Of course they do.

"Is there any other news?" Kareem asks.

I'm no longer hungry, but I make myself take another bite of the fig in my hand.

"Trouble in Karolene, but that is far from us."

It may be no more than Val was able to tell me, I remind myself, forcing myself not to engage.

"What trouble is that?" Huda asks, carefully not looking at me. I would hug her for that if I could.

"A rebellion on the streets, it seems. The Council has stepped in to quell it. It should not take long to return the peace."

Return the peace? The only peace Blackflame wants there is the silent, deadly power he held over those he'd subjugated. What is happening in Karolene? The soldiers and mercenaries held too tight a rein on the people—I cannot quite imagine a full-blown rebellion. With the portals closed, Blackflame could be doing anything.

I take a steadying breath, set down the tiny woody stem that is all that is left of the fig. Nothing I can do, I tell myself. Truly. Even if Kenta has gone back there, even if I have friends there whom I no longer remember, I'm in the desert now, with the only portal open to me deep in the Burnt Lands, and no portal open in Karolene regardless. The Shadow League is there. They'll be working to address Blackflame's actions.

Yet what little I recall tells me they likely don't have a mage on their side. Blackflame will have no compunction against using magic to destroy his opposition—not when no one is watching but the Council, which he holds in the palm of his hand anyhow. And then there's what Val told me—that Blackflame has called in "allies" from the Northland Council to support him there. What if this isn't a rebellion, but a people attempting to defend themselves from oppression?

"What of the other Kingdoms?" Huda asks. "Is there any news of note?"

I look up slowly and find Miragecleft watching me steadily. "Not that we have heard."

With a nicely timed clatter, his wife pours out the coffee beans from the roasting pan—still lightly green, perfect for making the green-beige qahwe the desert dwellers so love—and sets about grinding them. Kareem comments on the pleasant aroma, and the conversation turns to easier topics.

Once the coffee is ground and steeped with cardamom and served in tiny cups, Miragecleft finally turns to the business at hand. We spend the next hour and more discussing my study of the magic of the Burnt Lands, the stone-based magic and its latticelike structure, and the final working we achieved with the talisman's help. Where the desert tongue fails me, I switch to Tradespeak and back again—Miragecleft knows both, and I suspect Amina does as well. It is for my own friends that I do my best to keep to the desert tongue.

"The phoenix believes I'm more able to work with the draining spells because I've been marked with stone," I say as we discuss my methods in particular.

"You draw upon fire to encourage it to flow," Miragecleft says, his tone easy. Too easy.

I cannot discern what he truly thinks of me or my work. Still, the critical thing is his understanding, not his opinion—or rather, as much as I want his good opinion, I have little hope of gaining it. He knows I'm a rogue, after all, and treats me as a guest because of the phoenix only. If he's guessed I'm his dead brother's child, he's given no sign of it, despite how I've named myself. Perhaps that wasn't the giveaway I thought it was. I can't tell one way or the other. Best not to let that bother me.

"It's the fire that worries me," I admit. "The phoenix is able to work with the draining spells as I am with some effort, but fire comes naturally to him."

"You think that stone isn't as vital to your work, then."

I shake my head. "I think it might be harder to do the work without an affinity for stone, but not impossible. I don't know how to replace the ability to draw on fire to transform the stone."

Miragecleft grins and reaches a hand toward the banked coals of the coffee fire. At his gesture, a single, slim column of fire rises an armlength above the coals, liquid in its shape, twisting and furling. "We have fire. There is nothing simpler."

I watch him, entranced. Never mind that it didn't even occur to the phoenix or me that a mage might simply *build* a fire and channel what elemental magic they need from it. No, what enthralls me is the way his amusement transfigures his face, the crow's feet by his eyes, the laugh lines by his mouth, half-obscured by his mustache and beard. It is as if I've caught a living, breathing reflection of my father. Something inside of me stretches tight, balanced on the verge of shattering.

I look away, my shoulders hunching, and force myself to breathe.

"You are upset?" he asks, his voice cool.

I shake my head, one hand twisting in the fabric of my thobe. I make myself flatten my hand against my leg and say with as much truth and ease as I can, "No. That's brilliant. It makes everything so much easier."

He doesn't answer. When I finally look back at him, he's watching my hand, his expression inscrutable. My gauntlets hide most of my markings, but perhaps he knows exactly what he's looking for. I hold perfectly still, as if that might keep me safe.

Huda exchanges an uncertain glance with Kareem. Their

movement breaks my uncle from his thoughts. He shifts, takes a sip of qahwe.

Then he lowers the cup, one finger tapping the rim, and says, "For a talisman, or a set of them, to contain the magic of the entire Burnt Lands..." He shakes his head. "That would form a powerful artifact indeed, if it could be done. Who would keep them then? Or do you plan to hand them over to the Council?"

There is no way I would put such a talisman, or set of talismans, in the keeping of a body that elected Blackflame to preside over them. Especially not when that would put the talismans directly in his hands.

I shake my head, smile blandly. "It is for the phoenix to decide. I am only his helper."

"Only?" Miragecleft eyes me with faint amusement. "Indeed."

I look away. I can't seem to get used to seeing my father in him: that humor, the sharp intellect, the gentle but firm manner. I wish that I knew this man, that I could claim this relation and have his care, however unlikely that is. I may have desert blood, but I only know a handful of the customs that surround me—a foreigner in a home that can't be mine.

Stiffly, I tell my uncle, "I believe the phoenix intends to see magic returned to the Burnt Lands. I expect he will use the talismans to that end."

Miragecleft clasps his hands together, interlacing his fingers. "For such a large working, it seems the Council should at least be informed."

That would go over *wonderfully* for me. Though I suppose he is right.

"That is for the phoenix to decide," I repeat, figuring the phoenix will be much more successful in arguing this point than I will. Miragecleft may be older and wiser than I am, and claim more authority on any number of things, but the phoenix has him beat.

"The Council seems to be rather busy with other matters just now," Huda observes. "No doubt the phoenix will involve them once he has perfected the method he hopes to use. It is perhaps still a little early to bring them in. After all, if what bint Al-Ghaib has done cannot be easily replicated, then there will be nothing for them to see."

Miragecleft nods thoughtfully. "As you say."

"Excellent!" Amina says, clapping her hands together. "Now all that is settled, shall we not allow our guests a little rest before dinner?"

Huda's smile flashes past so fast I nearly miss it. "We thank you! We can make our camp at the well—"

"I would not hear of it," Miragecleft interrupts. "You are the guest of the phoenix, bint Ahmer, and our tents are ready to welcome you. Where the phoenix's work is being done, surely, we can join together."

Huda dips her head, her expression schooled into amiability. To refuse would reinforce the enmity between their tribes, especially as peace has yet to be formally established.

"We thank you," she says. "Indeed, let us hope that the phoenix may unite all of the tribes in peace."

CHAPTER 18
LULLABY

Our hosts prepare a feast for us that evening. We exit the tent where we've been made comfortable only to find the whole of the camp gathered together—there are well over twenty people here. A goat roasts over the fire, built up now, and the camp is in the final flourishes of preparing the meal. Kareem leads Laith and two other young men up to the well, camels in tow, and they bring back water for everyone.

The men gather separately from the women, but Kareem seems comfortable enough, and I have the distinct feeling Laith has attached himself to his guest to ward off anyone who might be looking for trouble. Huda and I join Amina in one of the larger tents along with the other women of the camp—an elderly woman, two middle-aged women, and a gaggle of children.

A great platter is set at the center of our group, filled with seasoned roast goat resting on a bed of fragrant yellow rice. We gather in a circle around it, each person taking from that portion of the platter directly in front of them. Huda seems to gather herself beside me, and then quietly partakes of what she is given. Amina deftly passes a particular delicacy across the platter to us— I cannot tell if it is a bit of organ, or some other choice cut. "Please eat, my daughters," she chides us, drawing a smile from Huda.

The goat is *delicious*, no doubt made all the more so by the fact that I have not had fresh meat since I left Fidanya. I can't recall if I was served any while being held prisoner by the High Council. The last I remember was the mouth-wateringly-good kebab roll Kenta bought for me as we walked the streets of Fidanya.

This dish is utterly different, but the companionship it comes with is equally precious. Huda remains beside me and these other women, these children—they are Miragecleft's relations, his cousins and kin. Which means they are also mine. It's a thought that staggers me with the beauty of it—and the loss. I thought I was alone, and yet here are relations of mine that I dare not claim —relations who might give me up as easily as my mother did. I don't know, and I don't dare find out.

Do I have other family that I have yet to meet? I had only really thought of my direct blood kin—my mother, and her now deceased parents; my father and his parents who disowned him; his brother who did the same. That my father's family is actually larger than four people, that each person around me is in some way my relation, seems unfathomable. I find myself listening to their voices, studying their mannerisms—the way that child tosses her head when she laughs, the way her mother smooths down her mop of curly hair. It's as if I'm striving to commit this family to memory, as if I might make them mine in my heart, even if I cannot do so in reality. It's a yearning that leaves me achingly hollow.

Once the platters are emptied and carried away, the women settle to telling stories, folk tales they all know by heart, but which I do not know at all, pieces of my heritage that I have perhaps never held. Huda listens avidly as well, and I wonder how many are familiar to her, and how many are particular to my family.

As the faint keening of the Howling Caves rises above the hills, carried by the wind, the stories take a darker turn. I sit quietly beside Huda and let this evening wash over me, the warm companionship of the women, the delight they take in the antics of the children, the stories that have been passed down, generation upon generation, like memories that will never be lost. I may only have this one night, a stranger in my uncle's home, which makes it that much more precious to me.

Eventually, I rouse myself and slip away to answer the call of nature. On my way back to the tent, I pass by a smaller tent I have yet to enter—and find my feet slowing to a stop. A woman's voice sings a lullaby within. In the past I cannot remember, I'm sure I've heard more than a few lullabies, but this one is different. It is familiar at a level that takes my breath away, my ribs throbbing with the force of it.

O CHILD OF MY SORROWS, O breath of my life,
  My brother has vanished across the sands
  His journey marked by the warbler's flight

SWEET MY CHILD, hold close my hands
  Let us ride together through the silvered night
  Until the guiding stars connect our hearts

I DON'T KNOW IT—EACH line is new to me—and yet it's as deeply familiar as the sound of my own name. I hold perfectly still, listening. On the other side of the fabric wall, a baby whimpers and then the woman's voice begins the lullaby again. I commit the sound of it to memory, the words and the haunting lilt of her voice along with the soft touch of the desert breeze, the starlit valley around us. I grasp all of it tight, as if I might create a new memory that can withstand what I might yet do with my life, to replace the old ones I have lost. There is nothing for me to hold here but this moment, and so I hold on to it with all my will.

"Hikaru?"

I turn to find Amina a few steps away, regarding me curiously.

"Sorry," I murmur, starting forward again. She falls into step with me. "I heard someone singing, and the song is one I thought I knew, from many years ago."

As soon as I say it, I regret it. What if this song is particular to the Bani Essam?

Amina tilts her head, watching me. "Songs have a way of staying with us."

I shrug. "I could be wrong. I'm sure many lullabies sound similar."

Amina gestures me into the tent where the women are gathered, and I'm glad to let the topic drop. I settle once more beside Huda, turning my face to a middle-aged woman telling a story of a ghoul who devours a child whole, and the child's poor father who kills the ghoul and cuts his lifeless daughter from its stomach. The storyteller describes his grief, and how he wraps the child in a blanket and returns to his wife, telling her that he has brought home a gazelle that can only be prepared in a pot that has never been used to cook a meal of mourning.

As I shift, my attention wandering, it finally occurs to me to wonder why Amina came looking for me. I had not been gone that long, nor is there anywhere else to go out here in the desert, the camp a beacon in the darkness. The simplest explanation is that she is keeping a watch on me. As Laith must be keeping a watch on Kareem.

If it were just Huda and Kareem receiving such attention, it might be due to the concern of a host aware that enmities may still be simmering beneath the surface. But I have no enmities here. There is only one reason why my uncle might put me under watch: so I do not leave without his knowledge.

I swallow hard. If he is watching for me to escape, then chances are he means to hold me for his own ends. He is, after all, a mage sworn to the High Council. I already know how justly the Council treats a mage charged with violating their oaths: Stormwind was innocent and still condemned to life imprisonment. If my uncle violates his oaths to shield me from the Council, they will hardly be more lenient.

I should have thought this through more clearly when the

phoenix first argued it, should have considered exactly what he meant to demand of his allies. I don't want to believe that my uncle will betray me—but he has no reason to keep my safety in trust beyond his respect for the phoenix, and every reason not to. It isn't a betrayal, it's wisdom.

Somehow, it still feels as if a blade has slid into my heart.

Around me, the circle sighs as the mother of the story reports that no one of their camp has a pot that has not been used to make a meal of mourning, and the father, revealing the dead child, tells her, "There is no family that has not tasted loss, and so must we. Here is our gazelle."

I look down and pretend the tears that blur my eyes are for the parents of the story, but they are for me: for my uncle who likely intends to betray me before the phoenix ever returns; and for my mother who looked me in the eye and told me she knew nothing of my family, disowning me in a single breath; and for my father, whom I remember with as little detail as I did the lullaby I heard but a few minutes ago. My father, who looks in my memories as his younger brother does now.

Beside me, Huda shifts, her shoulder coming to rest against mine. She is carefully not looking at me. In that care, I see her friendship, and know that regardless of what I have lost, I am still surrounded by love. Perhaps it is not from those with whom I share blood, but it is still strong.

I lean into her in return, and listen to the storyteller's next tale as I begin to plan our escape from my uncle's camp.

CHAPTER 19

THE BONDS OF BLOOD

I lie on my side in the dark of the tent, listening to the sounds of my relatives drifting off to sleep. Someone shifts to my right, and another sleeper lets out a soft snort across the tent. I suspect this is not how they usually sleep, but for tonight most of the women have gathered in this tent while their menfolk sleep separately, which means Kareem is not with us. Huda slipped out earlier, tailed by another young woman, but even so I think she must have been able to warn Kareem of our planned departure. At least, Huda returned looking as calm as ever, and lay down to sleep directly after.

I count my breaths, listening as the camp falls into silence. My uncle's wife has yet to return, though she prepared a goat-hair sleeping mat and blanket for herself before going out. I can't risk leaving until she's settled in to sleep or the alarm might be raised before we ever leave this valley. So, I wait.

The tent flap opens and falls shut around a figure. I watch as the woman—Amina—makes her way past the other sleepers, wending her way toward Huda and me. Her own sleeping mat is a little farther to the left. She passes it, turning toward us instead.

Huda makes no movement beside me. I keep my breath steady and watch through my lashes as Amina comes to a stop, kneeling beside me. My heart raps a staccato rhythm. Surely she

196

won't do anything here? My uncle would not send her to do his work for him, not when she has no magical inclination herself.

She taps my shoulder lightly.

I shift, opening my eyes to look at her. The tent is too dark to make out much more than her shape.

"Habibti," she murmurs. "Come with me."

I blink at the endearment, my fears falling away. One does not call a would-be prisoner "my beloved." Unless she doesn't know what my uncle intends and is used to using such endearments with others—which could be. She reaches past me to touch Huda's shoulder. My friend rolls away before Amina's fingers can make contact and sits up sharply.

"Come," Amina whispers again. She rises, grasping the strap of the bag Huda made me, and pads out of the tent.

Huda reaches for her own bag, then looks back at me—or at least, I see her head turn toward me. I dare not speak, so instead I stand up and start out as well. If my uncle intends to betray me, I would rather meet him head on than wait for him to come and drag me out. I consider calling Val, but I'm not yet sure what's afoot, and... if my uncle really is going to betray me, I don't want him with me, aware of my every emotion.

My aunt waits just outside. She passes me my bag wordlessly. I snatch it back rather more emphatically than I intended and quickly loop the strap over my head.

Huda steps out behind me. My aunt gestures to us to follow her, walking on silent feet around the tent toward where the camels rest.

Huda's hand finds mine. I give her fingers a squeeze. She lifts her other hand to point toward two more figures making their way over from the men's tent: Kareem and Miragecleft. Kareem is carrying his pack as well.

My aunt, my uncle—they're helping us escape? I can't help the hope fluttering through me, the buoyant rush of delight. If my uncle is helping me escape—regardless of whether he called Ravenflight here or not—then he isn't *really* betraying me.

"Bint Al-Ghaib," my uncle says as he joins us. Perhaps it is because of the dark, but I hear the thread of sorrow in his voice as clearly as if he wept.

"Yes, honored mage?" I return, because I dare not call him uncle right now.

"I ask you to forgive my failings. You must leave at once. A mage will arrive soon, perhaps even before dawn—one High Mage Ravenflight. You know of her?"

A shiver runs under my skin. "We have met."

Miragecleft reaches up to rub his mouth. "Then you know you must go."

He turns, gesturing for us to follow him to the camels. Both camels are saddled and ready for us. As we near them, I fall into step with Miragecleft, unable to leave without asking more. Perhaps it is foolish of me; I know what happened when I asked my mother to admit our relation. I lost her. To ask now, if my uncle is not ready to admit it... but I need some indication from him before I take my leave, some sign whether I might ever seek him out again or not.

As we reach the camels, I blurt, "If you know why Ravenflight seeks me, why do you aid me?"

Huda and Kareem exchange a glance and move quickly to their mounts.

Miragecleft grimaces. "I... never got on well with my brother. Rasheed was the coolness of our parents' eyes, and the better mage of the two of us by far. Resentment is a bitter brew to grow up on."

I hold perfectly still, wishing I could see him more clearly in the light from the crescent moon, but neither it nor the stars can light his expression.

"I was glad in a terrible sort of way when he left. The desert was wider, more open to me without him. When I learned of his death, and his wife's, I finally knew regret. They had a child, but I could get no word of her. And so, my resentment turned to ash."

"You—you looked?" I think I might weep here, on the side of a desert hill, while my uncle admits old wounds of which I know nothing.

He tilts his head toward me, his face in shadow. "I looked, my child. And I failed. Now, I have failed you again. When Ravenflight said she sought a young rogue named Kiki Hibachi, I did not imagine that was you. You were gone five years by then, an old grief with a different name. But then you came riding in company with our enemies, and I found my brother written in the lines of your face, in the way you hold yourself when you are wary." He gestures with his hand, and I remember how he watched me so carefully through our initial conversation—not just to read me, but to read my father in me. "He is there in the name you have chosen for yourself, regardless of what the Council calls you."

"Thank you," I tell him, my voice choked.

"Do not thank me, for I have betrayed you and now you must flee."

My uncle cared for me; he looked for me when he knew nothing of me except that I might need him—and now he risks the High Council's anger by sending me away before Ravenflight arrives. Because we are family.

"I hope you can return to us one day, habibti." He cups my cheeks with gentle hands and presses a kiss to the top of my head. It is a tenderness that tears at my heart.

I inhale shakily. "You were only doing what you thought right," I tell him.

My uncle grimaces. "I should have trusted the phoenix and asked you your story. Now there is no time for that."

He steps back and looks to where Huda waits, seated on her camel a few paces away, the creature still kneeling for me. "I am glad you have such friends as these. I will be proud to call their people our allies from this day forward, if they will have us in return."

Huda inclines her head in acknowledgement.

"Peace be upon you," he says, the traditional farewell another kind of benediction.

I pull myself away to scramble up behind Huda in the saddle before she commands it to stand. My aunt stands beside my uncle, and I reach a hand toward her, though I am too high, too far, to actually touch her.

"Come back to us," she says. "I would know you better, habibti."

"I will," I promise, just another impossible thing, but my heart swells regardless.

Miragecleft hisses softly, swiveling toward the far side of the valley. I set a hand on Huda's back, seeking with my mage senses, and catch the faintest echo of magic in the air. A ward?

"She comes," my uncle says urgently. "Go *now*. I cannot use my magic to aid you—Ravenflight knows my signature, knows all my tricks. You must get away on your own. I will do what I can to delay her."

"Hold on," Huda tells me. I barely manage to grasp her waist before the camel breaks into a rocking gallop, racing toward the ridge. Kareem rides before us, his bisht flapping behind him.

I don't dare look back—my balance is tenuous enough without twisting around, so I do not have a final sight of my uncle and his wife. Instead, I seal their words and the feel of their love— so unexpected and so true—into my memory.

We pass over the ridge, and my uncle's camp falls behind us.

We thunder down past the covered well, Kareem guiding his camel to the left, following the edge of the valley to a raised pass. My friends slow their camels as they reach the incline, for the path here is littered with rocks. Still, they keep a brisk pace.

My senses prickle and then magic blazes a path close around us, a blinding blue-white wall that encircles us.

"Stop!" I cry as we close the distance toward it. "Kareem, stop!" Huda pulls back on the reins, and our camel swerves to the side, our legs brushing against Kareem's camel as he reins her in as well, just shy of the wall. Still gripping Huda with one hand, I reach out to lay a hand against it. It doesn't hurt—but it is inarguably there, as hard and impermeable as any physical wall.

"What is it?" Huda demands, staring wide-eyed at the space beside us.

"Magic. A wall." It is formed from a mix of all the elements, as many spells are, but this has a little more stone to it, no doubt for having drawn on the desert around us. I know what to do with stone.

"We're surrounded?" Huda asks.

"Yes." I look back toward the far ridge. I can't see anything through the magic, but I know Ravenflight is there. Somewhere. "I need to get down. I might be able to take down the wall."

Huda gives the camel a command and it drops to its knees, rocking its way down until I can jump off.

"I'm sorry." I tell Huda, turning to face the wall. "If I can't take this down—"

"You will," Huda says shortly. "Do your work."

I don't answer, my vision already taken up by the wall. Ravenflight will be walking toward us—on foot or by camel or by wing—but she will have no cause to hurry right now, no reason to believe we can escape. Just as Blackflame's minions thought us secure. I must make every moment count.

I raise a hand to the wall's shining blue flow. It is hard to my touch, built to withstand attacks. But I'm not attacking, I'm simply urging it on, pouring in my own fire as it flows faster and faster. The pale wall brightens to orange as it swells and flows, and still I urge it on. It begins to wobble, glowing with heat as it loses its initial form. I am vaguely aware of my friends shifting away from it.

I hear a shout behind me that is not Huda, and bare my teeth. *Yes. Now.* My markings tingle as I turn the magic, channeling it from its circular path to arc down the hillside and across the valley. It slams into the shield protecting the mage standing on the far ridge. The magic sends her staggering back, the edges of her shield shredding, falling away with a scattering of sparks as she is driven backwards, disappearing over the ridge.

"*Now, Hikaru!*" Huda shouts, grabbing my wrist and yanking me to the camel. Had she called my name before? She shoves me up onto the camel saddle, then leaps up as the camel heaves itself to its feet once more. Kareem circles around behind us as if to protect us.

There is no sign of anyone behind us.

"Hold on," Huda says, reaching back to catch my hand and raise it to her waist, and then the camel is running, great rollicking strides that nearly knock me from my seat. I grab on to her waist, holding tight as the camel makes for the ridge. Our path is now lit by a gentle white light, allowing both Huda and the camel to easily navigate the stones underfoot. She's attached a glowstone to a strap that passes below its neck, made just for this purpose. Ravenflight won't need its light to be able to focus on us—and this way we can see our way forward.

We cross the next valley at a run, Huda guiding us toward the end where a low pass opens into the next valley. As we reach the end, Kareem curses behind us, the words unfamiliar but the sound unmistakable.

I twist, my hands still tight around Huda's waist, and spot a rider coming over the ridge. From this distance, I can't make out the details, but I don't need to. There's no glow of magic about them, no shield or spell held at the ready. "It's not Ravenflight," I tell my friends.

"Are there more riders?" Huda asks we speed through the pass. "Or just the one?"

"I only see one," Kareem says.

"Keep checking."

As we make the pass and swerve to ride along the line of hills, out of sight of the rider, I turn to get one last look. "Still one," I tell her. "Not Ravenflight, or she would have sent something after us by now."

"Perhaps it's her guide," Kareem says uncertainly. "I cannot imagine who else would be chasing us."

It makes sense that Ravenflight would have had a guide to escort her through the desert. But what guide would be so foolish as to give chase and leave their charge behind—especially after the magic I sent down on her? I have as little idea as Kareem who is behind us, but I don't want to find out.

"Do you have a plan?" I ask Huda.

"I'm borrowing your plan."

I blink at the back of her head. "What's that?"

"Run," Huda says, her voice unexpectedly bright with amusement. "In this case, to the Howling Caves, as the phoenix bid us. Not that I think it's a good idea."

"You can leave me there and circle back to the well," I tell her. "I'll call the phoenix now and you know how fast he'll come. I'll be fine."

Huda casts her eyes to the heavens. "I'm not leaving you anywhere," she says, and catches hold of my wrist at her waist for a moment as if to ensure I don't attempt anything stupid. Which is just a little embarrassing, but also lovely. "Hurry up and call him."

We should have called him already, but everything happened fast, going from *my uncle is aiding me* to *Ravenflight is on my tail* in less time than it takes to drink a cup of qahwe.

"His feather's in my boot," I say without great confidence. We're riding at breakneck speed over uneven ground and I am not a good rider at the best of times.

Huda's head bobs in response. "Can you light it now, while we ride?"

And keep my balance? "I don't think so. We'll need to slow down a moment, if we dare."

She glances over her shoulder, but our pursuer is hidden by the pass we just came through. Still, they should be nearly a valley away. She pulls on the reins, bringing the camel to a halt.

"What is it?" Kareem asks.

"Hikaru needs to summon the phoenix," she explains as I rock back and forth on the saddle in the process of yanking off my boot. I manage to retrieve the feather a moment later, aware of everyone watching me.

"Here," Kareem says. "I can hold it."

"Can you light it?" I ask, passing it to him. "I have a firestarter."

"Yes."

"Drop it as soon as you light it," I tell him and shove my

firestarter at him. It was one of only three charms that survived my exit from the Burnt Lands.

I have my boot only halfway on when Huda presses her camel forward again. I yelp and grab her waist with one hand, holding onto the top of my boot with the other as I try to shove my foot in the rest of the way. I manage it a moment later, and glance back to see Kareem already riding, and behind him a glowing orb burning bright in the sand. The phoenix will come quickly this time, as he has every time before. The only question is if he will be able to beat Ravenflight here.

"How far are we?" I ask.

"Two or three more valleys. It's on the other side of this ridge of hills."

"Do you think we can make it?"

Huda glances back past Kareem to the rider. "No."

I follow her gaze to see the rider already gaining the pass. He's closed the distance between us by half. *Kraken spit.* "Not a mage," I say, more to comfort myself than anything.

"But a faster camel than ours, carrying less weight. You don't have any tricks you can use, do you?"

The talisman bumps against my chest, in tandem with the camel's gait. "I can hit them with a burst of pure power. Only, if that isn't a mage—if they can't deflect it—it could kill them."

"Well," Huda says. "I've got my sling, and Kareem has his. Keep a watch. If you see the rider raise a weapon, tell me and we'll stop."

"Stop?"

"He's a warrior, is my guess. He'll know how to sling a stone while riding, and if he's brought his bow and arrow, that will be another problem. Either could easily kill one of us. Better to face him—with our slings or your magic, whichever we choose."

I shift in my seat, wondering how I'll be able to tell if he's got his sling out or not. The man rides crouched low, his camel racing over the sands. Like Huda's, it wears a special strap that passes beneath its neck and holds a glowstone to light its way. Which at least makes it easy to see how much closer they are getting.

As we reach the next pass, merely a narrowing of the space between the hills on either side of us, the rider raises his hand.

"What—" I begin, uncertain what he's doing.

Huda looks back as she tugs on her camel's reins, making us swerve from our original path just a few paces. Enough to keep us out of the path of airborne projectiles. Kareem, looking over his shoulder, shakes his head, saying a word I don't recognize.

"What?" I repeat.

"A stick," Huda tells me. "For making the camel run faster."

Ah. And, of course, we don't have one.

"Ibn Saleem!" the rider shouts at us. "Bint Ahmer, stop!"

Huda pulls on the reins, turning her camel as it slows until we are facing the rider. Kareem draws up next to us. "Are you sure about stopping?" he murmurs.

She ignores him. In the half-light of the glowstone, her features are bright with disbelief. "Ibn Hamza! What are you *doing* here?"

The rider—Laith—slows his camel. I have to agree with Huda —why in the world is he chasing us? Surely he's not going to betray me *and* his uncle?

Laith glances between the three of us before his gaze focuses on Huda, or rather on her hands. Even now, he's following desert etiquette, careful not to offend her by staring straight at her. "Bint Ahmer, the one behind you has deceived you and your family. She is wanted by the High Council of Mages for her crimes."

Huda exchanges a disbelieving look with Kareem. "Do you think I don't know that?" she demands. I find myself desperately grateful for Huda, her fierce friendship and deep loyalty.

"But..." Laith shakes his head in bewilderment.

"But? Shall I turn over one of the desert who has been chosen by the phoenix himself, for the crimes of her past? When she has already paid a full price?"

"She didn't pay—the crimes of her *past?* It hasn't been a month!"

"She was marked. That was punishment enough. Now the phoenix has set her a task, and she is doing more than generations of mages have, and you would betray her? And the phoenix? And your *uncle*?"

"My uncle," Laith says blankly. Yep, he has no idea.

"Laith," Kareem says with great aggravation, "when did you last speak with your uncle?"

Laith's eyes narrow. "Are you trying to suggest my uncle approves of your flight? *He* is the one who made the decision—"

"I cannot believe you," Huda says, cutting him off. Oh, she is *angry*. "Blood means nothing to you, does it?"

"Huda," I mutter. "What are you doing?" It was one thing for my uncle to deduce my parentage on his own—but he's sent me on, kept our connection secret even as he protected me. I didn't even pause to think what Huda thinks of it—or how she might use it. But telling Laith is something else entirely.

"Blood?" Laith echoes, starting to look frustrated.

"Have you not yet figured out who she is?"

"Huda," I say. "Don't—"

"He has a right to know," she says, loud enough for him to hear. In the light of the crescent moon, her face is all gray planes and determination.

"Know *what*?" Laith demands.

His camel takes a step forward, then another.

Huda turns a look of pure wrath on him, stalling him completely. "Miragecleft was not the only mage of your tribe, was he?"

I close my eyes.

Huda presses on. "He had a brother. A brother who died and left a daughter behind years ago. You did not care when she lived half a world away. I see now that you do not care even when you have shared your meals with her—even now that your own uncle has helped her escape. How do you *think* we got to our camels without anyone else noticing?"

Laith shakes his head, staring at me. "Wait, you mean—"

"I mean it is a shame when your own blood finds greater protection among your enemies than with you." Huda turns to me. "Tell him your father's name."

"I...." There is no going back from this. No starting over, and no unmaking this confession. My aunt and uncle might keep my identity a secret, not sharing it with their family, but if I choose this, I will be claiming it. Even if that gives me nothing now, perhaps it will mean a family one day—a home I can't revisit but that will always stand open to me, like a halcyon dream. I want it, however unlikely it is.

"Tell him," Huda says, her voice gentling but her expression still fierce.

I look Laith in the eyes. "My father was Rasheed ibn Shakir, called Coldeye." It feels strange to say it out loud—strange, and liberating.

Laith stares at me, speechless.

I go on quickly, "I ask that you tell no one, for if it is known, then those who hunt me will learn my birth name, and then I cannot ever hope to escape them."

"You see," Huda says, her tone daring him to choose wrongly.

"Rasheed Coldeye," Laith repeats, shaking his head. He opens his mouth to say more. Pauses. Clicks his jaw shut. He searches my face once, as if he might find his answers there. Perhaps he will.

"And now we are going to save the life of your family, ibn Hamza. As your uncle bid us—because he knew, even if you didn't. I suggest you do not stop us." Huda raises her brows in challenge.

"I—" Laith looks back at me, brow furrowed. "Are you my cousin in truth?"

I swallow hard. I did not expect this, somehow. "I do not know precisely how we are related, but if Rasheed Coldeye was your uncle, then we would be cousins."

He nods once. "Cousins through marriage."

Huda clicks her tongue, turning our camel away.

"I am coming with you," Laith says behind us.

Huda twists to stare at him in disbelief. "You cannot come with us! You have already slowed us down enough. Go slow down Ravenflight if you need something to do."

"I'm a fast rider," Laith says stubbornly. "And Ravenflight can fly. I doubt she'd pause for me." He pauses, and adds cheekily, "Stop slowing us down now, bint Ahmer."

She throws him an outraged look and urges our camel forward. I hold tight to her, trying not to laugh.

"Where are we going?" Laith asks Kareem.

"The Howling Caves."

"The—are you serious? What of the ghouls? And the spirit creatures every child knows to fear there?" Kareem must make some response—a shrug of the shoulders?—for Laith goes on, "This does *not* seem like a good idea."

Kareem gives a soft laugh. "It's the phoenix's idea, not ours."

And then our camels surge forward into a rollicking run, and there is no more talking. But even over the thump of the camels' flat feet against the sand, I can still hear the memory of Laith's voice naming me cousin.

Two gifts in one night. I have an uncle and now a cousin. It was worth this—Ravenflight's pursuit, fleeing into the night—it was worth every moment of it to have discovered family who will claim me.

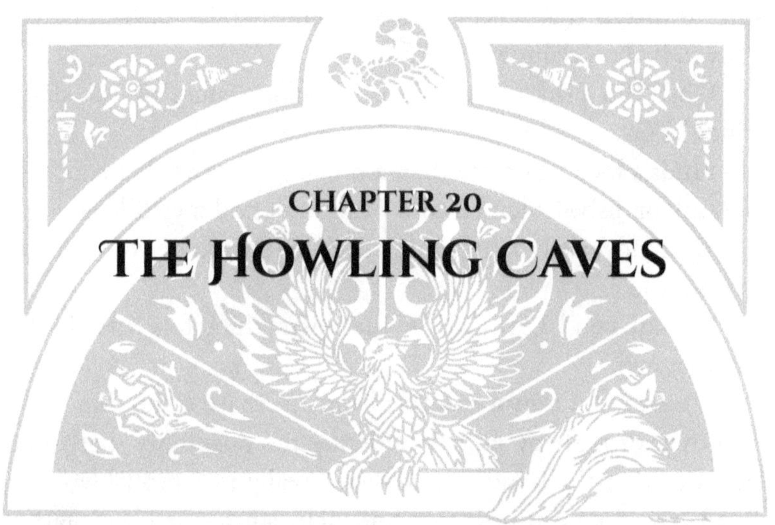

CHAPTER 20
THE HOWLING CAVES

As the ridge beside us dips to an elevated pass, Huda turns our camel toward it, allowing it to slow a little. The boys ride behind us, keeping a sharp watch for pursuit. For now, though, the desert lies empty behind us.

"We cannot drive the camels too hard," Huda tells me. "Not from a cold start. We will speed up again as needed."

I nod, even though she can't see me. "Huda, I—I am sorry I did not tell you my parentage."

She snorts. "I already knew."

Wait— "You *knew*?" I ask. "That my uncle—that I—"

"That you are of the Bani Essam?"

"Yes, that," I say, wishing I could see her face. "How did you know *that*?"

"When we first met, you asked about your uncle, and your father, and if the tribe had cared at all for your father's family after his death. There are not that many mages in the desert. There are even fewer who left the desert to study and didn't return, and only one of those who left for good who could possibly have been either mother or father to you."

The desert may be vast, and enmities may run deep, but the tribes sure do keep track of each other.

"Also," Huda says, "you have never claimed a family. I wasn't sure, at first, if that was because we were enemies, or because you felt you had no claim on your family."

Oh. "I'm glad the phoenix is making allies of the desert tribes," I say.

Huda's look, no more than a quick glance over her shoulder, is so full of disbelief joined with irritation I find myself laughing.

"I do not need the phoenix's intervention to be your friend," she tells me.

"Thank you," I say. "You're the closest thing to a sister I think I've ever had."

Huda doesn't answer immediately. Perhaps I shouldn't have said that, or perhaps she's considering the possibility that I have no idea what the bond of sisterhood really is. I probably don't. But I have a cousin now, and an uncle, so maybe I will start to learn. Maybe there *are* things I can have, even if I cannot keep them long.

"I am glad the phoenix brought us together," Huda finally says, reaching down to give my hand a squeeze where I grip her thobe.

One more thing to treasure while I can.

She guides her camel up the hillside, following a barely visible path toward the top. The hills here are rougher terrain, more stone and less sand than before, with places where the dirt has eroded away to leave sheer rock faces. There is no hurrying this ascent past a brisk walk. I keep a nervous watch on the valley behind us all the way up.

"There," Huda says as we crest the hill. The keening of the wind rises, whistling and shrieking across the ridge.

Before us, the valley opens up into a wide plain featuring a massive, solitary flat-topped hill with sheer stone sides riddled with holes and caves. It is huge, easily as tall and three or four times as wide around as the hill we are now descending, but it stands alone as if thrust up from the earth whole. The valley around it lies barren—no swath of desert grass rises from the earth, no thorn bush has found purchase in the dirt.

I have no difficulty grasping why the desert tribes consider this place cursed, even if this place is still alive in a way that the Burnt Lands are not.

I glance to the sky, using my mage sight, but there's no sign of the phoenix. Thankfully, there's no sign of Ravenflight either. Still, I don't like the idea of bringing my friends to such a place. "Are you sure about this?"

"The phoenix would not send you to your death," Huda says. "We have to trust in that."

"I'm not always certain he understands how easily we die."

Huda nods, her head bobbing up and down. "I cannot think of any other place to take shelter. Even here, Ravenflight may follow."

I glance back over my shoulder, scanning the hilltop, and my mage sight picks out a black fleck flying over the ridge, a faint sheen of magic enveloping it. It drops down, wings flapping as it speeds toward us.

"Huda," I say, my eyes focused on the bird. "She's here."

Huda shouts an order at her camel, and the poor beast breaks into an exhausted run, shambling down the hill toward the natural stone fortress before us. It is barely a thousand paces away, but it may as well lie at the other end of the desert.

"A bird?" Kareem asks, having twisted to follow my line of sight. He reaches for his sling and tugs it free. Already the raven has crossed half the space between us, feathers deep black in the early light.

"No," Laith tells him, for once in the know.

"That is High Mage Ravenflight. You cannot attack her," I call back to Kareem.

He hesitates. The raven passes us, sleek black body and wide wings, its shadow skimming across the earth. Its shadow? A moment ago, it was too dark for shadows to be cast, which can only mean—

"It's going to be all right," I tell my friends, my heart leaping. "Just keep riding, no matter what she does."

"But—" Laith begins.

Kareem hushes him and says, "Trust her."

His words make me straighten further in the saddle, still clinging to Huda.

The raven circles back around us, cawing. I raise a hand and wave cheerily, squinting against the burgeoning light. "Greetings, Ravenflight," I shout in Tradespeak. "I hope you don't mind, but we can't stop right now."

The raven caws once more and then folds its wings, swooping down to land before us.

It never reaches the earth. A light bursts through the valley in a ball of golden flame that streaks across the space before us. I squeeze my eyes shut as the camel lurches to a stop. A single, shrieking caw pierces the air, just audible over the rush of air and the keening of the wind.

I open my eyes to find our way clear, my vision marred by a blue afterimage from the phoenix's passage. "We're safe," I tell my friends. "Hurry."

There's no sign of mage or bird. I don't know if the phoenix killed her—I hope not, in part because such a death would be laid at my doorstep, and with it, more hunters dispatched to capture me. But there's nothing to be done now.

Huda drops her arm from her face, clicking her tongue at the camel. Fear gives the animal renewed energy, and it jolts forward in a staggering run, covering the remaining distance to the caves in the span of a dozen breaths. Kareem and Laith keep pace with us easily, riding beside us now.

"What *was* that?" Laith asks over the constant shrilling of the wind. "Did you call it?"

"Of course." I grin. "That was the phoenix."

HUDA GUIDES our camel to the largest visible cave at ground level—at the entrance, it is roughly camel height. Most of the other caves and openings appear to be higher up the walls, making it an easy thing to choose our entrance. Huda swings down in her usual, graceful manner, one foot set on the camel's neck as it lowers her down. Then she has the creature sit so that I can clamber off. The boys dismount beside us.

I take a step to the cave opening. It continues on into darkness, and even the light from the glowstone strapped to the camel fails to show the end of it. All I can tell is that it grows narrower and slopes down into the ground—a cavern that leads, perhaps, to a system of caves.

"The phoenix should be back shortly," Huda says. "Let us wait just within the cave."

I hesitate. More than anything, I don't want my friends to enter the Howling Caves with me. "He might return soon," I agree. "But it may also take him time to ensure Ravenflight does not follow him back here."

Kareem grimaces as he and Laith join us. "In the meantime, there may be other mages on their way, correct? Because of that flare Ravenflight set off. If they know anything of the desert, they will be able to follow our tracks well enough. If we remain here, they'll find us easily."

Huda nods. "What if Hikaru and I wait here, and you two take our camel on, leave them different tracks to follow?"

Laith shakes his head. "Once we leave this harder ground for sand, any capable tracker will be able to tell the difference in your camel's tracks, going from carrying two riders to none. They'll also be able to tell if one of us is leading your camel. It's not a giveaway, but it will be notable—enough that they might stop to investigate, or circle back."

Which is just as well, because I don't want any of them here. "You should go," I tell Huda. "Make it look like we're riding on. They won't expect me to stay at the caves."

"They'll still be able to tell the difference in the weight my camel is carrying," Huda says, looking to her brother. "If we leave Hikaru here at all, they'll know."

Kareem grimaces, casting a look around, and then blinks at the fallen stones. "We can try to disguise that. Let's load up the saddlebags with an equal weight to bint Al-Ghaib," he nods toward me respectfully. "If you are still guiding the camel separately, and we get close enough in weight, they should not be able to tell."

Laith nods slowly. "That could work, but you both know the stories of this place, even if my cousin may not. Perhaps it is better if we all continue on together."

"I don't want to leave you," Huda tells me in agreement, looking from me to the cave we stand before.

"It's fine," I say. "You'll lay a false trail, and I'll wait here for the phoenix. The only one who knows I should be with you is Ravenflight, and the phoenix has taken care of her. If another mage follows you, pretend ignorance. It should buy us enough time for the phoenix to rejoin me, and then find you."

I *wish* I had had a chance to try to repair Stormwind's necklace using the few ward stone beads I'd rescued.

Huda grimaces. "It's a good plan. I just don't like it. We'll circle back once it is safe to fetch you."

"All right," Kareem says, starting forward. "You both sort supplies; we'll get the rocks."

I nod, mind racing. "If you cannot find me, then that means I've had to hide myself, or I've gone elsewhere with the phoenix. Go to the well and I'll send him to you there."

Huda frowns as she opens her saddlebags and pulls out a few pouches of food—dried fruit and dates that she passes to me. I stuff them in the bag she made me, alongside my few belongings. She passes me a second smaller water bag to complement my own.

"Be careful," she tells me.

"I will," I promise, and shut my mouth to keep from offering false assurances.

Huda nods grimly.

Laith helps Kareem gather some of the rocks that lie just within the cave mouth. They cast anxious glances at the cave as they work, but say nothing. Once Huda has emptied the saddlebags, they set a few rocks at the bottom of each saddlebag, and then we pile the supplies that will stay with Huda on top of them, obscuring them from view.

"Quickly," Huda says, casting another apprehensive glance

toward the ridge. I've been keeping an eye on the ridge as well, and so far there has been no movement, but every additional moment we take makes keeping watch more nerve-racking.

"Find a crevice and stay quiet," Laith suggests, his brow creased with worry.

"We will be back as soon as it is safe," Huda promises.

I step back into the cave, deeper into the shadows. "Go on," I tell them. I want to tell them what I feel for them—and why not? "I love you all," I blurt. "Be safe."

Huda's face breaks into a smile. "We will see you soon, little sister." Beside her, Kareem nods in agreement.

The next moment, they are mounted, Laith whisper-calling a belated farewell, and then they are gone.

I allow myself to watch after them as they follow the cliff walls until they disappear beyond my sight. Then I turn and check my pockets for my charms—I forgot to retrieve the firestarter from Kareem, but I still have a glowstone and a seeker charm—which is good for finding things, but not much else. At least I still have the obsidian ward on its cord around my neck to keep from being found. Time to hide.

I start forward and something cracks beneath my boot. I fumble my glowstone from my pocket and freeze. The floor of the cave is littered with bones—thin, fragile things that look like twigs, and here and there larger ones with rounded ends, though many are broken. That's what Laith and Kareem were looking at. But why didn't they say anything? And what kind of predator would live here?

My gaze skims over the bones, the layer of dust resting over everything. There are the brittle, hollow bones of small birds. Those... perhaps gazelle? They are too small to be a camel's. But there are no tracks or droppings and the bones are old, the dust undisturbed. Whatever once lived here must be long gone— which at least explains the boys' silence on the matter.

I pick my way across the cavern, trying not to disturb the bones. I shield the glowstone, but I don't dare put it out—I need its help to get deeper, even if it risks drawing attention. The cave itself has a tall, sloping roof. Toward the center, the roof curves up to a circular hole, pitch black and, I hope, unused. I pass to the side of it and continue on to where the cave narrows into a winding tunnel. Within ten steps, I have lost sight of the main cavern.

The tunnel walls close in on me as I proceed. I go slowly, listening carefully. It's longer and deeper than I would have expected, which means if I can go only a little farther, I should be very well hidden. Then I can sit down and try to repair Stormwind's ward necklace.

Somewhere ahead—or perhaps behind me—a pebble skitters over stone. The sound echoes, small but unmistakable, making it impossible to tell where it started.

I jerk to a halt, extinguish the glowstone, and listen with bated breath.

Nothing.

I inhale shakily and open my senses. I cannot sense anything behind me, though that might be because of the weight of stone between me and the cave opening. Shifting, I peer around the turn before me. Past it, the tunnel curves into a larger, dark space —perhaps a cavern, perhaps merely a wider tunnel. All lies quiet but for the keening of the wind, muffled here. But there was no mistaking that sound.

I strain my senses, seeking anything—a whisper of magic, the rush of blood in a creature's veins, anything. At first, I catch only a glimmer of magic ahead, just enough to freeze my feet to the floor, and then, as my mage sight grows attuned to the space, I begin to catch more: the hum of wards, the flicker of blades charmed to cut through whatever they touch. The pulse of blood through the veins of at least a pair of large beings, if not more.

I need to go. *Now.*

I race up the tunnel, keeping my head low so I don't bash it on the stone roof, and my hands out to either side so I don't scrape against the stone walls. I still manage to graze my knee against a protrusion, though not so hard as to slow me. A glance back shows me the sudden movement of enchanted blades following me.

I enter the main cave and skid to a stop, bones crunching beneath my feet. A figure stands in the entrance of the cave facing me, blade drawn. Silhouetted against the pale moonlight, their features are impossible to make out, but their clothing is not. They wear close-fitting body armor, nothing like the desert people. But they can't be a mage—if they were, they would have attempted to subdue me by now.

"Who are you?" I demand in the desert tongue.

A light flashes behind me. I twist to see two more warriors moving silently up the tunnel toward us, one of them bearing a small, golden light in a tube, allowing them to point the light where they will—it skitters over me before shining into my face.

I step to the side, so I can see all of them together, the cave wall at my back.

The warrior at the entrance says, "The question is, who are you?" Their voice is heavily accented, and yet I don't recognize the accent at all.

"I am a friend of the phoenix," I say, really hoping the phoenix knew what he was doing. "He bid me take shelter here."

The warrior moves forward, coming to a stop a bare three paces away. The one with the light source lowers it. In its ambient glow, I can see that they've wrapped their helmets with turbans and drawn the long tail of the turban across their faces, obscuring their mouths and noses. Their eyes, though, are unexpectedly large in their face, the dark pupils elongated, coming to a point at the top and bottom. Like a snake's.

Not human, even if their form appears so, but I don't know what they are.

"Indeed," the warrior says. "Who is it you seek to evade by coming here?"

"An enemy," I say carefully. But I can't hide exactly what I'm dealing with. "A mage who would enslave me."

The warrior's brows rise. "Then let us offer you shelter. Quickly now."

They gesture for me to go back down the tunnel. The warriors there turn and begin the descent, moving fast.

"We will not be caught with you," the warrior says, gesturing again. "Move."

I hurry forward, the warrior behind me. Two steps into the narrower tunnel they pause and do *something*—I feel a faint brush of magic. When I look back, they have lifted up another golden light to illuminate our path. Behind them, the tunnel is sealed, stone closing the entrance to the main cave and a magical shield sliding into place that will make it nearly impossible for Raven-flight—or any mage—to detect anything here. It's both masterful and a little terrifying. Whoever, and whatever, these people are, they not only have access to charms, but they must have at least one mage at hand to create such protections.

The desert tribes may not know what lies within the Howling Caves, but I have the distinct feeling that their stories of people disappearing within them are truer than I would like to believe.

There are secrets that were meant to stay buried here, and I have stumbled directly into them.

CHAPTER 21
SHAHMARAN

The warriors lead me deep into the Howling Caves, through branching tunnels and paths that both ascend and descend. I become increasingly certain that they are also misleading me—purposely confusing our path so that I cannot find my way out again.

They must eventually decide they have done enough, for the tunnels begin to change, the stone underfoot smoothing out. The walls go from rough to smooth to decorated with a single strip of carving just above our heads on each side, a pattern of intertwining flowers and leaves. Then a doorway appears on one side, instead of merely an opening into another tunnel or cavern. The stone door is closed, its center carved with a circular symbol that might be a sigil of some sort, though I can't be sure. We continue down another corridor of doors, all closed but with more mundane engravings, and take a turn.

Another short length of tunnel brings us to a wide antechamber with glowstones set in sconces on the wall, though these stones are golden-tinged rather than the pale white of my own stone. They're as gold as the lights the warriors carry, though I have never seen such glowstones before.

"Wait here," the warrior says, gesturing to a stone bench

against the wall. I sink down gratefully. It's been a long day, and I am not at all sure how much is still left of it.

The two remaining warriors disappear through a doorway in the far wall—the flash of light they pass through giving me only a glimpse of more stone before the door closes once more. Only the warrior who spoke to me remains. They reach up to adjust their turban, letting the long end drop to fall over their shoulder. The fabric reveals a wide, long face, skin slightly lighter than Huda's golden tone, though not as pale as the Northlanders.

"Are we waiting to meet someone?" I ask, even though it's abundantly clear that we must be. None of them responded when I mentioned the phoenix. Does he even know these people are here? Will he even be able to find me past their wards? Or is all of this part of his arrangements for me?

"Our sovereign," the warrior replies.

"And is your sovereign expecting me?" I ask, the words slightly awkward. The desert tongue is highly gendered, but sovereign gives me little to go on. Better to repeat it than make a mistake in my references.

"Yes, though perhaps not at this precise moment," the warrior says with a hint of amusement.

So the phoenix *does* know about these people. That's a relief! I glance at the warrior's eyes again, taking in their distinctive shape, and remember the mosaic of a snake queen at the Mekteb in Fidanya. A mosaic whose artists, I'm relatively certain, had no idea what they were depicting with their fantastic portrayal of people with snake tails instead of legs.

"Shahmaran?" I venture.

The warrior smiles, a curving of their lips that shows the tips of their canines—fang-like and yet too slim. "We are the maran, yes."

A race of people gone so long they are considered mythical are the true inhabitants of the Howling Caves? I'm pretty sure that's a secret I have no business knowing. But the phoenix arranged this, and maybe he has a plan larger than I know of in bringing me here. Nothing for it but to hope for the best and keep my wits about me.

I dip my chin. "I am honored to meet you. I have heard tales of a people called the maran. I was told they passed from these lands during the Great Burning."

"Many things ended then," the warrior says. "We did not."

The door swings open to reveal a young maran dressed, I suspect, as a highly ranked servant. They wear a long-sleeved tunic that ends just above their knees topped by a second open-fronted robe—like a desert bisht, with wide arms, but it is only as long as the tunic worn underneath, and the cut is slimmer. It is held closed at the waist by a brightly colored sash. It is also embroidered in repeating patterns formed of black thread that remind me strongly of the patterns of snakeskin. Loose, pale-colored pants and a similar-colored turban complete the look.

"Sovereign Arnaz will see you now," the servant says, holding the door for us.

I follow them through the door, the warrior falling into step behind me. We come around a corner and the cavern opens up before us: rough, stone walls that jut high up, yellow glowstones set in lamps illuminating a generous natural spring that bubbles up to the surface beside us. Its waters flow over the mossy rocks to gather in a central pond. On the pond's far side, the water pours over a small dam of natural rocks to flow down between the long lines of cliff-carved buildings as a wide, placid stream.

Arched walkways and wide balconies line the cliffs, all of them overflowing with potted plants, though I see no sign of other people. But all around us is lush greenery: flowering plants clinging to the walls, small, slender trees spread along the far bank, a profusion of herbs growing in pots set onto ledges carved into the walls, their leaves fluttering in the cool night breeze. Far above, a swath of starry sky can be seen. This interior gorge is a haven of life, and the secret to the survival of the maran here.

As we walk, I open up my mage sight, and find myself awed a second time by the scale and subtlety of the spells here: everything from spells to keep the water flowing in the streambed, to purifying enchantments to keep it clean, to wind chimes that encourage the air to move, to the shield that envelopes the top of the gorge. This larger dome of spells is a ward, a shield, and, if I had to guess, a camouflage to hide it from outside notice. But what stands out as we progress down the gorge is how very brilliantly each spell interacts with water, from what flows before me to the humidity in the air, to the faint dew beginning to gather on the leaves.

It's no surprise that the maran have a mage. After all, I saw the way the maran warrior sealed the cave I entered from. Whoever they are, or have been through the generations, they are not just excellent at protections, but have mastered the element of water in order to keep this haven alive. It is a wonder to observe.

The servant turns, leading up a set of four stairs to an open veranda where someone sits. The maran sovereign. They are tall, with strong shoulders and an air of elegance and authority about them. They watch me steadily as I approach, their yellow eyes with their slitted pupils standing out starkly against the paler tone of their skin. Their hair, a variegated red-orange that reminds me of nothing so much as the colors of a diadem snake, is wound behind their head, the bulk of it hidden by a pale scarf draped artfully over their head and shoulders. Their nose, like those of the warriors, lies flatter, the nostrils angled similar to a snake's.

They wear little jewelry—possibly because I've roused them in the middle of the night. Their robe remains their main adornment: the fabric an exquisite jade-green jacquard with a woven leaf design, the sleeves widen into great bells that hide their hands from sight. The front is embroidered with gold wire in a floral and leaf pattern. They wear no sash at their waist, the two sides of the open front instead simply layered over each other. The flowing sleeves and straight lines of their robe perfectly complement the power and grace of their body.

The maran sovereign rises as we near, one beringed hand remaining on the arm of their carved seat. As we stop before them, they say, "I am Arnaz, sovereign of the maran. Welcome to my realm."

"I am honored by your kindness," I return, hoping that there is still an abundance of kindness left to be discovered. I use the plural masculine formal *your*, which can also include the feminine, because I don't know what else to do: the desert tongue is built for gendered conversation, but I have no overt markers for how to refer to Arnaz. The warrior never gendered their sovereign, and neither did the servant, and while Arnaz's clothing appears royal, I don't know enough of maran culture to consider them gendered any particular way. Which could mean I am absolutely flubbing this.

Arnaz's eyebrow quirks, and then they tilt their chin in an unspoken question.

"I am called Hikaru bint Al-Ghaib," I add hurriedly. I *definitely* flubbed the introductions.

"I wished to bid you welcome, bint Al-Ghaib, though it is late," Arnaz says, smiling faintly. "You will want to rest and take refreshment, I think, before we speak further. When you are ready, I would hear your story and what news you bear, but all of that can wait. There is no rush."

"I thank you," I say with some little relief: through the flurry of *yous* in their speech, Arnaz flipped back and forth between the masculine and feminine constructions without concern. Either they are just as unpracticed at desert grammar as I, or they are not used to such gendered language. I continue on, "I believe the phoenix should arrive shortly. I am very grateful for this shelter in the meantime."

"Indeed, we look forward to speaking with the phoenix again. For now, Rewniz will take you to your room and see that you have all you need."

I thank them again, and Arnaz dips their head, and that is it. I am ushered out by the same lead warrior, Rewniz, back through the hallway we entered the gorge from, and down a couple more, then through a doorway into a bedroom.

"This is your room," Rewniz tells me. "If it does not meet your needs, we can arrange new quarters, but we ask that you remain here until that time. There are many tunnels and we would not want you to lose your way. We will bring you food and drink. Is there anything else you require?"

I shake my head.

With a bow, Rewniz departs, leaving me to wonder just how long the maran are expecting me to stay.

I cross to a small side table and help myself to a drink of water from the ceramic pitcher and mug left there while looking over my room. It contains a single great divan against one wall, a black and red woven carpet at its foot, the aforementioned side table, and a few floor cushions stacked against the opposite wall.

The walls are hung with tapestries, but for the wall with the door into the hall. That one has a mosaic of painted tiles representing a tree-like figure with branches for arms, the sun rising over it. The tapestries present different stylized battle scenes, mostly of archers on horseback—though there are also a fair number of mythical creatures that I don't immediately recognize. There is a lionlike creature with a woman's head and a scorpion's tail that appears to be eating a warrior whole. And there are a number of snakelike dragons with long and winding forms, some with wings and some with feet—though perhaps they are meant to be a symbolic representation of the maran. I don't know enough to be able to tell.

Two of the tapestries have nothing but stone wall behind them. The third has a large, rectangular niche carved out of the wall, and a hook to allow the tapestry to be pulled to the side. Based on the small pile of folded linens carefully set at the bottom of the niche, as well as the two shelves above it, it functions as a wardrobe.

There are no other exits or entrances to the room, which is not particularly surprising—it is all carved out of stone, after all, and there would not be any windows down here. There are two small holes with grates, one that must connect to the hallway, though no light comes through it, and the other going up into the ceiling. That explains why the air down here feels fresh. No doubt there is also a good deal of magic as well as practical architecture at work to maintain the airflow.

I cross to the bed and take off my boots. My whole body aches from tiredness. Where will Huda and Kareem and Laith be by now? Will they have circled back to Miragecleft's camp, or kept going to further evade Ravenflight? There should still be some time before they attempt to retrieve me. I can only hope the phoenix arrives before that time and is able to let them know I'm well.

My mind wanders from my friends to Val, who met my uncle with me, and whom I promised I would call on if anything went wrong. I wince. Things aren't really wrong now, though, are they? I could sleep first and contact him after... though the longer I put it off, the worse it will go.

Sighing, I drop onto the divan and call out to Val, just a gentle speaking of his name in my mind. No response. Perfect. I lay my bag beside me and climb under the bedspread, snuggling down. The pillow is more of a stiff bolster than anything. I push it aside and let my body sink into a puddle against the mattress—and realize I've left the golden glowstone still lit in its niche. Ugh. Maybe I can sleep with it still shining? I don't know that I have the energy to get up and deal with it. I gaze at the mosaic with unseeing eyes, trying to decide how much I care.

Hitomi? Val says, his voice uncertain as he joins me. *Where are you?*

The How— I break off, thinking of the true inhabitants of the Howling Caves, and then of the stories my friends have. Ghouls? Spirit creatures? The maran have spent centuries building those stories. Now I know they are only that: stories. I should probably at least consult with the phoenix before revealing them as such.

The How? Val echoes, thoroughly confused.

I'm underground, I clarify as vaguely as possible. *With the phoenix's allies.*

Tell me your uncle didn't betray you.

He didn't! I can't help the grin that spreads across my face. *Or, I guess technically he did, but then he realized who I was and snuck us out of his camp in time to run. So, really, he didn't.*

Val takes a moment to digest this. *I'm glad of it. So, he knows who you are now?*

He and Laith both. Laith is my cousin by marriage. I sit up, despite the fact that I was too tired to imagine getting up for the glowstone a moment ago. *Val, I have so much family!*

That's good, Val says with some reservation. *Are any of them with you now?*

No. I lie down again, pulling the blanket over my head to block out the glowstone's light, and tell Val about our flight through the desert, Ravenflight's initial attempt to capture me, Laith's pursuit, and the phoenix's timely arrival.

I suppose someone was going to catch up with you eventually, Val says grimly.

I blink. *They already did once—I guess I didn't properly tell you. But that first time I was in trouble in the desert, when you couldn't come at once? And then when you did, the phoenix was already there? That was... a pair of Blackflame's bounty hunters.*

How did they find you so fast? Weren't you wearing a ward?

They had something from my old home with Stormwind—a spindle I used all this past year. It helped them to get close enough to find me another way.

I can feel Val's frustration, as well as something else darker. *Where are they now?*

Dead. The phoenix engulfed one of them in flame and... and I —he—the other mage was using me as a source, pulling magic through me in order to destroy my friends. I reversed the flow and took everything he had... I killed him.

Good, Val says ruthlessly. *I'm glad. But are you all right? With what you did, and with what he did to you?*

I know how to fight a mage who is trying to use me now, I tell him, pulling the blanket tighter around me. An image of Mountain flashes before my eyes, his body collapsed on the sand, his eyes wide and unseeing. *I don't regret what I did. I was glad too, when I realized he was dead,* I admit, my mental voice unsteady. *But I also don't want to be glad about killing. I don't want to kill.*

No, you prefer justice. But you are not in a position to receive it, or be protected by it, Val says.

I know, I agree. *But Val, that's the third person whose death I've caused. I killed Kol as well as this mage, and then there was also the mage who followed me through the portal into the Burnt Lands.*

As I recall, that one tried to throw you to that tentacled spell-creature—the kraken, as you called it.

I nod. I'd ended up tumbling down a stairwell to huddle amid the kraken's tentacles while the mage escaped to the building's rooftop. The kraken had promptly pulled itself up onto the roof after him and eaten him. *He wouldn't have been there if not for me.*

And the world is now that much safer, Val says, unimpressed. *While you're counting deaths, you might also count lives. You killed Kol and saved me. You evaded a killer mage who chose his own death—but protected that lycan captain from me and saved his life. And you drained a mage dry to save your companions, one of whom, if I recall correctly, is a child. You think a little too sharply in black and white, Hitomi. The world is full of greys.*

There are some things that are right or wrong, I point out. *I don't want to be a Blackflame, with no moral compass or conscience to speak of.*

Val's amusement washes over me. *You misunderstand him. I suspect he considers himself dedicated to a higher ideal. Perhaps, as you said, it's raising up the Northlands. That is his moral compass, and his conscience will remain clear no matter what he does, so long as he is working to achieve that. He will set fire to whomever and whatever he must to gain his ends.*

I don't want to become like that, I tell Val. *I don't want to excuse the violence I might do in pursuit of—whatever I think is more important.*

Considering you saw someone worth saving in me, the creature you were fairly certain would eat you, I don't think you're anything like Blackflame. His methods depend on a complete lack of empathy, a ruthless focus on his own aims with no remorse. Kol was much the same, but that his higher ideal was nothing more than his own prosperity. You, on the other hand, have enough guilt to make up for a dozen sadistic fang lords.

An unexpected laugh breaks from my lips. *I'm not sure that's a compliment.*

Neither am I, Val says, which makes me laugh harder.

I wipe my eyes and yawn. *Thanks.*

Where are you now? Some underground place, you said?

Yes. I'm with the phoenix's allies. They have a secret haven of sorts.

The phoenix and his caves, Val says with wry amusement. *I presume you're attempting to keep these allies' secrets. You're safe, though?*

Yes.

Then I had better let you rest. Call me again should you need me.

I will, I promise and close my eyes.

Val slips away as I sink into sleep.

CHAPTER 22
THE MAGES OF THE MARAN

The chimes above the door give a swift, short jingle, heralding my long-awaited summons. I sit on the carpet wrapped in a blanket to ward off the slight chill of the caves, my back against the side of the divan. I shed the blanket and stuff the handful of loose lapis beads from Stormwind's old necklace back in my pocket as Rewniz steps in. I still need a cord of some sort to restring them, but at least their spells still hold.

"Sovereign Arnaz will see you now," Rewniz says, their expression neutral.

"Alone?" I ask, pushing myself to my feet. I suspect it is early afternoon by now, though I have no way to measure time without a window to the outside world. Still, I slept long and uninterrupted, and have been up a little while.

Rewniz shakes their head, holding the door open for me. "The phoenix has arrived."

Oh *good.* I'll be able to send him to the well, so that my friends will know I'm safe. I follow Rewniz out, my step light, and my mind clicks back to their first words. *Sovereign Arnaz.*

I look sideways at Rewniz as they pace alongside me. So far, the maran I've met have used no consistent verbal gender markers, their ruler neither king nor queen. Which doesn't matter, per se, except the desert tongue is innately gendered, and I don't want to go into another meeting with Arnaz and accidentally insult them, or anyone else, for that matter.

Gathering my courage, I say, "If I may ask a question?"

Rewniz tilts their head.

"In speaking with your sovereign in the desert tongue, is it better to use the masculine or the feminine?"

They smirk. "We do not have such words in our tongue. It makes no difference in your language."

Oh, *interesting*. It's more like Tradespeak, then. Which, now that I think of it, is probably why I'm so bad at gendering things and people in the desert tongue.

Rewniz rattles off a trio of words; the sounds are lyrical and, while vaguely familiar, not any language I can actually place. "That is 'me,'" they say, pointing to themself. "'You,' but not as you have in this tongue. It is every 'you,' regardless. And we have only one word for a person or thing, more like... *yeye*."

I start. "You know Tradespeak?" I demand. The maran may be hidden, yet they've maintained ties not only with the desert people—somehow, enough to speak the language fluently as it is spoken in the present day—but also with the wider world. That opens up a *lot* of questions around how they've maintained their secrecy—and why.

Rewniz waves a hand, their expression flattening. Oh, they didn't mean to let that slip. "You understand? We do not need he or she. They do not matter."

I force myself to focus on this, hoping to allay their sudden tension. "So, when I speak to your sovereign—?"

"He, she, it does not matter."

I mull over Rewniz's explanation as we return to the interior canyon with its stream. We follow it to a wide staircase that leads up the side of the cliff wall to a broad stone balcony. The phoenix perches there on the stone balustrade, his tail sweeping down behind him, long curved neck turned to watch me come up the stairs. I feel a rush of pure relief as I spot him that leaves me grinning stupidly.

Arnaz sits on an ornate stone bench with a quilted cushion to soften its top, body turned toward the phoenix, but face toward me. They wear a new set of clothes, similar in cut and style to those they wore last night, though this time they wear a gorgeously wrapped turban strung with gems, their hair showing below it, pulled back over their shoulders. The morning light falling through the opening overhead gleams against the bright red and gold of the loose, bejeweled braid they wear. Their fingers gleam with rings, only a few of which they wore last night, and an emerald choker adorns their throat.

I raise a hand to touch my heart in a gesture of respect and bow from the neck. Arnaz dips their head in acknowledgement, but there's no missing the tightness of their mouth. They are already displeased, perhaps from their dealings with the phoenix?

"Welcome," they say, nodding to me, and then, as my escort disappears down the stairs, "Rewniz!"

They skim back up the stairs at once, bowing at the top.

"Request Mage Eshvat to wait on me here. And Kherbanu, if you can find her."

"As you wish," Rewniz says and departs nearly as quickly as they came.

"So," Arnaz says, returning their attention to me. I wait, meeting their gaze easily, as if I were already used to the very differentness of their yellow-gold eyes with their slitted pupils. "The phoenix tells me you are engaged in healing the Burnt Lands."

"I am trying," I say steadily, making myself keep my focus on them. I wish the phoenix had consulted with me first—though he has no reason to hide my abilities here, where the High Council of Mages can hold no sway. Except my markings will always keep me at a disadvantage anywhere there are mages. Not much I can do about that now.

Arnaz says, "I would have you speak of what you've learned with my mages."

The phoenix can do that well enough, and as the elder of us two—by far—it's his place to discuss it. But it's nice of Arnaz to invite my perspective. "It would be my honor," I tell them.

Arnaz offers me a smile that doesn't reach their eyes and turns back to the phoenix. They converse in a language that carries a vague sort of familiarity to it, lyrical as the desert tongue, but some of the sounds are different. I can pick out the occasional word, but the conversation flows too fast for me to grasp its gist. I take a step back and lean against the balustrade, listening with half an ear as I wonder what Arnaz, or the phoenix, would gain from my training the maran mages.

Arnaz can't mean for their mages to travel with us to offer their help... except that the maran clearly *must* leave their home somewhat regularly. If nothing else, the plants needed for the types of fabric Arnaz wears don't seem suited to such limited growing conditions as this slim gorge. Magic might be able to create the dyes for such vibrant colors, but it cannot change one material into something entirely different—and cotton takes a great deal of land to farm. So perhaps the maran mages *do* travel under cover of glamors—perhaps the phoenix always meant to call on their aid. And perhaps I can learn a thing or two from them about hiding my existence as well.

I glance toward the stair as a tall, slim maran strides up the last few steps. They are dressed in deep maroon robes with black and white embroidery along the edges. They have foregone a turban for a round, embroidered cap. Their hair is long, if thinning, their nose somewhat more hooked than seems typical, and their expression pinched.

"My liege," they say, sweeping past me without a glance.

"Mage Eshvat. You were not busy, I presume?"

I step sideways along the balustrade to catch Eshvat's expression. They raise their brows, smiling faintly. "It is my honor to serve. I can never be too busy to answer."

Arnaz allows themself an unconvinced smile. "I am glad to hear it. You see that the phoenix has come to call on us."

Eshvat bows to the phoenix, their gaze sharpening. "An honor, indeed."

"She has asked us to shelter the young mage beside you, Hikaru bint Al-Ghaib. The young mage has been studying a way to 'heal' the Burnt Lands and open them once more to human settlement."

Eshvat casts me a disbelieving glance that has nothing to do with Arnaz's accidental switching of pronouns, thanks to the desert tongue. "Is that wise? We would have even more humans coming through to contend with then."

"A consideration," Arnaz agrees. "I suspect the phoenix will continue with the project regardless. As such, I believe it wisest to see that it is done in a way that does not threaten us."

I exhale softly, not having realized till this moment how worried I was. Arnaz knows what we're doing and supports it—which means it will be all right. Even if I know the maran's secret, Arnaz won't attempt to keep me here any more than they have attempted to constrain the phoenix. There are definite benefits to having his protection.

"I believe Eshvat will serve your effort well," Arnaz tells the phoenix.

A flicker of light catches my eye. I tilt my head to the side to see it better: a small blue-white bubble floats up from below, coming to rest half-hidden behind the stone supports of the balustrade. A listening spell of some sort, perhaps?

As Eshvat asks a question of Arnaz, I shift, looking about for the maker of the bubble. There. An older maran sits on one of the stone seats in the circle below—this must be the second mage, Kherbanu. They are a wizened old creature with a bulky turban set atop flyaway white hair and a wrinkled face. They sit with their knees sticking out, their maran-style jacket and pants showing the bony lines of their body, a long wooden staff lying across their lap. They lift a finger and point at me, grinning as if we were accomplices in a trick played on our elders.

I dip my head a fraction, an answering smile on my lips, and return my attention to the other occupants of the balcony. Whatever their game is, it's not for me to interfere. Eshvat is now discussing our current plan for unraveling the spells of the Burnt Lands with the phoenix. As I expected, it is the phoenix who is best suited to describing our efforts. He explains our base concept simply and elegantly, from the flow of fire and stone to the talismans to capture the magic.

Eshvat frowns. "But this is exceptionally dangerous. Should it go wrong, the whole of the surrounding desert may be flattened by the magical backlash."

"We are aware of the danger, and have developed a method to reduce the possibility of such a backlash," the phoenix says, and describes the use of the Barrier as a shield.

Eshvat grimaces. "I do not think this wise, my liege," they say, turning to face Arnaz. "The risks are too great." I stare at them. Are they really so sure of themself that they would contradict the phoenix without even looking into what we have accomplished thus far?

"The risks are even greater if the Barrier collapses while the draining spells remain whole," the phoenix says coolly before turning to face Arnaz. "Perhaps you have a second mage we might meet who may actually help us?"

Eshvat's complexion darkens.

"Mage Kherbanu is older and... eccentric," Arnaz says. Their words are light, but the look they bestow on Eshvat could liquify stone. "Perhaps, Master Eshvat, you would consider listening more thoroughly."

"I heard that," a loud, shrill voice calls up the stairs. I glance down and am unsurprised to see the older maran with the staff: Kherbanu. "If you wanted me to come, my liege, you would have called your meeting somewhere without stairs."

Arnaz touches the tips of two fingers to their forehead, eyes closed, and sighs. "I did not think," they say, their voice pitched to carry.

I watch Kherbanu haul themself up the stairs one by one, their right foot first each time. "Did not think," they repeat, their voice carrying quite as effectively as Arnaz's. "Your mother always thought. I don't see any reason why you shouldn't too."

Arnaz sets their hands in their lap and waits with the patience of the severely afflicted for Mage Kherbanu to reach the top of the steps. They eventually do.

"You," Kherbanu says, pointing their staff at me. It is topped with some sort of faceted pink rock, and a few short lengths of cord swing from it with a random assortment of bits and bobs tied to them—a bit of carved bone, a scrap of leather, a few pale beads. Charms of some sort.

"Yes?" I straighten, amused despite myself at their use of the masculine "you."

"Do you think this," they whirl the staff around, nearly knocking Eshvat in the head, "*plan* of yours will work?"

"I think it might," I say as Eshvat takes two quick steps away. "We must still work out the final details. And plan for the—for what might go wrong."

"Desert tongue isn't your first, eh?"

"No," I agree with some relief.

"Then? What do you prefer?"

"Tradespeak."

They snort and switch over at once. "Should have said so, young mage. Would have been easier on Eshvat here too."

"I speak the desert tongue quite well, thank you," Eshvat says with stinging politeness.

"It's a fine line between confidence and arrogance," Kherbanu agrees. "Now then, say your piece, young mage."

"We haven't worked out the intricacies of the plan. We must be very careful to guard against the ramifications should anything go wrong. I would not endanger the desert tribes or your people, nor would the phoenix. But we think it may be possible to open the Burnt Lands. They are... a blight, and their existence impacts everything around them. Further, as the phoenix said, the Barrier is weakening. It cannot hold much longer, and if it collapses while the draining spells still hold sway, that will be a catastrophe."

"Mmm," Kherbanu says. Then they turn and spit a red stream over the balustrade. Eshvat makes a disgusted sound at the back of their throat.

"Your thoughts, Kherbanu?" Arnaz asks.

"Overly idealistic, young, and brazen. I've no idea of their magical ability, though." Kherbanu eyes me brightly. "Shall we test you?"

"No," I say firmly, keeping my tone polite.

"I'll vouch for her ability," the phoenix volunteers.

The corner of my lip twitches in amusement.

"I meant," Arnaz says tiredly to Kherbanu, "what are your thoughts on this plan?"

"Oh, the plan. The plan." Kherbanu taps one finger against their lips. "As plans go, it will take some more planning."

"It is dangerous," Eshvat puts in.

"So is walking up those stairs. You see I still took the risk."

Eshvat glares at Kherbanu. "Far more dangerous than that. It could easily fail and destroy the desert—it could even touch us here!"

"Bah. We have you to protect us. Surely you can manage a ward strong enough to keep a backlash so many hours distant from bothering us? Our deepest caverns are already designed to offer every magical protection we know; you would only have to strengthen them."

"I—well, of course I can strengthen our wards! But they've no plan worth speaking of. Surely even *you* can see that."

"I did just say it would require some more planning," Kherbanu replies, smiling serenely. "And it seems if we *don't* plan, we shall have the draining spells to contend with shortly regardless. If you can manage to see to our wards, I will see to this plan."

Eshvat bristles, then turns to the phoenix. "I recommend you take your plan to the so-called High Council of Mages that governs the human lands and have them assemble a team of experienced mages to plan this properly. Attempting to unmake the draining spells with the help of a half-trained child can only result in disaster."

I clench my jaw to keep from snapping at the mage. I am nearly an adult, even if my level of training might—*might*—be debated. Stormwind was quite thorough, though there are still some things I likely need to learn. Or there were, before I lost my ability to cast spells. What I lack, really, is experience, and the phoenix has that in droves.

The phoenix turns his regard on Arnaz, his eyes glimmering. "This is your decision?"

They gesture toward Kherbanu. "Let us hear from my other mage."

"What do you want to hear? I told you: they need to plan more. How should I know who would do a better job of planning?" Turning to the phoenix, they continue, "Honored one, have you tested these theories as yet?"

Kherbanu knows we have, has already heard all this via their listening bubble, but they are wise enough to pretend they haven't. Or perhaps just mean to make a point of Eshvat's refusal to lay any store by what we have done.

In a few broad brushstrokes, the phoenix once more outlines my work collapsing the draining spells by the banyan, my destruction of the tentacled spell-beast, and finally the greater vein of magic I created from the edge of the Barrier.

"Ooh," Kherbanu says, their lips jutting out in the shape of an O. "Very good for a half-trained child. Let me congratulate you."

They dip their head at me, eyes twinkling.

I nod in return, well aware of Eshvat's glare.

"My liege," Kherbanu says, turning to Arnaz. "I suggest a planning meeting."

"That is what this is," Arnaz says.

Kherbanu waves their hand dismissively. "I don't mean *your* planning whether or not to aid the phoenix. I meant *us* planning how to free the Burnt Lands from the curses that hold them in thrall. We will, of course, have to travel there to get a good look at them. One can't just work on theories from a distance."

Arnaz raises their brows with a mix of disbelief and amusement. "Are *you* planning to travel there?"

"Of course. Eshvat has already said they're going to strengthen our wards. *One* of us will have to go take a look. Or," Kherbanu shrugs, "we expect that our young mage will at some point run off with the phoenix to the Burnt Lands, put their plan into motion without any help at all, and," Kherbanu swings their staff again, the leather cords flying around to slap against Eshvat's arm, "*blam!* We have a problem that a bit more planning and a modicum of courtesy might have avoided."

They turn their gaze on the phoenix. "You *were* looking for an *experienced* and *wise* mage to help, were you not?"

I bite the inside of my cheek to keep from laughing, well aware that they're commenting on Eshvat as much as they are on my own youth.

"I am," the phoenix says.

"Well, then," Kherbanu says, as if that has decided everything. "I'm going back down these dratted stairs. You may join me in my study when you're ready."

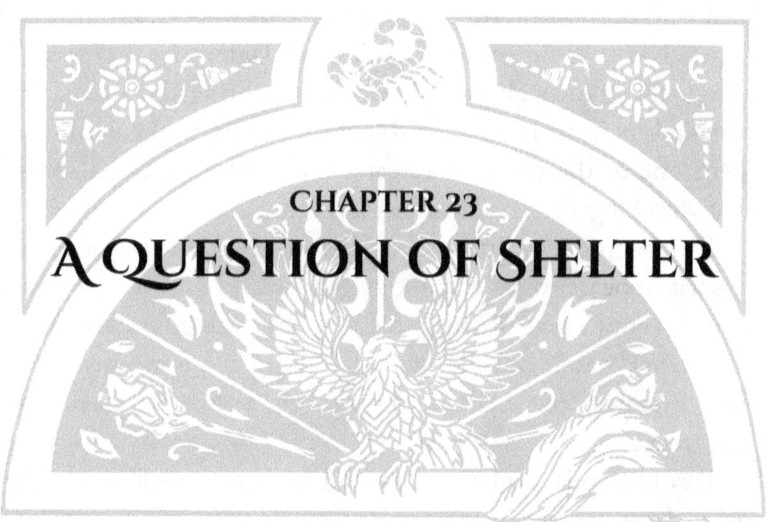

CHAPTER 23
A QUESTION OF SHELTER

Sovereign Arnaz keeps the phoenix and me a few minutes longer, as if to make the point that they are, in fact, the one in charge, before dismissing us to join Kherbanu. We follow Rewniz out of the canyon into the warren of tunnels once more, leaving Eshvat to make their shamefaced excuses to their liege by themself.

The wider halls Rewniz conducts us through now are lived in, completely unlike the empty corridors I walked before. Here, doors stand open, the sound of voices echo down the hall, and thrice we pass small groups of maran who step to the side to allow us passage. They are a variety of ages, from the portly middle-aged maran who stares at the phoenix with wide eyes, to the bright young face of the maran half their height who peers around their leg at us. There are even a pair of maran who are likely about my age—or at least, they look to be close to adulthood, even if the maran might age differently. They stand in a doorway chatting, their conversation falling to silence as they spot us. I smile uncertainly. They exchange a bright look and then beam at me together, eyes alive with curiosity. I can't imagine they get too many visitors down here.

Kherbanu's study is perfectly ordered, containing shelves

filled with bottles and stoppered jars, a great wooden cabinet, and a central work table with stools. A dusty lantern hangs from the ceiling, the golden glowstone within it lighting the room. The mage hovers in front of the cabinet muttering to themself, then opens one of the doors to reveal a shelf of books and a second shelf with longer rolls of aged leather.

Kherbanu doesn't turn around as we enter, just waves a hand in what appears to be a random gesture and says in the desert tongue, "Find a seat. Rewniz, habibti, close the door behind you and keep a watch outside, would you? Don't want any young ones listening in. Let me know when Eshvat makes her appearance."

Rewniz nods. I glance toward Kherbanu, wondering what makes them so sure the other mage will join us.

"And thank you for coming to tell me of Arnaz's summons before you went to get Eshvat. Much appreciated," Kherbanu adds.

"It was my pleasure," Rewniz says and closes the door behind them.

I take a seat on a stool and the phoenix hops up to sit on the one around the corner from mine, bright eyes watching me carefully. We haven't yet traded a private word, and while there's a great deal I want to ask him, I don't dare speak now.

"They aren't *quite* fluent in Tradespeak," Kherbanu tells us, effortlessly changing languages. They pull out one of the long rolls from the shelf, using one hand to keep the others in place. "Didn't want to make an issue of it."

"Of course," I say, wondering if that had been the one source of Rewniz's tension when I asked them about Tradespeak.

Kherbanu sets the scroll down on the table and opens it, weighing down the edges with polished stones to reveal a map, the ink faded but still legible—each place name is labeled in the desert tongue, and again in a script I do not recognize.

"Is this your language?" I ask, brushing a finger over the characters. They are rounded and flowing, like the desert script, but with angled lines connecting to the curves, or sitting on top of them like little hats, and more than a few bisecting lines.

"Yes, that's marani," Kherbanu says, setting down the last paperweight. "Now, here are the Burnt Lands at the center. You see the old city of Bayt al-Mawt here," she says, pointing to what must be the city I accidentally stumbled into on my way through the portal.

"That *can't* be its name," I protest. Absolutely no one in their right mind would name their city *House of Death*.

Kherbanu chortles. "It is now, child. Had a much prettier name before the Great Burning. Something along the lines of Fruit Basket or—"

"Al-Rawdah Al-Muthmira," the phoenix interrupts. "It means the fruitful garden."

"Yes, that," Kherbanu says. They point out the second abandoned city to the north, where I've had no cause to go, and then trace the unnaturally smooth edges of the Barrier around the Burnt Lands. It really is almost perfectly circular. And *vast*. Looking at this map, I can see I've only really traced the edges. The closest I've gotten to the center is the phoenix's haven, and it is only perhaps a third of the way there.

"To do the amount of work needed and make sure the Barrier doesn't fall—that will take more than one or two mages," Kherbanu observes, turning to the phoenix. "Do you have a plan to find more mages? I assume the mage that chased your young friend here is not among your allies."

The phoenix clicks his beak. "Unfortunately not. However, I've sent word to the other desert tribes for both their elders and their mages to meet us in a week's time. The mages will each help begin the process from their station at the edge of the Barrier."

"And the elders?" Kherbanu asks.

"They must establish peace with each other before the Burnt Lands are opened," I say. "They have enough enmities now. If we open the Lands to them as things stand, in all likelihood there would be a war over the new territory."

"It's a dead land, isn't it? Not worth much."

"Not now," I agree. "Within a few years it should begin to improve, to grow more like the surrounding desert, with grazing for their herds." I know for a fact there are underground water sources—that alone will constitute riches in the eyes of the desert dwellers.

"Mmm. So. Making peace between warring tribes and healing a cursed land. You must think quite highly of yourself."

"I—" I blink. They watch me expectantly, as does the phoenix —who is the whole reason I'm even here. "It needs to be done," I say. "That's why the phoenix asked me to join him. The Barrier is slowly failing. If some further good can come from our actions, we would be foolish not to try for that—or to try to prevent any possible evil."

"Ooh," they say. "A sense of honor too. That will get you killed, my dear."

"No getting killed," the phoenix breaks in gruffly. "We are trying to keep everyone alive here."

Kherbanu flaps a hand at him. "Yes, of course. But when one has a martyr type on one's hands, one must be aware of it."

"I'm no martyr," I say, irritated. But even as the words leave my lips, I wonder if that really is what others see in me, if it's more accurate than I want to admit.

"Mmm, well, maybe I'm wrong. But tell me this, are you afraid to die?"

"Of course I don't want to die!"

Kherbanu rolls their eyes. "This child," they say to the phoenix.

"Do be kind," he tells them. "She's very young."

"Kind? *Pfft.*" They eye me with disappointment. "There is a great difference between fearing death, which you don't seem to, and not wanting to die. Just as there's a great difference between not wanting to die and wanting to live."

"I do want to live, though," I say.

Kherbanu turns to the phoenix. "You know this one much better than I. Do they?"

The phoenix studies me, and I'm suddenly afraid of what he will say. "I have only known you a short while," he finally says, "but it seems from what I have seen and what you have told me, that wherever you see a fire burning, you throw yourself in the middle of it."

"That's because *someone* has to do these things," I argue. "No one else was going to help Stormwind, and you were the one who *chose* me to help in the Burnt Lands."

"I did," he agrees gravely.

I look from him to Kherbanu, and think of how many people have asked me what I will do next. All I ever answer is "run"—and not in the way of Osman Bey's farewell. I don't want to die, but maybe Kherbanu's right: I don't know how to live either. Maybe some part of me has been looking for a worthy death because I haven't believed I have a worthy life... or that I can choose to live it.

I don't know how true that is, don't know how to even begin changing it. I'm not even sure I'll have the chance to—which I suppose is half the problem: not believing I can.

Kherbanu shakes their head, tutting softly.

Thankfully, the next moment, the faint sound of a voice snapping an order comes through the stone door to us, followed by the jingle of the door chime.

"That will be Eshvat," Kherbanu says. Raising their voice, they call, "Come in, then."

Eshvat sweeps into the room, their face set in an expression equal parts irritation and distaste.

"Took you long enough," Kherbanu observes, gesturing to the remaining stool at the table. "Do sit down and stop glowering. We've been waiting *ages* for you to arrive so we might begin."

"Indeed," Eshvat says and sweeps a hand over the stool's seat first, flicking off imaginary dust specks. "Let us not waste any more time, then."

"Agreed," the phoenix says with a slight edge to his voice.

Eshvat presses their lips together, but their ears, framed by their cap, darken with embarrassment.

I look down to the tabletop so they won't note my amusement.

The phoenix lays out each part of what we've learned and accomplished with enough detail to keep the mages' questions few and far between. In the end, Kherbanu doesn't think our plan is as bad as all that. It needs to be tested by additional mages, and ideally, we should conduct another, larger experiment, trying to reach to the center of the Lands from the Barrier. For that, Kherbanu would need to travel to the Burnt Lands to make an attempt with us, testing out our methods.

"You cannot seriously plan to travel there," Eshvat snaps. "The stairs are enough of a challenge. What if you should meet with one of these spell-creatures?"

"Your concern is heartening, dear Eshvat," Kherbanu says, smiling so warmly it almost undoes the sarcasm in their voice. "But if you are not willing to go, it seems I must. Unless you have changed your mind?"

Eshvat draws themself up. "If we are committed to seeing this plan through, then it is only right that I should make the journey."

"Mmm," Kherbanu says, their eyes twinkling. "That is honorable of you, indeed."

I frown to hide the smile I'm fighting—they've known from the beginning that Arnaz intended to send Eshvat. I've no doubt the maran sovereign made it clear to Eshvat where their duty lies. Kherbanu is perfectly happy to let the younger mage do the work.

They turn back to the phoenix. "You realize that once you start this flow of yours as you plan to, from multiple points, you'll have no control over it. That is what concerns me most."

"That's why we need a focal point to anchor it and absorb its power," I agree. "Otherwise it could go anywhere."

They snort, but it's more amusement than derision. "You'll have to make sure your mages can find those anchors—or talismans, as you call them."

"True," the phoenix says steadily. "The talismans will have to be created and placed first, and then we can test it. I was able to bring the necessary stones with me." He glances to me, and explains, "That is what I had gone to do while you traveled to meet the Bani Essam."

I nod, remembering that much.

He looks back to Kherbanu. "I will require your aid to form them into talismans."

"I presume there is a particular reason why our young Hikaru cannot do such work," Kherbanu says, "despite being such a well-trained mage that they have found a way to do what your other mages could not."

"I think I've gotten this far through a fairly unusual course of training, and a bit more exposure to the element of fire than is typical," I say, keeping my tone casual, and very carefully *not* looking at the gauntlets that hide my markings.

"Meaning a coincidence of particular experiences," Kherbanu says. "You still haven't answered my question."

I flash them a grin. "I have: I don't have the training. To make the talismans, we want someone who actually knows what they're doing."

They purse their lips, making them jut out, then tilt their head, allowing my explanation to pass. "And you?" they ask, turning to the phoenix.

"There are some forms of magic and casting I find challenging. This is one of them." He says it so simply, with such a complete acceptance of what he can accomplish and where his limitations lie, I find myself staring. I've never really accepted my limitations—not that I can remember, and if burning myself to a cinder by my sunbolt is any indication, I never have at all. I've never taken no for an answer, finding a way around the obstacles before me to accomplish the impossible.

Now, that calculus has changed. While I'm still pushing my limits in some ways, there are other limits that I cannot escape, caged as I am by my markings. I cannot cast spells. I cannot create new charms. This is my new reality. I've been angry, I've grieved, and I've—well, I've tried to forget how deeply things have changed. I've even told myself I am resigned to the future I chose. But this—a simple, quiet acceptance of one's abilities? This I've never even imagined.

The phoenix continues, "We'll need to create a second set of spells once we're done, to return the magic in the talismans to the land itself."

Eshvat's brows shoot up. "You will have just created the greatest talismans in existence. Would it not be wiser to keep them out of human hands altogether?"

"That's why the phoenix will keep watch over them," I point out.

"Your human mages will still have to set the spells you've described. I do not think you can trust them near the talismans once they contain such power."

"What do you propose?" the phoenix asks coolly.

Eshvat makes a sweeping motion. "Send them here. We are hidden from humans and can keep them in safety. I can easily create the spells you require."

"No."

Eshvat blinks, brow furrowing. "No?"

"Absolutely not," the phoenix says coldly. "The talismans are not for you to play with, nor to gain power over those who do not know of your existence. They will contain the power of a whole land, drained from the earth and air, and we will use them to restore that land—for which purpose, they must remain within the Burnt Lands. There is no other choice, certainly not these far-distant caves. Do you understand?"

Eshvat's ears burn dark red, their face a tightly set mask. "I understand very well."

Oh, dear. I am not at all sure it was wise of the phoenix to deal with them so.

"Excellent," Kherbanu says cheerfully. "So the talismans must be created and a place for them set. You want a spell that will channel the magic back into the earth, but it will have to be a great one to reach the whole of the Burnt Lands. And it will have to be cast *after* the talismans are created, correct? So that their magic isn't absorbed into the talismans." Kherbanu taps their lips, thinking. "That may require more than one mage. Have you considered using the Barrier to redirect the talismans' magic back into the land? The Barrier is designed to contain, after all."

The phoenix ponders this. "I am not sure the Barrier can be adjusted to perform anything beyond its current function without risking its integrity. But perhaps one of the desert mages may aid me in creating a model spell we might utilize to mimic the draining spells instead—a network to return magic rather than drain, centered in my haven."

"Do you trust these desert mages?" Kherbanu asks, eying the phoenix askance.

"Enough to know they will not betray their own people," the phoenix says. "That is all we need."

"Mmm," Kherbanu says.

"There's too much risk," Eshvat interjects, shaking their head. "I tell you again, go to the humans' Council and have them do this properly."

"And let them lay claim to the talismans?" I demand, turning on Eshvat. "Can you imagine such power in their hands? Can you imagine them agreeing to give the talismans up at all?"

"Burying them in a hole is hardly going to keep them safe," Eshvat says, their words dripping derision. "That is your plan, is it not? The phoenix will keep them in his *haven*, and there they will stay until someone either agrees to selflessly feed that magic back into the earth, or," they shrug, "steals them while the phoenix sleeps."

As much as I hate to admit it, they have a point. The phoenix cannot remain on guard continuously. Surely there is a desert mage that *can* be trusted?

I smile slowly, meeting the phoenix's gaze. "Harith Stonefall," I say, naming the rogue hunter who came for Stormwind a lifetime ago—the same mage whose life I saved, and who aided me in return, and gifted me Zahra. "He resigned from his position with the Council and will have returned to his tribe by now. He is a skilled high mage, and lives by his honor. You can trust him."

"That is only one mage," Eshvat argues.

"I will seek him out and speak with him," the phoenix says, eyes bright. "I don't need many. I only need the right mage to work with me to figure out how to return the magic to the land, and keep the talismans safe until they are drained. An ex-rogue hunter may be just the thing."

Eshvat looks unimpressed. "You would have us enter the Burnt Lands on the hope that you might not only drain the draining spells themselves of their power, but also that such a vast amount of magic contained in a handful of talismans will be returned to the land rather than abused—when you cannot guarantee any piece of this?"

"If you do not wish to go, stay," I say, my patience running thin. "I have entered the Burnt Lands with much less to give me hope, and I will do so again."

"I doubt that," Eshvat replies, smirking.

Oh, to wipe that look off their face. "Doubt what?" I demand through gritted teeth.

"That you are going anywhere at all. Did you really think our sovereign would let you leave the caves, now that you know our secret?" They laugh, a huff of amusement that has my hands curling into fists. They spread their hands, smiling that ugly smile of theirs. "Welcome home, little mage."

"Oh, stuff it," I snap. "I'm not staying here. Surely your sovereign has more honor than to imprison a guest of the phoenix."

I don't truly believe that—I'm quite certain Arnaz will be as ruthless as necessary in protecting their people's secrecy. But I know the phoenix, and I can't believe he would allow my imprisonment. I turn toward him, expecting him to be ruffled with irritation, ready to argue for me.

He isn't looking at me.

Surely not. *Surely not.*

"Phoenix."

He shifts from one foot from the other. Still, he doesn't look at me.

"We leave in the morning," Eshvat says pleasantly. "It's already set. I'm sorry to disillusion you, but it is the phoenix and I that will be departing, not you."

"Phoenix." My voice comes out hard and sharp. "Is this your agreement with the maran? You told me to take shelter here. Is *this* what shelter means to you? That I remain a prisoner the rest of my life?"

"Mageling," the phoenix says quietly, finally turning his head to meet my gaze. He hesitates, his eyes dark with some emotion I cannot name. "You will be safe here."

What? He agrees with this—*chose* this for me?

"Child," Kherbanu says softly. "You knew the stories of our caves before you ever took shelter here. There is no leaving."

I pay them no heed. Pushing myself to my feet, I turn toward the phoenix where he perches on his stool. I'm angry, but my chest is tight and my throat hurts, and I can't say why my face feels so wrong.

"Well?" I ask as Eshvat leans back, arms crossed and a smile sitting on their arrogant mouth. "You can't really intend to leave me here. You said you needed me to teach the mages we work with."

The phoenix shifts, his eyes darker than I've ever seen them, and I know. *I know.* The knowing breaks something inside of me. He knew me, I believed he cared, and now—this?

"The Council will never find you here," the phoenix pleads. "It's the safest future I can give you. You will live, and you will be safe."

"I don't want *safe*," I say, my voice rough as the truth of it hits me. I want family and friendship and *care* and none of that is in these cursed caves. "*I don't want safe.*"

"Child," he says.

"Don't. Just don't. Go save the Burnt Lands, if that's all that matters. Don't make excuses to me about how it's easier for me to be imprisoned than freed to an uncertain future. My future isn't yours to choose."

"Every time you step outside the Barrier, Ravenflight and every other—"

"*Don't.*" I walk to the door, then turn back to him, chin raised. "You release me of my debt."

It isn't a question, but he still bobs his head.

I nod, as if that seals all that is between us, and let myself out.

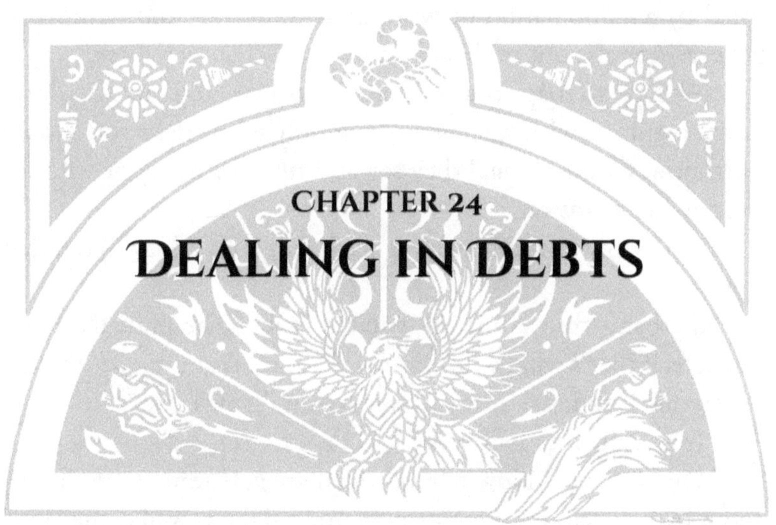

CHAPTER 24
DEALING IN DEBTS

"You young people are *so* dramatic," Kherbanu says, sweeping into my room some three hours later without so much as a by-your-leave, their staff with its plethora of charms in hand.

I have spent the intervening hours alternately lying on the divan and pacing the confines of my room, my eyes dry and my heart aching. I'm going to leave, that much I know. At least Huda and the boys should still be at the well, waiting for me. But I haven't even asked that thrice-cursed bird-brain what happened to Ravenflight. And regardless, escaping before the phoenix himself leaves wouldn't end well—not if he has promised the maran my captivity in order to keep their secrets. No, he needs to be beyond their call before I make a bid for my own freedom. I'll have to wait, which is just as well, since I've no idea *how* I'm going to find my way out of here.

"The phoenix isn't all that young," I say now in response to Kherbanu.

"I wasn't—oh, child!" They snort a laugh. "Never mind such nonsense." Kherbanu glances about my room and grimaces. "This is a terrible place to work. You had better come to my study."

I raise my brows. I have no doubt that they knew my room was hardly a mage's study, which means their visit was likely motivated by a combination of wishing to collect me and wishing to get everyone else out of their own room. "What for?" I ask.

"We have to shape the talismans, of course. You said you don't have experience with such work, so it only seems right you should learn now. Come along," they say and turn for the door without waiting for an answer.

I school my features, keeping my hands lax, and say, "I'd rather not."

Kherbanu throws me an irritated look. "The phoenix won't be there, if that's what you're worried about. As I came *all the way here* to fetch you, the least you can do is walk me back."

"It's hardly four hallways."

"On old knees! Now tell me, what are you going to do in this room by yourself, hmm? Nothing! You might as well come along and learn something."

"I don't owe the phoenix anything anymore," I say, my voice tight. Kherbanu will figure out soon enough that I'm marked, whether or not I try to use magic in front of them. I'm either going to have to escape before they do, or decide if I trust them enough to tell them.

Just the idea of trusting a mage with my secret makes me tense up, but in some ways Kherbanu reminds me of Stormwind—and Harith Stonefall. Kherbanu's a bit rough around the edges, but I suspect they might be equally honorable in how they deal with people. Eavesdropping on conversations aside, Kherbanu never hesitated about helping the phoenix once they knew the stakes.

Kherbanu sighs. "It's unfortunate, really, that there was a debt between you two to begin with. It makes it much harder to be friends. One should never deal in debts with friends."

"We were never friends." The words are hard to get out.

"That may be, but I've no doubt the phoenix cherishes you. I suspect you are so deeply angry only because you love him in return, foolish bird that he is. Friendship is an impressive amount of trouble, is it not?"

"If he was my friend, he wouldn't leave me here," I snap.

"If he was your *wise* and *thoughtful* friend, he wouldn't,"

Kherbanu agrees. "But—correct me if I am wrong—he is trying to protect you from a variety of people who would see you dead, or worse. While knowing you are likely to throw yourself into the middle of the next available fire because *someone* has to. Being overprotective, he does not realize that burying you alive is not the answer."

My brow furrows. That's rather strong language for one's own home.

"Yes," they say, as if in challenge. "We are all buried alive here. There's no reason to add to our number."

"No reason?" I echo. "Are you planning to help me escape, then?"

"I'm not planning on stopping you," Kherbanu says frankly, reaching out to pat my shoulder. Given that they think me a fully able mage, that's as good as opening the front door for me and reporting on the weather. "In the meantime," they continue, "I would like your help. Unless there is something else?"

"There is," I say. Kherbanu has been honest, and now they're giving me their support—though it will gain them nothing. I can either try to hide the truth and expect they'll discover it sooner than later, or tell them on my own terms, and have the chance to gauge their reaction. "The phoenix hasn't told you everything about me."

"No? They do like to keep their secrets. Calling you *bint Al-Ghaib*, for one. A little obvious about keeping that secret, if I say so myself."

"This is different—and he knows it. This isn't a secret I can keep for any length of time. I don't know how he thought he could leave me here with it for the rest of my life."

Kherbanu chews this over quite literally, as if getting the taste of my words on their tongue. "They did say your magic working is inhibited in some ways."

"I'm marked," I say, shoving up a sleeve. It's the work of a moment to unbuckle the gauntlet I still wear, baring the markings. "It means I cannot cast spells anymore."

"I have heard of the practice," Kherbanu allows. "Are you

bound as well? That may present some challenges in keeping you safe here."

"No, and I intend to keep it that way."

"Indeed," they say. "I don't suppose I might take a look at those?"

I flex my fingers, letting my sleeve fall down to hide most of the markings. I can't help the dread curling in my belly. "What do you mean to do?"

"I've never actually seen such markings before. It's not as if we do such things to our own children. I am curious, and of course one wonders if there's a way to undo them."

I ignore the rush of hope I feel—the possibility that Kherbanu might discover something the average Council-trained mage would not. There have been hundreds of years of source slaves, and not one has escaped the prison sentence of their markings. Instead, I opt to make sure Kherbanu really doesn't betray me. Meeting their gaze, I say coolly, "If you attempt to bind me, I will wrap my magic around your core and rip it out."

"So dramatic," they mutter to themself before saying, more loudly, "You've done that before?"

"Yes, to a mage who attacked me."

Kherbanu grunts and stumps around me to sit on the divan, laying their staff beside them. "If you are concerned by anything I do, you may bop me over the head with that. Now come, let's have a look."

I shake my head, glancing at the staff. The action is purely symbolic. Kherbanu can defend themself from their own staff easily enough. But laying it down is a sign of trust, a sign that Kherbanu wishes to be found trustworthy. It suggests that we are at least allies. Even with the phoenix's betrayal fresh in my mind, I find I want to take this chance now.

Kherbanu holds out their hand to me expectantly. There is something strangely familiar about their actions, about that hand waiting for me. An offer, an opportunity, a kindness—I don't know which. Perhaps it doesn't matter. Sitting down, the staff by my side, I put my fingers in theirs. Their skin is dry and smooth and unexpectedly cool. The maran appear so like humans in so many ways, the realization that they might actually be cold-blooded takes me by surprise. Though it does explain how they don't seem to mind the cooler temperatures of the caves.

Kherbanu's magic slides through my hand, making my markings thrum. Their eyes narrow. I wait, teeth gritted, as their magic flows through me. I can't help the memory of another mage's grip on my hand, the way he pulled on my magic so hard I flailed in his grasp, desperately drawing on the magic around me to feed his demand. But this is nothing like that. Kherbanu doesn't hurt me, nor do they attempt to draw through me. I took their hand of my own accord and this, now, reminds me of when Brightsong sent her magic through me weeks ago, singing her soft spells of healing.

Kherbanu lets my hand go with a dry laugh. "The nerve of that phoenix! Vouch for your magic, will he?"

"I did much of my work in the Burnt Lands as I am now," I say. I buckle on my gauntlet again, keeping my focus on it, though I desperately want to know their thoughts on the markings themselves. When I finally look up, I find Kherbanu's gaze on me, the slitted pupils in their amber eyes clearly visible this close.

"Well, this explains why the phoenix wasn't taking Eshvat's advice to work with that Council of yours."

I shrug. "He could have, given that he's planning to leave me here. There's nothing stopping him now." Well, except Black-flame being in charge. I doubt the phoenix would want to risk his taking control of the talismans as well.

"Mmm," Kherbanu says.

I'm beginning to think that each of their *mmms* has its own meaning. This one seems to imply that they know more about the phoenix's decisions than I do. I hate to admit they might.

"Well, I've never seen the likes of those markings before. Set from the inside out, I take it?"

I nod.

"They've only made it to the surface on your arms and hands, but they're woven throughout you."

"Can they be—unraveled?"

Kherbanu frowns. "I do not think so. What holds them all together appears to be the thread of your life."

I drop my gaze, shoving the rush of anguish I feel. It's no worse than I expected.

"I suppose you know perfectly well you're marked by both stone and fire," they say, pushing themself to their feet. I pass them their staff. "Absolute disaster of a child, aren't you? Where are your parents, if I might ask?"

"Dead or disowned," I answer. "Or both."

"Disowned by you?" Kherbanu asks.

"No," I say, the word catching in my throat. I push the thought of my mother away, and think instead of my uncle, and Laith, and find myself lifting my chin defiantly. "No," I repeat.

Kherbanu stands a long moment, looking at me. Then they stump over to open the door, motioning for me to follow. "I think you'll find the phoenix your friend yet."

CHAPTER 25
SHAPING A TALISMAN

The phoenix brought with him a variety of diamonds, the largest a bevel-edged jewel the size of my thumbnail. I turn it over once in my hand, aware I'm handling more wealth than I'm likely to ever see again in my life. There's a faint line of grime along the back edges—this diamond apparently had a setting not all that long ago. I wonder what it was plucked out of. My best guess is a crown. Or a scepter, I suppose.

"The rest are smaller," Kherbanu says, unceremoniously dumping out the remaining contents of a small velvet pouch onto the surface of their worktable. These diamonds are flat and straight edged—and all different shapes. Uncut diamonds, some as large as my pinky nail, looking like bits of broken glass. "We'll start with the smallest, and work our way up."

"Why isn't Eshvat here?" I ask, shifting on my stool.

"We agreed I am better at such work, and they are *terrible* at working with others. I should know; I had the bulk of their training. Now, pay attention." Kherbanu pulls around their stool to sit beside me, and then selects one of the smaller uncut diamonds and lays it out in an open space on the table. "A talisman is a vessel. We are simply adjusting its structure to store more magic than it currently holds."

I nod. Everything naturally holds a hint of magic—unless, of course, the draining spells have been at work. A talisman capital-izes on the crystalline structure of gemstones to allow for a greater weight of magic—a similarity to the draining spells and their ability to hold power that I had not previously considered. At any rate, diamonds have the strongest such structure, thereby creating the best vessel. Rubies and sapphires are not that much farther behind, but for our purposes, using the strongest vessel is the only risk worth taking.

The process is surprisingly simple. Kherbanu taps out five points of magic around the diamond and then sketches a sigil I've never seen before, the lines bright and steady in my mage sight. They then infuse the sigil into the stone, drawing on those five points of magic. Kherbanu remains still, their hands cupped around the stone until the stone itself glows, its structure meshing with the inflow of magic, and then everything fades away. It's... the opposite method to what the phoenix and I have developed in the Burnt Lands. Here, the flow of magic alters and strengthens the structure. There, we use an outpouring of fiery magic to over-whelm the structure until it softens and breaks down to join the flow.

Kherbanu wipes their brow with the edge of their sleeve. "Forgot how much effort that takes. Did you note the sigil?"

I shake my head. "I didn't recognize it, and I wouldn't be able to form it myself, regardless. I can only channel raw magic. I can't form it as I channel it."

"Try anyhow."

"I'd rather not. We can't afford to damage—"

"You won't harm the diamond if it doesn't work, child. Just *try* it."

I do. As expected, my efforts come to nothing, the thread of magic I channel unable to do more than loop over itself in infan-tile mimicry of the sigil.

Kherbanu grimaces, spits into their pot by the door, and creates a second sigil themself, this one a slap-dash, malformed affair. "Fine then," they tell me grimly, centering it over the diamond. "Fix that."

It takes four tries and a fair bit of swallowed curses, but I manage it. After all, I've been playing with spells for weeks now. A sigil is a little different, but in the end the idea is the same. This one is composed of sharp intersecting lines, not unlike the structure of the stones we are working with, only there are added connections, and some of the lines are broader. The end result is a complex, multi-edged sigil anchored by the cardinal points.

"Excellent," Kherbanu says. "Now, infuse it into the stone yourself."

"But—"

"Stop arguing!" they say, lifting their hands away before I'm quite ready.

I yelp and steady the sigil. "You might have warned me!"

They cast their gaze to the ceiling. "I did. Now, press the sigil down, and draw on those points of power I laid out for you."

I do, following their instructions as they walk me through meshing the sigil with the structure of the stone. It snaps together far more easily than I expected, the magic smooth and cool at my fingertips as the diamond absorbs it.

"I don't believe it," Kherbanu says testily. "It ought to have been harder than that."

"Why?"

"Because stone is" —they pause, looking at me, and finish brightly— "*exactly* what you are predisposed to work with! How very convenient. Here, we'll get these all done this afternoon, I'm sure, with energy to spare."

I cough on a laugh. Kherbanu immediately begins the next one and hands it off to me with an even sloppier sigil than before. By the time we get to the fifth one, they're barely doing more than forming the initial, shaky shape of it before passing it over to me. By the twelfth small talisman, I've broken a sweat, but I also can't remember being *this* excited to work. Because I'm doing it, I'm taking a half-formed mess of a spell and building off of it—even restructuring it—to complete it. The proof is piling up before me. It's a small spell—sigils are simple in structure by nature—but this is one more thing I thought I could never do again.

"Last one is the big one," Kherbanu says, sweeping the small talismans all together into their pouch once more. They walk over and pour a mug of water from a pitcher on a side table. "Have a drink first."

I take the proffered ceramic mug and quaff the water in three big gulps. I don't realize my hands are shaking until I set it down with a slight thump.

Kherbanu's brow furrows. "Are your markings worse?"

I shake my sleeves back to inspect my markings, then unbuckle a gauntlet to see them better. The markings are darker, as they often are after I've been working with magic, the skin around them faintly inflamed, impacting the colors I had inked. I flex my fingers, my skin tingling, but it isn't painful.

"It hurts you," Kherbanu notes, perturbed.

"A little, but not much. It's nothing like the first time, or even the first few."

They sit back, lips pursed. "Have you ever worked with another mage?"

I hesitate. "There was that mage who drew on me once before—the one I killed. They were going to use my magic to kill my companions."

Kherbanu's brows shoot up. "Not a friend, then. Anything else?"

"I've seen—I've seen a source slave after another mage drew on him. It hurt him a lot more than this. But... the phoenix and I thought that it had to do with choice. When the mage who attacked me took my magic by force, it felt like my arms were burning. But now, when I choose this work? It's just a little uncomfortable, and it's gotten easier since I first began trying."

Kherbanu rubs their mouth, stretching the soft skin of their face taut before letting go. "Would you channel to me once, to test that?"

"I'd rather not," I say lightly. "Anyhow, the phoenix needs that last talisman, doesn't he?"

"You and all your rathers—sometimes there are things that

need to be done whether one would rather or not." They sigh. "Another day, then. Ready?"

I nod.

Not twenty minutes later, Kherbanu passes me the finished talismans and tells me to take them to the phoenix myself. "Don't tell me you'd rather not. You're unlikely to see that fool bird again; you'd better give them a chance to make things right before they go. You might even give it a whirl yourself. Rewniz will escort you."

The next moment, Kherbanu shoos me out of their rooms into the custody of the ever-present Rewniz, with strict orders that they are to take me to the phoenix. I pocket the pouch of talismans and follow my escort.

I'm tired out, and while Kherbanu has managed to present various arguments to excuse, or at least explain, the phoenix's action, I'm still angry—and hurt. But if I never see him again, remembering that I went stalking out of the room in a haze of hurt and fury is not the ending note I want. Kherbanu is right. I'd rather part ways without feeling betrayed. Only I'm not quite sure that's possible.

Rewniz leads me along a set of hallways that look vaguely familiar, though it's likely just the band of carving and the style of doors. Then we take a stairwell up I've definitely never seen, and follow a short hallway only halfway down. Rewniz opens a door, poking their head in first before ushering me through to a small balcony overlooking the gorge. This one is higher up than where I met Arnaz, without access to the walkway and stream far below. Rather, one can see some distance along the gorge, the rock walls interspersed with balconies, the stone around them smoothed and carved with images of fantastical creatures interwoven with flowers and vines.

Plants in pots spill out along the edge of each balcony and line the balustrade of the phoenix's balcony. The phoenix himself perches on the back of a sturdy chair woven of thin wooden stems braided together. Its mate sits opposite him, with a small table in between. He opens his beak to greet me and then pauses as Rewniz steps back out again.

"Your talismans," I tell the phoenix, placing the pouch on the table.

"Will you sit?" he asks.

The words, *I'd rather not,* rest on the tip of my tongue, but Kherbanu's already taken me to task for them. At the same time, I don't *want* to sit. There's too much nervous energy running through me, and I'll end up just fidgeting in my seat. "I'll stay a little," I say, walking over to the balustrade instead. I turn and lean my back against it, watching the phoenix.

He shifts his weight from one foot to the other. "I apologize. I should have consulted with you before coming to the maran."

He should have *consulted* with me? "You mean, before you decided to leave me to lifelong captivity? You knew what I would have said."

The phoenix resettles his wings, sending a scattering of sparks to the ground. A pair land on the wooden chair. When they wink out, they leave two tiny black spots behind. "I did not truly believe you would need to enter the caves. But I thought that if you did, it would give you a chance to stop—to stop running, to breathe in safety, to put down roots and consider what you would like for a future, any future."

He sighs. "You are so young, child. Every step you take is dogged by hunters. But here, even if they manage to find you, Arnaz has promised they will not take you. There is nowhere else you can find such safety, not even in my own haven. Here you might have the chance to learn to live."

I nod slowly. It's the third impossibility. I just hadn't counted on the phoenix bargaining my freedom to achieve it. To him, safety is a cave hidden beneath the dangers of the world. Of course he would see nothing wrong with what he has chosen. It's misguided—an explanation but not an excuse—but it's still love.

"You should have discussed this with me," I tell him.

"I know." The phoenix bobs his head. "I feared for you, and

so I acted as I thought best. But I should not have taken that choice from you. Forgive me."

Why does he have to sound so reasonable? It makes it even worse that he knows me well enough to know that the safest place for me would be a place without a single fire to throw myself into, even if I wanted to. It's so *annoying*.

I turn around, glaring out over the gorge. The last rays of sunlight stretch out over the edge of the gorge, gilding the higher balconies in gold and reflecting off the stream far below. It's beautiful, which does not help my mood at all.

"You are young," the phoenix says, bringing up yet another exceedingly annoying line of argument. "Perhaps you have never made a decision for a friend, trying to help them or keep them safe. Perhaps you have never left them out of the choices you have made in order to protect them. I hope you never have to. I hope that if you ever do, you are wiser about it than I. You would think, after all these years, I would know how to handle such things. But I am only what I am. I ask your forgiveness, Hitomi."

His voice is achingly sweet, laden with centuries of small griefs. I stare out over the balustrade blindly, his words settling into me. Because I have done this. I hid my story and the dangers that followed me from Huda on our journey back to the desert. I slipped away from Kenta while he was trying to protect me, leaving him to return to Fidanya alone instead of accompanying me to the desert as he wished. Not because I didn't want his company, but because I thought I knew better what was right for him, and what he needed to do. I took away my friends' right to make their own choices because I thought I knew better, or I didn't want to risk their lives. But it was *their* lives at risk, and their right to choose. Perhaps if I were their guardian, the decision would be different. But they aren't children, and I had no right. If all of that was in just the last few weeks, chances are I have done it more than a few times in the life I don't remember.

"You're wrong," I say, turning to the phoenix. My voice is soft, a little too small. I clear my throat and try again, more clearly this time. "You're wrong. I've made this mistake too. I can hardly judge you for doing to me exactly what I've done to my friends."

The phoenix blinks. "Then there is space for forgiveness for both of us, I think."

I smile tiredly. "One can hope. For myself, I forgive you. Thank you for caring." I also won't trust him again, at least not as blindly as I did before, but I suppose that's how relationships are: complicated and flawed, however beautiful.

"Thank you," he tells me, his tone oddly formal. "You have given me hope when I thought there was little; companionship when I had grown used to emptiness. I am honored and grateful to have known you. I will never forget the days we have shared. I hope I will yet see you again."

That is something: that whatever I do to myself from here, whatever memories I might accidentally destroy, some part of me will live on with the phoenix. But more than that is the recognition of mistakes made, the deep ache of his voice when he speaks of hope and companionship, the realization that he acted out of friendship more than anything... this makes all the difference. I look across the balcony at him, and feel the urge once more to wrap my arms around him. Which—why not?

"I'm going to hug you," I tell him, starting forward.

He has just enough time to say, "What?" before I reach him and bend to wrap my arms around his warm feathered body. I don't pick him up, just hold him where he is, perched stiffly on the chair. His feathers are silky smooth and edged with a heat that doesn't quite burn me—perhaps because I am marked with fire, or perhaps because the phoenix has had half a breath to temper his heat. It doesn't matter. His body relaxes and he curves his neck around my shoulder, resting his head against the back of my neck. His breath releases in a soft sigh.

I hold this moment with me long after I end the embrace, long after I wish the phoenix farewell and let myself out, long after I return to my room to sit alone in the quiet. It is a moment I hope to hold with me for the rest of my life.

CHAPTER 26
A CELEBRATION OF FIRE

A trio of maran descend upon me no more than a half hour later, taking my measurements and chattering away in a mix of the desert tongue and their own language. The eldest, who—if the maran age as humans do—may only be a handful of years older than I, explains that there will be a feast in my honor. "We have brought clothes for you, and will help you prepare, yes? It will be so fun!"

I smile and nod and allow them to proceed, wishing Kherbanu had given me some warning. The one who spoke is named Tahmineh; they are tall and slim with dark brown hair with golden highlights. The other two maran's names I catch and lose, but they are both cheerful and industrious, and set to work altering the clothes they have brought along in order to fit me as well as possible.

In short order, I find myself outfitted in a pair of flowing cream shalvar edged in black, with a long-sleeved tunic with an upright collar worked in yellow embroidery. It seems to be a fancier version of the standard base layer among the maran—further, the shalvar bears a striking resemblance in name and design to the selvar worn by the local population of Fidanya, though there is definitely some variation at play.

This base layer is topped with a matching yellow jacket with

embroidery down the front edges. I pull the jacket on gratefully—
it is of a thicker fabric and will hopefully do a better job of
keeping me warm than my thobe has. At my waist, Tahmineh
binds a bright crimson sash with yellow tassels and a hint of black
embroidery; it brings the whole outfit together. Finally, they help
me tie up a matching turban—a soft cream accented with yellow
and red embroidery.

The mystery of all these fabrics—when there is nowhere to
properly farm what would be needed to make them, and the
maran are utterly isolated here—is one I can at least poke at. I
reach up to brush the fabric of my turban with my fingers. "This
is so soft," I exclaim, not even having to act. "What is it made of?"

"Oh, it is—ah," the young maran cuts themself off, glancing
about at their companions for help.

Tahmineh offers a reassuring smile. "It's all right. I'm sure our
friend will learn our ways soon enough." They turn to me. "It is
cotton—very fine. My family, and Gul's," they indicate the maran
who first spoke, "we are gatherers. Our best gatherers make trips
to trade for the things we cannot make here."

"You do what?" I say, taken aback.

"We, ah, travel? To get supplies?" Tahmineh says, forehead
wrinkling.

So they *do* leave, and regularly at that. That might be something I can use as I plan my escape. I reply as casually as I can, "I
have heard of people disappearing into the caves, but not of
anyone leaving them."

Tahmineh winces. "Our mages can create—what do you call
them? Spells to change our looks? So we cannot be recognized."

"Glamors," I say, nodding. "What of the desert folk who have
come here in the past? Sought shelter in your caves?"

The maran exchange a concerned look. Tahmineh says, finally,
"We have only had a few such people enter our caves. Mostly we
try to scare them away. Perhaps you might ask Sovereign Arnaz
more about them?"

I've gotten more information from Tahmineh in the last three
minutes than in my multiple meetings with Arnaz. Still, I don't

want Tahmineh to regret their openness. "Of course," I say with a cheerful smile. I'll just circle back with more or different questions later.

Tahmineh, happy to have escaped such a fraught subject, helps their companions open up a stiff, flat-bottomed bag they have brought. Together, they remove a number of small pots—makeup, if I'm not mistaken.

"Will you keep your arm covers on?" Tahmineh asks, indicating my gauntlets.

"No," I say. They will shout that I am hiding something at an affair like this, where they will be terribly out of place—and where no one is likely to know what my markings are anyway. I push up my sleeves and unstrap the gauntlets, drawing gasps of delight from the maran as they see the mix of markings and inkings on my arms, from the flame-colored firebird on my inner arms, to the amethyst and cobalt touched inkings on the backs of my hands.

"Oh, those *are* lovely," Tahmineh breathes. "You must show them to my mother's sibling! They are an ink artist. If you would like?"

I blink and find myself smiling. "I would like that."

Tahmineh turns happily back to the makeup. While they apply kohl to my eyes, Gul does the same for the other maran, and then they switch, that we might all be ready together. After the kohl, there is a reddening ointment for our lips, and creams to hide blemishes. I cannot remember taking part in anything like this before—being part of a gathering of young people, readying ourselves in pretty clothes and makeup for a coming festivity. My uncle's family threw a feast for us, and between the food and stories it was a marvelous affair, but Huda and I merely attended it as we were.

But despite the cheerful company of these young maran, and all they are doing to make me feel welcome, I feel desperately alone. Because this feast is still different in another way. It is being held in my honor, yes, but I am as much a captive as the desert folk Tahmineh will not speak of. I too will never be given the privilege of leaving these caves of my own choice—a privilege they grant at least some of their own.

The maran with me now are wonderfully amiable, their intentions kind, but none of it can be truly deep or genuine so long as I remain a prisoner here. Nor can I find joy in preparing for a feast being held to celebrate my imprisonment.

MY MARAN COMPANIONS lead the way down the halls to the feast, my assigned guards trailing behind us. We pass a few groups of maran, all dressed for the occasion. None of the simpler clothing I saw earlier is visible now. Even the most modest of families seem to have a set of clothing for celebrations.

Eventually, we reach a large set of doors at the end of a wider hall. These doors are full wood, ornately carved and inlaid with metal in a gorgeous curving geometric pattern reminiscent of interwoven vines.

"We call this the Great Hall," Tahmineh tells me, opening the door and ushering me in.

And great it is: a huge cavern, stalactites wider around than the trunks of hundred-year-old trees hang down from the soaring ceiling, each of them hollowed out and carved into natural chandeliers, golden glowstones shining from their depths. More glowstones have been placed in carved nooks all along the stone walls in dizzying patterns of swirls and waves. The ground underfoot has been smoothed out and laid with a mosaic in another geometric pattern with interwoven floral elements. The tiles are so polished they reflect back the light of the glowstones.

A central aisle has been cleared to the other end of the hall. On each side, multiple rows of cushions have been laid out to flank fabric runners on which the food will be placed. There must be enough space to seat five hundred comfortably. The hall is already half full, some of the guests sitting, others leaving behind an item to claim their spot before crossing the aisles to greet friends and loved ones. The maran themselves are a whirl of color, from their embroidered jackets to the bright scape of turbans and caps.

Taken together, the hall is breathtaking, utterly different from anything I've seen before while also strangely familiar. I stand for a moment gawping before I realize my escort is waiting patiently. I offer Tahmineh a sheepish grin, but they and their companions are beaming: if I wanted to pay them a compliment, I couldn't have chosen a better reaction.

"Look, there is—how do you say? Sheikha Kherbanu," Tahmineh says and leads us up the aisle to the dais at the other end. Here, a series of low tables have been set side by side to cross the width of the dais, with cushions on the far side, allowing the nobility to see across the whole hall.

Kherbanu stands among a knot of maran in exquisite clothing. Their overlayers are made of silky brocades with repeating patterns picked out in embroidery at the lower hems. While some wear turbans, others have opted for a small cap, some with an added silken scarf pinned to hang down their backs. They smile and nod at us. Despite their gorgeous clothing, it is their eyes that stand out, the slit pupil particular to the maran as striking as the colors of their irises—amber and gold and bright green alongside the more familiar brown, though even the brown holds glints of gold and amber.

This seems like such an incredible society, and for the first time it occurs to me to wonder *why* they have hidden themselves away. It seems a shame that no one else might meet them, and that they may only know their own people... and those they have taken captive. Though even here, I see no sign of any other humans, no glimpse of any desert folk.

"Welcome," Kherbanu says, dipping their head toward me.

I return the gesture, and Kherbanu introduces me to their companions. All five are adults, though none seem to be quite as old as Kherbanu themself. I store their names away, smiling politely, deeply aware of how keenly they inspect me.

"Will the phoenix join us as well?" one of them asks hopefully.

"I'm afraid not," Kherbanu answers for me—which is good, since I had no idea. "He has already left to see to some work of his, but if that is successful, we may yet hope to welcome them back with a feast."

Yes, he will be busy now, between brokering alliances among the tribes, gathering the mages, and ensuring Eshvat's safe travel. I am glad Kherbanu gave me the chance to make my peace with him before he left.

"How do you find our home?" one of the others asks, a shrewd-eyed, middle-aged maran whose jacket makes me think of a peacock, from the shimmering emerald of the brocade, to the paisley designs picked out in blues and greens and creams. Zohan, Kherbanu had named them.

"It is marvelous," I tell them. "Not what I expected when I first took shelter here—though I did not know what to expect."

They laugh, but the sound has an edge to it. "No," they agree. "We are not generally expected."

I consider them, thinking back over the architecture and mosaics and carvings I've seen here, and where I've seen the closest similarities. There was the Mekteb with its arched walkways and mosaic-lain entryways. But before that... "I think that I have seen some aspects of your architecture among the old ruins of the Burnt Lands."

A third maran, quiet till now, perks up—a gawky, long-limbed person with an unusually earnest expression. "I am curious about the differences you might have noticed," they say, happily ignoring the grimaces that break out around them. "I have worked to make a study of our history, and—"

"Perhaps after dinner?" Kherbanu interrupts, rather mildly for their usual tone. "Sovereign Arnaz is entering, you see. We will need to take our places."

The maran immediately bobs their head. "Whenever you are free," they tell me.

I nod in response. It *would* be interesting to discuss such things, in large part to gain a sense of the history of these people.

Kherbanu's group breaks up, and Tahmineh and the younger

maran take their leave as well. Kherbanu leads me over to our places at the table on the dais. At the far end of the room, Arnaz has entered with a small entourage, including what I assume are a handful of nobles as well as, unsurprisingly, Mage Eshvat. They make their way to the nobles' table, and Arnaz takes their place at the center of the table, pausing only to smile and nod to me and bid me welcome in a voice that naturally carries across the dais. Once they seat themself on their own impressively ornate cushion with an additional back support, we settle ourselves.

Arnaz has placed us only three cushions over to their right—a position of high respect without actually putting us beside them. Kherbanu settles themself with a grunt beside me. I spot Eshvat on the other side of Arnaz, only one cushion over from them. To my other side is an elder maran who nods kindly at me, wordlessly pats my hand, and turns their attention elsewhere. When they speak, it is to their other neighbor, and in their own tongue.

Turning to Kherbanu, I ask when the phoenix will circle back for Eshvat. "They leave at dawn," Kherbanu tells me. "Why? Do you intend to try to follow them?"

"No. I have no wish to travel to the Burnt Lands again," I say honestly. I'd love to see them restored, but I have no wish whatsoever to go haring through the spell-cursed Lands as they stand, hoping I'll survive the next hour.

"Good," Kherbanu says. "That's at least one step in the direction of wanting to live."

I huff a laugh. "I am not as bad as all that."

"Mmm," Kherbanu says, lowering their voice to a bare murmur. "Might I add that, while you are hunted, you may as well stay here. Once your hunters give you up for dead, you'll have rather more chance of surviving."

I tip my head to the side, acknowledging their argument. The phoenix had promised to tell my friends I would not be coming back to the well to meet them, which means no one is waiting for me. There is no harm in waiting, though I am not sure Raven-flight will give me up so easily. Especially not after the phoenix tore her away at the moment she found me.

Kherbanu adds, casually, "In fact, there is a mage wandering around the outside of our caves, just now."

"What?" I ask, startled. I glance across the hall toward the great doors, as if Ravenflight might come sweeping through them at any moment.

"There's no need to worry," Kherbanu says, patting my hand. "We've had more than one mage come poking around our home before. We have our methods for keeping them out."

I nod, glancing down to my hands with their markings. The phoenix chose this place precisely because the maran have successfully hidden here for centuries. I can take heart from that, and from the fact that Kherbanu is clearly unworried, sitting beside me at a feast. Still, some part of me remains tense. I won't feel better until I know this mage is gone—and if it *is* Ravenlflight, I'm not at all convinced she'll leave without proof that I am no longer here. Nor am I sure how Kherbanu or Arnaz can give her that.

I look up as a servant sets the first course before me: a savory fish soup. A trio of musicians take up a quiet melody, providing a haunting score for our meal. I do not recognize their instruments, though they are generally familiar: a stringed instrument not unlike a mandolin, a woodwind that somehow looks more like a trumpet, but for its flutelike holes for the fingers, and a handheld drum.

We work our way through course after course—first the soup, then a modest salad of fresh herbs and lettuce topped with thin slices of a deep-fried root vegetable that reminds me of potato but bears a hint of sweetness. After this comes a spread of seasoned rice served with roasted mushrooms and vegetables at the high dais, though I note the rice does not make it to the rest of the hall. It is all delicious, and I am happy to split my attention between the food, the music, and observing my hosts. Kherbanu makes the occasional comment to me, but mostly their focus is on the maran down table.

The maran speak in their own tongue, but now that I can give it my full attention, I can pick out words here and there that have the sound of the desert tongue. Not all of them make sense: the repeated mention of dwellings, and the much grimmer allusion to sunshine must mean something in context that I cannot suss out on my own. This haven of the maran is a whole world of its own, one with politics at play of which I have no understanding.

I turn to Kherbanu, and ask in a whisper, "It sounds like they are discussing sunshine, but... sunshine as a person?"

Kherbanu snorts. "You've keen ears, haven't you?" They lean toward me. "A sunshiner is a maran who believes we need to bring our people back out into the light, leaving the caves and making our existence known again. A dweller, on the other hand, thinks we are best protected and served by remaining as we have been."

I raise my brows. "What is your stance?"

Kherbanu purses their lips, eyes bright. "*Mmm*. I serve our sovereign, as you know."

I am quite certain Kherbanu does nothing they don't want to.

"Is Sovereign Arnaz a dweller, then?" I ask, keeping my voice low.

"Of course. Else they risk losing some of their power. Right now, everything and everyone who enters or leaves must go through them. Every resource we have is assigned at the end by them, even if we have committees and a council to make such decisions. It is in their best interest to keep things as they are. So, here we are," Kherbanu says, gesturing to the great hall with its mosaics and stalagmite chandeliers, "dwelling beneath our rock."

"Careful, honored one," the maran from their other side says. "There are many keen ears here."

Does *everyone* listen in on each other's conversations?

Kherbanu shakes a finger at them, and I catch a glimpse of peacock colors. "I've no worries about that, Zohan. I've a measure of our guest, and they bring nothing with them if not chaos. I am quite looking forward to what they will do for us."

Oh, certainly, first Kherbanu tells me I should want to live, then they hope I'll end up in the midst of their own personal bonfire. Which I probably will, intentionally or not. But really, how can I be blamed for what Kherbanu is planning?

Zohan sits forward, their bright green gaze moving from Kherbanu to me. "Really? You are a mage, yes?"

Kherbanu smirks. "We don't need magic for sunshine, do we?"

Zohan eyes them shrewdly. "We get it from glowstones now, so yes, we do. But what do *you* think our guest will do?"

They get sunshine from *glowstones*? I glance out across the hall, taking in the golden light spilling from the stalagmites and wall niches, so different from the pale white light I am used to. Sunshine. That's *brilliant*.

"I've no idea," Kherbanu says in answer to Zohan, "and I don't expect them to tell me either, but I've certain hopes we'll see the sunlight yet."

I force my attention back to the conversation. "I didn't come here to play at politics," I say carefully, wondering if it is even possible to stay out of this fire. Or if I want to—because if walking in the sunshine means not only that the maran will come out, but that their prisoners will be freed.... I try not to sigh. I am so *very* tired. While I care about the people here, I can't find the energy to think further than that.

Zohan exchanges an amused look with Kherbanu. "Everything is politics," they tell me. "Your being here, your simple existence, it's all political." They shift their attention to Kherbanu. "We have had important guests join our ranks before, and nothing has changed. Why would it now?"

"This time is different," Kherbanu says comfortably. "As you are so fond of proverbs, I will remind you that seh raahi vaalii chahaar maeshoohah."

They turn their attention back to me and huff a laugh at my befuddled look. "It means there are three ways but four beloved ones. Work it out, child."

Three ways? Four beloveds? I have *no* idea.

Fortunately, Zohan takes pity on me. "It means that though there are different ways to do something, in the end, it also depends on *who* is involved."

That makes sense. It is not just what you know, or what you

plan, but who you know—who gives you their support. Which—yes, I've learned the truth of that often enough. Between escaping Kol with Val, and escaping the Mekteb with the help of a whole crew of people, but especially Osman Bey and the phoenix.... It was the beloved ones, ones whom I had really only just met but who gave me their trust, that made the difference.

In an undertone, Kherbanu tells Zohan, "This time, we have the opportunity to establish ourselves as offering aid to our neighbors in need through the intervention of the phoenix. It is not an opportunity that is likely to come again."

Zohan tilts their head. "Offering aid?" they echo, the words slow and careful, as if they're not sure they heard Kherbanu right.

Kherbanu tsks softly. "Did Arnaz not consult the Convocation? What *will* they think?"

Zohan sets their spoon down, glancing toward an approaching servant who brings the next course. "Let us speak again in private."

"Yes, of course," Kherbanu says, waving a last mushroom toward the other end of the hall. "The dancing is about to start."

I watch avidly as a line of dancers sweep in through the great doors, taking up position in the center of the hall. The first set, staggered across the wide aisle, are ostensibly facing the dais. But a second set lines up behind them, facing each side. They are dressed similarly to me, with a gorgeously embroidered overlayer, but theirs is light and silken, with a lovely flow and flare. The under tunic has a matching wide skirtlike flare and goes nearly to their ankles—but sports long slits that become apparent as they begin to move. Their pants underneath are slim, accenting the shape of their legs, and they wear circlets on each ankle that tinkle with the sound of bells as they move. In lieu of turbans, they wear matching caps with long drapes of silken fabric hanging from the back.

The musicians strike up the first number, and the dancers begin to sway, moving in graceful fluid motions so that hardly a single bell sounds, the hands and arms moving in intricate patterns. This dance is all subtlety and elegance, the flow of their clothes emphasizing their movements in gentle sweeps and shifts.

The next dance takes full advantage of the tinkling anklets the dancers wear. They begin slowly but, as the dance progresses, move faster and faster in synchronized sweeps, stamping and twirling to create a ringing accompaniment to the musicians' offerings. The dancers reach out their hands to each other, touching fingers, then brushing shoulders, then dancing hand in hand as the song crescendos.

"This dance is a celebration of fire. It is, after all, a source of heat, warmth, and provision," Kherbanu tells me softly. "As you have fire in your blood, perhaps you may feel the resonance."

I nod, watching the final twirling, stamping, connected rush of life before me, and think of the fire that lives within me, the stone that has marked me as well, the combination I have used within the Burnt Lands to try to end the spells there, to bring life. I have never thought of fire as life-giving. It has been an instrument of death for me, of self-immolation and killing. But here is another story, and I want nothing more than to feel fire as these dancers portray it, with love and light and life.

CHAPTER 27

VENOM

I wake to the sudden, harsh jangling of chimes, sometime in the late morning. I roll to my feet from the divan, one hand grabbing my gauntlets from beside my pillow.

Rewniz shoves open the door, their face grim. "Forgive the intrusion, but Sovereign Arnaz will see you. At once."

"All right," I say, strapping on my gauntlets, aware that something has gone wrong. The phoenix and Eshvat should already have left—I heard the morning chimes some time ago and drifted back to sleep to make up for my late night. But if it hasn't to do with them.... "What's happened?"

Rewniz shakes their head. "Come," they say and pivot on their heel, striding down the hall. I follow, hurrying to catch up. The two guards from outside my door fall into step behind me.

"It's the mage who was hunting me last night, isn't it?" I ask, my stomach sinking.

Rewniz glances over their shoulder to the guards behind us. They don't speak the desert tongue, and perhaps that's enough to allow them to answer, "It is. We have not been able to convince him that you are not here."

Dread twists in my gut. "Is it a woman mage with dark hair?" I ask, knowing better than to assume "him" means it's a male. "She calls herself Ravenflight?"

"That's the one," they agree and pick up their pace. "We cannot afford for him to come any deeper than she has. Nor can we take such a one prisoner—it is dangerous in its own right, and their disappearance would only bring more mages down on us."

I should have known Ravenflight wouldn't be shaken quite so easily, no matter how sure the maran are of their wards, or how far the phoenix carried her.

We follow a maze of tunnels that grow progressively narrower and rougher. Rewniz pulls out a golden glowstone to light our way as we travel further out towards the exterior caves. To where Ravenflight waits.

I press forward to match their step. "Does your sovereign plan to give me up?"

Rewniz clears their throat. "We are playing a game for your life," they say, tone neutral. "It has its risks."

Most games do when you're playing against mages.

"You will need to play along," they add, meeting my gaze.

"I'll do my best," I promise. "Thank you for telling me."

They don't speak further, nor can I read anything into the silence. My fingers close on the splintered stub in my pocket, all that is left of the crow statuette. I have nothing to protect myself with if Arnaz loses their game—or decides to give me up—but surely they wouldn't? Not when they have promised the phoenix to shelter me?

If only I knew how honor worked among these people, I would have some idea of the risks I'm running. But I don't—and I can't guess at what point danger to their home may outweigh harboring a fugitive, no matter what debts might be owed or promises given. What do the maran prize most? Loyalty? Family? Whatever it is, without knowing for sure, I'm not going to be able to speak to it now.

Abruptly, Rewniz comes to a stop, holding up a hand. I wait, listening as the two warriors behind us stop as well. They are perhaps ten paces back, as if waiting there to catch me if I try to run.

Rewniz puts out the glowstone, plunging the tunnel into

darkness. It takes a moment for my eyes to adjust, and then I can see the brightness at the end of the tunnel.

Rewniz turns, silhouetted by the light filtering in. "Come."

I grip the wooden shard of the crow statuette in my pocket, its rough edges biting into my palm, and start walking again.

I know I'm walking into trouble. I know it from the way Rewniz watches me, gauging each step. They are worried I'll run. Whatever future lies around the bend ahead—whatever game it is Arnaz is playing—it is not something I want to face, and they know it. As do I, because what waits for me is Ravenflight, with the life and death of a source slave in her hands.

I take a slow, steady breath. Val's not going to be able to help me outrun this, nor do I want to necessarily turn tail and run through the warren of tunnels behind me—that would only lead to more trouble. This is something I need to face. The maran tried to shelter me; it is no fault of their own that they did not understand what hunted me, that all they have left is a game to play, one last bid to keep me alive and imprisoned, but not enslaved.

So.

I raise my chin, give Rewniz a smile that feels old before it ever touches my lips, and stride past them around the corner.

"Ravenflight," I say, my voice confident, carrying across to the other end of the cave where she stands, tall and braced for trouble. Her robes are a nondescript gray in the light of the pale glowstone she has set down beside her. We are still not at the exit—Rewniz was right that she has progressed deeper. I take three more steps before turning my head to look straight at Arnaz where they stand, flanked by a pair of warriors, one of whom also bears a pale white glowstone.

Arnaz looks nothing like royalty now. Their fine clothes have been replaced with a desert thobe and pants, a leather belt at their waist with an old saber, and all but their eyes obscured by a mottled and stained kufiyah. What Arnaz looks like—what all the maran look like—are a group of bandits who have taken the caves as their shelter, relying on the place's reputation to keep the tribes away.

"Is this the child you seek?" Arnaz asks in the desert tongue, glancing from me to my hunter. Their pupils appear perfectly rounded, a glamor so delicate not even Ravenflight has caught it.

"Yes," Ravenflight says. She carries herself with the honed grace of a warrior, dark hair bound back tightly. Her hands, lifted slightly away from her side, are holding a spell at the ready—perhaps it is even a binding spell meant especially for me.

"What will you do with her?" Arnaz asks. "You say she has done wrong. What is her fate at your hands?"

"I will return her to the High Council of Mages," Ravenflight says, voice neutral.

"Before or after you bind me as your source slave?" I ask lightly.

Her answer is smooth, but I catch the flicker in her eyes. "I will do what is necessary."

"Against a child?" Arnaz queries. "That seems harsh. What child deserves slavery?"

"I—did not choose this," Ravenflight says. For the first time, I hear a note of uncertainty in her voice.

"You are to be my master," I retort. "You *chose* that."

"At the behest of others," Ravenflight agrees, meeting my gaze. "I think perhaps because I do not *wish* to have a slave."

"So what? You'll still be my master, and you'll still use me if I'm there."

"Someone will have to be your master," Ravenflight says steadily. "At least I do not intend to harm you."

"Just enslave him," Arnaz agrees, earning a sharp look from Ravenflight... because they gendered me wrong in a tongue that should have been their first. Oh dear. Arnaz continues, "There's no harm in slavery, it would seem?"

Ravenflight grimaces. "There is little choice here. The girl must come with me and face the punishment the Council has ruled for her. The Council will not stop, nor will I, until she is in their custody and her sentence has been completed."

Arnaz tilts their head, considering.

It is possible I have only this moment to escape. A vision of another mage flickers before my mind's eye, collapsed on the ground, eyes unseeing. There is an escape. There is always an escape. But I would rather have another option.

I take a slow breath and let my senses expand. There is the glow of magic about Ravenflight's hands. I can hear a faint rustle as one of the warriors shifts, can sense the warmth of the desert air flowing into the cave. The light beyond is bright and golden, a thing of this moment and yet as lasting as the greatest of human monuments. But for all that, I sense no other escape.

"I am afraid it must be your choice," Arnaz says to me. "You have before you slavery at the hands of this person who claims they will not harm you. What shelter I can offer you in turn is only what we have here: to be buried beneath a rock. What is your choice?"

I meet their gaze. *Buried beneath a rock.* I have to trust now, trust that Kherbanu used these same words to Arnaz, that to the maran it means survival. They need to provide a body, and I must trust what Rewniz offered in telling me they were playing a game. They will fake my death and "bury" me beneath the Howling Caves to live with them. I raise my chin and say, "I would choose shelter over slavery, no matter if I never saw the sun again. Wouldn't you?"

Ravenflight takes a quick half-step forward, expression sharpening. "Our agreement was that you would hand over the girl alive."

Arnaz murmurs something in an undertone, eyes hard as jewels as they meet my gaze. Then they turn back to Ravenflight.

"Agreement?" They flick their fingers. "You said you were seeking the girl, dead or alive."

A hand grasps my right arm. I turn my head just as something pierces my biceps, a bare finger's breadth from my nearly healed wound. I swallow my cry, a small choked sound that doesn't carry, as Rewniz releases me. Cupped in their hand to hide it from Ravenflight's sight, they hold a tiny leather bag, no bigger than my thumb. It ends in a snake's fang.

I stare at it. The pain in my arm is already fading, replaced by a stab of cold that shoots up my arm and pierces my lungs. Wait, this was supposed to be a game. Rewniz *told me* to play along. I'm not supposed to die now—did they think I was asking for that? Surely, I didn't read Arnaz's question so completely wrong?

Ravenflight says something, voice sharp, but I don't catch her words. I look up to Arnaz. The cold wraps around my heart, my lungs already so heavy I can barely breathe, and then shoots out through my arteries, riding through my blood like fire formed of ice. I don't want to die. I didn't *mean* that. There's no coming back from death, and I haven't figured out yet how to live, how to love my life. I can't die *now*.

Ravenflight takes a step toward me, brow furrowed as she realizes she's missed something. The binding spell in her hands winks out. My legs fail, spilling me sideways toward the ground—only, Rewniz is there and lowers me down gently. Ravenflight surges forward, but Arnaz's warriors slide into the space between us, swords drawn. They cannot fight a mage, but perhaps they do not need to—they just need to slow her.

"It's too late," Arnaz says, their voice clear and ringing. "The venom is lethal, and she is already lost. This meets your approval, yes?"

"*No.*" Ravenflight pushes past the first of the warriors. "Step away—I may be able to help her."

"She does not require your help," Arnaz says coolly. "She chose this. You heard him yourself."

I can no longer blink; my eyes are frozen open. My lips harden, the cold a numbing fire that takes away my life heartbeat by heartbeat. I cannot feel, cannot move my lungs to breathe—I have been frozen from the inside out. Darkness grows at the edges of my vision. I don't want it, don't want this death that I chose by accident. *I don't want it.*

I shove my consciousness back, away from my eyes, as I used to slip sideways when I shared my body with Val, and I find myself slipping out altogether. It is as easy as stepping out of water, my skin still damp, only there is my body before me, laid out upon the ground, Rewniz crouched beside me. My eyes are open, glazed and unseeing.

I'm dead.

"We will bury her in the caves," Arnaz says, their voice strangely distant even as it comes easily to my ears. "As she wished."

No, no, no. That's *not* what I wished. I've gotten this all wrong, and now I'm dead for it. Rewniz *said* it was a game.

Ravenflight drops to her knees beside my body, reaching out to press her fingers against my throat, seeking a pulse. She snatches her hand back. "She's frozen!"

"Yes," Arnaz says. "The poison turns the blood to ice. What other proof do you require?"

Ravenflight doesn't answer. She bends her head, her lips moving, then reaches out and tries to close my eyes.

"It won't work."

"She was hardly more than a child," Ravenflight snaps, turning on Arnaz. "What would she know of death, to choose it?"

"Perhaps she knew enough of slavery, to know better than to choose that," Arnaz says. "You were the one who made that her only choice."

But I might have *escaped* slavery. If only Kherbanu hadn't spoken of their living here as being buried—if I hadn't read Arnaz's words as such, I could have chosen differently.

And now I'm dead.

It's not scary—even now, I don't fear death. Perhaps I never have. I have seen a soul rise from a prison of blood magic, and I *know* this isn't my end. There is something past all this, there is some order to the universe, some power I can trust in.

But this is the end of everything here for me. I was just starting to think about what I wanted for myself, what such a future might look like. Now I will not have that: not the family I have only just found, not the days I could've filled with memories, not anything I could've been.

Ravenflight says, her voice strangely pained, "I demanded the girl alive."

"You said you wanted her alive, and if that were not possible, you wished to see her body. There it is."

I don't want to hear anymore. I slide away from the cave, my heart aching—even though it is also somehow frozen below me. I float into the sunlight. It is bright and beautiful out here, the desert stark and yet bursting with life—thin blades of grass on the hills, thorn bushes raising their needled branches, a sand salamander sunning itself on a rock, and a pair of scorpions there, facing each other in a silent standoff. I don't want this to be the end—I want to still be a part of the beauty of this world, even with all the pain of my life, *especially* with all the years I've burned away. It's not fair that I cannot even bring with me the years I've lost now. I have only one year of living left to me. It isn't enough. Even if I had the rest, it still wouldn't be enough.

Ravenflight steps out from the cave below, crossing the sands to the pair of camels waiting by the far hills, a second person squatting by their side—her guide, no doubt. She stands by her camel, head bowed, and does not move to mount. Her companion rises, shifting uncertainly from foot to foot while they wait. Is she sorry? Well, so am I. I don't want to be here, a spirit upon the wind, my body lost to me, mourning the life I could have had. I want to be *living*.

I don't know what has tethered me to the earth still. The spirit I saw rising from the blood sigil in Kol's tower seemed to know exactly where it was going. I am—just here. I can sense my body faintly, a vessel I was once intrinsically connected to, but as I concentrate, I find I can feel something else as well. A faint pull on me, no more than an eddy in the air currents around me, and yet I'm sure of it.

With no other focus, I turn and follow the pull across the desert sands.

THE WORLD DISAPPEARS in a blur of bright light and golden

earth that deepens to green until finally I slide to a stop atop a horse.

I blink.

No, not me, but the eyes I look through. I feel a rush of relief so deep it staggers me. *Val?*

Hitomi? He startles, one hand darting out to grasp the saddle. *What's wrong?* he asks urgently.

He must have picked up on my relief. *I'm just really glad to see you,* I tell him. Being able to say goodbye to him seems so important now, but I don't want to do it yet. Surely, I have a few minutes?

Why were you looking for me? Val asks, and I can sense his worry, the edge of fear to his thoughts.

I look about keenly through his eyes. Unfortunately, I don't recognize the rolling fields interspersed with groves of trees. It could just as easily be the land outside Fidanya as the wide fertile plateau leading up to the mountains where Stormwind made her home. At least he's left the portal town with its mages behind.

Hitomi? Val prods, that fear suddenly sharp and cutting. He's afraid for *me? How did you find me? Where are you now?*

I went for a walk, I say, trying to smooth things over. *You said I should try it sometime.*

I'm relatively certain I said nothing *of the sort.*

I'm going to miss this friendship, how easy it is to talk to Val. Even when I'm keeping secrets.

Why are you still traveling? I ask, cutting off his next question. *And don't tell me some rubbish about how you often travel.*

Val hesitates. *My prince asks it of me.*

I wonder if Val can tell when I try to hide something as easily as I can when he does. *Did your prince send you to find me?*

He sighs. It's strange, a detached sense of his chest rising and falling. But I can also sense his regret, as if this were something he hadn't wanted to admit quite yet.

You can tell me, I say softly.

A pause.

He's concerned that you may inadvertently betray me to the

Council—especially if they use force. If that happens, I cannot be near our home.

No, that would betray all his people to the Council. If I had eyes, I would close them. Instead, I merely rest there, still and unmoving, wishing I could undo all these things I've set in motion.

He's exiled you, I say for Val.

I can return with you, or.... He shrugs.

Or after I die, I supply.

You'll live a long while yet.

I suspect he's trying to comfort me, but I find I don't like it at all. *I'm pretty certain I just died.*

Val tenses, his hand jerking on the reins. The horse snorts, shaking its head in response. *The hell you did,* he snaps. *That's not possible. Where are you, and what the hell is happening now?*

He's *furious.* I can hear it in his voice, feel it in the coil of his body. I didn't quite expect that. *I'm sorry. I just—I made a mistake.*

So help me, if these allies of the phoenix have done something to you—

They did, I admit, and then plow on quickly, *But I think it was my fault. They were asking me one question, and I thought they meant something else.*

Hitomi, where are you right now?

He's going to come get me, or my body. Even though he's only one person, I'm pretty sure he'll be able wreak a significant amount of havoc. I don't want him fighting Kherbanu, or even Rewniz, who told me to play a game that cost me my life. Only...

Why isn't it possible that I'm dead? I demand, which seems like the most pressing question, really.

Because you're here, talking to me, Val says impatiently. *Once one of us dies, the bond is broken. You don't just,* he waves his free hand before him, *float about visiting people. You go on to the next life.*

He's right. If I were standing, I would sag with relief. As it is, I feel like I'm melting further into Val, except he's all tense muscles and wrath.

Hitomi, I am only asking one more time, and then I'm coming to find you one way or the other. Where are you? And what *happened?*

I don't think I've ever seen him this angry. *Ravenflight found me,* I explain quickly. *The people I took shelter with injected a poison of some sort into me, because I told them I'd rather be buried beneath a rock than be a slave.*

Are you— Why would you say that?

Because they *live under a rock!! I thought they meant they'd fake my death to trick Ravenflight into leaving! I don't want to die; I want to live. I just—I haven't figured out how.*

The truth of that admission hurts, especially saying it to someone else, to someone who knows me so well. I feel shaky and small, and so indescribably sad. Because how can a person not know how to live? How did I forget this? How does one lose something so vital, something they must have been born with, and not recover that from the ashes when they burn everything else away? I don't just want to burn; I don't want every fate I choose to become a fire that will consume me.

Val takes a slow breath, pressing down on his anger, and the fear that is shaping it. Because he *is* afraid for me—beneath all that anger and then fear is a quiet sort of love for me, the wayward child he has given a part of his life to, and whom he wants to see live and thrive. The truth of it wraps around me, warming me, as if I were cradled against his soul.

In that way, he's not so different from the phoenix. That anger and fear is because he too wants to protect me—from myself, from my decisions. Perhaps he didn't bury me beneath the rocks, but he did take me to a remote mountain valley to study under a mage who had isolated herself from the wider world. He just didn't predict the world coming after her. Since then, all he has done is try to give me another chance to live, time after time.

Val says, with a gentleness at odds with the emotions I can feel him battling, *Perhaps they did understand you. You are not dead, and not all poisons kill. Some just paralyze. Will you tell me where your body is now?*

I owe him that much, even if I don't want him to come walking through the tunnels to fetch me, leaving a handful of mesmerized maran in his wake. Although he clearly isn't near the desert, at least not yet, so there's some safety in that. *I'm at the Howling Caves, near the lands of the Bani Essam,* I tell him. *But I don't want you to come here yet. Let me find out what's really happened first.*

I will check on you shortly, he says, without making any promises whatsoever. I have to hope he means he'll visit me as he has before, through our bond, not in person.

I can come back to you, I offer.

If your body is weak, it's best for you to stay with it.

Makes sense. *I'll call you, then,* I tell him. *When it's safe for you to visit.*

Make sure you do soon, then, he says. For all his attempts at gentleness, there is a hardness to his voice he can't quite disguise, the anger and fear coalescing. *Else I will check on you whether you call me or not.*

I'll call you, I promise. *Thank you.*

I slip from him easily enough, eagerly following the faint hint of a connection I still have with my body—because I *am* alive, and however much that might hurt, I cannot wait to reclaim myself.

The world blurs past, and for just a moment I catch a glimpse of myself lying unnervingly stiff beneath a blanket, someone leaning over me, and then my spirit snaps back into place, and all is darkness.

CHAPTER 28
WATER

Across the room, a figure sits on a stool. I blink slowly, my eyes burning each time I press my eyelids together. I recognize the dark line of the staff leaning against the wall, bits and bobs dangling from the top, before I recognize Kherbanu themself.

But I am alive, that much is real and true. I am so desperately grateful for it, even as I struggle back to consciousness.

"Waking up, are we?" Kherbanu shifts, the lines of their body blurring together.

I open my mouth to ask a question, but my tongue is too heavy to form it.

They grunt, then push themself to their feet. "Easy, child. You've had a bigger dose than you should have, not that it didn't help." Kherbanu chuckles, shuffling along the far wall to a door. I watch the shadows of it shift and realize they've opened it to speak with someone outside.

My body is heavy and cold—so desperately cold. I'm not shaking, not yet, but if I don't soon, the cold could very well be the death of me. No, that's not right, because I was frozen solid before.

"Let's see how you are," Kherbanu says. Even standing before me, they're not quite in focus.

"C-c-co...." I manage.

"Mmm, yes, you'll be cold. We've got stone warmers all around you. Another blanket, maybe?"

They move away, then return with a mass they shake out and spread over the blanket that already covers me. I can't see it clearly, can't tell anything past the fact that it is brown. Why can't I see properly?

Kherbanu's hand touches my forehead. I jerk away reflexively from the coldness of their touch. They click their tongue at me, and even if I can't make out the expression on their face, I can hear the irritation in that sound.

"H-h-how?" I ask. Dead but not. Dead enough that Ravenflight, mage and rogue hunter that she is, left me for dead. And yet here I am, waking up, my body fitting me no better than a glove made for a larger hand. I cannot quite reach my fingers, find the tips of my toes. What sort of paralytic *freezes* a person?

"Answers later," Kherbanu says, patting my cheek. It's the touch of a person who has known the young and the infirm, and I find it unexpectedly comforting. "Close your eyes and rest. We'll speak when you're warm again."

THIS TIME, it's someone else sitting in the chair. They seem to be looking toward the opposite corner of the room, and I watch them for some time before closing my eyes again. I consider trying to turn over, but not only do my eyes still hurt, but so does the rest of me. Every breath aches, my belly burns, and my arms and legs feel heavy and useless. I do not want to risk waking the pain that may be slumbering in them. So I wait, eyes closed, until I am no longer waiting at all, but waking again.

Kherbanu is back, their staff laid across their lap, their face no more clear than the first time I saw them.

"I can't see," I rasp, making Kherbanu jump. Had they been dozing?

"Can't see?" They rise and stump over to me. "At all?"

"No, I—" I break into a hacking cough that starts in my throat and spreads to my chest and will not stop.

Kherbanu waits beside me, and then their fingers brush my shoulder and a curl of magic unfurls within me, easing the contraction of my lungs until I can breathe again. I lie still, panting.

This weakness is familiar to me, a place I have lived before, drifting in and out of my days while my body tightens its hold on me once more.

I never thought I would be so *grateful* to be here again, in a body that can only just hold me. But I am. I'm ecstatic to be back in this small anchor to the world. I want the days ahead, whatever they bring. I want the possibility of the future that I thought I'd lost. I want more than I've been giving myself, and that starts here, in this quiet. Even these moments, fractured as they are, are precious.

"Let's sit you up," Kherbanu says. "You'll need some water."

They help me up, supporting my shoulders as I waver there, pain bleaching the edges of my vision.

"Here, child. Drink this."

They hold a cup to my lips. I drink slowly, each sip something I have to work up to. But my body needs this, and I will give it as much as I can. It isn't water, but a healing tisane of some sort, bringing a warmth that spreads through me more than a lukewarm tea might impart. Kherbanu waits until I've finished, then helps me lie down again.

"You can't see clearly, is it?" they ask, setting the cup down somewhere beside me on... a table? The floor? I don't turn my head to look.

"Yes," I say.

"That'll be the venom we used."

I shake my head, because it's easier than speaking. At least the pain seems to be easing under the influence of the tisane.

"That was our own maran venom. In small doses, it causes

paralysis. In larger doses—have you ever seen a frog freeze? No? Ah." Kherbanu shifts. "There are some species of frogs that, when the temperature gets cold enough—when ice touches their skin—it sets off a reaction so that they freeze from the outside in, their organs going dormant until even their heart stops beating. Usually, it is a slow process. But we have made some adjustments to our maran venom to make it faster acting without proving fatal. It tips the balance from warmth to cold in a body. In a word, you froze through. It works best, of course, in creatures not quite so warm-blooded as humans."

I close my eyes, try to grasp what they've told me. Frozen from the inside out, like a frog? It sounds absurd at best. Far more frightening, though, is the possibility that my vision might be permanently damaged. "My eyes?" I ask.

Kherbanu waves one blurry hand. "Nothing to worry about! They should heal up fine, they just need a little time. You, and your sight, should be back to full health within a couple of days, I would say."

Their voice is a little too cheery. There is definitely *something* they aren't telling me, but I can't think what. Nor can I spare the energy to worry. There is still time left for me to ask later, so I close my eyes and sleep.

As Kherbanu expected, my strength begins to come back relatively quickly, though their prognosis of being back to normal within a couple of days was far too optimistic. Over the next day, Kherbanu—having appointed themself my chief nurse—plies me with bland soups, herbal tisanes, and the occasional touch of magic to ease the things their medicines can't help. My eyesight slowly comes back into focus, first what's near and then, slowly but surely, things at a distance, though I suspect it will be some days before I recover my full sight. At least I'm no longer bedbound, but able to get up and shuffle about my room and sit where Kherbanu directs me.

My night's sleep is broken by aches and unexpected cramps, and I find I do not want to get up the following morning, despite Kherbanu's insistent prodding. I lie with a sheet pulled over my head, considering the golden light permeating the fabric, and how much longer I can manage to convince Kherbanu I need to sleep. The quiet is punctuated by the occasional sound of a page turning and, once, the unmistakable sound of Kherbanu spitting into the pot left by the door for precisely that purpose.

But I am alert enough to know I should call Val—that I should have done so sooner, but for the exhaustion I am dealing with. Now, I snuggle deeper into my nest of blankets and call out to him.

He responds almost at once, his presence there, in my mind, alert and laced with worry—and relief. *Interesting. Is that a sheet?*

I let out my breath in a huff, glad to feel Val here, his voice light but not artificially so. There's no anger or fear now, just concern. *Yes,* I tell him. *It is.*

"Are you finally awake, bint Al-Ghaib?" Kherbanu asks.

And who is that? Val asks.

I let out a groan, which I hope will keep Kherbanu away for at least a few more minutes. *An ally of sorts? They're hard to read, but they've been taking care of me. You see I'm all right.*

I see a sheet, Val says. Then, *Did you forget you were supposed to call me?*

I—

Kherbanu tugs the sheet off my head. I yelp, squinching my eyes shut.

"It's not that bright, child. I've a meal for you at the table. Let's see you sit up."

I roll gingerly onto my side, my arm over my face. "In a minute," I rasp.

They hesitate. I can just see the hem of their shalvar brushing over their slippers from beneath my arm. "As you like."

Kherbanu moves back to the table.

Why do I get the feeling you're hiding them from me as much as you're hiding me from them?

What do I know about your feelings? I grouse, slowly pushing myself up to a sitting position. *They're yours, not mine.*

As long as I don't look toward Kherbanu, Val should not notice their maran features.

Val hesitates, and I feel his worry again.

I'm fine, I tell him. *You were right—it was a paralytic, augmented by magic. I'll need time to recover, but Ravenflight is gone, and I'm safe.*

Buried beneath a rock.

Yes.

How long will you stay there?

I hesitate. I don't have answers.

Val goes on, *I came to check on you after you left.*

Oh. Oh dear. *I didn't sense you.*

Even when you were awake, you seemed slow. I didn't say anything.

Which means he may already know that I'm not among humans. *What do you know of these people?* I ask.

A pause.

"Come and eat, Hikaru. You need to build up your strength."

I dip my head. "I'm coming," I assure Kherbanu, but I don't stand up yet. *Val?* I query.

I don't recognize their eyes.

I clench my eyes shut.

Or their noses, he adds with a hint of humor. *I've heard tales of the Howling Caves—it has just taken me some time to remember them. Will these people allow you to leave? Because the existence of such tales would suggest they paint themselves as demons and let no one go.*

He's not wrong. *The phoenix wanted me to stay here with the maran,* I say finally. I rub my face, aware of Kherbanu's watchful gaze.

They call themselves snakes?

How many languages do you even know? I slide my feet into the slippers Kherbanu has provided me, and then pause, my gaze fastening on the rather less-hard bolster that serves as my pillow.

Hitomi, Val says, his voice perfectly steady. *Is that your hair?*

I reach out a hand, brush it over the scattering of locks that lie against the fabric. They're not long—perhaps no longer than my fingers—with a very slight wave to them. They're also not attached to my head anymore. I reach up and run a hand through my hair. My fingers come away with more hair caught between them.

Yes, I say in answer to Val, even though the answer is abundantly obvious. I grin. *Don't worry, I'm not very attached to it. At least not anymore.*

Not funny. The last time you lost your hair, we weren't sure it would ever grow back.

I shrug. What else can I do but find a way to laugh?

"Is that your *hair*?" Kherbanu asks, apparently just catching sight of what I hold in my hand. And also perfectly echoing Val.

I drop the hair onto my pillow. "I'm afraid so. Must be a warm-blooded creature problem. I'm sure it will be fine." After all, it's not like frogs have hair to lose when they're frozen solid.

Kherbanu starts to rise, but I wave a hand at them and shove myself to my feet instead, body aching. I shuffle over to the table under their careful scrutiny, thumping down on the cushion before it. After all, if Val has already seen Kherbanu, and neither has recognized the other, then I might as well have something to eat. Maybe it will help me keep what hair I have left.

As Kherbanu ladles out a bowl of thick mushroom soup for me, Val asks, *Are you a guest here, or a prisoner?*

A bit of both, I expect. Honored prisoner, or the like. You promised not to come here, though.

I made no such promise.

Didn't he? No, I don't think he did. It's bad enough he knows the maran exist. I can't imagine how a meeting between them all would go.

Still, I argue. *I'm not in danger, and they* did *protect me from Ravenflight. Wherever you're going, you should keep going there.*

Should I? Val asks, sounding unaccountably amused.

I take a sip of soup to give myself time to think. It's thick and almost creamy, and utterly bland. I dip my spoon in and then I notice another small lock of hair lying beside my bowl. I'm definitely losing my hair. I blink, make myself focus.

Val *can't* enter the Howling Caves, or accidentally cross paths with Ravenflight. Both would be catastrophic, just in very different ways. Although... maybe I'm making decisions for him that it isn't my right to make.

Listen, I say grumpily, *there's a well belonging to the Bani Saqr not far from here. Huda and Laith and Kareem were going to wait for me there, but the phoenix will have told them I'm not coming. So, it should be quiet there. But... I don't know if, or when, I'll leave. I don't think you should go there, because I still need to recover and decide what I'm doing.*

I'll keep that in mind, Val says, which likely means he'll ignore my thoughts completely.

He's been traveling for a little while now—days? A week or two? But while I once thought he might be going to some specific destination, now I know he's on the move because of me, because his prince exiled him. Which means he may not have anywhere in particular to go. The thought rankles. *Does your prince still want to meet me?* I ask.

Yes, although I don't know that you need to meet him, he says, surprising me. *For now, you should rest up. I'll check back in a few days.*

Wait, I say, bending my head over my bowl in the hopes of evading Kherbanu's attention a little longer. *Have you heard anything further about Blackflame? Or Karolene? I heard that there was a rebellion there, and that the Council was taking action to quell it.*

I don't know much for sure, Val says slowly. *But rebellion isn't the word I would use. Invasion is perhaps a more accurate term. The Northlands have landed a fleet there. There are whispers about violence—possible mass killings—but nothing is known for sure. With the portals closed, news travels slowly and changes over the valleys and mountains and seas it crosses.*

A shudder runs through me. I set my spoon down with a

clatter against the wood. My fingers brush the fallen lock of hair beside it.

"Child?" Kherbanu asks. "Oh, your poor hair. Let me have a look now."

You'd better go, I tell Val, pressing my eyes shut.

Perhaps I shouldn't have told you. There's nothing you can do.

That may be true, but I'm still glad to have some idea that something is wrong. *It's fine. Thank you for telling me.*

I'll check in on you again soon, Val says and slips away just as Kherbanu closes their hand around mine, having pulled their stool close enough to reach me.

"I'm just going to take another look," they say, their magic slipping through my veins.

I gaze down at my bowl and consider the news Val has shared. It's not that different from what my uncle said, only one step farther along. The Northlands are invading with Blackflame's blessing, and I'm... sitting under a rock with my hair falling out around me. The phoenix has moved on to healing the Burnt Lands without me. I need to reconcile myself with that, accept that I had my uses there, and now am done. Going back will only put me in the path of mages who will recognize my markings; and the phoenix left me here to learn to live, not to be useful.

For the first time, it occurs to me that Ravenflight will have reported my death to the Council. Within a week, the hunt to recover me will have been called off, Blackflame's unofficial bounty cancelled. My "death" at the hands of the maran wasn't just a wake-up for me, for how much I want to live. It was also an absolute gift: the chance to live without having to flee constantly. The time I have now, I can use—to heal, to allow myself the grace to breathe and think more than one step ahead of where I stand. I rest in that thought, in the heaviness of knowing that I cannot just go on surviving. That living is a different thing altogether, and now I must find a way to it.

I also know that I don't want the story of my death to reach Huda or Laith—and especially not Kenta, who thought me dead after I killed Kol and disappeared. Moreover, I want to be there for each of them—to be there *with* them, alive and enjoying one another's company. I want to share a meal and laugh together and not worry about what use I might be, or how long I have.

Kherbanu withdraws their magic and sets my hand down carefully. "Ah," they say and pause.

"Yes?" I ask, pulling my attention back to them.

"I'm afraid there isn't much I can do for your hair." They rub their mouth, giving me the distinct impression they're trying not to say anything more.

I have no such compunction. "Your venom froze me from the inside out. The last time I lost my hair—"

"You've lost your hair before?" they exclaim.

"The last time I lost my hair," I repeat patiently, "I burned myself from the inside out and marked myself with fire."

"You really shouldn't make a habit of such things."

They're telling *me?*

"Was the venom Rewniz used augmented by magic?" I ask, trying to keep my tone casual. It froze me, which would suggest there was water magic at work—unsurprising, considering the surfeit of water workings in the hidden gorge with its stream and bounty of greens.

Kherbanu looks at me from the corner of their eyes. "Of course. Otherwise, it would be quite fatal in warm-blooded creatures."

"It drew on water, didn't it?" I ask, even though I know.

Kherbanu presses their lips together in a wrinkly grimace and offers me a grudging nod. Because of course it did. But was it enough to affect my core magical balance? The balance I already threw off with my sunbolt, and then by absorbing the backlash of magic from my first encounter with the great tentacled kraken in the Burnt Lands? Fire and stone, and now water.

"You'd better just say it out loud," I tell them. "I've done it again, haven't I?"

Kherbanu huffs. "More accurately, Rewniz—and by extension, Sovereign Arnaz—did it. But yes, it would seem that you have a new balance at your core."

I drop my face into my hands, my shoulders shaking.

"We didn't intend it; it's just that the dose you received was rather more than it should have been. I assure you, Rewniz is sorry for it." They pause and then, as I am still struggling to look up, they say, "Come, child, there's no reason to weep. It will be a challenge to manage, but there are certainly worse fates."

I raise my face to them, shoulders still shaking, unable to speak.

"Are you—are you *laughing*?"

"You did call me a disaster of a child, didn't you?" I manage to gasp. This is definitely a disaster. I've been marked by *three* elements? All by accident, too. No wonder Kherbanu wanted to know where my parents were.

"There are—*well*," Kherbanu says, appearing flustered for the first time since I met them. "The elements balance each other. The fact that you were able to work with the sigils for the talismans before this shows you've some natural balance. We'll work through this together. It will be fine."

Right. "Just how typical is it for a mage to be marked by an element?" I ask.

They clear their throat. "It's not particularly common so far as I know. But," they raise their brows, "I live under a rock. I can't say in truth what's common in the wider world."

"You have books," I point out, wiping my eyes.

"They are old."

"So is magic. Do you know anything about what happens when a mage is marked by more than one element?"

They chew at the bitter nuts that stain their teeth, thinking. Considering they don't seem to be the type to ponder their words for long, that's hardly a good sign. "Their magic would be more volatile unless the elements balanced each other. Fire for water, earth for air. Although it's not always so simple as that. Earth is often a better balance for water than fire, and fire can be balanced by any of the elements, if done properly."

I'm pretty sure I haven't done anything properly, all told, but it's heartening to hear that the various elements within me aren't likely to cause me too much harm.

"Air is by far the hardest to balance, and you've managed to avoid that one, at least," Kherbanu observes.

I guess it's a good thing I didn't try to just blow Kol away with a hurricane, then. I force myself to focus on Kherbanu. "Have you ever heard of a mage being marked by three elements? Or all four?"

They snort. "There are tales of a mage who lived long before the Great Burning who was marked by all four."

"What happened to them?"

"They died young. In a war, I believe—it tends to be wars that involve spells strong enough to change the balance of elements in a person's body. They ended up burning the surrounding landscape to a crisp before creating an abyss that swallowed both armies. A river reportedly still flows through the canyon left behind, though it may have dried up by now." Kherbanu shrugs. "That book is near on three hundred years old. At any rate, I'm sure you won't do anything of the sort."

I eye them in disbelief. They clearly don't know me well. "Are you?"

Kherbanu spreads their hands. "You cannot cast spells, my child. The trouble will be more what happens to you if your elements are thrown off balance *within* you, than what you might do to the world around you."

Oh.

I meet Kherbanu's steady gaze and find myself grinning fiercely. I wanted freedom, didn't I? This is one form of it—without my markings, my magic might become so volatile I could simultaneously burn, bury, and flood a place. With them, it's all contained. I'm not a danger to anyone but myself—and that's something I can learn to manage. I have the time and space now to figure out how to live with this. "That's not so bad, then," I say, running my hands through my hair and pulling out a few more loose locks.

"You're losing your hair."

"It won't be back," I agree cheerfully. "Do you know, I think I might have my scalp inked to match my hands. Tahmineh said their relative does inkings. What do you think? Shall I ask them?"

Kherbanu coughs on a laugh. "I was wrong. You're not a disaster. You're an absolute terror."

I meet their gaze and let the laughter I'm holding spill out of me.

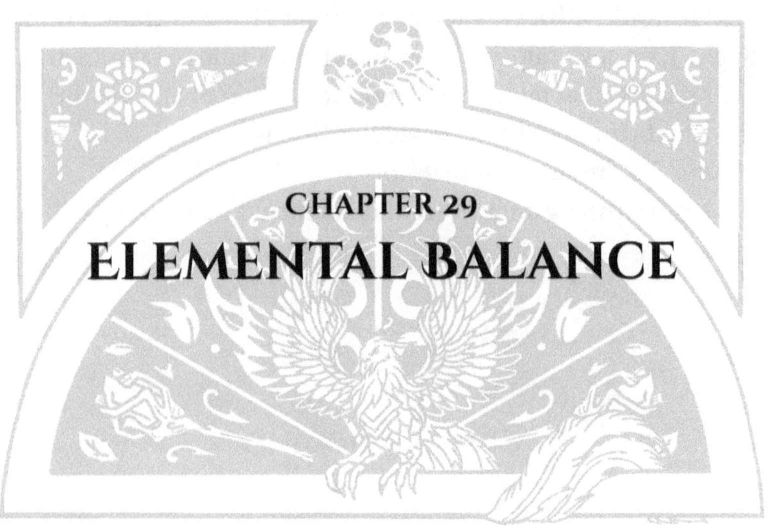

CHAPTER 29
ELEMENTAL BALANCE

The maran have a method of measuring their days composed of a system of deep yet bright tones that reverberate through the living space, making everything hum. The morning tones clear the air, the afternoon tones energize, and the evening tones—the two times I've noted hearing them—are gentle and calming. Now that I recognize them at least in part, I'm better able to measure the passage of time.

After the morning tones, I join Kherbanu in their rooms. They have an unfortunate preference for making me move as much as possible in order to regain my strength. We also entertain Tahmineh and their relative, who come for a visit.

Dalileh is in fact a *master* inker. They are delighted to visit me and see my own inkings—an opportunity they weren't able to take advantage of at the feast except from afar. To be offered the canvas of my now nearly bare scalp has them absolutely thrilled.

"Oh yes," they say, turning my head just so. "The rest of this should fall out shortly. And the skin is not irritated at all! I can sketch you a few designs tonight, and we can start whenever we have something you are happy with. There is plenty of space to work where the skin is already bare."

It is rather heartening to have someone look at my bare scalp with delight. There's an odd sort of familiarity to the smooth feel

302

of my scalp, the touch of air against my skin. It's mine—not just my scalp, of course, but this life I lead, where I keep losing my hair. Adding inkings allows me to make it even more mine.

We discuss designs over a cup of tea—or an herbal tisane that fills the same role. Dalileh presses me to share what I want for myself. I'm not sure at first, but the more I think on it, the more I know that I want these designs to be as much me as I am a part of all the different pieces of my life. I want something reminiscent of the desert—I think of Huda's facial inkings and ask for sharply angled lines worked into the design. I ask for touches of the inter-laced lines and arches and geometric designs of the lamps in my uncle's tent. And I ask for all of these to be interwoven with hints of the Eastern kingdom my mother hails from. Just as my father has relatives I never imagined, my mother may too. Perhaps I have cousins out there, aunts and uncles I know nothing of—and I will claim that part of me now, even if I have never met them. And finally, I ask for shadows and flame—for forgotten memories of my life in Karolene, and the fire that burned it away and made me anew.

Dalileh promises to return before the evening bells with some sketches for me, and I can already see their thoughts turning, the images shifting and forming behind their eyes. They depart with Tahmineh in tow and a strict directive for me to drink as much water as possible.

I down a cup of water as instructed, gather the blanket Kherbanu has loaned me, and snuggle up in a corner despite their reproachments to go sleep in my own room. "Don't want to," I tell them, stifling a yawn. "I like how busy it is here."

It feels so full of life, nothing like the distant quiet when I thought I was dead, my body a thing apart from me and my future gone. The clatter and noise of this life is a welcome accom-paniment to the rest I am seeking.

Kherbanu shakes their head at me, lips pursed to hide their smile. I drowse through the afternoon bell, paying little mind to the visitors who traipse through to consult Kherbanu—and catch another glimpse of me. At least a couple of them have come to consult Kherbanu regarding their health, as evidenced by how the old mage peers into their mouths or lays a hand on an aching limb. They speak mostly in their tongue, and I find it behooves me to look small and inconsequential in their eyes: a child curled up in the corner to nap. At any rate, if they are looking for an impressive magic worker, they can go right back to looking at Kherbanu.

Eventually, the stream of visitors dwindles to nothing. I rouse and join Kherbanu at the table for a light afternoon repast. Remembering the comment Zohan made at the feast, connecting sunlight to glowstones, I make it my business to ask about the golden glow of the maran's stones when every glowstone I've seen before glows pale as moonlight.

"We have your white-colored glowstones as well," Kherbanu tells me. "But we miss daylight here. We have only what falls within the gorge. So, of course the mages of generations past found a way to capture such a glow for our glowstones, that we might have daylight within even the deepest and darkest of our rooms. If I am not mistaken, it took many years to perfect. I doubt your human mages would see any need to spend so much time on so specific a task when your average glowstone works perfectly well for your needs."

"Will you teach me how you do it, though?" I ask, as if I can form the spell myself. I can't, but I wonder if I could take a regular glowstone and alter it to glow as the maran's stones do. There is something truly life-giving about the golden glow of their stones.

"Here," Kherbanu says, passing me one of theirs. "Study that and tell me what you have learned tomorrow."

I turn over the glowstone in my hand. "Is it made with actual sunlight?"

Kherbanu's lips quirk. "You're the one who is supposed to tell me."

I close my eyes, reaching out with my mage senses. The glowstone warms in my hand, calling to my blood. Definitely a base of fire, then. How appropriate if this is a vessel for sunlight, much as

I made myself into a year or more ago. I could have just thrown a bucketful of these at Kol and been done with it. I choke on a laugh.

"Are you quite well?"

"Never been better," I assure them.

"Good then, put that away for later. If you are well enough to study, then you are well enough to investigate much bigger questions."

"Like what?" I ask.

Kherbanu looks heavenward, an apparently universal reaction to being faced with the foolishness of youth. "Child, do you not have a new element at your core?"

I grin. "I do, though I'm not sure how you intend me to study it. I suppose you're going to dunk me in a stream and make me spout magic?"

As it turns out, that is *exactly* their plan.

We make our way to the inner gorge with its stream, the afternoon sun shining down to light the central space and warm the air. I don't realize how cool the caves have felt until I step into the bright wash of light, the sun warm against my skin. I raise my face to the sunlight, basking in it.

"Fire at your heart first," Kherbanu says with some amusement. "Go on, then, take off your shoes and see what you can feel."

They gesture with their staff to where the path widens into three broad steps down into a shallow wading area. Kherbanu takes a seat on what they call a char pai—a sort of wooden frame similar to a cot, strung with rope woven together to make the top. It is bare of any mattress, but the rope weaving seems to have some give. Someone has pulled the char pai right up to the edge of the wading pool; it seems Kherbanu has been planning this outing for a little while at least.

I shuck off the embroidered leather slippers I've taken to wearing since the feast and dip my toes in the water. It's cool, but just here at the base of the stairs there is a natural soft reddish-brown stone underfoot that holds the sun's heat, warming the slow-flowing water. A little farther in, the stream deepens; the swift flow there will no doubt be a good bit colder.

I don't particularly want to go for a swim, even if these waters are warmer than the crystal-clear waters of the lake in Stormwind's valley. This past summer, Stormwind, unappeased by my assurance that I probably knew how to save myself, saw to it that I learned the basics of swimming. Some of it came to me naturally, as if my body remembered what my mind did not. Nevertheless, she was a diligent teacher and I am no longer at risk of accidental drowning. I still don't want to swim today, though.

I sit on the final step, soaking my feet, and rest in the quiet. A faint breeze stirs the air, rustling through the branches of the slim trees behind us, and over the tops of the bushes and potted plants that dot the wide stone veranda, whispering through the gorge with its abundance of greenery. The twittering calls of small brown birds fill the air—desert sparrows or their brethren, flitting among the rocky crevasses and carved balconies. There are also a good number of maran on those balconies, some of them leaning out over carved balustrades to catch a glimpse of me. I pay them no mind—they've every right to their curiosity, after all. Instead, I focus on the opposite bank, with its mosaic-laid path and the arched doorways to the hidden interior.

In some ways, this is the phoenix's haven come alive: the stream, the trees, the sheltering walls, a whole community living their lives among them. All of it cut off from the wider world. Small wonder he thought it a good place for me.

"Oi, child," Kherbanu says. I look up just as they dip the end of their staff into the water and flick it at me, splashing me.

I laugh, raising a hand helplessly. "What?"

"What are you going to learn by staring moodily into space, hmm?"

I shrug, spreading my hands. "What shall I do then?"

"*Try* something, child," Kherbanu says, their words punctuated by a rather more emphatic splash.

I duck and wipe the water from my face, still smiling. Then I close my eyes, seeking with my mage senses. I am unsurprised to find magic at play here, charms and wards to protect the water from pollutants and manage its flow. My focus now is the water itself, the lazy lapping of water over my ankles, the swift cold flow of the deeper waters.

I draw in a little magic, my markings barely twinging as I absorb the flow, and feel it meld with my blood. It's as if I've taken a drink of water that has gone straight to my veins, cool and refreshing. With my eyes closed and my focus on myself, I can feel the fire at my core warming the water, feel the strength of stone in my bones as water flows over it—all of it together and yet separate. Which is good. I'm not sure a core of steaming lava would be healthy for me.

Kherbanu pokes my arm with the end of their staff. "What are you smirking about?"

I open my eyes. "I can feel the water within me," I explain. "It is thankfully not doing anything too drastic."

"Of course it isn't. The elements are not drastic. People are."

I raise my brows. "Have you ever seen a storm?"

They wave their staff. "That is different. This—this is just the elements within you, at peace."

"I suppose it is my goal to maintain that balance," I say dubiously.

"If you'd like to live, yes."

I consider them, their words: that the elements within me, that my *magic*, might be a source of peace, unlike the destruction I've wrought with it. It's me—or rather, it's the people who wield the elements that cause drastic things. Which makes it that much more important to practice peace at heart—not just with my magic, but with myself. A deceptively simple observation I'm pretty sure I'll actually be rubbish at doing.

Kherbanu sets their staff down across the char pai and takes me through a series of exercises designed to increase my awareness of elemental water and help me build my skills in using it. There's something to be said for having access to a teacher whose magical tradition has focused on water for hundreds of years—which is no doubt how I also ended up getting marked by it. Guess I wasn't going to get the one without the other.

Once I've gotten a sense of the water currents, of how warm and cold interact, of how currents can curve and run into each other and then diverge, Kherbanu introduces me to more unusual flows. We begin with the small eddies around a set of stepping stones and progress to little whirlpools. Kherbanu teaches me to create them as I learn their structure—how they are formed not of one current but the meeting of two, swirling together. I love them, love the strength and flow and circular power, and the secrets hidden from sight that hold it all together.

Kherbanu laughs, shaking their head at me. "You should have been a water mage first."

"I'm good at it because I've been working with fire and stone," I argue. "Lava flows too, you know."

"*Child.* What has the phoenix been teaching you? A vortex of lava is *much* less forgiving. Do not do any such thing."

I snort with laughter. "Take it up with the phoenix. I'm just doing what my elders tell me."

"Water," Kherbanu says sternly. "What I'm telling you is water. Only."

I grin and bend my attention to making another tiny whirlpool.

Within a couple of hours, my energy is spent. Kherbanu takes me back to my room to sleep until the evening bells, when Dalileh shows up with a shallow wooden box filled with wax—a sort of portable wax tablet that they can draw on and then smooth out and reuse as many times as they like.

They pass me the wax tablet, on which is sketched a top view of a person's head, and then two side views. The designs cover the top of the head, creating a sort of artistic framing of the face as they wrap around the side and around each ear. There are arches and sharp angles and swooping embellishments and curling flames.

I trace the lines with a finger. "I love it," I say, and pause as I find myself staring at a gorgeously rendered lotus flower. It is very much symbolic—but my finger still shakes as I look at it.

Dalileh, unaware of my reaction, takes back the tablet and begins to ask questions. I give them my full attention with a sense of relief, glad to discuss the rest of the design. Over the next hour they adjust and fine-tune their design. They leave the tablet with me, so that I can continue to study the design they created and ask for any changes in the morning. Perhaps I will ask for the lotus flower to be replaced with something else. It would be simple enough.

Come night, I lie nestled on the divan, thinking of the last time I saw lotus flowers, the only time I can remember them at all. Perhaps I was surrounded by them growing up, but I don't remember that. I drift into a shadowed dream of lotus flowers floating on a pond before an ornate gazebo, a glimpse of blue silk at its heart. My mother, back from the dead and garbed in silks in Blackflame's home, while I scrabbled for survival—and tried to escape the fate he had decreed for me. I wake with my cheeks wet with tears, my heart twisting in my chest like a feral creature.

I wipe my face angrily with the edge of my sheet, furious with myself, with these tears I cannot explain or banish. Kherbanu and their people may not be my friends, but I'm not *alone* here. I've still got my connection to Val, and Huda is waiting for me somewhere in the desert. My uncle has claimed me; he *looked* for me when my father died and my mother disappeared. He tried to find me, he wanted me, even if my mother did not.

"It wasn't me," I whisper aloud to the faintly lit corners of my room. "It was her. It was never me."

And then I am crying, embracing my grief as it floods through me, deep within the stone walls that are both shelter and prison to me. Because however complicated my life and relations are, here is a truth I have needed: my mother did not abandon me because of *me*. It was not something I did, something that was wrong with me, something I could not be for her. She left me because *she* chose to, never looking back to the child waiting for her on the streets, doggedly remaining before the inn that would no longer harbor me, squatting in doorways and trusting in her promised return when she had already turned away from me.

That isn't what family does. Family does what my uncle did, seeking out a lost child until all traces are gone, and grieving them afterwards. I was not some terrible, flawed creature, that my mother could not love me. Or that she could seem to love me and then walk away. Or that—five years later—she could walk into my room in the infirmary at the Mekteb and tell me to my face that she did not know me or my family, that she had only a passing knowledge of me, but that she still did not wish me dead. As if that is all one can ask of a mother: that they do not wish you dead.

The flaws are all hers.

This grief, however, is mine: mine to hold, mine to feel, mine to allow out. I cry without holding back, letting the tears wash out the pain, undeserved and unearned as it is, so that I can allow other things in: my uncle's love, my friends' care and kindness. I weep until I am emptied out, my eyes aching and my throat raw.

Then I curl up beneath the blanket and rest in a newfound peace.

CHAPTER 30
A PROMISE MADE

Over the next couple of days, I spend a portion of each morning and afternoon working with Kherbanu, slowly exploring my connection to water and the intricacies of water magic. Kherbanu takes a keen interest in my studies, including suggesting gentle experiments between my various elements. Our conversations are fascinating and the exercises they set me are challenging but satisfying.

We also venture into the deepest caverns together to review and strengthen the wards and shieldings there. I mostly just follow along, tired from my water work but curious nonetheless. In addition to asking Kherbanu to ensure the strength of the magical protections here, Arnaz has also sent down work crews to clean and store supplies.

"They aren't taking any chances," Kherbanu says after greeting one such crew. "The phoenix may be perfectly comfortable that your method will work and keep the whole of the desert safe. Arnaz will have the whole of us come down here to wait out the process."

"It's wise," I allow, looking out across the cavern we stand in to the interconnected tunnels, the faint light of the departing crew's glowstone still visible. In some ways, it reminds me of the phoenix's haven. There, too, the draining spells passed over the phoenix and his band of refugees. "Do you have a water source down here?"

"A small one." Kherbanu rests a hand on the cavern wall, bringing the ward there into focus. "I'll show you later."

I nod and settle myself on the floor to rest while Kherbanu mutters over the ward.

Beyond that, it is a quiet time. I am aware of how Kherbanu's other duties and politicking brush shoulders with our time together: the maran who come to Kherbanu for health concerns, the one meeting they leave for without explanation—sunshiner politics, perhaps?—and the careful way they assure that the other nobles never manage to chat with me alone. Not that I mind; the less I know what's at play at a granular level, the more I can just let Kherbanu continue their clearly subversive work. If I had to pick a side, I would choose the stance of the sunshiners, same as Kherbanu. A life in which one cannot leave one's home is a life of imprisonment, no matter how loving that home.

When I am not with Kherbanu, I put myself fully in Dalileh's hands as they ink my scalp. The last of my hair falls out, leaving my skin smooth and unblemished, the perfect canvas for their work. Kherbanu provides an ointment with a mild numbing agent to be applied before Dalileh begins their work, and a second healing balm to be used afterward.

Dalileh spreads out their work, but even so, they are done by the end of the second day. They bring a polished silver tray and hold it up for me to inspect the tattoos. They are done primarily in black ink to match the markings on my arms, and stand out starkly against the pale skin of my scalp. The design, with its arches and interwoven curves, is gorgeous. The shadows Dalileh added in deep blue add both meaning and visual depth.

As part of my care, I must keep it bandaged initially, and out of the sun for the next week or two. Not that there's a lot of sun down here, but the one place I go—the gorge with its stream—is also the one place with direct sunlight. I learn to loosely tie the turban I was gifted, and call it a win.

I'm with Kherbanu during the afternoon tones the following

day, carefully stringing the last of the lapis wards from Stormwind's old necklace onto a new cord. Kherbanu finds the wards fascinating, and is working on making their own set as I repair mine. There are only five beads left in total, but I've strengthened and adjusted their enchantments to allow them to be strung farther apart. I knot on the last bead, wondering how and where Stormwind is now. Has she managed to stay ahead of the hunters on her trail? I can only hope she has succeeded where I failed; at least her hunters would have no reason to suspect the direction she might take. The Council knew I owed the phoenix a debt, which meant they knew exactly where to look for me.

The chimes at the door sound suddenly, three jangles in quick succession. Kherbanu turns, brow creasing, as Rewniz lets themself in. Their gaze flicks to me before focusing on Kherbanu. They rattle off a sentence in the maran tongue, voice clipped.

Kherbanu's eyebrows shoot up. They ask a short question.

Rewniz twists to shut the door, their gaze darting out to the hallway as it closes. What follows is a short conversation, Rewniz looking grim and shrugging their shoulders at one point, and Kherbanu eventually huffing in irritation before turning back to me.

"It seems Mage Eshvat has returned," they explain. "Our sovereign has called a meeting of the Convocation, though Rewniz has no detail on why. Perhaps only to share what Eshvat has accomplished."

"The Convocation?" I echo, having heard this reference a few times now.

Kherbanu waves a hand. "It is what we call the group of nobles who theoretically guide and support our sovereign—two members from each noble family join the Convocation, and together they decide our path. Although there are always more politics at play than just that."

"So, Arnaz does not actually rule alone?"

Kherbanu shakes their head. "No. Although they did not consult with the Convocation until after they had promised Eshvat's help to the phoenix. I suppose Arnaz is offering this as a balm to their frustration, that Eshvat report back to them all together now."

"Then Eshvat's work with the phoenix is done?" I ask, and even though I expected this—it was the whole point of Eshvat going with the phoenix—I feel unaccountably low. It's not like I thought I was the only one who could really help the phoenix; I knew that wasn't true. But... I suppose part of me still wanted to see things through to the end.

"It would seem so," Kherbanu says. "I will have more information for you shortly. Will you stay here or return to your room?"

If I leave, my armed escort will follow me like a pair of sharp-edged ducklings, as Arnaz has not yet allowed me free movement in the caves. Nor have they attempted to wring an oath from me to stay, or placed any kind of binding on me to keep me here. I suppose I had better start putting together an escape plan before such an option occurs to them.

"Well?" Kherbanu asks.

I glance up to see them by the door, ready to depart, Rewniz already in the hallway. I don't really want to be tailed by my escort again. "I'll stay," I tell them.

I pace the workroom after their departure, trying to gather my thoughts. I am more or less recovered from the maran venom, and the last of my bruises from my encounter with the great desert kraken have faded in the meantime. Even the old wound to my biceps from Osman Bey's crossbow bolt has nearly finished healing, in large part thanks to my time in the phoenix's haven. I'm relatively whole, though my endurance may still not be what it used to be.

I run a hand over my smooth scalp, grip the back of my head. What am I worried about? It's in Arnaz's best interest to make me a willing member of their society rather than attempt to bind me or harm me in some way. I'm not really worried about that. I suppose I should plan my escape, and yet... I don't know what I will be running *to*, anymore.

I think through my options because, for once, I'm not in

danger. There's time to plan, and this isn't about saving anyone other than myself. I can't remember a time when I considered my own desires in my choices, rather than having to consider someone else. It's a welcome sort of difficulty, to think this through, if a little scary… because I'm not really sure *what* I want.

I can't go back to my uncle, as much as I may want to. In all likelihood, he's left for the meeting of the tribes. Huda and Kareem and Laith will also have moved on, believing from the phoenix that I won't be returning to them. Val is still traveling. Even if he decides to come here—I did, after all, tell him where to look for me—I don't know where we would go from here.

Further, somewhere out there are likely more minions of Blackflame, still searching for me. They will hardly have gotten word of my purported death so soon—not when Ravenflight and the official side of the Council aren't directly connected to Black-flame's unofficial bounty hunters.

I flex my fingers. I can't risk it. Not when there's no reason. I would only be exchanging a comfortable imprisonment for the life of a fugitive, risking my friends' lives in the process. And for what? So that I can run from one place to another, unwanted and unneeded? Or maybe go to Karolene and offer to channel magic for the Shadow League, as if that will make a difference in the face of a Northland invasion. Foolishness, all of it.

Grimacing, I drop onto a stool before Kherbanu's worktable and pull out the glowstone they gave me to study, along with my own glowstone. I don't have answers, or a future I know I can survive. But that was the phoenix's unwanted gift to me: to have the time to ponder what is possible, rather than what isn't. I don't have to answer this moment, or tonight, or even tomorrow. I just need to keep asking the questions and see if I can find my way to something better.

Focusing on the golden glowstone, I work through each layer of the maran enchantment, comparing it to the glowstone I brought with me when I entered the Howling Caves. There is fire at the core of this golden stone, as I knew from before, and I am only just—*just*—beginning to grasp how it was done when Kherbanu sweeps into the room, their face a study in fury.

My hand clenches around the stone as they dip their head at me and stump past, their staff smacking against the stone floor with each step. They pour a cup of tea from the pot set up on its enchanted warming tile, then stare at the mug for a long moment, before huffing and turning around to regard me. "We are going to have to leave, very shortly, and very carefully."

"Leave?" I echo, sliding the glowstones into my pocket and slipping off the stool. My future has narrowed down into a single thread again, as simply as that. "What happened?"

"That pompous *mushroom* of a maran has betrayed their work."

"Eshvat," I say with a sudden, dreadful understanding. "What do you mean *they betrayed* their work? What did they do? Did the phoenix not realize?"

"I doubt it," Kherbanu says, waving a hand. "If the phoenix knew, Eshvat would hardly look so smug. I've sent Rewniz for your things. You'll have to help me gather mine." They take a large, slurping sip from their mug and set it down with a small thud that sends liquid splashing over the edge. They wipe their hand on their tunic, hissing with frustration. "*How* we're going to fix this, I don't know, but I'm hardly going to stay under this rock and let it happen."

I flex my hands, feeling my inkings twinge, aware that I'm drawing on magic instinctively. I take a slow breath, releasing the magic at my fingertips. "We're... *you're* leaving for the Burnt Lands?"

"What do you think? The last time I sent someone off to do a good deed, we ended up with a possible magical disaster on our hands. Of *course* I'm going myself this time."

A magical disaster? I force my jaw to relax and say, "Tell me what it is that's going to happen while we find your things."

Kherbanu, as it turns out, has never packed for a flight of survival. They watch with dismay as I lay out a sheet and place their belongings in the center. I allow them only one change of clothing, one extra set of spare socks and underthings, a single pouch of herbs and ointments... one or two sentimental objects should they never return. There is a certain sense of unreality to it, as if it is only a dream, a happening-again of Stormwind's departure from her valley, and then mine.

While I pack, I have Kherbanu's dry recital of events to keep me grounded. "Our sovereign reminded us that we took in a traveler at the request of the phoenix as payment for an age-old debt. We then also sent a mage with him to complete the work he required."

Also? Was Eshvat's work not part of their repayment? Or does Arnaz simply not want to present it as such? "I see," I say, folding Kherbanu's spare tunic.

"The Burnt Lands act as a second protection for us, reducing the number of humans traveling nearby," Kherbanu explains. "Should the Lands be healed and become livable, Arnaz argued our own home may be endangered. This is only an extension of dweller logic—that our survival is hinged on our secrecy, and anything that jeopardizes that must be dealt with accordingly."

I hadn't considered the possibility that Arnaz would have kept their own priorities secret—that they would have sent Eshvat under false pretenses, claiming to help the phoenix while planning to protect their own people's interests. Arnaz themself argued that it didn't make sense, that the Burnt Lands would be opened at some point anyway. Had they not meant their words?

"And?" I ask, sweeping the charms Kherbanu has chosen into a pouch and adding it to the small pile of belongings in the center of the sheet.

"Eshvat has ensured that the experiment will fail. They believe there will be an explosion of magic that should destroy the surrounding lands as the draining spells pass over them. We are to retreat deep underground in two days' time to keep ourselves safe. The draining spells will purportedly not reach so deep, and our wards will be able to protect us from what stray magic does."

"An... explosion? The *draining spells*?" I shake my head, look back at Kherbanu. "What did Eshvat do? *Specifically*?"

"They introduced flaws into the talismans we created. I believe they left the big one alone, but most of the smaller ones will fail. When they do, they'll release the magic they've absorbed, and of course all the magic flowing toward them will have nowhere to go."

An explosion of magic, as Kherbanu said, that the larger talisman won't be able to contain fast enough, if at all. The shock-waves will ripple out, slamming into the Barrier— "They want the Barrier to fail."

"Yes."

"The draining spells will be let loose then, whatever of them have survived." And if they're at all functional at that point, which they likely will be, they'll have all the magic they need to self-heal and spread. It will be just as the phoenix said—they will race across the desert, draining the land as they consume the extra magic taken from the Barrier, and then slow as that runs out.

Kherbanu nods. "It will be worse than the Great Burning itself, because at least then people knew to run."

I shudder, and my mind twists back to Kherbanu's description of Eshvat's smug certainty. It must have been a planned betrayal—Arnaz clearly supports Eshvat's actions. No, Arnaz *planned* for them. Why else did they have Kherbanu strengthen the shieldings in the deep caverns, send whole work crews down to clean them out and set in a store of supplies? Arnaz wasn't just being careful; they were preparing for exactly what they had planned.

I am so *tired* of betrayal. I don't care if the phoenix's actions were well intentioned, and I don't give a damn if Arnaz saved my life by tricking Ravenflight into leaving me for dead. I should not have been left down here as thanks for my work, and Eshvat sure as hell should not have planned the fall of the Barrier.

"Our only option is to get to the phoenix in time to warn him," Kherbanu says heavily.

There are only two days before the maran go deeper underground. I close my eyes, my mind racing. That must mean at least three days before the phoenix attempts to take down the draining spells. Arnaz would surely plan to get their people to safety early.

Which gives us—nearly as little hope. Escaping the maran, even if Kherbanu is with me, finding Huda or any of her people, and then riding to the meeting of the tribes to warn the phoenix, assuming he is still there.... I can't see that far ahead. Yet, if the phoenix doesn't discover what Eshvat has done, if the Barrier collapses, the draining spells will cut through every living thing in the desert. Only the maran in their deep underground haven have a hope of remaining safe—just as the phoenix and the children he rescued remained safe below the banyan tree. Though the spells would devastate their canyon, and leave them trapped beneath the draining spells with whatever spell-creatures have survived. How could they take such a risk?

The first evening tone sounds, reverberating gently through the room. How has it gotten so late?

Kherbanu, apparently thinking the same thing, says, "We must move quickly. Are you well?"

As well as I can be, but there's one thing I still need to be sure of. I meet Kherbanu's gaze. "Did you have any idea this is what Eshvat intended?"

They straighten to glare at me. "Do I look like a murderer of babies and the elderly and everyone in between?" they demand.

"No, but neither does Eshvat or your sovereign, yet here we are."

Kherbanu lets out their breath in a sigh. "I'm not your enemy, nor the phoenix's. Think, child! I am planning our escape right now. I wouldn't be doing that if I intended to keep you prisoner here."

I look down, chagrined. "Thank you. I guess—I guess I am just tired of being betrayed. The phoenix was only the most recent." At least he'd been well intentioned, unlike Eshvat. "I want to be able to trust in my friends and allies, but I can't seem to tell who will stand by me and who won't."

Kherbanu grimaces. "Fair enough. I'll make you a promise,

then: I've no intention of betraying you, but I'll tell you if I have to, so you won't have to fear it."

"You'll warn me?" I say in disbelief. That's not how betrayal *works*. Surely Kherbanu understands that.

"I *did* start by saying I wouldn't betray you. Right now, I need to fix what Eshvat has done, so how about we stop worrying about my wording?"

"Right," I say and clear my throat uncomfortably. I'm not sure why their promise eases my tension, but I'm grateful nonetheless. "So, we ride for the Barrier and try to find the phoenix to warn him. Do we—do your people even have camels we can steal?"

"No."

I grimace. We'd better hope *someone* is at the old well. I'll take anyone at this point, even Ravenflight.

The door chime sounds. I grab the two ends of the sheet and swing Kherbanu's belongings around in a quick, tight twist, leaving them fully wrapped at the center. I hold the lumpy package in my arms, fighting the desire to hide it behind me in what would be a blatantly guilty move. But it is only Rewniz, carrying my gauntlets as well as the small woven bag Huda made for me, stuffed with my thobe and other spare clothing. I'm wearing my maran clothes today.

"You were mostly already packed," Rewniz says to me, brows raised with curiosity.

"I like to put things away," I say, which is perhaps not completely accurate. I do like to keep things organized, but I've never allowed myself to think of this place as a home, even if I don't know what I'm doing next. Having my bag ready was nothing more than instinct, when I've had to move on constantly since I left Stormwind's valley. From how naturally it came to me, I suspect I might have lived that way before as well, in the life I can't remember in Karolene.

Rewniz's gaze focuses on the bundle in my hands, and then they turn sharply toward Kherbanu. "You're not going as well? Tell me whatever is in that bundle is for the mageling."

"I'll tell you no such thing."

Rewniz passes my bag and gauntlets to me without looking away from Kherbanu. I nearly drop the gauntlets and end up setting down Kherbanu's things to strap them on. They're easier to wear than to carry anyway, and I'm going to want to start hiding my markings again.

"Will you not consult with the Convocation?" Rewniz presses.

"Arnaz made no consultation on assigning whole peoples to their deaths," Kherbanu points out. "But you needn't fear: I've spoken with Zohan already, and I'll have my glamor to hide my true appearance."

I knew Zohan was influential from their seat at the table at the feast, but this suggests they're very much Kherbanu's ally. Interesting.

Rewniz purses their lips. "You're sure about this, then? It is dangerous out there, and such a journey will be very difficult."

"I'm *sure* Eshvat needs to consider what it means to kill a person, let alone a whole people. I knew they were an arrogant fool, but really, I did not realize that they don't see the desert dwellers as people at all. That is far more dangerous than what you might expect from your average pompous mushroom. And if that human Council of Mages ever discovers Eshvat's part? We will be destroyed as certainly as the desert dwellers Eshvat has no thought for."

"Yes, but the journey itself—" Rewniz begins.

Kherbanu pats their arm, cutting them off. "Yes, yes, I know it's a hard journey. I've got the mageling to guide me, and between the two of us, I expect we'll be quite a force to be reckoned with. As long as we actually leave, and don't spend the next week arguing over our competence."

Rewniz gives a soft, dry laugh. "Heaven forbid I ever stand in your way, closest of mother-kin."

Oh, *that* explains why Kherbanu trusts them implicitly.

"Perhaps I might come with you, though," Rewniz adds,

glancing between us. "I am sure you can protect yourselves, but I might offer some support."

"I think not," Kherbanu says. "The Convocation cannot afford to punish me, but you are another matter. No need for you to risk yourself. Although," Kherbanu says, turning to me, "I shouldn't make decisions for you. You're dead for now, child. You realize that, don't you? As long you stay here, within our wards, what hunters yet seek you will give you up for dead and you can go on living among us. The moment you step out there and start playing with magic, you risk the chance of calling back their notice. Nor will our sovereign appreciate your betraying the shelter we've granted you."

"I appreciate the shelter," I say coolly. "But I'm done with living under a rock. I have friends in the desert who need to know what Eshvat has done. The phoenix must be warned."

Kherbanu nods. "There's that sense of honor again. Very good. Let me weave something to hide you, and we'll be on our way."

The shadow enchantment Kherbanu lays on me is wonderfully fine, settling over me like gossamer. It is subtle enough that I will need the help of other shadows to fully disappear—which means it is also subtle enough that Eshvat would not even notice it at work, should we have the bad fortune of crossing paths with them.

I slip the strap of my bag over my head and shoulder, then tie the ends of the sheet crosswise over my chest, Kherbanu's belongings hanging at my back and freeing my hands.

"Do you have a plan of where to go once we reach the desert?" Kherbanu asks, making Rewniz squeeze their eyes shut in worry.

"We'll start by going to the well at the campsite I was staying at before I came here. Possibly, there will be folk there who can help us. Either way, we'll be able to make our way from there, as long as your people's warriors don't catch us before then."

Kherbanu shakes their head. "I can deal with a pair of warriors. It won't be a problem."

Rewniz swings open the door and we step out to the sight of a dozen armed warriors heading toward us.

"Correction," Kherbanu mutters. "That will be a problem."

CHAPTER 31
ARREST

Kherbanu directs me to the side with a quick—and wholly unnecessary—tilt of their chin. I keep Kherbanu between myself and the warriors, moving back at an angle to lean against the wall. Here, I'm shielded by both their bulk and the faint shadow they throw. Unfortunately, I can't see Kherbanu's face from here, but I can read the slight tension in Rewniz's shoulders. The lead warrior dips their head, and while their manner and tone as they speak is respectful, their face is far too grim for good news.

Kherbanu grumbles a reply and points their staff down the hallway—the same direction as my room, though it could be something else as well. The warrior shakes their head, and gestures back the way they came. Is Kherbanu being taken into custody?

Kherbanu says something short and harsh, and in the warrior's response I catch the name *Arnaz*. Well, that's no surprise. Arnaz likely doesn't want to risk Kherbanu doing anything about what Eshvat has set in motion. I slip my hands into my pockets, but I have hardly any charms, and nothing that will do me any good. Nor does Kherbanu need my magic; they've got their own. Just because they choose not to cast a spell at a dozen of their own warriors doesn't mean they can't if they need to. Better to follow along and see what's happening than do something rash.

I wait as Kherbanu stumps forward, Rewniz falling in beside them. They pass through the group of warriors, the lead warrior falling into step on Kherbanu's other side, and the remaining warriors following after. I ease out of my leather slippers which have a tendency to pat against the stone floors, pick them up, and follow after the warriors barefoot.

We pass from the halls I know relatively quickly, ascending one staircase that Kherbanu takes at their own pace, grumbling about the lack of courtesy young people have nowadays. I suppress a smile—not that anyone can see. I'm not sure if this is an act, or if Kherbanu really is that unworried about what politics are at play now, but I'm glad they can project such confidence.

I wish I had the same. With the shadow enchantment, I still have a good chance of escaping the caves. From what I've observed, and the one time Rewniz led me to the outer caves to confront Ravenflight, I think I can patch together the way out. But there are still so many unknowns, and here I am, walking into trouble again when perhaps I should have opted for the unknowns of escape.

I can't reach Huda from here, can't contact my uncle, and the phoenix didn't leave me another feather—that would have been far, far too easy. He meant to leave me behind, and now I have no way to reach out to him. Taking a slow breath, I call out the only other way I can, using the bond I still have. *Val. Valerius—can you hear me?*

I wait, counting off every curse I know in silence, raining them down on Eshvat's arrogant head. It's an absolute relief when, halfway down the next hall, as we pass a small knot of maran whose attention remains riveted on Kherbanu and their escort, Val slips into my awareness. *What's wrong?*

Eshvat—the maran mage who went with the phoenix—they've damaged the talismans that were meant to hold the magic of the Burnt Lands. The maran expect the Barrier to fail when the phoenix makes the attempt to unravel the Burnt Lands. It will release the draining spells across the desert—killing everyone in their path. At least until the spells slow, but that will be well past the desert itself.

That is certainly a problem, Val says slowly. *I'm not convinced it's your problem.*

I nearly stumble over my own bare feet. I pause, heart thundering, but the warriors ahead of me didn't hear my misstep. I start forward again, furious. *What do you mean?*

I think your problem is getting free of the prison the phoenix left you in. He and his parcel of mages can worry about the unmaking of the Burnt Lands.

They won't know—

It is their work to know. You are not responsible for this.

I straighten, fingers clenching into fists. *Yes, I am.* How can he not understand this? *And you're responsible now too—because you know. We both know and it is up us to act.*

All very idealistic, Hitomi, but you're shut tight in an underground prison and—

You're not. And I'm going to get free. I just—I'm asking you to find a way to tell the phoenix to look for what Eshvat did.

Because you don't think the phoenix will notice.

I don't know *that he will. It's too much of a risk to assume so.*

A silence. I can sense Val's frustration, but not much else. It's as if he's letting me that close, and then shielding the rest of his emotions from me. I can't guess at what he's thinking. I remain quiet as we turn into another connecting hallway, determined to let him speak first.

The phoenix recognized me as a breather when he saw me looking out of your eyes.

A shiver runs through me. I wrap my arms across my chest, as if that could explain it, and concentrate on following the warriors ahead of me. *I—I remember.*

Now he keeps company with mages.

Yes. There is no getting around this, no pretending it might be otherwise. The phoenix will know Val for what he is. The mages, if they realize it, will consider him their enemy.

I can't risk it, Hitomi. I've already put my own people in enough danger. If these mages get a hold of me, they'll find you. And between us, they'll unravel where my people are as well. Even without you, they will. I don't know that I can survive another tower if it's mages holding me there.

I swallow hard. I understand. I do. He has to think of his people, and his own survival, but... *They'll all die, Val. Not just the mages, but the tribes. Every single person, every child. Val, I... I know I tend to throw myself at every piece of trouble I come across. But this is Huda and... and my* family *who will die if the phoenix isn't told. I've only just found them. I can't lose them now. Please.*

It's selfish of me to ask him to risk so much. I know it is, and I can't help asking, *begging* him, anyhow.

He's silent as we turn down a wide hallway with bands of glass mosaic at shoulder level. I don't know where we're going, but if Kherbanu and I can't get away, if there's no one waiting at the well, if we can't reach the phoenix ourselves....

I'm sorry, Val says, his regret washing through me. *I cannot do this thing. You said you're going to get free. When?*

I don't know, I say, swallowing down the rush of helpless grief that floods through me. He wants to help. I'm just asking too much. He's helped me every single time before this. Of course, he has to think of more than just me and the fires I throw myself into.

I go on, *Kherbanu and I were going to leave—and now there are these warriors.* I know he can see them through my eyes. *I'll have to help Kherbanu get away from them, and then we'll leave from there.*

The warriors pause before an ornate doorway. *You should go,* I tell Val.

I'm still here for you, he says. *I just can't seek out the phoenix.*

I nod. *Thank you.*

Without another word, he departs—one moment there, the next his presence fading.

Before me, the lead warrior opens the door and bows as they

step in. I hear the distinct cadence of Arnaz's voice. And then Eshvat, sounding far too smug and righteous.

Kherbanu lifts their chin, standing before the door, and the warriors shift, their hands going to their weapons. Kherbanu glances back at them, sharp eyes missing nothing. A look of regret passes over their features and then they step into the room. Rewniz makes to follow them, but the lead warrior shuts the door, shaking their head, and points back down the hallway, speaking in clipped tones.

I lean into a closed doorway, where a shadow might naturally fall, and watch Rewniz pass, expression grim. I don't dare walk between them and the warriors at their heels. Instead, I wait, barely daring to breathe, wondering if they will notice me—a deeper shadow than what one might expect—but they continue on.

I take a slow breath, watching them turn the corner, then start after them with soft, quick steps. I don't know precisely what is happening, but whatever it is, it can't be good. Kherbanu is under arrest—that is the only thing that would explain the warriors reaching for their weapons, or Eshvat's tone. They smarted under Kherbanu's sharp tongue and dismissive manners, and now their time has come. I don't know what they intend to do to Kherbanu, but I've been on the receiving end of magical imprisonments, and I don't wish any of them on my newfound mentor.

Unless someone helps Kherbanu, they aren't going to get out of this very easily. And right now, I need a mage to help me—to escape, to get to the phoenix, and failing all that, to do something about the talismans. We will just have to be one another's best allies.

I break into a jog, scanning the hallways as I hurry after the warriors, slippers clutched tight in my hand. I am not sure where Rewniz is going, and I'm not sure I can afford to follow them for much longer. We've already left the more ornate upper hallways. As Rewniz turns down another hall, I catch the sound of a familiar voice, faintly muffled.

I plaster myself against a wall, keeping my head down so I'm not quite at eye level, and wait five heartbeats as I listen. The warriors pass out of sight, but the voice has also quieted. I grimace, turning on my heel. The doors here are all closed. I'm just going to have to risk this—the longer I leave Kherbanu with Arnaz and Eshvat, the higher the likelihood that, if things have gone wrong, I won't be able to help turn it around. I have to try one of these doors, for better or worse.

I glance down at my shadow enchantment, my mage sight bringing it into focus. I may need it again soon—perhaps very soon, if I don't play this right. Working with quick, deft movements, I snip apart the web around me and wrap it around the glowstone I had in my pocket. The stone disappears into liquid shadow. I slip it back into my pocket, where the darkness will put the least possible strain on the enchantment. Then I slide my feet back into my slippers and pull the chime for the nearest door.

After a moment, the door swings open to reveal a waist-high maran in what can only be a nightshirt, pale white cotton falling to their knees. "Oh!" they say with delight, looking at me. "You the traveler!"

They speak a heavily accented version of the desert tongue I can only just make out, and they definitely just used the male form of "you." It's also nothing short of a miracle that they are learning the desert tongue at all, and happened to be behind this precise door.

"I am," I say, dipping my head as I grin. "I am looking for a friend. Can you help me?"

The child straightens up proudly. "I be your friend! Come!"

From the other side of the door, a voice calls a question in the maran tongue. My new friend turns to holler back an answer, and the next moment a middle-aged maran steps into view, pulling the door farther open. They stare at me, and I offer a hesitant smile and bob my head in greeting, wishing I could have just dealt with the child. This maran is slightly taller than me and still dressed for the day, though they've done away with whatever turban or head covering they might have been wearing to reveal a head of deep brown hair streaked with gold. The maran really have the most gorgeous hair.

"A friend," the adult maran repeats with a considering look, placing a hand on the little one's head as if to gently restrain them. They hop around excitedly, but don't actually attempt to jump on me as they clearly wish to.

"I am looking for a friend," I explain. "But I am happy to make one too. Perhaps you can help me?"

The maran glances down the hallway in either direction, no doubt wondering where my guard has gone. "Of course, honored one," they say. "Whom do you seek?"

"I need to speak to a maran I met at the feast, called Zohan. Perhaps you know whom I mean?"

"Of course," the maran says. "Elder Zohan is among my kin."

Is everyone related here? Well, actually, they might be. Four hundred years in a closed community can't be good on some fronts. I shake the thought from my head, forcing myself to focus. "Can you take me to them?"

The maran tilts their head. "Is something wrong, honored one? Should not Sheikh Kherbanu be with you?"

I sigh, waving a hand and doing my best not to show my frustration. "Kherbanu sent me to find Elder Zohan, but I have mixed up the directions."

"Oh! I see," the maran says, their expression clearing. "I can take you. It is something important, is it not? Come, it is not far."

"I come!" my little friend cries, darting out to grab my hand.

I glance up questioningly at the adult maran, who hesitates. Feeling rather bad, I say, "I must hurry. Maybe we can visit later?"

The young maran sighs and drops my hand and I feel a pang at this small deception. I know no more if I will see this child again than I do if I will survive what lies before me.

I bid them goodbye and gratefully fall into step with my escort. We hurry down the hall, turn in the opposite direction Rewniz had taken, and take one more turn into a wide, well-lit hall with mosaics underfoot in addition to the band of mosaics at shoulder height.

The maran stops before a carved wooden door, pulling the silken rope beside it to ring the chimes within. A younger maran opens the door, and after a few words with my escort, leads me in and goes to fetch Zohan. My escort bids me a pleasant farewell and departs.

The room holds a trio of low sofas constructed similarly to Kherbanu's char pai, except that they are all large squares instead of rectangles with two sides and a same-height backrest, all of them lined with bolsters. The woven ropes that form the surface of the char pai are topped by a thin but well-stuffed mattress, which is in turn topped by a silken carpet. All three char pais' carpets are well worn, shiny in spots, but no doubt still priceless—perhaps brought in a century or two ago and carefully cared for since. At the center of each sofa rests a silver tray with four empty cups, set upside down, as if this were both a sofa and a table. Despite how inviting the sofas look, I find myself too nervous to sit, and instead stand by the door.

"Ah, welcome, young mage," Zohan says with just a hint of confusion, stepping in from the far door.

"Elder Zohan," I say carefully, remembering how my escort referenced them. "Elder Kherbanu mentioned you were not pleased with the news shared earlier today."

Zohan makes no response but to raise their brows in question. Kherbanu was clear, though, that Zohan was both a sunshiner and disapproved of Eshvat's scheme. I'll have to trust in that.

"Mage Kherbanu and I were together in their study when a dozen armed warriors came to the door," I continue. "Kherbanu hid me among shadows before opening the door, perhaps believing trouble was afoot. The warriors escorted Kherbanu to a room not far from here. When they hesitated to enter, the warriors all reached for their weapons."

It's not perfectly accurate, but it's close enough to what happened. Zohan lifts their chin, gaze focused intensely on me.

I go on, "I waited beneath my shadow spell and heard both

Sovereign Arnaz's voice and that of Mage Eshvat. Mage Kherbanu entered the room aware of the blades at their back."

Zohan hesitates. "Did you hear anything of what was said?"

"It was in your language, honored elder. I could not understand it."

"A dozen warriors," Zohan mutters. "What do you think happened?"

"I think it was an arrest," I say baldly. "I believe Kherbanu meant to undo what Eshvat has set in motion. If your sovereign arrests Kherbanu...."

Zohan grimaces. "Then there will be no outside world for the rest of us to desire."

I shudder. I had not thought of it quite like that, but it is absolutely true. Destroy the world around the caves, and remove all hope for rebellion within. It's brilliant in a brutal sort of way.

"Can you help Kherbanu?" I ask.

"How long ago did this happen?"

I don't understand maran conceptions of time enough to answer in a way that they would understand. "Not very long; I followed Rewniz a short distance away from that room, then knocked on a door and was escorted here at a fast walk."

"So, they may yet be there."

I nod.

Zohan considers this a moment or two longer—far longer than I would like—before turning back to the adjoining room. "I will be ready in a moment," they say, and leave me to wait.

Thankfully, within a minute, they return in company with two other maran. "Let us go," Zohan says, without further explanation.

I dart out of the room and lead them at a brisk pace back the way I came. There's likely a faster route to our destination, but I don't know that hall well enough to describe it to Zohan. So, instead, we hurry past my little friend's door and around the corner to where I last saw Rewniz, and then back through a trio of hallways to the door Kherbanu disappeared through.

Zohan pulls the chime-rope, and without a moment's pause,

shoves the door open and steps in, calling a cheery greeting. The two maran follow directly behind them. I pause, my fingers going to my pocket. If things have gone sideways within, then....

I slip the shadowed glowstone from my pocket and peel off the enchantment, settling it over myself and sealing it shut once more. Then I slip through the still-open door. Stepping around the back of the rightmost maran, I press myself against the wall—nearly knocking over Kherbanu's staff in the process. I grab hold of it before it can fall, and quickly slip a strand of the shadow spell around it before pausing to get my bearings.

The room appears to be a meeting room of sorts, the walls lined with the same sort of sofa-tables that Zohan had in their front room, only these sport wool carpets rather than silk ones. Eshvat and Arnaz stand side by side, as if we have interrupted a private conversation. They are both dressed in the traditional clothes of their people, Eshvat's jacket a dark blue brocade, and Arnaz in emerald embroidered with amethyst. Both have clearly dressed for the meeting earlier today, Eshvat with their turban decked with jewels, Arnaz beringed and bejeweled as they were at the feast.

Kherbanu, in stark contrast to them, sits two sofas down, feet on the ground and back slumped, their face pale beneath the loose folds of their simple cotton turban. They are also, strangely, quiet. Far more concerning than Eshvat's arrogant demeanor, or the cold, cutting sounds of Arnaz's response to Zohan, is the absolute lack of grumbles and sharp comments from the old maran.

As I reach them, I bring my mage sight back into focus, and catch sight of a tight web woven around Kherbanu. Where the shadow charm lies against my skin softly, only a whisper of a presence, this spell is all large, great ropes wound tight. There is nothing subtle or gentle here, nor is there much in the way of nuance. It is a prison, the magic strong as bars. Although, without nuance, it hardly seems like it could hold someone as wily as Kherbanu.

I slip to my knees beside Kherbanu, and under cover of the

conversation between the other maran, whisper, "I'm going to help you out of this."

Kherbanu blinks, and a smile flickers over their lips. "There's a corner I can't get, looped around my shoulders," they murmur.

I tilt my head, catching sight of their hand resting against the edge of the sofa on the other side of them. Slender threads of magic run from their hand to each set of loops Eshvat has fashioned. No, they really hadn't thought this through. Kherbanu likely would have gotten free in the next few minutes had I not arrived to help them.

I slip around to their other side and reach toward the magic banded around their shoulders. Gently, I tease out a thread of magic, channeling it down to their hand. They catch hold of it with perfect control.

"Under the sofa with you," Kherbanu mutters.

I hesitate, and they jerk their chin down even though they can't see me, their attention on Zohan as the maran turns toward us. Arnaz says something, and Zohan, dipping their head, asks Kherbanu a question in marani. Kherbanu tilts their head, the jut of their chin telling me exactly where I need to be. They offer Zohan a clipped answer. Eshvat frowns, watching Kherbanu a moment longer before returning their attention to the distraction I've brought. Zohan really is doing a good job in that quarter.

"*Child,*" Kherbanu all but hisses.

With a faint sigh, I lay the staff on the sofa beside them, releasing the strand of magic that hides it from view, and then drop down to crawl beneath the wooden frame. Except I still have Kherbanu's belongings in their makeshift sheet-pack on my back, so I end up having to worm my way underneath like a top-heavy beetle.

The next moment, Kherbanu rips apart their cage, the magic flashing blue in my mage sight. They toss it back at Eshvat, their voice breaking through the room at the same time, loud and unamused.

Eshvat yelps, raising a hand to bring up a hasty shield that barely protects them—and doesn't protect Arnaz at all. The spell rebounds off Eshvat and wraps tight around their sovereign instead. Arnaz staggers to the side with a shriek as the spell seals itself around them.

Zohan helpfully cries out, jumping in front of Eshvat to grasp at their sovereign's arm, and seemingly accidentally sending Arnaz toppling to the ground instead, arms now bound at their side.

Eshvat turns on Kherbanu, fury in every move. The spell they send at the older mage is meant to incinerate—all fire and fierce heat. Kherbanu isn't expecting it. Even with their staff in hand, they barely manage to shield us both from what would be a killing spell. I reach out, and do what I do best, channeling the magic rushing around the shield before it can curl around and burn us, and winding it into a tight ball. The shadow spell around me catches against the edge of the magic I hold, fraying and falling to pieces, but I haven't time to worry about that.

I channel a bit of the fire-warm magic in my hand into the shield, strengthening it as Kherbanu holds it steady. Kherbanu straightens infinitesimally, my aid easing the strain on them. They say something sharp and mocking.

Eshvat staggers slightly, having expended rather more magic than they intended. They stare at Kherbanu in dismay, then look from Arnaz upon the floor to Zohan crouched in the way of any help Eshvat might offer there, to the maran at the door, staring with wide eyes. Witnesses, I realize. That was a brilliant move by Zohan, so long as we all survive.

As Eshvat gets their bearings, Kherbanu murmurs, "I'm going to take down their shield. Then I'll send a sleeping spell at them; can you make sure it gets to them?"

"Yes," I say, shifting forward to the very edge of the sofa.

With an impressive amount of daring, Kherbanu drops their shield, a new spell already prepared and in hand, and sends it hurtling across the space to Eshvat. The spell crashes against their shield before disintegrating, taking the shield with it—which is exactly what Kherbanu intended.

"Now," Kherbanu murmurs, already weaving their new spell. I channel a single thread of magic up to connect to their spell, connecting as Kherbanu tosses it forward and immediately attempts to bring up a new shield. I only just manage to keep my connection, sending my thread of magic looping out around the forming shield.

Kherbanu didn't aim the spell any more specifically than Eshvat's general vicinity. The younger mage is already bringing up another shield—hasty and half-formed, but enough that the sleeping spell won't hit them. Except Eshvat isn't expecting me; a fact Kherbanu is absolutely depending on.

I tweak the spell, pulling it sideways, so that it drops down to bounce across the floor, slowing to a stop near the edge of Eshvat's shield. The spell is already weakening—it wasn't meant to hold together on its own, but rather latch on immediately to its target. I draw on the magic around me, channeling it through the thread to the spell huddled before Eshvat, inert and unthreatening.

Faintly, I hear Eshvat laugh, no doubt jeering at Kherbanu for such a failed attempt. I concentrate, watching, and catch the edge of Eshvat's shield shifting as they move. They haven't created a full shield to encapsulate them, just a single side facing Kherbanu. Which means, yes, *there.* I send a pulse of focused magic through my connection. The sleep spell skitters sideways and—with a final nudge—tumbles around the edge of the shield to Eshvat's feet.

They yelp, attempting to dance out of the way, but the magic brushes their ankles, and the next moment they are falling, their face pale and eyes already fluttering closed. They don't even blink when their head hits the wooden edge of the sofa behind them. They sprawl at its foot, breathing heavily.

"Well done," Kherbanu says to me. "I wasn't sure the spell would last, but you took care of it."

"You didn't do too bad yourself," I say, crawling out from under the sofa, wishing the shadow spell had outlasted Eshvat's attack. I am reminded yet again of how undignified it is to worm one's way out from under furniture while others watch. I don't mind Kherbanu seeing, but both Zohan and their pair of witnesses watch me curiously. I feel about as impressive now as I did clambering out from beneath Stonefall's bed at the Mekteb while he watched me from above. I feel my face flushing and hope no one here can see my embarrassment through the golden tones of my skin. They probably can.

Slowly, Zohan straightens from their crouched position next to their still magically bound and distraught ruler. Arnaz spits a curse at Kherbanu—or at least, I assume it is such from the general sound of it.

Zohan shakes their head in response. "I am afraid, on behalf of the Convocation, I must place you and Mage Eshvat under arrest. You have endangered not only the safety of the desert, and so our own survival—for there is no surety that we could withstand what will sweep across these lands due to Mage Eshvat's actions. Further, you have turned upon your opponents here with unsanctioned and unprovoked violence."

Ah, he said that for me, for when Arnaz responds in furious tones, keeping to their own language, he replies again in Tradespeak. "You may defend yourself at the trial, for I have no doubt there will be one. You and Mage Eshvat as well."

Arnaz looks daggers at Zohan, but holds their silence.

Eshvat, however, lets loose a great, unrepentant snore.

CHAPTER 32
A THIEF OF SORTS

It takes several hours to sort things out. Once Arnaz and Eshvat are officially under arrest, the Convocation gather to decide the maran's path forward. And while Kherbanu *could* run off into the desert with me, it seems they'd prefer to leave with their people's blessing. I can't fault them, it's just that there is precious little time to waste on anything that doesn't involve survival.

I pace Kherbanu's rooms, Tahmineh and Dalileh my companions and unofficial guards for the time being—my actual armed guards who usually wait in the hall were relieved of their duties thanks to Zohan's orders.

"You should rest," Dalileh tells me. "Once you start your travels, you'll be pushing hard to reach your destination, will you not? So, it is best to start off refreshed."

They're not wrong. I sigh and grab a blanket and settle down in my favored corner, to Dalileh's horror.

"There is a *divan* in the next room," they tell me. "And a sofa as well."

"I'm fine here," I assure them, and my body—perhaps much better at understanding my needs than my brain—prompts me to yawn. I curl up and drift into a light sleep, only waking when—finally—Kherbanu returns.

"Awake, child?" they ask, peering down at me, staff in hand.

"Yes," I say, surfacing from under the blanket with only one relatively mild flail of my arms. "Can we go?"

If we still have to sneak our way out now, I'm going to find a way to leave little gritty spells behind in everyone's beds. I can probably repurpose half the glowstones down here to that end. The maran will never know what hit them.

Kherbanu pokes me with their staff, which sends me to my feet faster than expected. As I stumble to keep my balance, they say, "You young people have no patience. I need your help with a spell, and we must tie up a loose end or two. Then we can leave. Rewniz will accompany us, and we go with the blessing of the Convocation."

"What spell?" I ask, grabbing my bag and Kherbanu's makeshift sheet-pack. I would have repacked it by now if they actually had a bag, but something about never leaving their homes means the maran don't seem to have much need for good-sized traveling bags.

"I'll tell you on the way," Kherbanu says, nodding to Tahmineh and Dalileh. I take my leave of them, thanking them both for their help—and Dalileh, again, for my inkings—while Kherbanu nips into their bedroom to retrieve a small pouch.

As we hurry back through the halls, Kherbanu briefs me on the status of the Convocation's two prisoners. Arnaz has been released from their magical cage and placed in a holding cell, awaiting their trial. Eshvat, however, remains caught in the sleep spell, now snoring away atop the sofa beside which they fell. The trouble is maintaining a binding on them that they can't attack with magic once they wake.

"What do you plan to do?" I ask, glancing with concern at Kherbanu. They move briskly, but they also lean on their staff rather more than they did before.

Kherbanu, misreading my concern, pauses to offer me a hard look. "Nothing permanent, mageling. Eshvat has not been found guilty of anything. I've a pair of metal bands here that were used once before to seal a mage's abilities within them—it's a temporary sort of measure, as the spells weaken over time and an accomplished mage can take advantage of that. The bands should hold Eshvat for the better part of two weeks, though, which should be enough for the trial, given that it begins tomorrow and I've given my testimony to the prosecution already. You'll need to speak with them as well."

I shudder. Kherbanu raises a brow, then gestures me on. "You don't wish to?"

"No, it's fine," I say, not knowing how to tell them that I've stood trial before the High Council, that the prosecution I faced was cold and hard and empty of mercy. Or that the idea of facing a prosecution now, even just to share my testimony against an injustice I witnessed, still fills me with dread. I'm not fine, I'm scared. But it's something I'll have to face, because what Arnaz and Eshvat stand for—what they have set in motion, and what they intended in binding Kherbanu—will never be okay.

We find Eshvat snoring away on their sofa table, sprawled rather messily as if whoever lifted them could not be bothered to make them comfortable. I can relate, though I don't like it. Grimacing, I pick up their wrist from where it dangles over the edge and set it on the sofa beside them. Then I wipe my fingers on my shalvar.

Kherbanu extracts the bands from the pouch, and I have a moment of vertigo staring at their silver finish, the sigils etched into them. The only marked difference from the cuffs Blackflame's minions used on me is that these are not connected to each other, and each sports a small emerald set into the metal—a talisman to keep the spells active when not in use, and no doubt the reason that they could have been stored for decades, or more, without the spells fading to nothing.

"Have a look, then, and see what you can do to strengthen them," Kherbanu says, dropping the bands into my unwilling hands. I fumble them, and have to steady myself to keep from sending them skittering across the floor.

"You can do it, child," Kherbanu says with unexpected gentleness.

Oh. They don't really need my help. They want me to understand these spells so if something similar is ever used against me, I'll have some knowledge, a starting point to break myself free.

I offer Kherbanu a wan smile and turn my attention to the bands. I start by recharging the talismans, gathering and channeling the latent magic around me into them until they fairly glow with stored magic. It doesn't take very much. Then I work my way through each sigil, testing its form and function, smoothing snarls and strengthening weak spots. I revise my opinion of the spells' age—they must be at least a century or two old, the talisman recharged a few times since their making, but they're showing their age. Everything I learn I commit to memory in the hope that I will never need it, but the knowledge that I might.

When I'm done, Kherbanu makes a quick study of them, then slips them over Eshvat's wrists. They contract, thickening around Eshvat's wrists until they are just snug enough that no amount of tugging will remove them.

"That's done, then," Kherbanu says.

"Young mage," Zohan says from behind me, startling me. I don't know when they arrived. "If you will come with me, you may give your testimony to the Convocation's representative, and then you and Mage Kherbanu may depart to seek the phoenix."

If we can find the phoenix in time, which is not guaranteed. I glance back at Eshvat, still sleeping, then focus on the jewels bedecking their turban. "A moment," I say, my mind racing. "Mage Kherbanu, you said that Eshvat introduced flaws into the talismans we sent with the phoenix."

"Yes?" Kherbanu says.

"With your permission," I nod to include Zohan, "I would take Eshvat's jewels in reparation, to form new talismans. If we cannot reach the phoenix, then the talismans themselves must be replaced at the center of the Burnt Lands."

Zohan glances at Kherbanu, as if seeking confirmation of this plan. Kherbanu nods slowly. "It is a sound idea, mageling."

So I go to meet the Convocation's representative with an

armload of half-stolen jewels—the turban with its carefully attached gems, three large bejeweled bangles, and four glittering rings. I suppose I still am a thief of sorts.

My takings do not make it any easier to sit before the trio of maran who await me, Zohan to one side and Kherbanu to my other. I walk through the events of Kherbanu's arrest and rescue, and for the first time, find myself being truly honest with the officials listening to me. I don't know what testimony Kherbanu gave, and so must assume they did not lie. Nor is there any reason to—stating that Kherbanu meant to undo a wrong is hardly a crime, and so our preparations to sneak out are the actions of those who care for a people's survival, rather than criminals intent on law-breaking. Even if I must then admit that I did not tell Zohan the full truth when I went to ask for their help. Zohan merely nods, as if they assumed they didn't have the whole story, and Kherbanu gives a small, amused snort.

Still, I clutch my hands together, aware they are damp with sweat, and twice have to pause so my voice does not shake. How this is more frightening than facing Blackflame and the rest of the High Council, I don't know. Unless I am simply still carrying that with me.

Kherbanu lays a gentle hand on my arm as I finish answering the last of the maran's questions. "Well done," they say.

I force another smile, aware that the day is slipping away. How much longer until the phoenix begins his work? Bringing Arnaz and Eshvat to justice will not matter if the draining spells are still unleashed across the desert.

By the time we step from the room, it is deep into the night. Kherbanu's steps are dragging as we make our way back to their rooms. Rewniz waits in the workroom, dressed for travel, a large pack full of supplies by their feet. Such are the benefits of having support: an actual pack built for travel, with the food and water we'll need to make it more than a day or two. Not to mention a warrior to carry it all.

"Here," they say, reaching to take Kherbanu's makeshift pack from me. I pass it over, and while Rewniz makes quick work of putting away Kherbanu's belongings, I wrap up Eshvat's turban and slip it down to the bottom of my bag, along with their stolen jewelry.

"Do we rest or leave now?" Rewniz asks, strapping their pack shut again.

Kherbanu grimaces and eases down onto a stool. "I do not think I have much left in me today. Let us start in the morning. As it is, I doubt any of us know the desert well enough to navigate it at night. Unless, child, you know how to read the stars?"

"No," I say regretfully. I may have been learning, but I don't know the stars that well. Further, I recall little from my midnight ride to the Howling Caves.

"I have received instructions on landmarks from one of our gatherer families," Rewniz says. "But they will be harder to recognize at night."

It's not a long walk to the camp well—if we covered it in a half hour or so of breakneck riding, surely we ought to be able to walk it in a couple hours? But from the look of it, Kherbanu doesn't have that in them, and we might be more sure of not going wrong if Rewniz and I can actually see where we are going. A darkened desert offers little in the way of landmarks.

"By first light, then?" I ask, trying not to give in to a creeping sense of foreboding at such a necessary delay.

Kherbanu nods. "At first light."

CHAPTER 33

A PACK OF TROUBLE

B y the time we reach the final pass to the campsite, the sun is rising, casting deep shadows across the valleys. I don't recognize the hills per se, and my friends' camel tracks have long since been swept away by the wind. Instead, we follow the landmarks Rewniz was told to look for, Kherbanu stumping along beside me, slow but steady.

Now, they pull out a pair of charms from their pocket and inspect them briefly before passing one to Rewniz. "Your glamor. Might as well put it on."

Rewniz slips on the ring. The glamor is so subtle I don't immediately catch the shift in the line of their nose, or how their pupils have rounded out. They grin, and their canines are no longer sharply curved. If they have any other physical markers of their maran heritage, they're well hidden by their clothes. A quick glance at Kherbanu shows the same effect of their glamor. It is just subtle enough that even another mage would be unlikely to mark it as a true disguise rather than a small vanity—to hide a blemish or improve the line of one's nose. Perfect.

"Hikaru?" a voice calls.

I twist around, my heart leaping. On the ridge of the hill before us, a figure rises to their feet. "Who—? *Val*?"

The speaker starts down, toward us. All but his eyes are

344

covered by his kufiyah, his thobe and bisht giving only a vague sense of height and strength. "I'm glad you made it out," he says, his violet gaze taking in our little group. His voice is as familiar as my own. "I was beginning to worry."

"*Val*!" I cry, stepping forward. Then I'm running, not even questioning this happiness crashing through me, this absolute *relief*. Even if he can't go to the phoenix, he's here, somehow, impossibly, and—

"It's all right—Hikaru?" he says as I throw my arms around him, slamming into his torso. His feet are braced and arms held uncertainly above him. And then, carefully, he pats my back. "It's all right," he repeats, but this time the words are different. Gentler.

I hold him tight, my face pressed into his bisht. I'm a good bit shorter than he is, my head definitely not even in the neighborhood of his shoulders. "You're here," I say into the rough cotton. "How are you here? And did you bring a camel?"

"I brought two," he says, his voice laughing.

It is *so* strange to hear it with my ears, to feel it reverberate through his chest. I drop my arms and step back, realizing belatedly that a physical hug is a bit different from a mental presence.

"I was worried we wouldn't make it in time," he goes on, as if it were perfectly normal for me to have tackled him with a hug. He reaches up and pulls down the end of his kufiyeh that was tucked up to shield his face. The hair peeking out from under its edges is dark as night, his skin more tanned than I recall but still pale in comparison to mine. "Admittedly, you told me where you were days ago, but when you called for me yesterday, we were still some distance away."

"We?" I echo, bewildered.

He nods his head toward the pass. "I thought you might need a guide, and that the best guide might be a friend. Or three?"

"What?" I say blankly.

He makes a shooing motion, but he's smiling, just a crook of his lips, his eyes laughing. "Go see."

I turn, cast one glance toward Kherbanu and Rewniz who are

watching us with great interest, and sprint for the pass. A friend. *Three friends.*

I hurtle around the edge of the hill into the next valley, one hand holding my turban in place, and spot no fewer than *five* camels standing near the well, a pair of small travel tents, and a trio of people gathered before the small cook fire.

"Huda?" I call, flying across the sand toward them.

"Ukhti!" Huda cries, as if I were truly her sister, breaking into a run to meet me.

I laugh despite myself, despite the betrayal I am trying to make right, because in this moment, this is everything I needed: my friends gathered together, a path forward clear before me.

The other two figures start after Huda belatedly. "Cousin," one of them cries, bright and cheerful. I catch the gleam of a crooked grin on familiar features. *Laith?* "You have returned to us!"

"She was *our* guest first," Kareem says, elbowing Laith as they thunder toward me.

I gasp a laugh, already out of breath, and then Huda envelopes me in a hug. I hold her tight, aware that we are both laughing with relief, holding tight to each other. Eventually, Huda leans back to exchange the customary three air-kisses, from one cheek to the other and back again. The boys have come to a stop a few feet away, grinning.

"How are you all here?" I ask. "I thought the phoenix told you I wouldn't be returning."

"We stayed anyhow," Huda says, reaching out to take my hand. "We were concerned about you."

Behind me, Kherbanu snorts a laugh. I hadn't realized they'd already caught up to us. "With good reason, I'm sure," they say dryly.

Huda dips her head respectfully toward them.

"Did you meet Ravenflight?" I ask.

Huda looks back at me with suspiciously wet eyes. "She came to the well to rest for a day before leaving to report to the High

Council. She told us you were dead." Huda's hand tightens on mine. "That she'd seen your body."

"I'm sorry," I repeat softly. I had worried about this, had hoped that my friends wouldn't mourn me, but I had no way to reach them. "But then how are you here?"

Laith gestures toward Val, who has come up beside Kherbanu and Rewniz. There is just a bit of awe, and pride, as Laith says, "Rahhal Al-'Ajami arrived among my people, asking for me by name."

Rahhal Al-'Ajami—is that Val's name among the desert dwellers? While I recall a good bit of Val's stories of his travels through the desert, I'm also relatively certain he never mentioned gaining enough of a reputation that the people of other tribes would have heard of him. From the look Laith sent his way, though, it's clear his reputation precedes him.

Laith goes on, "He assured me you were still alive, that your death had been a trick to end Ravenflight's pursuit once and for all. We were able to catch up with bint Ahmer and ibn Saleem, and circled back to the well late last night."

Late last night? "When did... Al-'Ajami come find you?"

"Just yesterday," Laith says. "It was a blessing our friends had not ridden far and we were able to reach them."

Our friends? I glance from Laith to Kareem and Huda... and note the faint rose tint to Huda's cheeks. Now *that* is interesting.

"We had ridden to join a nearby camp of our relatives," Kareem explains. He glances toward his sister, then adds carefully, "We were about to set off to the meeting of the tribes when Laith and Al-'Ajami arrived. I believe," he glances at Laith, "you were only so close because you intended to do the same."

Laith now very carefully is not looking at Huda. "Yes," he agrees with impressive brevity.

I'm missing something, though I'm not sure what.

"You have some very good friends," Kherbanu says, with peculiar emphasis.

Oh, I've been appallingly rude. "Forgive me, I should have introduced you…" Only we have not actually discussed a name for Kherbanu, not to speak of a mage name.

"I am a mage," they say firmly, and pause. They don't have a name saved up either.

Their given name will work, but they still need a mage name or they won't be able to pass as a noncriminal human for even a night. I cast around for some example of their magical abilities, and come up with the most obvious. "High Mage Kherbanu Frozenfrog," I say, using the desert tongue except for their mage moniker, which is traditionally given in Tradespeak.

Kherbanu stares at me, aghast. Even Rewniz seems taken aback. I grin at them both. As far as I'm concerned, it's fair payback for losing my hair to Kherbanu's magically augmented venom. Val's eyes bulge comically, but the rest of my friends, not knowing Tradespeak, dip their heads at once and welcome *Mage Frozenfrog* to their camp.

I introduce Rewniz next as Kherbanu's kin, and their lack of any known last name is not questioned by my friends, because the desert folks are the *best* at not questioning guests. I am coming to absolutely love that about them.

"Come sit and tell us your news while you take a quick refreshment," Val suggests. "Even if we must move on, you will need your energy."

Kherbanu gives a heartfelt sigh of agreement.

As soon as we are seated around the fire, a cup of water in each of our hands and a loaf of barley bread and a bowl of olives set out before us, I turn to my friends. "We need to find the phoenix as quickly as possible."

"What is wrong?" Huda asks. Laith glances once, quickly, at Val, before returning his attention to me. Val himself just regards me steadily. If I needed a reminder that he is older than any of us, except perhaps Kherbanu, this is it: the way he just waits, quietly. The boys seem like—well, like *boys* beside him, the same as Huda and I must seem no more than a pair of girls. Or, as Kherbanu would have me, a disaster of a child.

"There is a great deal wrong," I confirm to Huda, to buy

myself time to actually *think* about how to present what Eshvat did without simultaneously damning the maran in my listeners' minds.

Thankfully, Kherbanu knows what they wish to say. "The phoenix called on my people to send a mage to work with him, to lay the groundwork, if you will, for the rest of your desert mages," they explain. "I am but one of two mages among our people. Being older, it seemed wiser for the younger mage to go in my place. But the mage who aided the phoenix in my stead carried a secret directive: our leader did not wish for the Burnt Lands to be opened."

Huda's eyes narrow as she turns to them. "What do—ah," she breaks off, and then says, carefully, "I do not understand what this means."

Oh, she doesn't know which form of *you* to use in the desert tongue for Kherbanu. Neither do I—which is why I've been so happy to use Tradespeak instead. Unfortunately, that's not an option for Huda. So instead, she's restructured her sentence completely.

Kherbanu, unaware of this new complication, goes on, "They vandalized the phoenix's work. The spells will not collapse safely as the phoenix planned. They will instead break through the Barrier. If they do, the draining spells will spread through the desert. They may well destroy everything in their path for a few hundred miles." They pause. "Even if the draining spells do not expand, the explosion of magical power caused by the Barrier's collapse might well destroy much of the desert."

My friends stare at us in horror. Then, Huda says, "Surely the phoenix will notice what this mage has done?"

"He would have no reason to look at the talismans again," I argue. "Once they've been formed, they don't naturally break down for decades, sometimes even centuries, if they have enough magic to sustain them. We can't trust that the phoenix would think to inspect them again."

"How is this possible?" Laith demands, glancing from

Kherbanu to me. "Who is this mage—who is this leader, that they would order such a thing? What enmity do they have with us?"

Well, so much for not asking questions of one's guests, though I can't fault Laith for breaking with etiquette, considering the gravity of the offense.

For the first time since I met Kherbanu, the older maran looks genuinely humble. "I beg your forgiveness on behalf of our people. Our elders were horrified, and I have left my home with their blessing to try to stop what was put in motion. That is how I came to be here now, in company with your friend."

"Please," I find myself saying, "Let us not now blame a people for the actions of their powerful. The mage and the leader have been dealt with, and Mage Frozenfrog has ventured forth to make things right. What matters now is that we reach the meeting of the tribes in time to warn the phoenix. The mages who have gathered to help him can study the talismans, find what this mage has done and correct it. We must get there before the phoenix moves forward."

"The meeting is far and may already be over," Kareem says. "We will have to skirt the Burnt Lands to reach it. From here, it may take as long as three or four days."

That's too long. Arnaz gave the maran only two days to go underground, and I'm not even sure if today would count as the first day or the second. I had hoped they were being cautious, but if the phoenix called the tribes together while Eshvat was still completing their work, two days from now may be all we can hope for. I hesitate, my mind racing. "If the talks have been completed, the phoenix will have bid the mages to stagger themselves along the Barrier."

"So, we might meet with a mage while riding the Barrier," Laith says.

"Or we might not," Val points out.

He's right—there's no certainty. While I want to hope for it, we need more options. The one option I really don't want is the one at the bottom of my bag. "Is there any way to get there faster?" I ask with a touch of desperation.

Huda and Laith shake their heads. "A pair of us might ride ahead as fast as possible, but it would be the same path. We would save no more than an hour or two."

Which leaves us with the worst option possible.

"How long would it take to ride to the center of the Burnt Lands instead?" I ask.

Kareem hesitates, glancing toward Val. Huda says, "We don't know the Burnt Lands as we do our own, but I would estimate it at about two days. More or less. Does anyone else here know better?"

Well, those are the two days we possibly have, if Arnaz wasn't counting yesterday. One can also hope they counted in an extra day for safety, in which case we *might* be all right.

"Two days sounds about right," Kareem agrees slowly. "If it can be done, and if there were good reason to attempt it."

It can, but I wouldn't have survived either time without the phoenix. Or Val. That doesn't mean I'm not willing to try again, but I don't like the risks. Two days in means that is where our path will end. We won't have time to come back out before the phoenix begins his work. Even without a backlash to worry about, the amount of magic on the move could be extremely dangerous, though theoretically survivable.

Taking a slow breath, I say, "We need to replace the flawed talismans, so that—if we do not find the phoenix—their work will not fail as we have described."

Val closes his eyes in sudden understanding, then nods, refocusing on me. "Crossing the Burnt Lands is no small endeavor, but it can be done. Let us start by traveling to the Barrier. If we can find a mage within a short distance, then we need not worry about crossing into the Burnt Lands."

Is he going to come with us, then? I study him uncertainly, not sure if something has changed, or if he simply intends to part ways with us before we meet anyone.

"That would be convenient," Kherbanu agrees, taking a second slice of bread from the plate. "I will try to signal to what mages might be about when we get closer."

"Are you comfortable meeting them, then?" Val asks, leaning back to assess both maran. Because *of course* he recognizes Kherbanu from seeing them through my eyes in the caves, regardless of the minor glamor they're wearing now.

Kherbanu studies him. "No more than young Hikaru, I am sure," they say. "But what must be done, must be done."

Val glances at me, and then offers Kherbanu a conciliatory smile. "It is the same with me, honored mage. It seems we are a pack of trouble come together."

"What do you mean?" Kareem asks, brow furrowed. "Are you *all* also hunted?"

I choke on a laugh and take a bite of bread to keep from having to speak.

"Subtlety, child!" Kherbanu chastises him. "Do young people know nothing, nowadays?"

"Apparently not," Val says, winking at Kareem. "You young ones ready the camels while our guests complete their meal. We must make what haste we can."

Huda, Kareem, and Laith step away from the fireside, Laith calling back a question to Val. As he answers, Kherbanu leans toward me and murmurs. "I'm very curious how you got a message to your friend from our caves."

"I have no idea what you mean," I say uncertainly.

Kherbanu snorts. "He did say you spoke with him yesterday. Which *ought* to have been impossible with the wards we have in place." They wave a hand in amusement. "But by all means, keep your secrets."

CHAPTER 34

LIKE THE TALES OF OLD

The camp is packed in no time. Val helps Laith and Kareem load up their camels, having already taken care of his while they took down the tents. As it turns out, in addition to the spare camel Val brought along, Laith brought a camel for me from his uncle's herd—given to him before Mirage-cleft left for the meeting called by the phoenix. With two extra mounts, and my having brought two unexpected companions, only one camel will have to carry two riders. My friends quietly agree among themselves that I have more riding experience at this point than Kherbanu, and as an elder, they will need the extra support.

Only once we are all mounted and moving do we hash out our destination along the Barrier. The choice lies between the dead city I first came through, the point that the phoenix last brought me out, and a point in between the two. It seems unlikely a mage will be stationed at the city considering its only access from the desert is a bridge across a deep gorge. A mage would have to risk the possibility of pack creatures gathering on the other side, with no way to avoid them and still access the draining spells. Conversely, the point the phoenix led me out through last, while ideal for reaching his haven, might add a little more time onto our journey toward the center of the Burnt Lands. We therefore opt for an accessible part of the Barrier a little closer along our path than that, and so hope to shave a couple of hours off of our journey.

With our specific destination decided, we shift to traveling in a string—Kareem in front, followed by Huda with Kherbanu, and then Rewniz, their camel's lead connected to Huda's camel. I go next, glad to have my lead connected to Rewniz's camel. Laith brings up the rear, assuring eyes on the many inexperienced riders in the group. Val rides separately from us as our scout, ranging ahead, then falling back to watch for trackers.

An hour into the ride, Val brings his camel to walk beside mine. I can't sense his emotions, can't read him as I've grown used to being able to in the conversations we've had this last month and more. But I can sense *him* now, the reality of his presence, in a way that I can't quite explain, whether he's beside me or far enough ahead he's out of sight. There's just a thereness to my sense of him when before there was not.

"Are you really going to ride with us?" I ask. "Or will you part ways before the Barrier? It's all right if you need to—I understand you need to protect your people. You've already done so much, meeting me here, bringing my friends here too. You don't have to do more."

"I knew you would need them. It seemed kinder not to leave them grieving your supposed death longer than necessary." Val looks over the head of his camel. "You realize that if we find a mage in place of the phoenix, they may take you prisoner. And if we don't, and you enter the Burnt Lands to place your new talismans, you may never leave again."

I do know it. "What else would you have me do?" I ask.

"Ride," he says quietly. "Ride as hard and as fast as you can away from these lands."

Is that why he's still here? To ride with me? But no—he brought my friends *for me*. He already knows I won't walk away. "I can't," I say simply.

"You can. The Council believes you dead. Leave now, and you have a chance of outrunning these other fates. Two days' ride from here and with a ward to shield you, you will outlive this madness."

"At what cost? If the phoenix doesn't find out what Eshvat did—if the talismans aren't replaced in time—the desert and all who call it home will die."

"Then warn them." He says it easily, as if it were the most reasonable thing possible. "Tell them to leave. Everyone you care for is either already with us, or within a short ride. So warn them, and then take yourself to safety. Let their warriors carry your message to the phoenix. Let Mage Frozenfrog take the talismans into the Burnt Lands—it was their colleague who betrayed the phoenix in the first place. You owe him nothing anymore."

I take a slow, deep breath. I don't owe the phoenix anything, that much is true. But Huda and her family, Laith and my uncle and the family I barely know—even if I warned them all, even if they rode to safety, would that be enough? Would I be able to sleep at night, knowing there were other families, children and grandparents, mothers and fathers, who died because I was not there to help reach the phoenix? Does it matter that I don't know their names, will never meet most of them? That there is no debt here to speak of?

"That's not...."

"Not what?"

I straighten my back and meet Val's gaze steadily. It's hard to say this, to speak it out loud, but I know I need to. "That's not what I want," I say firmly. "You're right; there aren't any debts left. But I love this place and its people, the family I have that I don't yet know, and the people I have never met—and never will. If there's a chance that I can stop the Burnt Lands from destroying them, then I will, as much as for them as for me."

"Good."

"Good?" I echo, taken aback.

He smiles ruefully. "If I'm going to keep you company on this venture, then you had better not be doing it from some misplaced sense of duty. Doing it for yourself, because it gives you something to keep living for? That's different."

It wasn't just the phoenix and Kherbanu who were worried about me, then. I run my fingers over the rough weave of the blankets draped over my saddle and let his words sink in—the worries, and the reason he's still here. "You don't have to stay with me," I say finally, looking up. "The risks are the same for you as for me—more, with the secrets you need to protect."

He looks away, considering my words. "Nevertheless, I will take the risk."

I drop my gaze to the gauntlets that hide my markings. "Why are you doing this?" I ask.

He is quiet for a moment, the only sound the creak of saddles. Then he sighs. "Because you are right."

I hold his words close, not having realized how much I needed to hear them. If I am going to die, knowing that I am not alone in seeing the necessity is a gift. Likewise, knowing that Val is here not merely out of duty, but out of love—even if he will not say it in so many words—heals another part of me that withered when my mother turned away from me. I hold that feeling close, the warmth and peace and gratitude of it, resting in it.

Val continues to ride in silence beside me. I let myself look at him, tracing the changes in him since we last met. He seems—healthier. Better than he did even over those last days at Stormwind's cottage. The ensuing year has allowed him to recover in a more real yet intangible way after what Kol did to him. More than merely being able to eat again.

"You'll tell us if you need to rest," he says, as I continue to study him. He's letting me look, aware of my gaze.

Embarrassed, I turn away. "Yes," I agree, trying to collect myself. "I'm pretty well recovered from the venom. I suspect it's Kherbanu who will need more rest than I."

"We'll call a rest in a few hours, without telling them why. As it is, you and I cannot afford to push ourselves too hard now, before we enter the Burnt Lands."

I nod, glad to have his experience at hand. As much as I want to rush ahead, pushing myself to the limit, collapsing halfway through the Burnt Lands will only ensure our failure.

"You have a good head for these things," I say, remembering how he paced himself a year ago when we escaped Kol, and carried me when I actually did collapse. Because he's been more open now than in the past, I try pushing for a little more from him, as lightly as I can. "How did you end up in that tower, anyway? Did you plan something criminal by any chance?"

He looks at me, startled. "Surely you don't think I'm a criminal?"

I snort. "I have rogue hunters after me, and if any of them knew about you, they'd be after you too. Criminality isn't always about ethics. Sometimes it's about who makes the rules."

Val laughs. "I know that. I just wondered how you see me."

That's... unexpectedly vulnerable, coming from Val. Gently, I say, "As a friend, of course... So, the tower?"

Val reaches up to smooth his kufiyeh. "No crimes, I'm afraid. It was more of a hostage situation gone wrong."

Hostage situation? My eyes narrow. "Wait a minute. Hostages are important people."

"Not always," Val says as casually as if we were discussing horse lineages, or strains of cabbage. "Sometimes they are just convenient."

Maybe generally, but I suspect not in this case. "You were important."

"You're making me regret riding up next to you," Val says with some amusement.

I snort. "Doesn't matter where you go, though, does it? Can't get away from me. So, your prince, whom you had to go back to, who just *exiled* you—how *exactly* are you related to him?"

I half expect Val to brush me off, but instead he says simply, "We're brothers."

I nearly fall off my camel. "You're a *prince?*" I demand, scrabbling to keep my balance.

Val reaches over to steady me. "In a manner of speaking. My brother's the eldest and rules our land, and has a daughter of his own who will take up his mantle in due time, assuming she passes our council's examination. I'm the spare."

"Wait, wait, wait," I say, unable to contain myself. "You were a *prince* locked in a *tower* who needed *rescuing?* This is even better than a fireside tale!"

He drags a hand over his face, but his eyes are definitely crinkled with amusement. "I will remind you that we rescued each other."

"Yes, yes, I'm sure that's how most stories *actually* go, but you're the heroine of your own tale!!"

"In most such tales, the rescuer," he tips his head toward me, "marries the one requiring rescue," he looks down at himself with great discomfort. "However, I am *significantly* older than you, and also—"

"That would just be wrong," I agree cheerfully. "You probably have a long-lost love though, who will set everything to rights."

Val stiffens—it's just the slightest tension in his shoulders, but it says far more than the too-casual way he waves me off. I open my mouth to tease him, and realize I've probably said more than enough already. He's been exiled because of me, which means if he *does* have someone he loves, he left them behind on my account, after having already been separated for a year thanks to Kol. Which isn't funny at all.

"Well," I say, pretending I haven't noticed a thing, "it's still a good story as it is."

"Which we do not need to tell anyone."

"But don't you think little girls *need* stories about rescuing princes from towers?"

He pinches the bridge of his nose. "No one needs such stories."

I roll my eyes. "Everyone does, but I'll keep quiet about it for now, just for you. Once we sort things out with your prince—excuse me, your *brother*—we can decide how we want to tell it."

He laughs helplessly. "You are—"

"An absolute terror," I provide, grinning. "Kherbanu thinks so too."

WE BREAK at midmorning for a short rest, then in the midafternoon to sleep through the hottest hours of the day. Kherbanu is exhausted but grimly ready to continue. As evening settles in, we stop to stretch our legs and cobble together a cold meal, and then mount up again. My legs are achy, unused to riding once more—if I ever really got used to it. At the same time, all I want to do is send the camels racing forward, their brisk pace rubbing at my patience. But, as Val noted, we will need our strength, and so too will our mounts.

At each break, I have Kherbanu cast the base spells for some of the jewels I carry, and I finish the work of making them into talismans. By dinner, we have spelled all but the smallest of the jewels.

I keep a watch on the horizon, and am beyond grateful when my mage sight shows the faint white dome of the Barrier in the distance. Kherbanu sends messages winging away in the hopes of their reaching a mage stationed nearby—but we all know it is a slim chance at best. Such messages, sent over a short space and to a specific target, have the same chance of arriving as a handful of butterflies might passing through a meadow rife with birds. Which is why mages don't generally bother trying to use them. Without a certain target, Kherbanu's messages are merely a hope sent out on the wind. It is worth the effort, but none of us rely on it.

Finally, near midnight, we reach the Barrier.

Kherbanu grumbles wearily as they heave themself off Huda's camel with Rewniz's aid. Given how tired and sore I am, I can't imagine how the older maran must feel. As it is, I know they've struggled to sleep whenever we've stopped, unused to the constant desert wind, the overwhelming prospect of the wide-open desert. Leaning heavily on their staff now, they stare up at the Barrier in fascination, then cross to take me by the shoulder. "Show me," they say.

"Perhaps we should send up a signal first," Val suggests, coming up beside us. "If the phoenix and his mages are keeping watch on the Barrier, they may see it and come to investigate."

"Oh, yes, of course." Kherbanu sets their staff into the sand before them, angling the quartz at its top toward the sky, and sends a shaft of rose-colored light shining up into the air. Far above our heads, it explodes in a flowerlike design of sparks, bright in the night sky. "That ought to do it," they say. "If anyone is looking, which they may not be."

That is the problem, precisely. Such a signal will only work if the right person is within sight, awake, and watching the skies. None of those are a given, let alone all three.

Val keeps a watch for us as I lead Kherbanu forward to study the Barrier. Everyone else is busy with caring for the camels and setting up camp.

"Go slowly until you hit the draining spells," I caution Kherbanu. "You don't want to stay long among those." They nod, and I step into the pale white light. The Barrier feels the same as it always has, and though I spend a few moments assessing the flow of magic, I can find no cause for alarm. At least it remains as strong as it was when I first assessed it.

I press forward another foot, step through to the other side. The draining spells still swirl up against the Barrier, roiling and eddying, thick and viscous as old blood. Here, a step past the Barrier, the land is precisely as I remember, a faint sheen of magical strands spreading through the earth, and the air utterly parched. I tug on Kherbanu's hand, pulling them through after me.

"*Wai barman!*" Kherbanu gasps as they cast around. I may not know marani, but that sounded appropriately horrified. They drop my hand to grab my shoulder.

"Is something wrong?" Val asks, stepping through after us.

"It's just empty," I tell him, trying not to breathe too deeply. The absolute lack of magic is always a shock, even though I've experienced it a few times now. Kherbanu knew what to expect, but they clearly did not realize what it would actually feel like. I'm not sure any mage is really prepared for something like this.

Val nods, looking around slowly. In the dark, with the moon waxing but still not full, it's hard to tell much beyond what is immediately before us: a wide plain, empty but for a littering of rocks, and in the distance the dark bulk of hills. I wonder if the Burnt Lands feel any different to him than the desert behind us.

"I'm going to assess things a bit," I tell Kherbanu. They let go of my shoulder with a nod.

Sitting down, I tease a thread of magic from the sapphire talisman I wear, using it to reach the draining spells underfoot, just as I have a hundred times before. I follow the veins of magic out across the Burnt Lands. I don't spread my awareness wide, not wanting to exhaust myself unnecessarily. Instead, I traverse a single pathway, doubling back to try different branches, assessing what I find.

I find the slight snarl of magic, still repairing itself, where I drained the great tentacled beast. And farther away from that, even, I find a steady loop of magic, small but unwavering, which must be the entrance to the phoenix's haven. I go on slowly, not pushing myself but letting my consciousness flow with the magic, and finally, finally, I find what can only be the talismans.

Beneath them is a great, messy knot of magic, impossible to miss, and difficult for the draining spells to self-heal. More than that, the draining spells around the knot are linked to the talismans. Even now they feed into them ever so slowly, the connection tenuous—but not so fragile that it might break. Rather, if the veins collapsed together into a greater vein, they would easily flow into the talismans. The talismans themselves are placed closely enough that they will function together to draw in the magic—if one fills too soon, the others will continue to absorb what remains.

At least, that must have been the phoenix's plan. If most of them fail, the surviving talismans won't be able to absorb the sudden release of magic, and the shockwave would travel out again. If most of the draining spells have already been dismantled, they won't be able to absorb the resultant shockwave either—leaving the Barrier as the final, flawed defense. It's *possible* the Barrier will survive it. But it's really, really unlikely. Once the Barrier goes down, the surviving spells will self-heal and spread, accelerating as they absorb more and more magic. Eshvat's plan is both simple and utterly diabolical.

I pull my consciousness back into my body and sit a moment, breathing in the empty air.

"Done?" Val asks from beside me. Kherbanu has gone to the other side of the Barrier and is about to send another streak of pink light into the sky. We'll have to spell the last of the jewels as talismans tonight—better to do it before we sleep than start the morning newly tired.

I sigh and haul myself to my feet. "Yes. The phoenix has set the talismans he had; all that is left is for the attempt to be made. If Eshvat spoke the truth and the talismans are flawed—and I can't imagine they lied—then the danger is as great as we feared."

Val grasps my shoulder, meeting my gaze with perfect confidence. "Then we ride. Together."

It's not a promise of everything working out, of our reaching the phoenix in time, or stopping what could amount to cataclysmic destruction. It's only a promise to try. A promise that I am not alone, that I have others to lean on just as they may lean on me. I'm not sure why it makes me want to cry.

"Together," I agree.

CHAPTER 35
CROSSING

As dawn begins to lighten the horizon, we make our final plans. Kherbanu only somewhat reluctantly agrees that they can best aid our efforts by riding the Barrier, sending up signals at intervals and attempting to draw the attention of any nearby mages to deliver our warning. Kareem agrees to be their guide, and Rewniz elects to accompany Kherbanu as well. This is the territory of the Bani Saqr, which means that Kareem will be more familiar with it than anyone else here, barring Huda.

The rest of my companions, as it turns out, intend to come with me. I had expected Val, but Laith and Huda take me by surprise.

"I see no reason why I wouldn't come with you," Huda says, eyeing me severely. "It seems to me that you'll need someone with you who has been used to traveling the desert recently. And you should hardly travel alone with a male, however trusted, when you don't have to. Since we are more or less sisters, you can't refuse me."

"I...." I say, unable to form a coherent argument while just wanting to hug her.

"And since I *am* family," Laith says, not to be outdone, "you can't leave me behind either."

Huda, her expression hidden from him, rolls her eyes, grinning.

Val says carefully, "You must both understand the odds of survival are low. Once we enter the Lands, there is a great likelihood that we will attract the spell-creatures. Bint Al-Ghaib has fought them before, and I have seen them. The chances of all of us surviving every encounter ahead of us are... not very high."

Huda's laughter falls away and she purses her lips, looking no less committed than before. Laith just nods.

Val goes on, "Further, if Mage Frozenfrog and your brother are not successful, we will be caught within the Burnt Lands when the phoenix begins his work. Regardless of whether or not we are able to replace the talismans successfully, there will not be enough time for us to travel out of the Lands. To be caught within such a magical maelstrom could be deadly—we might survive it, we might not. You must understand this."

Kareem looks from Val to Kherbanu and then to me, his expression drawn. But our survival is not up to them either—it is out of everyone's control. No matter how hard they ride searching for a mage, if there is none posted between here and the meeting the phoenix called, they won't be able to stop this working. Once Val and I step into the Burnt Lands, we will never be able to travel fast enough to replace the talismans and leave again. Even just reaching the talismans feels uncertain.

Huda drops her gaze, and I can see her thinking of her family, the people she may never see again. Even Laith looks subdued.

"I will come," Huda says, her voice firm.

Laith nods, then offers me a crooked grin, strained around the edges but still there. "Can you imagine what our uncle would say if I let you go without me, cousin? I would probably be exiled for my selfishness. You had better have pity on me and let me come."

I shake my head, smiling despite myself. "It isn't my choice, or his."

"No," Laith agrees. "Still, I would not watch you leave without me, knowing I might aid your journey. As Al-'Ajami says, there are many dangers ahead of us. If I can protect you from some of them, and so ensure our people's survival, then I cannot walk away either."

Rewniz, who has remained a quiet but steady presence through the whole of our journey, says now, "Perhaps one of you would travel with Mage Frozenfrog and Kareem ibn Saleem, and I might take your place with bint Al-Ghaib. I am trained as a warrior, after all."

Laith frowns. "I am perhaps not as accomplished as you, akhi, but I am yet capable."

Val tsks softly, glancing toward the brightening skies. "We do not have time left to argue. Those who are coming into the Burnt Lands, bring your camels to the Barrier. We will need a camel each for our party."

We rise and pack the last of our belongings. I have already changed out my maran clothing for my desert garb, knowing it would be more suited for the ride ahead of me. Now I pack my remaining clothes into a saddlebag, making my own little bag light enough that I can sling it crosswise over my shoulder and head, resting against my back for easy access.

Eshvat's turban and jewelry remain safe within it, along with the last of my charms—the broken-edged seeker; the lapis ward string I repaired with Kherbanu; the shattered bit of the crow statuette Val made me a year ago which holds only memories and no magic at all; and my two differently colored glowstones. I stand a long moment, my hand brushing over these little vestiges of my life, as I remember the phoenix's treasure room, the detritus left behind by the mages who died in the Burnt Lands, my own broken spindle. It seems an unspeakable tragedy that all that should be left of a life are a few small bits and pieces.

"Child," Kherbanu says from behind me.

I turn, forcing a smile.

They watch me with unaccountable sorrow. "If I were just a little bit younger and stronger," they say finally, "I would make this ride for you. But I think you have a higher chance of success than I, and in saving this land, that is what matters. I—I am sorry you must pay such a price."

I take a slow, uncertain breath, and feel my eyes filling with tears. Kherbanu sighs and gathers me into their arms. I lean my head against their shoulder, and let myself feel for just a moment. I don't know why it hurts to hear their words, to know that someone else would do this for me if they could. My heart feels simultaneously shattered and healed, and I rest in Kherbanu's embrace as if it were the safety I know I can never attain.

"There, child," they murmur. "There, child." It is a soft observation that gives no false comfort, just care and sorrow and company. It is everything I need.

I pull away sooner than I would like, swiping my arm across my face. "Thank you," I tell them. "I am grateful for everything you've taught me and given me."

"And I, you," they say.

I smile in return, allowing myself to accept this rather than question it. I am just beginning to understand that connection goes both ways. That to refuse love given is to hold my own back. I want to be able to love and be loved for whatever time I have left.

"Take this," Kherbanu says, pressing their staff into my hands. "There is nothing here I cannot cast of my own accord. Perhaps it will be of use to you."

I curl my hands around the smooth wood, my fingers brushing the thin fabric they have wrapped around the upper part of the staff. The charms hanging from their cords swing back and forth from the top, the rose quartz nestled among the twisting nest of carved wooden branches holding it in place. This staff is a work of art and time, something that Kherbanu must have kept with them for decades, the spells so expertly woven as to feel as if they were a single casting instead of a dozen layers seamlessly fused together. The quartz itself contains its own small reservoir of magic, a simple talisman to serve my needs.

"Thank you," I tell them, my voice catching. Despite having given it to me with so little fanfare, it is a great gift indeed.

I unloop the chain of the sapphire talisman from my neck. "You should keep this in return," I say, passing it to them. I won't need more raw magic in the Burnt Lands than their staff can offer me, and this will ensure they won't tire themself out drawing on magic to send up the signals we so desperately need someone to notice. Perhaps it will lend their story the credence needed to get whatever mage they meet to pay attention—it's heavy and gaudy and just the sort of thing a mage would take note of and respect, even if they don't recognize it as being from the phoenix.

"And this," I add, passing them my old seeker charm. "There's one on your staff I can use. Perhaps this will come in handy for you."

Kherbanu takes it solemnly, cradling it in their hand, as if it were the greater treasure by far. "Go in peace, child," they say. They lay their hand against my cheek for a single, sweet moment before stepping away to rejoin Kareem and Rewniz.

We depart all together as the dawn lights the sky above the far hills. Kareem, Kherbanu, and Rewniz follow the Barrier toward the set meeting place of the tribes, while Val, Huda, Laith, and I ride through the Barrier. I point us in the direction of the snarl of magic marking the placement of the talismans, and my friends do the actual navigating.

We travel quickly, making our way through dead valleys and over windswept ridges as the sun rises over the hills. An hour goes by, all of us anxiously scanning the land, and then another hour. I use my mage sight, watching for the telltale movement of magic that would be the spell-creatures approaching, and still I sense nothing beyond the spells underfoot.

The hills grow higher, more rugged. Anxiety gnaws at my gut. When it was just me alone, spell-creatures found me quickly enough. It seems strange that we have gone farther than I ever have without sighting even one. I wish the phoenix were here to fly overhead and tell me what he sees. Granted, then we wouldn't need to be racing across the Burnt Lands in search of him.

We ascend yet another low ridge to look down into a wide

valley, the hills throwing their shadows across the sandy expanse below.

"There's a thickening of magic there." I point halfway down the hill and over to the right a good three hundred paces. "I'm not sure what's caused it."

Huda squints, bringing her mount to a stop as she looks, but there's nothing visibly unusual from here. "Do you want to check it?"

I really don't. I examine the spot with my mage sight anyway, of course. The network of magic pulls together until it forms a rope that appears to run through the hills a distance nearly half as long as the valley behind us. It's not *messy*, and I don't think it has anything to do with Eshvat... but I can't tell what it actually is. "I don't like it," I say.

The camels shift restlessly, well aware of our tension. A dry breeze blows, cooling the sands and leaving me with the taste of dust on my lips.

"Do we avoid it?" Laith asks.

I nod. Whatever it is, distance seems like a good idea.

"This way," Val says, gesturing toward the other end of the valley. "Stay close together."

We start down, the camels picking their way over the scattered brown rocks. I divide my attention between scanning the valley for other dangers and keeping an eye on the veinlike rope of magic.

It takes me far too long to realize that the vein is moving.

"Stop." I twist in my saddle, staring through the bright daylight at the vein of magic. It shifts again—

"Up," I say, gesturing frantically. "Fast—get back over the ridge. *Now.*"

Huda shouts to the camels, Laith yanking his mount around. Val keeps his camel beside mine, his face turned toward the far end of the valley. We surge back up the hill, but not fast enough. Nowhere near fast enough.

The vein of magic bursts from its tunnel, a spell-creature as wide around as a horse is tall, and indescribably long: a worm taken to obscene proportions. It towers for a moment over its hole, the sunlight gleaming off a set of wide black pincers—or are they jaws? Along its sides, small, sickly appendages wave slowly, as though tasting the air. Vaguely, I recall the phoenix speaking of sand strikers lying in wait for prey to pass through the mountainous regions of the Burnt Lands.

"Wait—" I gasp, clinging tight to the saddle as our camels race for the ridge. It's checking for us—if we hold still—

The sand striker darts forward, straight over the rock-strewn hillside toward us. More and more of its long, segmented body comes out of the tunnel as it moves. It crosses the distance between us in the time it takes for Huda to shout for her camel to run faster.

"*Jump!*" I cry, twisting toward Laith, just behind us. The nightmare creature slams down barely twenty paces away, skidding over the rocks toward Laith, its jaws wide and gleaming. Val vaults from his camel in a leap that no human could make, one arm out to sweep Laith off his saddle. He shouts as they tumble down. I cannot see where they land past the camel, can hear nothing past the camel's terrified shriek.

The sand striker snaps its jaws shut around the camel, cutting off its scream with a sickening crunch. Dark liquid sprays as the creature rears up, its jaws folding in to shove the already silent camel down its massive throat.

"Laith!" Huda cries, panic edging her voice. Among the rocks, Val pulls Laith to his feet. I glance toward the sand striker, towering over us, my hand tight around Kherbanu's staff. It will turn its attention back to us any moment.

I tease a bit of magic from the rose quartz at the top of the staff and send it slicing across the distance to the sand striker. It's a horrifying thing, this creature without eyes or brain, its only purpose to hunt and kill what crosses its path. Its own structure is solid, unsnarled, but I've learned enough now that I don't need a natural flaw to work with.

What I do need is a way to dispose of the magic I'm about to release. I'm not about to save us from a spell-creature only to slam my friends with a magical backlash. I shove a hand into the bag at my back, fingers closing on one of Eshvat's rings, and throw it toward the sand striker, keeping a thread of magic connected to it.

As I did with the great kraken, I need to create a flow of magic through the spell-creature, and then channel that into the talisman. I reach back up through the connection I've created to the sand striker, take hold of a separate, central strand that reaches to its jaw, and snap it free. The sand striker stills, the only movement that of its gullet slowly moving the camel down. I urge the magic along the strand, drawing the thinner connecting strands after it.

The creature shakes itself. Faintly, I can hear Huda's voice, and Val shouting back to her—or perhaps to me.

I catch a second strand, snapping it free and funneling the two strands' magic together. *Flow*, I command, and urge it on, funneling my own fiery magic into the sharp-edged strands, drawing on the connected latticework of spells to drain the magic from the outer reaches of the sand striker—the tip of its tail anchored into the hill, its pincers.

The creature rears up even farther, letting out a roar that reverberates through my bones. The camels scream in return, and I have a dim sense of Huda fighting to keep control of our mount. But the magic of the creature is flowing now, dissolving its own structure in a fury of liquid stone.

Out, I command as the magic cascades up the spell-creature's body to its awful maw, and then slams right out of it. I channel it, my hands moving as I shape its arc, the staff slipping from my grip. But I have the sand striker's magic now, the stone in my body singing to it, and it is only a matter of gently guiding it into the talisman waiting in the rocks below me.

I can hear shouts, vague and unformed, even as I hold the channel steady, the magic tearing out of the creature and streaming into the talisman. In another half breath, it is done.

I find myself slumped over my saddle, Kherbanu's staff teetering sideways on my lap. I blink slowly, my mage sight still bright in my eyes.

"Hikaru?" Huda asks, and I realize she's right beside me on

her camel, an arm out to hold my elbow, keeping me steady. The camels are still wheezing in the aftermath of their terror, the sound rubbing at my nerves. "Hikaru."

"Mmm?"

"Are you all right?"

I nod woozily, glance about for Laith and Val. "Are they...?"

"We're fine," Val says from somewhere to my other side. I turn my head to see him and Laith on one camel, and beyond them, the rocky desert valley. The sand striker has fallen and rolled to the bottom of it, great stone segments of its body broken apart by the impact. I somehow missed that happening.

"Would it be safer to go around?" Val asks, nodding toward the valley and its contents.

I shake my head. "It is undone," I say, my mind beginning to focus. "The danger is in other spell-creatures coming to investigate what happened."

He nods. "Could you ride with bint Ahmer? That will distribute our weights better, and you can rest a bit."

I don't think it will make much difference to the camels; I am not *that* much lighter than Laith. But I am tired, and that is likely Val's greatest concern. Magic working comes at a cost, even if I've learned to manage it better. At least my markings only ache a little.

"Here," Huda says, bringing her camel a step closer, so that we are side by side, my knee brushing the back of her leg. She takes Kherbanu's staff, tucking it snugly into a loop among the saddlebags. Then she grasps my arm and steadies me as I scramble from one camel to the other.

"Can you get the talisman I threw?" I ask Val as I settle myself. I point in its general direction, and he dismounts to look for it. Laith swings over to my vacated saddle with far greater grace than anything I can manage. I catch a glimpse of the corner of his thobe splattered with darkness—not his, but the camel's blood. That was terribly close.

As if reading my mind, Laith says in accents equal parts awe and delight, "That was *incredible*. The stuff our stories are made of!" He waves a hand at the broken creature. "You saved me, cousin."

I feel my cheeks warm in embarrassment.

"So did Al-'Ajami," Huda teases, a grin pulling at her lips. "Don't forget him." I've never seen her so relaxed around Laith. Belatedly, I remember the panicked way she called his name when the sand striker swallowed his camel, and we lost sight of him and Val for a moment. Teasing him is the only way she's going to let herself show her relief.

"Did you *see* him leap across the space to me?" Laith demands, all oblivious. "You are both magic, aren't you?" he says to me, clearly not expecting an answer. He shakes his head, awestruck. "Incredible."

"It was," Huda agrees in an undertone.

"The phoenix and I worked together to develop the method I used," I tell her. "That's the only reason I could do it so effectively."

"You've mastered it then," she says, glancing back down into the valley. I am grateful for her respect, and that's she's tempered her reaction. Laith's awe is more than enough for me.

"Found it," Val says, walking back to us. He tosses the ring to Huda, who catches it deftly. She passes it back to me, and I slip it into my pocket, testing it—it is not even a quarter full, which gives me hope that the wealth of stones I carry will actually be able to absorb what the diamonds Eshvat sabotaged will release.

"I guess we know why the phoenix didn't bring you this route," Huda says dryly.

Laith give a high, slightly panicky laugh. I know the feeling.

"Quickly now," Val says, swinging up onto his camel. He leads the way down into the empty valley, past the great stone carcass of the sand striker. It is larger even than I thought at first. The rough-edged round segments of it rise above our heads like massive stone discs, heat rising in waves from their surface, and a strangely metallic scent permeating the air. The pincers and various waving appendages have fallen and lie shattered among the rocks. It's surreal to pass among the wreckage of the creature, the dull stone dark in the late morning sunlight, as if it were absorbing the light itself.

As we crest the next hill, I keep a nervous watch on the land around us. The blast of magic I released from the sand striker would have acted as a beacon, even if it remained focused as I channeled it. It may well have drawn the attention of spell-creatures for leagues around, and it's foolish to assume that we won't cross paths with them. We'll need to get as far away as possible quickly, before they converge on us.

Val turns his camel, his gaze coming to rest on me. "We cannot cross here."

I look down, but where the valley floor should lie runs a deep gorge with steep walls, like a chasm leading into the depths of the earth. There is no way our camels can cross here.

Huda points to the northwest. "The hills fall away there."

Val shades his eyes as he studies the direction she indicated. "We'll be able to move faster there, and avoid any more of those sand strikers." His gaze flicks back to me. "It will add a little time, but it is better that than losing more time to chasms we must find a way around, as well as the possibility of another attack. We must weigh time against survival."

I nod. I want to argue that I can undo the next sand striker as easily as I did this—but it's exhausting enough continuously scanning the hills with my mage sight. I am wearing myself out quickly; signing up for more magical battles than necessary would be foolish.

We follow the ridge down into the next valley. We pass through that valley in quiet, and then another. As I scan the third with my mage sight, I stiffen.

"Hold," I call, my voice low and urgent. I lean forward, focusing on the shifting spells over the earth, the touchpoints they create to the draining spells.

"What is it?" Huda asks, as Laith and Val turn back to us.

I tilt my head, watching the compact spell-infused bodies race over the dirt, the flicker of legs.

"What is it?" Huda repeats, turning to squint through the overbright sunshine.

"Pack creatures," I say, my voice rasping. I blink away my mage sight as I point. Without it, they look like nothing so much as a small dark clump flowing over the far hill.

"Can you tell how many?" Val demands. "I can't count them."

Even with my mage sight, they surge together a little too closely to count, but I estimate anyhow because of all of us, I've the clearest sense of them. "A dozen or so." I frown, trying to focus. "The longer we stay ahead of them, the more I can pick off before they reach us." Once they do—it doesn't bear thinking. "We need to go." I glance toward Val beseechingly. I need to focus on the spell-beasts; I can't also take charge of our movements.

I needn't have worried.

"You go ahead," Val orders Laith. "Take us over that ridge, then angle east toward the next valley opening. I'll ride at the rear. *Move.*"

I close my eyes. Once again, I draw out a strand of magic from the rose quartz, channeling it to the earth below, and follow the strands of the spells underfoot to the pack creatures racing across the earth in the valley behind us.

I can't fight them all. Not one by one, picking them off as they run. But... maybe I can use the power of one to unravel the others. Or at least slow them down. I reach up into the first spell-creature, trying to grasp the magic at its core, but it lifts its paws as it runs and I lose my connection before I can establish it. I try again, and again, aware that I am sweating, sliding into Huda as the camels pick up their pace.

"There's one," Val says as I try again, which can only mean they've come over the ridge we just crossed ourselves.

The next time a paw hits the ground, I twist a thread of fiery magic around it and *yank*. The creature stumbles, which is more than long enough for me to grab the magic at its core. I twist and slam two cords together to create a flow, and then blast the magic through its body toward the other running figures. There is no elegance in this, just fury and brute power and desperation.

I have two channels of magic to follow, and I follow them both, because there are a dozen creatures and I've only undone one. The first blast of magic slams into the torso of another creature, and I use its force to break apart the core structure. The other blast of magic I don't manage to aim quite so well—it flows right through the third pack creature's legs. I grasp the threads of magic and rip them away before curving the slowly dwindling magic to hit another pack creature. The third creature shrieks as it falls, its legs turned to stone beneath it.

I laugh, a hoarse, half-hysterical sound. I don't have to unmake them; I just have to take off their legs.

I arc the magic around, bringing it back toward the front of the pack, slicing over the ground and dragging at each spell-creature I touch along the way until bits and pieces of their spells come away to join the larger flow. I can hear Val shouting something, see the frontmost pack creature leaping up in a strange sort of double vision of reality overlaid with magic. My heart stutters, and then my magic catches up as I drag it forward in a whirlwind, flying through the creature as it unaccountably rebounds back into the flow. It shrieks, turning to stone as I liquefy its spell-structure and whirl the magic around one last time. Except, there is nothing left to chase us.

Grimly, I slow the magic, bringing it arcing back in a great lazy loop and drawing it into Kherbanu's staff. I've depleted some of what the staff offered. It's no talisman, but it was built to house magic. It takes most of what I've stolen from the pack creatures, giving me time to pull out Eshvat's ring and add the remaining magic to its stores.

"Well done," Val says.

I turn toward him slowly, my awareness settling back into me. His sword is drawn, and there's a line of blood against the fabric of his sleeve—there must be a tear, though I can't see it.

"Did it—did you...." I can't quite find the right question. I shake my head helplessly.

"I knocked it back," he says, watching me steadily. "You did the rest."

"Oh." I rub my eyes. "The magic I released will draw other spell-creatures. We need to ride."

Val gestures and we start moving immediately. I sigh in relief.

"Eat," Huda says, passing me a pouch of dates.

I take them gratefully, savoring each sweet fruit as we ride on and scan the land for more dangers.

CHAPTER 36
A RISING STORM

We leave the hills behind for rolling dunes and wide-open flats filled with sand. Val sets a brisk pace for the camels—it seems the sort of thing they will be able to keep up for leagues, while still reserving enough energy to run if needed. I keep a note of the placement of the phoenix's talismans, but as I widen my awareness, searching for spell-creatures, I find the little loop of magic I know so well: Morningmist's work, marking the entry to the phoenix's haven.

"Pack creature in a *pit*," I mutter, turning my head toward it as I blink away my mage sight.

"What is it?" Val asks sharply.

"Nothing. It's just," I gesture with frustration, "the phoenix's haven lies there. Do you see those bumps? That must be his town."

Laith grimaces. "Then we might have traveled the route you last took and spent less time in the Burnt Lands than we have, and avoided the sand striker as well."

I remember suddenly how he spoke so animatedly of camels with Kareem. Was his camel that died a favorite?

Huda squints toward the buildings. "It would have taken half a day's travel to reach the place where Kareem and I met the phoenix and Hikaru—we've cut that a fair bit, to have neared his haven already. This route was faster, though likely more dangerous."

Val glances at me. "How much longer to the center where these talismans are placed?"

I shake my head as Huda shrugs. "It's hard to judge distances with my mage sight. Maybe three times what it would take to reach the phoenix's haven?"

Val casts a glance at the sky. It's three hours past sunrise, nearing on midmorning, which gives me a sudden, utterly unfounded hope that we'll make it safely to the talismans, and perhaps back again. Wouldn't it make the most sense for this sort of work to be done in the morning? Surely no one starts such work after lunch.

I try not to get my hopes up as we press forward. An hour later, I've watched the phoenix's haven grow closer, the banyan's reaching branches a grey mass just slightly taller than the visible buildings. And then, as we continue on, it slowly recedes again.

"So," I say to Huda, resting my head against her shoulder for a moment. "Tell me something new."

"New?" she echoes, and I have the distinct feeling there's *something* she has to share, even if she hasn't yet decided how to do so.

I lift my head to scan the land again. "If you like. To pass the time."

Huda rolls her shoulders back, then casts a glance at Val— ahead of us—and then Laith, bringing up the rear. "There is a bit of news. You know Karrem and I stayed with ibn Hamza at the well until Ravenflight came there and told us you were gone."

"Yes," I say, guilt tugging at me. "I'm sorry."

She waves a hand, still looking ahead so I can't see her expression. "We grieved you, offered the prayer for the dead for you, and parted ways."

Somehow, I never thought of that—that they would not only grieve me, but that they might pray for me, perform the ritual prayer that is a right of every believer. Even though they did not know my faith, they offered me the greatest respect they could.

"Kareem and I rode to a nearby valley to join our cousins' relatives and decide our path from there. They had some news for us." Huda casts a look over her shoulder at me. "As part of the peace talks, my parents agreed to my marriage."

"What?" I say blankly. "I thought you said it wasn't likely that —I mean—"

"I know," she agrees. "I did not expect it either. That is why my parents were not at all concerned when I came to meet you instead of joining them at the meeting of the tribes. But our relatives informed us that Kareem should accompany me there as soon as possible."

Wait. My brow furrows as I remember Laith saying how he intended to ride to the meeting as well... "Who will you marry?" I ask.

Huda dips her head, faintly embarrassed, as she says, "It seems Hamza ibn Mansoor was impressed with me when we crossed paths with him in the lands of the Bani Essam and I demanded an escort of him."

I remember Huda telling me Hamza ibn Mansoor was the greatest warrior of his tribe. He had complimented her courage— and allowed his only son to head our escort. My eyes nearly bug out.

Huda glances back and coughs a laugh at my look. "Yes," she agrees, meeting my gaze. "That was my reaction too. It seems I am to marry Laith ibn Hamza."

I open my mouth and close it again. Laith, judging by his bright looks and crooked grins, *definitely* likes Huda. She, on the other hand, has always treated him with a sort of brusque and careful distance. Except when he nearly got killed, and that concern on her part was very quickly hidden. "Um," I manage. "Wait, so this whole journey—?"

"We've known we're riding in the wrong direction to get married?" she says, humor tinging her words. "Yes."

"No *wonder* he insisted on coming with us."

Huda snorts. "I'm sure it was a consideration, but you've a

measure of Laith by now. He would have come with you regardless."

True. But I can't quite wrap my mind around Huda expecting to marry Laith in the next few days and then—being *married?* "Are you all right with it?" I ask hesitantly.

"With riding into a spell-infested land to save our peoples together?" Huda asks, grinning. "I suppose so."

"And being married?"

She sighs, looking ahead again. "For the sake of peace? Yes. It would be quite hypocritical of me not to be."

"Yes, but I mean, to Laith...." I sneak a look back to where he rides, kufiyeh askew, utterly oblivious to our conversation.

Huda shrugs, and I wish she would turn her head back so I could read her expression even just a little. "I would rather him than someone I had no idea of. I hope he is not too disappointed himself. That will make it much harder."

I blink. "Um, I think his father must have asked him, though, don't you? If he meant to ask for you specifically?"

Huda glances back over her shoulder at me, brow furrowed. "I suppose he might have," she allows. "At least, Laith doesn't seem upset."

No, he seems pretty well pleased to me, now that I think about it. But Huda might need to figure that out on her own. Or Laith might need to convince her of it. "Guess I better make sure we survive this all, then," I say, the words coming out grimmer than I intend.

Huda gives a soft laugh. "Was this not the news you were asking for?"

"I had no idea what I was asking for," I assure her. "None at all."

"I know," she says lightly. "But I am glad to have told you."

"I'm glad you did too," I say. "If we survive this, that will make you my relative."

"We are already sisters at heart," she says severely. "Laith knew you second."

I laugh. "True. Sisters come first, anyhow."

"Always," Huda agrees.

I lean forward to wrap my arms around her in a backwards hug. She raises a hand to pat my arm where it crosses over her other arm.

"There," Laith says from behind us, his voice raised.

What? I let go and twist to look for what he has spotted, my mage sight showing me no sign of spell-creatures. But there, far to the left, a faint bright light cuts upward along the edge of the Barrier. It is curved and formed of bright green, nothing like Kherbanu's signal. Oh no.

"A signal," Huda says, her voice bleak.

I swallow hard, scanning the Barrier as far as I can see. From here, at least, nothing else is visible; no other answering signal curves through the sky. Which may just mean we are too far from those points to see anything.

"And not Mage Frozenfrog's, I would say," Val agrees, drawing his camel around to join us.

"No," I say.

"Our path turned out to be the shortest to the phoenix's haven from where we began, and that signal was even farther away," Laith says as he reaches us. "We are likely closer to it now than our companions are."

I cast around helplessly. "We can't make it to the talismans," I say. "They're still too far, and the mages will work quickly now that they've begun signaling each other." Nor am I sure we'll make it to the signal we saw.

"How much time do we have?" Val demands.

None. They're beginning. We'll be caught within the Burnt Lands as they unmake the spells. We'll die, and if the phoenix hasn't discovered Eshvat's work, we'll only be the first.

"Hikaru," Val says sharply.

I push down on the panic. "We have only a few minutes," I say, since I need to give him something. The signal—if I've read its purpose right—will alert the mages staggered along the edges of the Burnt Lands. Only once all of them have responded in kind will they begin their work. Five minutes? Ten at best? Nothing certain enough to promise.

Huda twists to look at me. "You have your talismans that are still whole. Is there anything you can do with them from here?"

No. What can I possibly do? I swallow, my throat dry, and remember Val's words from earlier. "I—I can try. I need to think."

"Good," Val says, turning his camel to the side. "We'll ride for the phoenix's haven while you plan. Tell us if you need to stop."

"The haven?" I echo as Huda turns her camel as well.

Val shakes his head. "It's a good thing we're with you. I intend to see us survive; you take care of saving the world."

Huda lets out a sharp-edged laugh, and then the camels leap into a run. I grab onto her waist to keep from falling and try to focus my thoughts on what I can possibly do with an armload of talismans, far off from center of the Burnt Lands and unconnected to the flow the phoenix's mages will create.

But all I can think is that we should have left the Howling Caves without waiting for the Convocation's blessing. I should have pushed the phoenix to take Kherbanu instead of settling for Eshvat. I *really* should have bopped the phoenix over the head and told him not to be a fool when he decided to abandon me to the maran. He may have done it out of love, but settling for someone who was clearly not fully reliable in the first place was never a good idea.

None of it matters. What matters is this moment, my friends urging our camels on faster, a spot in the distance that we can barely hope to reach, and a cataclysm of magic that will envelop the whole of the desert. Even if Val's intuition is right and the phoenix's haven might shelter us, everyone else will die.

"Can you signal the mages in some way?" Huda asks as I cling to her. "If we saw their signal, they might see yours."

My mind races. Unless I release a blast of magic as great as the sand striker held, they're unlikely to notice raw magic. Remembering the signal Kherbanu sent up, I brush my hand against their staff, strapped to the saddle where I can easily reach it, thinking.

No, I need something brighter than that, something that will rise even higher.

I thrust my hand into my bag and grab one of my glowstones —it's the old one I brought with me, pale white against my palm. I focus my attention on it, altering its base spells until it will glow as bright as a small sun, shifting its colors for just that brief time to a bright red through the equivalent of a crystalline filter—the filter will fall apart quickly, but not as fast as the glowstone will burn out. I take another strand of magic from the quartz and loop it around the glowstone.

"We need to throw this as high as possible," I tell Huda, still clutching her waist with one hand.

"Here," she says, holding out her hand for it. "I'll use my sling."

"Do you want me to?" Laith asks, riding alongside us. He glances back toward me, and I realize what he won't say—that my presence gives Huda less space to move her arm.

Huda passes it to him without a word.

"I'll light it once it leaves the sling," I tell him. "Get it as high as you can."

He nods. I wrap one hand around Huda, my other closed around the staff, and watch as he whirls the sling once, twice, and on the third round he releases the end, sending the glowstone arcing up into the sky.

I touch the magic connecting it to my staff, and urge the stone higher, fueling its flight. As it hurtles toward the top of its arc, I light the stone. It shines for five brief, blood-red heartbeats, piercing my vision, and then it burns itself out, arcing back down to the ground.

I blink the streaks from my vision. So short. It was so short—

"There," Laith calls, pointing.

For one giddy moment, I think he means the mages have responded, but no, he's pointing to a slight rise in the land before us, the dunes having slowly given way to harder dirt, the same deep-cracked parched land I remember. Across that rise skitters a massive scorpion, its pincers dripping sunlight.

Severed sand strikers! That glowstone will have acted as another beacon to every blasted spell-creature left in the Burnt Lands, whether the phoenix noticed it or not.

I focus on the scorpion as it charges headlong toward us. It's almost automatic now, pulling the thread of magic from the quartz, reaching out through the draining spells, following them up to the scorpion itself, melding the threads, and so dissolving the scorpion's spell structure. I pull a measure of magic back to the staff, replenishing the quartz as the scorpion crashes to the ground, its legs splintering beneath it.

Barely three breaths later, we race past its broken body, giving a wide berth to the creature and its stinger, not quite drained of magic and still jerking as it slowly turns to stone.

We ride hard, the camels panting as they race over the ground. Val rides in front, seeking the safest and quickest route. He's doing his job; I need to do mine. I close my eyes, thinking about what the phoenix is setting in motion, what I designed. If anyone can stop this, it *ought* to be me.

"Huda," I say, "I'm going to talk this out loud, see if I can find a way to turn things around."

"Go ahead," she says. "I can listen."

I start with what I know. "Eshvat weakened the talismans. As they fail, they'll create a cascade of magic expanding out again. In theory, that magic will have to fight the flow of the magic already coming toward it. But it will likely be vast enough it will over-whelm the inward flow."

I pause, thinking about what I've learned of water from Kherbanu, because molten stone will flow as water does. "No, that's not right. The magic will explode outward and upward, and create a countercurrent over the original flow," I say slowly. "That current will run up against the Barrier. Even if the first impact doesn't overwhelm the Barrier, the Barrier will fall as the pressure increases—as the original inward flow reaches the center and reverses to join the countercurrent, rushing back out to the Barrier."

That doesn't leave me a lot of options, though. Still thinking out loud, I say, "I can't stop the talismans from failing—not from here. I can't stop the countercurrent from rushing out. And I can't anchor the Barrier from here or strengthen it enough to withstand the magic that will come at it."

"What can you do then?" Huda presses me, and I can hear the edge of urgency to her voice. "What's left?"

I don't know. Once the magic reaches the Barrier, what *is* left? "Maybe that's the moment I need to focus on. The moment the magic begins to build against the Barrier. That's where the flow has to change."

A wind whips past us, and I duck my head, blinking the grit it throws up from my eyes.

Huda reaches one hand up to adjust her scarf. "Sandstorm," she says. "Cover your face and eyes. The sand will blind you otherwise."

I scrabble awkwardly to adjust my scarf, untucking one end and wrapping it around my face. The thin, dark material creates a barrier I can still breathe through, protecting my eyes and mouth from the worst of the grit. But the burgeoning darkness from the storm makes it difficult to see—in clear daylight, there would be no such problem.

With one hand, I grip Kherbanu's staff. Since our fight with Eshvat, Kherbanu has added a shielding to the charms tied to the top—one I haven't seen before, though perhaps that's not saying a great deal. Based as it is in a white stone, the shielding moves with the staff, keeping everyone around it within its protective barrier. The moment I activate it, though, we'll bring the spell-creatures after us. I'll have to wait until we can't wait any longer—until the risk posed by both wind and magic rises too high. The phoenix's town is just ahead of us now, and under our feet the network of spells shines bright.

And then the latticework of magic beneath our feet brightens and begins to liquify.

"Huda!" I shout as the sand begins to heat with it. "Go left!"

Huda hauls on the reins, shouting, and the camel stumbles to the left, Val and Laith following suit.

"Go!" I shout as the sand behind us begins to melt and shift in a long, jagged line that grows smoother as it heats, the magic underfoot flowing toward the center of the Burnt Lands. I hadn't expected the magic to actually *melt* the Burnt Lands, even if that's what fire and stone do together. But this is a great deal more power at work than any of our experiments entailed.

"What was that?" Laith calls.

"Magic beneath the sand," I shout back. "They're starting."

Which means neither the phoenix nor the mages saw the glowstone. Of course they didn't. They're not watching the center of the Burnt Lands, they're watching each other. Or maybe it burned out too fast for the phoenix to see, and no one else took it seriously. Blasted mages.

We charge across the parched wasteland that lies between us and the phoenix's haven, the sand-laden wind obscuring our destination. This sandstorm isn't natural either—it's a result of the magical upheaval taking place. The winds pick up, screaming over the earth. Huda's camel stumbles beneath us, then regains its balance. Even with its double eyelids to protect against the sand, it cannot see the rocks underfoot clearly enough to travel with speed. I can hear Huda talking to it, urging it on, her tone gentle. Val is nothing more than a vague shape to my right.

With a growing sense of desperation, I activate Kherbanu's shielding charm. The dust around us begins to settle at once, the wind battering at the edge of the shielding. We're nearly to the town now.

"Handy, that," Val says dryly, tugging down the edge of his kufiyeh to see better as Huda and I adjust our scarves, the camels continuing on apace. Laith shakes the sand from his kufiyeh. At least we're all still together. If a spell-creature manages to find us through this storm, I'll just deal with it. There are enough massive shifts in the Lands' magic now, though, with the great vein of magic flowing behind us, that I don't think they'll pay attention to one little shield.

"Faster," Val says. The camels lurch forward, kicking back into a run. The buildings of the town rise up around us, the winds screaming through them in an eerie echo of the Howling Caves.

I cast my mage sight forward and spy the little loop of magic at the entrance to the haven—it's still holding, no major vein of magic running past it. Thank God for small mercies.

"What about that moment?" Huda calls back to me as we pelt down the road.

"What moment?"

"When the magic reaches the Barrier?"

"I'm thinking," I say, trying to focus again. Magic flowing outward, building against the barrier like a flow of lava against a dam, and then breaking through. Unless there's a way to release the pressure.

I think back to my work with Kherbanu, to that stream, the impossible quiet of those days, learning about the ways water can flow—not just currents but vortexes and whirlpools. If the magic is flowing out over the land and building at the base of the Barrier, then what I need is another flow—one drawing it up the inside of the Barrier and down again, to the talismans *I* have. I need to create a whirlpool of liquid stone, drawing from the top down, so that when the countercurrent flows to the Barrier, it will naturally be drawn *up*, along the dome of the Barrier, and back down again. If I can create a whirlpool strong enough—and if the Barrier can hold long enough—it might just work.

Out of the sand-obscured darkness, a forest of limbs rises: the banyan tree.

Huda reins in our camel, urging it to sit.

"Show them the way in," Val shouts at me as I scramble off. I can barely hear him over the tearing winds. He's doing something to his camel's pack.

"Not without you," I snap back. "What do you need?"

He shoots me a furious look and then orders, "Grab what food or water you have and let the camels go."

Ah, that's because he's hoping for our survival. For that we will need food and a few supplies, especially if the desert itself is destroyed. The camels will no doubt do better seeking shelter on their own than remaining here.

Huda and Laith are nearly as fast as Val in unstrapping the most vital items from their camels. They don't attempt to unsaddle the creatures, just pull free their halters. Huda lays a hand on her camel's neck, then turns to me.

"Hurry," I call out, and Val and Laith are with us a moment later.

Together, we stumble through the branches and pillar-like roots of the banyan to the phoenix's haven.

CHAPTER 37
SPINNING MAGIC

We send Laith and Huda down through the trunk of the banyan to the root-bound room below it, each of them taking some of the supplies with them. Val goes after them, throwing the rest down into the room before coming back out to rejoin me. I take the time to test the magic in the draining spells at my feet.

It's still there, but I have the sense that it will tear away soon. When I cast my mage sight out, the vein we crossed over is more of a river now, the heat of it spreading out to liquify the stone latticework underfoot and draw it after.

It's awesome in an absolutely terrifying way.

"What are you doing now?" Val asks, projecting his voice to be heard over the winds.

"I have an idea," I say, even though it's more of a hope than anything. "I think you should go below."

"I'm not leaving you."

"No," I say, looking past the shielding to the vague shape of the banyan around us, the reaching hands of the branches. "You can't help me with this kind of magic working. But if you go down and join me through our bond... maybe that will be a help." I can sense him looking at me, but the wonderful thing about

389

being actually next to him instead of having him in my head is he can't tell I'm absolutely lying. "You'll be able to steady me if I need it."

Val reaches out and sets a hand on my shoulder. "I'm right here, and I'll see this through with you. Stop wasting time and do what you need to."

Damn it.

"Come on, then," I snap, stumbling on the occasional root as I hurry out from beneath the questionable shelter of the banyan tree. Val follows behind me. I make it a few dozen paces past the last reaching bits of the banyan's canopy and come to a stop. From the bag still resting against my back, I pull out the array of talismans I've brought with me: the bangles and rings and jeweled turban all go in a heap on the ground—all except the ring that stores the sand striker's magic.

I sit down a few paces from them, Kherbanu's staff across my lap. Val settles a little off to my side. I pull out the ward string made of Stormwind's beads and pass the ends to Val. As he clasps them shut, enclosing us, I carefully tweak the wards' structure to allow magic to pass out while still protecting us from what lies beyond. Then I thread Eshvat's ring into one of the staff's carved wooden curls that holds the rose quartz. I bind the two together with a loop of magic and connect a second thread from the ring to the wards. Hopefully, such a store of magic will keep both protections steady. Any magical backlash will flow around us instead of overwhelming us, as a stream passes over a rock—so long as these hold.

"What are you going to do?" Val asks.

"Try to bring the magic down to the talismans from above. Like a whirlpool."

Val casts a look up, through the flying sands, and then down at the talismans right in front of us. "All right," he says, mostly to himself.

I take a thread of magic and loop it around the talismans before feeding it into one of them, the flow slow and steady. As the thread expands with the flow of magic, the other talismans should easily start drawing it in as well. Then I fashion a stronger thread and send it up, up, *up*, arcing through the magic-less air as the glowstone did, seeking the top of the Barrier.

I push with all my might, leaving my body behind to follow the thread of magic even as I urge it along, reaching for the very top of the spells contained within the dome of the Barrier. The draining spells here are more of a magical mesh than a latticework, fine as a sieve, draining every drop of sunlight and moonfall and lifebreath from the air.

I know how to work with these spells, perfected the technique with the phoenix. Now I draw on the stone of the sand striker already infused in the ring, and the fire in my bones, and the truth of how water flows, carried in my veins, to liquify the spells my thread touches. I fashion the stream of molten stone into a swirling loop. It isn't yet a whirlpool, but it offers the beginning structure for one.

I center it over the thread I followed up from Kherbanu's staff. Riding the magic, I cast around, aware of my body breathing hard and fast somewhere far away, aware of dirt pressed against a cheek that seems to belong to another person.

As if from afar, I feel the earth shudder. I can hear Val faintly, his voice muffled in the ears I have left behind. The phoenix's talismans have failed. The first wash of magic is flowing over the land. It parts around the protections I left behind and flows on to wash over the camels and any other creature so unfortunate as to be caught in the Burnt Lands. And still it flows, vast as the land itself, an ocean of molten stone rushing toward the Barrier.

A hundred *thousand* curses on Eshvat's head.

The loop shudders. I throw everything I have into it, steadying it, urging it on. I draw in ever more magic from the edges of the draining spells. Then the magic surge that rocked the earth below hurtles up the sides of the Barrier, as unstoppable as a tidal wave.

I don't want to stop it, though. I want to draw it on. As the magic rises to the forming whirlpool, it crashes over it, threatening to overwhelm it, to drown it before it can fully form. But, as

Kherbanu taught me, whirlpools are formed by opposing currents. This is what I *want*, the magic flowing up the Barrier from different directions, one side calm, while the magic flowing from the other directions rages past. We are not at the center here, and that is unexpectedly a blessing.

I draw on the crashing magic and the currents pour in from opposing sides, widening the loop and sending it spinning faster and faster. I pour all that I have into it, urging the molten currents to flow, reaching down now, into a slowly forming vortex.

I am fire and water and stone.

But I am not strong enough. The magic tears at my edges, flaying me. I will disintegrate here, and my body will die below, and the Barrier will fail, and a whole people I have never met will die because none of us—not the phoenix, not the gathered mages, not my friends and I—could stop what has gone wrong.

No, I scream into the magical storm.

This whirlpool will reach the ground. It will draw that tidal wave of magic after it—that wave of fire and stone. And the talismans will be enough to take the brunt of it. But the whirlpool still wavers, shifting its focus, teetering on the edge of tearing apart. And then the single thread I've spun up from the staff wavers and begins to fray.

The thread. I have used the phoenix's understanding of stone, and Kherbanu's teachings of water to get me this far. But I've still always thought of this magic as thread—that is what saved me when I first faced the kraken, seeing a seam that could be opened, rather than fiery stone. Around me, the whirlpool wobbles and dips, the currents too fast, the structure unsound. But one cannot spin thread without a spindle to center one's work, winding the thread around it.

I only have minutes left, a handful of breaths before the thread I have connected to the talismans fails. If I must die, then let me be the spindle that wraps these threads of fire and stone around it, let me be the central axis around which the whirlpool forms. I tear myself from the edges of the fiery vortex and throw myself into the wobbling center, spinning faster and faster as I go, drawing a river of molten magic after me even as I cling to the single, fraying thread that connects me to the talismans.

I am the center of it all: fire and stone together, flowing like water, the power of the greatest of storms concentrated into a single focused path. Around me, the magic streams like rivers of lava, molten red and glowing orange, streaming ribbons of heat and searing the air.

This must be done, I tell myself as I spin. Curving and curving, the speed at which I'm moving ripping at me, flaying me in a way that would have taken my skin had I worn any.

I know now that I don't want to be here, in the very center of this fire, giving my life—because a noble death is still death. I want so much to live, despite the pain and sorrow and abandonment, because there is so much more out there. Just as the elements balance each other, so does life when you're living it instead of hiding from it. I've only just started trying to live.

I think of Val waiting beside my body below, and Huda and Laith sheltering beneath the banyan tree, and the phoenix somewhere at the edge of this storm. I want to tell them I'm sorry. I'm so sorry. I wanted to stay with them. I don't want to leave them with my body, and no tomorrows left for us to sit together and sip qahwe and laugh and love.

But this must be done. *It must be done.*

I press the whirlpool down, strengthening the thread as the finest tip of the whirlpool spirals down it, slowly but steadily, the whirlpool centered on me now. I can barely think past the searing magic, my blood and bones singing with it. It's growing, reaching toward the talismans below, but I'm dwindling at the same time and I don't know if I can hold it long enough. I don't know if I can keep myself from dissolving into the flow around me. *Oh God.* I hold tight, all that is left of me a sense of my will and the fiery magic that is everything around me.

A light arcs through the sky above, a line of magic passing through the Barrier and skimming the edges of the whirlpool to spiral down to me. For a moment, I can see nothing but the brilliant light of it as it draws alongside me, and then my vision clears and I find the phoenix on wings of fire beside me, bright even against the backdrop of the whirlpool. The blues and purples of his shadows have never looked more beautiful—a sudden, deep relief from the magic that consumes me.

Hitomi, he says as the whirlpool spins around us. He is steadying it with me, the relief of it enough to bring me back to myself, my thoughts reforming. *How are you here?*

I've brought new talismans, I tell him, focusing on him. I'm not sure how we are even speaking; perhaps it is some special magic of his. *They can absorb this, if I can just keep it steady long enough.*

His head tilts, one beady eye trained on the ground below. Somehow, though the whirlpool spins on, it is still and quiet here in the center of it all. Beyond us, the winds whip trails of fire, and the whirlpool itself flows in shades of molten stone. He looks back at me. *Child, you must go.*

Doesn't he understand? *This work must be done.*

It must, but you are not going to go like this, he says, his voice in my mind achingly sweet. *I will see this work done for you and you will owe me another debt.*

What debt? I ask as we slowly sink toward the ground, encased in the tip of the whirlpool, the magic still roaring silently past us on every side.

You will live. That is your debt to me.

But what about you? I cry. I was willing to die here, even if I didn't want it. But if the phoenix is speaking of debts, of *living* as a debt, then he can't survive this either. He won't rise from this any more than I might.

I can't let you do this, I tell him. *Your life for mine—that's not fair! You're the phoenix. This land needs you. I need you.*

All things have an end, he tells me. *I have lived hundreds of years. This is my time. I can accept this end, as long as it is not yours as well. Your story needs to go on.*

The love of his words, the truth of his life, lived and relived, ending here so that he can give me the chance to live when I am only just figuring out how—it *hurts.*

I can't, I tell him.

I am not corporeal in this space—I have no physical body—and yet my eyes fill with tears that float away, drifting through the air before they disappear against the whirling fury that surrounds us.

Of course you can, he tells me, the winds sliding through his tail feathers, filling his wings. *You want to live; you're still holding on. Look. You have kept a connection not just to your talisman, but to your body. You are still holding on.*

I cast my gaze down, and see that it is true. That the thread I hold is twofold, separating near its base—one looping down to the talismans, and the other turning to pass through Kherbanu's staff to my hand. As the whirlpool strengthens, its tip slowly sinks toward the ground. When it reaches the separation, it will consume me on its way to the talismans. Every quiet moment we remain here, we sink a little closer to the ground, and my body.

There is little time, the phoenix tells me, so very gently, reminding me unexpectedly of Val. *Come, child, pass me the first thread, and follow your own back to your life.*

I look toward him, my tears like pearls in the air.

You can do it, he says.

I can, even though it hurts. The threads are wound around and through me, having turned with me as I made myself the spindle-like axis of the whirlpool. I separate them as if I were drawing apart a length of yarn, my tears still falling from my eyes. But I choose this now: to live, for myself, for the people I have left below, to be with them. Even as my heart breaks.

The phoenix's wingtips slide against my fingertips, and the whirlpool shudders, the thread I hold twining along his body.

Phoenix, I say, grief and love filling me.

I see the pride in his eye as he lifts his head, the whirlpool centering now around him, the wind whipping faster. *Fill your life with living,* he tells me, as if it were a debt of love he might lay upon me.

I love you, I tell him, shifting back, my life-thread slipping free of what he holds.

Be the impossible, my child, he says with wings upraised, the molten magic rising above him.

I will try, I promise, and then I am falling away, out of the stillness and through the wrath of the whirlpool, holding tight to the single, fine thread that connects me to my body below.

CHAPTER 38
HEARTSTONE

I slide through the empty air beyond the whirlpool, the thread I hold gossamer fine, almost rubbed away by the molten magic I have passed through. It is too thin, too hard to follow. My hold on it dwindles as each moment passes. I cannot find my way down, and my body is slipping away from me, even though I am seeking it now. I can't lose it, not when the phoenix gave me this chance—

Something tugs me forward, a connection that materializes within the thread itself, strong and pulsing with life. I find myself speeding across the darkness toward a body that is breathing again, calling to me as if it could guide me home. Does a body know its own name?

I slide into my skin, aware of a searing heat before me, the roar of magic made almost corporeal. The whirlpool must have touched down, connecting to the jumble of talismans.

My body shudders as I return, my breath rasping raw in my throat.

Stay with me, Val says urgently.

Here, I tell him. It was him breathing for me, him steadying my heartbeat. The bond we share is what brought me back here. Relief courses through me, and gratitude—his and mine, and then he is gone, back into his own body.

I tighten my hold on my body and realize I'm leaning against Val, who has propped us both up against the pillar-like roots of the banyan. Even without consciously using my mage sight, I can see the whirlpool pouring into the talismans, the crimson and orange of molten rock, the air whipping by at impossible speeds. The heat is scorching.

"*Hitomi.*" Val grasps my shoulders.

"Here," I repeat, my voice lost before it leaves my lips.

"We need to get to the haven," he shouts in my ear, barely audible over the whirlpool's roar. "Can you stand?"

The next moment, he pulls me to my feet. I stagger but manage to keep my balance. He presses Kherbanu's staff into my hand, the shielding somehow still active. It's the only reason we're not being flayed alive by the flying sand, or turned to ash. No—there's also the ward string. Val snatches it from the ground, unclasping it, and Kherbanu's shielding shudders as it takes the full brunt of protecting us.

"Come," he shouts, and half carries, half propels me toward the trunk of the banyan. It's a lot closer than I expected—he must have carried me away from the talismans.

I look back as we reach the crack, searching for any sign of the phoenix in the maelstrom of fire and stone. There is none.

"*Hitomi,*" Val shouts, holding me tight. "*Focus.*"

I force my attention back to him, to surviving. "Yes."

"Can you go ahead?" I nod, and he lets go of me, taking Kherbanu's staff back that I might enter the banyan first. I pause at the hole I must jump through, my head pounding. I'm too unbalanced to land safely. I'm going to break a leg or sprain my ankle or—

An arm wraps around me from behind, and then Val pushes us both off. I let out my breath in a wheezing squeak as we land, but Val somehow does something—I can't even focus on what, my eyesight fracturing from too much magic working.

"Hikaru!" Huda cries.

I hear Val responding to her, and then saying, "I think it worked. We can only wait and see now."

The phoenix, I want to tell him. But I have no more words left. As he lowers me gently to the ground, I slip into unconsciousness.

I HALF ROUSE to the vague sound of voices. A conversation slips in and out of my hearing, not quite real enough to wake me. Instead, I float along just beneath consciousness, aware that I am wrapped in something rough but warm. There is only gentleness here, the world a distant, muffled thing.

I could rest here a hundred years. I understand the stories of those who sleep through a century, why they wouldn't want to wake themselves. Why they'd let it all slip away. They've lived what lives they could, and the darkness is kind and undemanding. In this halfway place, the present is as unreal as the past, the future comfortably distant.

But the phoenix set me a debt, and I must learn to pay it. Even a month ago, I would have thought I didn't deserve this gift of my life, this last show of love from the phoenix. I would have dishonored his sacrifice by only focusing on what was lost, instead of what was given. But I understand now, even if I wept as I accepted it. Even now I grieve, my heart aching for the phoenix, who embraced the whirlpool, who took my place at its center so that I could live. And for what he called a debt, but was really his love.

"Hikaru," a voice calls softly but insistently. "Hikaru, can you hear me?"

"No," I rasp, without opening my eyes. My throat is parched, my lips cracked and tasting of dust and bitterness. It was so much better before I felt my body about me. But no, even this is good, painful but real, a reminder I'm alive.

Huda's arm comes around my shoulders, levering me upright. "Good. Can you stand?"

"A moment," I tell her, taking a mental catalog of my body. I'm mostly terribly achy and exhausted, but not hurt.

"We can't stay here much longer," she says, keeping her voice calm, kind.

I force my eyes open. Huda appears tired and drawn in the light of the pale glowstone that is, strangely enough, set atop the still-standing stone remnants of the pack creature that followed me down here eons ago. Its head is no more than a shapeless nob, its spines broken away so that it appears to be some sort of strangely made hump-backed little table. I stare at it, blinking.

Here are the things none of us expect to become.

"We need to make our way down to the cavern and find a spot to hide," Val says. I pull my attention away from the pack-table to see Val standing by the tunnel to said cavern. If Huda looks tired, he looks exhausted, shadows below his eyes, and his expression drawn. His thobe and bisht are darkened with dirt and ash, and his kufiyeh is missing altogether. He's tied his hair back tightly from his face. He says, "There appears to be a dragon on the way."

A *what?*

Val nods, interpreting my look correctly. "Since dragons fly rather quickly, we need to move."

I stagger to my feet, Huda taking the blanket from my shoulders. "It can't fit, though." No, wait, that's not right, as I learned at the Mekteb.

"It can if it's able to shift to a human form," Val says, apparently equally well-versed in magical flying reptiles with smaller mammalian alter-forms. Really, sometimes I don't understand magic at all.

"Where's Laith?" I ask, glancing around again. It's just me, Val, Huda, the glowstone on top of the pack-creature table, and Kherbanu's staff on the ground. Huda picks up the staff and passes it to Val.

"He's started down with our bags already," Huda says. "You go behind Val; I'll come at the back."

What follows is an exceptionally long and miserable crawl down the tunnel to the phoenix's main cavern. By the time I make it out the bottom, my arms and legs feel like jelly. I lie down on the wide stone shelf at the exit, dimly aware of Laith asking if I'm all right, and decide that moving again is overrated.

"Hitomi?" Val says with that gentleness that I have never

really appreciated before. It is something he reserves for me, a love and respect I never knew how to accept. I let it shore me up now, remembering how I heard it echoed in the phoenix's voice. "Is there somewhere here we can hide? In case the dragon brings mages with it?"

"Treasure room," I tell him, waving across the cavern.

"Excellent. You can direct me."

He kneels beside me, and the next thing I know, Huda and Laith heave me up onto Val's back to wrap my arms around his neck. He rises, wrapping his arms around my knees to keep me up, and starts across the cavern. It's at least more comfortable than being thrown over his shoulder like a sack of potatoes, as he carried me out of the tower in Kol's fortress. Huda and Laith follow us, carrying our belongings divided between them, though Huda keeps hold of Kherbanu's staff for me.

The small, relatively hidden room that contains the phoenix's treasure trove is difficult to locate in my current state. Eventually we find the slim hall-like tunnel leading back to the room with its piles of forgotten belongings. Val lets me down at its entrance, the tunnel too low to allow him to carry me. I'm steady enough to stumble along, a hand on the tunnel wall to either side.

"Val," I say as I walk, my brain beginning to process again. "How did you know a dragon was coming?"

"I went up close to dusk, once the winds died down, just to see if—to see what I could find. Your talismans are all there. I didn't touch them, but I found something else among them that I could not make heads or tails of. I brought it down for you to check. At any rate, I saw the dragon as I was coming back to the tree. It was still far, but it seemed likely it was headed this way."

My brow knits as I parse all of this. It seems a great deal of information, not all of it spoken. "What did you go to look for?" I ask.

Val sighs. "The camels. There's no sign of them. They may have survived, or they may have been destroyed by the magic. I couldn't tell."

Oh. That sounds like a problem for future Hitomi to worry

about. "What was it you found?" I ask instead, stepping into the treasure room.

He steps in after me and takes a small stone from his pocket, offering it to me on the palm of his hand. It is a strange, lumpy shape, its color a deep red that glows faintly in my mage sight. But there is no pulse to it, nothing beyond that last lingering light. I blink away my mage sight, my head pounding, and the stone is just a dull red thing, inert.

"What is that?" Laith asks as he and Huda crowd in beside us. "Is it a talisman?"

I shake my head. "No." It is something far more precious than that.

I think of the phoenix, able to fly like a star arcing through the sky. The phoenix, drawing the current to the talisman. If anyone could rise from such a conflagration, he could have.

But he didn't. There, on Val's palm, lies his heartstone, its fire gone.

There will always be death. It is the only surety any of us has, a truth phoenixes are well familiar with. Of all of us, only he had even the smallest chance of surviving—or rather, rising again. He didn't expect to; otherwise, he would not have laid the debt, or love, he did at my feet. But knowing that does not make this final, incontrovertible proof of the phoenix's fate any easier. The truth of it fills up my ribcage with sorrow and with love, with an unspeakable gratitude for what he gave me.

A phoenix's heartstone is a thing of great power, as rare as it is incredible. It has been fought over by armies and mages alike. It should flicker with fire as the phoenix had, pulse with magic as his heart once beat. But this does not. Its magic is now drained and captured within the talismans that had lain beside it.

The magic that lights it now is nothing more than a fading echo. The phoenix cannot rise again, and no one will come to fight over the right to raise him from his newfound youth and so gain his grace.

"Hitomi?" Val asks, the heartstone still cradled in the palm of his hand.

"He's dead," I say, and my voice cracks.

"Who?" Laith asks, twisting toward me.

"The phoenix. He drew the magic down at the end—and that is his heartstone."

Huda hesitates. "But—he's the *phoenix.*"

"All things have an end," I say, remembering the phoenix's words. "He chose this, that we might live."

Val takes my hand and places the heartstone in it, closing my fingers around it. "I am sorry," he says.

I remember how the phoenix grieved the children he lost crossing the Burnt Lands four hundred years ago. He died making the Lands safe once more, died so that I could live, so that the desert could prosper. I did not know that grief could hold such beauty, that gratitude and love and loss could go hand in hand like this.

Huda wraps me in an embrace, and I realize my cheeks are wet with tears. "Come," she says. "Come and sit and grieve."

I sit on a blanket someone has laid out on the floor. Laith puts out the glowstone before it can be noticed should anyone enter the cavern, and together we sit in the dark. I rest my head against Huda's shoulder, feeling her shake with her own sorrow, no less real for how little she knew the phoenix. He has been a part of her life in ways I cannot fathom, a story of hope in a dead land, passed down for generations.

Mostly, I let my tears fall for myself, and grieve the friend I have lost. Memories flow, of his flaws and kindnesses, and the feel of him, warm in my embrace as I held him that last time in the Howling Caves.

He gave his life for me, relinquishing the lives he might yet have been born to. As I once hoped that some part of me might live on with the phoenix, now it is his life and love I carry in my living. This is how he will continue in the world, the gift of his life melded with mine. So, I must learn to treasure this one small life I have.

CHAPTER 39
GUARDIAN

Eventually, we hear movement in the main cavern.

By unspoken agreement, we remain still and silent. It is hard to tell what is happening out there—only the occasional scuff of a shoe against stone reaches us, and once, the barely audible murmur of a voice. Whether it is one speaker muttering to themself, or addressing someone else also present, I cannot tell.

It would be exceptionally helpful to have someone among our number with preternaturally good hearing. Val can move quickly —and use his gaze to control humans, an ability I have conveniently allowed myself to forget, but he can't hear any better than the rest of us.

After a time, I attempt to use my mage sight. The phoenix and I had discussed the possibility of the talismans being brought to his haven, for spells to be set here that would funnel their magic back into the Lands. With his death, there will be no one to watch over the talismans, and no surety that they would actually be brought here. Unless the phoenix chose someone to take over in his stead? Unfortunately, my head is still too wooly, my senses overtaxed, and I cannot make out anything beyond the stone before me.

Footsteps sound suddenly, heavy and slow and louder than

any I've heard before, stone crunching like gravel underfoot. That would be the dragon then—though they must be a shifter to have made it down here in the first place. Not a good sign that they're back in dragon form, though.

"It is time to show yourselves," a voice says, the resonance of it huge, filling the cavern and echoing down the tunnel to fill our own little room. "I can hear the four of you. Come out and tell me why you are here."

So much for hiding.

Huda's hand closes on my wrist, and I hear Laith shift. Val lets out his breath in the faintest of sighs. "Ready?" he asks, as if we've planned this, or maybe just to make sure I can stand.

"Yes," I say, pushing myself to my feet.

There's no escape from this room without facing the dragon, and without the phoenix to champion us, I'm not sure how we'll escape what waits in the next room—unless it is the one dragon I've met before. Which seems vanishingly unlikely, but one can still hope.

I turn over the phoenix's heartstone in my hand as we shuffle toward the faintly lit tunnel. Wouldn't any dragon potentially be more forgiving if we came out bearing the phoenix's heartstone, intending to lay it to rest? I would do it anyhow, but perhaps if I start with that, the dragon will look on us more kindly.

Val puts a hand on my shoulder as I reach the doorway. "Do you want me to go first?" he asks, voice low.

"No," I tell him. "Not this time."

He drops his hand and falls in behind me as I make my way out.

A great creature fills the cavern before us, its neck long and snakelike, a slim, horned head peering down at us, and from its back, a pair of great leathery wings flexing slowly, sending a faint breeze to tease the edges of our clothing. A pair of glowstones placed before it lights the central space and brings the dragon's features into silvery relief.

"Ah," the dragon says, lowering its head to eye me. "It is you, little mage of many names."

It takes me two tries to speak. "M-master Jabir?"

"I should have expected you," he says, lifting his head again to look over our little group, his horns nearly brushing the great stalactites hanging from the cavern roof.

"You're a *dragon*," Laith says, as awed as I am. It is one thing to think *dragon*, or to see one from afar as I have once before, and a whole other thing to meet one face to face.

Jabir smiles, leathery lips drawing back from sharp teeth. "Indeed, young warrior. More than that, I am a Guardian." His gaze swings back to me. "I have left the Mekteb to guard the phoenix's haven until my aid is no longer required."

"We would not cause trouble," I assure him. "We only—"

Jabir snorts, and then he begins to rumble with laughter, the sound echoing off the cavern walls until everything vibrates with his mirth.

I feel myself flushing. *Really*. It's not like I said something that outrageous.

"I think," Val murmurs from beside me, "that he knows you almost as well as I do."

"Oh, hush."

There's no talking over a dragon's laugh, so I wait with growing annoyance until Jabir finally calms his amusement and returns his regard to me.

"We bear the phoenix's heartstone," I say somberly, as if he hadn't laughed at all. "I would lay it to rest here. We will depart as soon as it is done."

"Ah, child," Jabir says, tilting his head to inspect us. His gaze catches on my hand, clutched around the heartstone. Perhaps he can sense it even as it is nearly drained of magic. He knew I carried the phoenix's feather with me when I first entered the Mekteb, after all. He goes on, "I am glad you recovered his heart. Were you here, then, when the other talismans failed?"

I nod.

"I knew there must have been someone here, to begin what the phoenix ended with these talismans." He nods to the flat-topped stalagmite where the phoenix's nest sits. Instead of moving the nest, Jabir has used it: at its bottom, a score of colored gems glitter, the great diamond the phoenix acquired at their center.

I move forward, Val walking with me. In the light cast by Jabir's glowstones, the stream flows steadily, the various plants and little trees casting their small, uncertain shadows. They are no longer quite so green, their leaves beginning to yellow. Since I left, the phoenix must not have been able to spend as much time here as he used to, and now his light is gone altogether.

I cross the stream slowly, come to a stop before the stalagmite bearing the nest with its talismans. Not a single one of the smaller diamonds I spelled with Kherbanu lies among the colored gems. They all failed, just as we expected. Had Eshvat sabotaged the larger diamond, there is no way the smaller gems I brought could have absorbed the full magic of the Burnt Lands. Even looking at them now, it's mind boggling to consider the amount of magic that one diamond must have absorbed—perhaps an equal amount to the fiery whirlpool the phoenix guided down to the talismans I brought.

In my mage sight, the talismans blaze with magic just barely contained, from the smallest ruby to the great diamond. All around them lies a net of interconnected spells. Wards. Protections. And there I can see channeling spells as delicate as spiders' webs, drawing the magic of the talismans down into the earth and across the stone floors to curve up the cave walls and spread out into the earth from there, like a gentler, sweeter sibling to the draining spells that once held this land in thrall.

These spells were laid by a master. There is a beauty in the very nuance of the magic flowing around me, in the subtle complexity of each connecting thread as it creates just the right flow, a balance as unshakeable as the great banyan's trunk overhead. Rather than the molten wave of magic that I contended with, this offers the land the equivalent of a misting rain: something that can soak through the earth slowly but surely, permeating each stone it touches with a gentle magic that heals rather than destroys.

Behind me, Val shifts his weight, the movement enough to bring me back to my purpose. I turn over the phoenix's heartstone in my fingers, and then lay my burden in the hollow of the phoenix's nest, just shy of the talismans and their protective wards. I do not want to let it go, but there is nothing left to do, and the phoenix is beyond feeling any of this. I move my hand away, the heartstone blurring in my sight.

Jabir lets out a soft sigh and then—the shadows flicker. I look up to find him shifting from ancient dragon form to aged human, as if he were being concentrated down to his very essence, the shadows melding around him to obscure the process. It is over in the space of a heartbeat or two, leaving an older man of apparent desert descent before us. He wears a thobe and bisht, not unlike Val, but his pants beneath his thobe flap around knobby ankles, and he somehow carries a wooden staff that came along with his clothes.

"It was done well," he tells me, his voice sounding small now that it is only human. Though it isn't small, it's perfectly normal, if a bit dry from however many decades or eons he's lived. I nod, and step away from the nest as he says, "You were right."

Val curses, swinging around to search the shadowed depths of the cavern, but it still takes me a moment to understand Jabir isn't talking to us at all.

"Who—?" I twist toward the far end of the cavern, the tunnel up to the banyan, searching for the telltale flow of mage's robes in the darkness.

A figure rises from the shadows below the wide shelf leading to the tunnel. It is tall and slim, and sports a desert thobe and bisht. "I am glad of it," he tells Jabir, his voice warm. "Well met, Hikaru."

"*Stonefall?*"

He starts toward us, crossing the distance at an easy pace. "I believe I have you to thank for being singled out by the phoenix. He asked me to cast the final spells on the talismans here, to return their magic to the land."

"I thought that was Jabir," I say, bewildered.

"I gathered the talismans," Jabir says. "First from where we placed them with the phoenix, and then from outside this haven. It is Stonefall who has cast the spells you were just now studying. He developed them together with the phoenix."

I nod.

"Do you trust him?" Val murmurs, stepping forward to stand beside me.

"He helped me escape Fidanya—he gave me his horse."

"He moves like a rogue hunter."

My stomach twists. "He was one."

Val dips his head, his face thin and hard.

Jabir falls into step with Stonefall as the mage reaches him, and together they cross the remaining distance to us. At the same time, Laith and Huda walk forward to join us, lending their support to our number. Even if numbers are not how this game will be won. No, the best I can do is provide a focal point, so Val can go on passing as a human for as long as possible, and perhaps make it out of here untroubled.

"How did you guess it was me?" I ask Stonefall.

The corners of Stonefall's lips press downward, fighting a smile. "I asked myself if there was possibly another mage, marked by stone and fire, indebted to the phoenix, unknown to the rest of us, and reckless enough to attempt to create a new focal point, drawing on their own essence, when our first plan failed. Strangely enough, I couldn't believe it."

"I'm not *that* bad."

Stonefall grins. "I could not believe there was another mage quite like you, but word was you had also died. I am glad to see that was wrong, though I wonder at it. Ravenflight is not known for making mistakes."

"I, uh," I hesitate. Stonefall has aided me before; surely I can bring him around now?

Huda steps up beside me. "It is better that Hikaru's survival not be known," she says firmly. "We wish for her to live now."

It is an unconscious echo of the phoenix's words, the gift of his actions. I raise my chin, regarding Stonefall and Jabir together.

This is my life, and I will claim it for the sake of those who love me. "I intend to go on living," I tell them. "I ask of you your grace, for me, and for my friends. We came here only to aid the phoenix and prevent the failing of the work he began."

"*That* is what I want to hear about," Stonefall says, his focus sharpening. "I am glad you want to go on living—I have no reason not to support you in that—but how could you have known the talismans would fail?"

"I will tell you, though the story is perhaps best told by a mage you have not yet met."

Laith nods. "Mage Frozenfrog," he says helpfully.

I have a moment of absolute delight watching Jabir and Stonefall stare at Laith, their brows shooting up in astonishment.

"Mage Frozenfrog," Jabir repeats, as if he can't quite believe the words coming out of his mouth.

"Yes," Huda says, eyeing them curiously.

Stonefall coughs delicately into his fist.

"Right," Jabir says. "I will look forward to meeting them. First, though," he turns his attention back to me and says, "a phoenix's heartstone should never be left emptied."

"Will—will giving it magic help him come back?" I ask, barely daring to hope.

Jabir sighs. "I doubt it. There have been phoenixes that died and never returned. But as a mark of respect, it should not be allowed to go dark." He turns his gaze to Stonefall. "He died for the Burnt Lands to be made over. Perhaps you and the young mage might connect his heartstone to the magic of the land he hoped to save."

Stonefall dips his head and crosses the remaining few paces to us. My friends step away, allowing him to join me at the phoenix's nest. He makes a soft sound, looking at the little heartstone, cradled among the feathers and twigs of the much larger nest. Then he clears his throat and says, "I will adjust the spells to touch the heartstone as well. Is this where you want it to rest?"

I nod.

Stonefall bends his attention to the spells, working slowly but carefully. I watch intently as he works, ignoring how using my mage sight builds a slow ache behind my eyes. I've overextended myself, but a few minutes now won't cause any harm. I'll have time to rest my mage sight later.

The rest of my companions fan out around us, watching as well, though they can't see the way Stonefall expertly melds and parts the threads of the spells, drawing forth a single loop of thread.

"May I?" I ask hesitantly. "I would like to add a hint of fire."

Stonefall passes me the loop, watching with avid interest. Holding it, I reach deep inside of me to where my sunbolt slumbers, the fire lodged within my bones. I draw up a single spark, letting it brush against the stone within me, and slide through my veins to flow with the water within me. Finally, I feed it with the magic of the air around me, air the phoenix once breathed and warmed with his light. I want all four elements, for though a phoenix is fire, it is also a creature of the world, requiring a balance of all things. The spark strengthens until it is a steady flame of magic, pouring from my fingers to meld with the thread. Gently, I wrap it around the stone, thread and flame together.

Be warm, I think, gazing down at the heartstone as the magic I have shaped flows through it. I cannot bring the phoenix back, but I can offer him this final farewell, of companionship and light. *Be warm*, I think again, and lift my hands away. The heartstone glows at its core, outer stone deeper than any ruby, a spark bright at its center.

I sit back slowly, rubbing my palms as if I might hold on to the warmth still tingling through my hand. The heartstone brightens the nest, its light spilling over the edges. It is no more than a memory of the phoenix's fire, but it still makes my heart ache.

Stonefall rises and steps back quietly.

I gaze down at the nest, the heartstone glowing gently, the jewels glittering around it. At the edge of the nest, a single curling feather is caught, yellow shifting to orange and tipped with red, still pristine. I lift it up, holding it gently: one last feather to keep, but this one I will carry carefully instead of shoving into my boot. I know it won't last; one day I will lose it, or it will grow ragged and break. But for as long as I might carry it, I would like to keep it.

"Come," Stonefall says. "Let us all take refreshment, and then perhaps you can tell Master Jabir and me how you came to be here."

"*And* what happened to your hair," Huda says from behind me. I turn to find her eyeing me severely.

"Oh," I say with some confusion, "I forgot." I reach up to touch my bare scalp.

"You wore a turban and then a scarf," Val tells me helpfully, "right up until the winds whipped it away while you were fashioning your little storm up there."

"Oh, right," I say, smiling faintly, the feather still soft against my palm.

"I cannot believe you forgot about your hair," Huda says, shaking her head. "Even if those inkings are quite lovely."

Stonefall makes a slight choking noise and gestures across the cavern. "There is much to talk about, it would seem. Perhaps over qahwe?"

Val dips his head, watching Stonefall cautiously, as if he were a new kind of creature never encountered before.

A dragon, a breather, and a rogue hunter sit down together for a cup of coffee, I think, as we follow Stonefall to where he's left his gear.

Pretty sure I can make the end of that story work out.

CHAPTER 40
EVERYTHING WARM

Two rounds of qahwe and a long conversation later, I have shared my story, augmented by Huda and Laith's observations and additions. While I don't tell everything from my sojourn with the maran, I do promise Stonefall the chance to speak with Kherbanu once we meet again. I describe the whirlpool I created, and the phoenix's choice to take my place. It is hard to speak of, even though I have already told it once, but Stonefall and Jabir listen quietly.

In the end, Jabir says only, "It was well done."

Stonefall, in turn, tells us of his work with the phoenix, and how things unfolded as he stood at the edge of the Barrier. "I believe every mage who stood at its edge did their utmost to steady it, once we realized the power overtaking it from the other side. I did not expect us to succeed. While I have studied the Barrier before, I doubt any of the other mages have done so. We could not have held it in place more than a few minutes, if that, had you not drawn the magic away into your whirlpool."

It is awe-inspiring to realize how vital it was that each and every person there did what they could. The Barrier would have fallen without Stonefall and his cohort of mages, just as it would have fallen without the talismans Kherbanu spelled, or the whirlpool I conceived, or the phoenix's aid in focusing it and

413

completing my work. It would have also failed without Val to protect my body and life while I worked, without Huda and Laith's expertise in guiding us through the desert, without so many great and little things.

We succeeded only because we each tried.

By the time we are done sharing our stories, it is the tail end of an incredibly long day. Even if I slept through a few hours of it, I still feel stretched thin from what I've been through—and my companions appear utterly exhausted. Even the qahwe cannot keep us awake.

By unspoken agreement, we lay out our blankets. We have only the one that Huda wrapped me in before, though Stonefall came prepared and shares his supplies. Between his two blankets and a spare bisht, there are covers enough for the men, and Huda and I share our blanket.

Jabir kindly transforms back into dragon and his bulk warms the cavern to a comfortable temperature over the course of the night.

Come morning, we gather our belongings. I leave behind only one thing: the golden glowstone Kherbanu gifted me, linked to what remains of the magic in Eshvat's ring. Stonefall helps me create a spell that will tie the glowstone's brightening and dimming to the rising and setting of the sun, and we leave the ring and glowstone together at the center of the tiny grove. When I look back before leaving the cavern, the glowstone shines like a miniature sun surrounded by the slender trees the phoenix so loved. Eventually, the glowstone will run out of magic and the trees will die. But that day is not today, and that is all that matters to me.

I cast one final look at the faint red glow emanating from the phoenix's nest, and then I turn with my friends toward the tunnel up to the banyan tree. A faint *halloo* drifts down to us.

"Did you hear—?" Huda asks, brow furrowed as I stick my head into the low tunnel, listening.

"*Is anyone there?*" a voice calls, the words somewhat garbled by the distance they have traveled.

"Let me go first," Val says, and the next moment he is past me and halfway up the tunnel, because *of course* he can scramble through such a tight space like a godforsaken spider. I shake my head. *Breathers.*

By the time the rest of us make it up to the root room, it's to the wonderful news that Kareem, Kherbanu, and Rewniz have arrived.

I send Huda up first to her brother, then haul myself up the rope after her. Laith passes Kherbanu's staff up to me through the entryway and then I sidle through the crack in the trunk into a different world.

The morning sun paints a stark picture. This side of the tree has been stripped away, though behind me some part of the banyan I remember still stretches out like a small, debris-strewn stone forest. But here, a few broken stubs of the great branches stick out like misshapen lumps overhead. The rest of what once crossed this space—the spreading branches, the pillar-like support roots—all of it is gone, their remains merely coarse grit that crunches underfoot. Before me stretches a strip of debris-littered dirt, dark with ash, and then a vast circular swath of utterly scorched earth.

The buildings that faced the banyan on this side are as torn apart as it is, whole sections missing. Only a segment of wall toward the back remains. The ruined buildings are likewise littered with debris—whatever the whirlpool tore from its place but did not actually suck in. Everywhere lies proof of its destructive power, now contained within a scattering of talismans.

I can almost hear Kherbanu saying dryly, *You young people are so dramatic.*

I cough on a laugh, and Kherbanu themself stumps over to fold me into a hug. "Oh, child," they say. "We feared you had died."

I hold them tight, and then step back again. "The phoenix gave his life to focus the magic here," I tell them.

"Oh, my child," Kherbanu says softly, watching me steadily.

"Will you walk with me and tell me what happened? I know only what I saw from the Barrier."

I nod, offering them back their staff. Kareem calls a greeting to me, standing beside his sister. I wave to him, nod to Rewniz. Then, I walk with Kherbanu across the blasted landscape, following the edge of the square around what remains of the banyan.

I launch into an unabridged version of events, none of it hard to speak of until I reach the phoenix's words to me in the center of the whirlpool. The tears come as they did before, but they no longer hurt so keenly. There is just a faint ache where a part of me that was broken has healed, the phoenix's love carrying me even as I grieve him.

Kherbanu says, thoughtfully, "So, the phoenix chose you."

I hold their words within me, a light to warm my heart, and admit, "He did." Is it strange to realize I will cherish the debt the phoenix gave me as much as I hope to cherish my life? It will keep him close to me always, even as I struggle to figure out what it means to live.

Kherbanu raises their eyes to me, their gaze steady, looking right into me, seeing the things I don't say, the things I don't want to acknowledge. "Tell me, child, what is it you want next? Everything you have done has all been debts and responsibilities. Your debt now is to live, and for that you must choose: what do *you* want?"

I glance at them askance. "There are always responsibilities," I argue. "I have promises I've made, people who are giving up things for me that I need to do right by. I can't just suddenly decide nothing matters except me."

"No," Kherbanu agrees. "I don't mean you should turn your back on everything. But can you not find a way to" —they wave a hand— "come out from beneath the rock you've been living under, and walk in the sunlight a bit? You see I am doing that myself while I carry my people and their needs, and all my responsibilities, with me. What is it that you want—what is your sunlight?"

I turn the question over in my mind. "I don't know," I admit.

Kherbanu rubs their hand over their mouth, pulling down so firmly that, for a moment, their wrinkles all but disappear. "Let me ask this another way: what are the things you've taken away from yourself? What are the hopes you should have nurtured instead of burying?"

I rub my arms, not sure what I want to say, how to find words for these truths. I think of Osman Bey's farewell: *Run far, run fast, keep the wind in your hair.* If I could choose where to run—for myself, not for others—where would I go? If I could choose that wind in my now-gone hair, where would it take me?

And even still, I don't know. I've never asked myself these questions before.

Perhaps it will be easier to start with the things I don't want. I don't want to remain in the desert the rest of my life, joining Huda's family and learning to live among the desert folk—or even going to live with my uncle. Maybe one day, but not yet. I also don't want to go with Val to meet his prince, no matter if that prince is his brother, because that will be one more person trying to control me or decide my fate, and I don't want that. I don't think Val does either, even if it means his exile, and for now, I can let him make that choice.

What *I* want is to see Kenta again, and tell him I'm sorry for abandoning him, for taking away his choices when he was trying to be a true friend to me.

I want to travel with Huda and Laith to meet their families, and celebrate their wedding with them, because Huda is like a sister and I want to be there for her as she has been for me.

And then, finally, I want to take what I've learned, marked as I am but still more than capable of working with magic, and go back to Karolene. I want to see the streets I barely remember, and taste the food I've forgotten, and ask the Shadow League if I can help fight back against Blackflame. Because Karolene is home most of all to me, even as I've lost so many of my memories of it. If Karolene is burning, then I want to offer my fire as a weapon in return.

"I know what I want," I tell Kherbanu, my voice steady once more. They eye me expectantly. "First, I have a wedding of a very good friend to attend, right here in the desert."

"Weddings are good," Kherbanu allows.

"Then I wish to make peace with an old friend, which is certainly also for me."

"Because you feel guilty?"

"Because I cannot feel better until he knows I'm still alive—that I intend to go on living. And because I abandoned him when he was helping me, and I need to apologize for that."

Kherbanu makes a face but allows this to pass. "After that?"

"Then I want to go back to the land that—that *I* adopted, and see its streets again, and find the people I once knew, and offer my magic working to help protect it."

"It's under attack, isn't it?" Kherbanu says. "Or in danger in some way. And you are going to try to convince me that this is the path you want your life to take, the fire you need to throw yourself into. For you."

"Well, yes," I admit. "But I haven't let myself believe I *could* go back. I want this, very much." I suppose figuring out how to live is a process if you're not used to doing it.

"Mmm. Well, it's a start at least." Kherbanu turns toward where our companions are gathered, leaning heavily on their staff. "Though I cannot *imagine* getting on a camel again for at least a month."

I cough on a laugh. "I'm not planning to leave the desert right away," I assure them. "I have a wedding to attend."

"You," Kherbanu says emphatically, "are going to bed early every night for the next week."

"Unkind!" I cry. "Surely, I can stay up late if I take naps during the day? I'm quite certain weddings are celebrated at night in the desert tradition."

"Not my concern," Kherbanu says and passes me their staff with such abruptness that I find myself holding it before I realize what they've done. "It seems, since you are intent on seeking trouble, you had better keep that by you."

My hand tightens around the smooth wood. "This is too much," I protest. It was one thing for Kherbanu to lend me their staff, decades in the making, when I was riding into the Burnt Lands in a desperate attempt to save the surrounding peoples. It's very different to simply give it to me now, when there's no imminent danger, and no indication that we'll meet again once I finally leave.

"It's a stick with a rock on it," Kherbanu snaps. "Now give me your arm so we can go back to the others."

I do. Kherbanu threads their arm through mine and leans on me just a little as we walk. The staff feels comfortable in my hand, and I have to blink to keep my eyes from filling again. This is love that I hold in my hands; it is friendship and care and everything warm. I'm unutterably grateful for it. "Thank you," I finally say. "I will treasure it and keep it by me."

"You had better, you absolute disaster of a child," Kherbanu says and pats my arm kindly. "Now, let's go see what your friends have decided. I can only hope they have decided a nap is the best way forward."

I laugh and lead them back to where my friends are gathered. There will be plenty of time for me to decide where I will go from here, and how. For now, I am happy to rest in the company of my friends, and begin finding ways to walk in the sunlight again.

Acknowledgments

Debts of Fire has been a very long time coming, and I am so grateful to the readers who have stayed with me, waiting patiently for Hitomi's next adventure. This story was incredibly difficult to write, with all its myriad griefs and joys, and the emotional truths Hitomi has had to face. I give my heartfelt thanks to the many beta-readers, writers, and friends who have helped me find my way through this story in order to bring it to you—I could not have done this alone.

Many thanks to Shy Eager, Anne Hillman, Christine Elizabeth Kelly, Ashley Lambert, T.L. Shreffler, Charlotte Michel, and Elisabeth Wheatley for an initial beta read of an extremely flawed and broken story, and to W.R. Gingell for helping me to pin an ending on that first draft.

Sincere gratitude to the Highlights Foundation and Doris Duke Foundation for their work in creating the Muslim Storytellers Fellowship—and thus the community and love that has carried me through much of my time writing this book. Extra special thanks to fellow MSF storytellers Diana Ma, Loretta Chefchaouni, and Heba Helmy for a second round of beta reading, and for letting me get away with a draft that was suddenly, sadly, without an ending (again!). Sorry about that cliffhanger; I didn't know what happened next either!

I am eternally grateful to long time Writing Circle cronies and author friends AC Spahn and Anela Deen for yet another round of beta reading, accomplished in stages as I battled to make my way through my draft, and for the insight that finally helped me find my way to the ending this story needed. Additional thanks to my dear friends Virginia McClain and Emily Lo for a final, high intensity read to catch lingering issues and tighten the storyline. And of course, deep gratitude to Laurel Garver for her line-editing wizardry, and Batool Al-Khawaja and Diana Cox for their proofreading prowess.

Just in case you imagined I did the rest myself, I am so very grateful to Iris Bauer, Emily Lo Gibson, and fellow authors Tansy Rayner Roberts and Kel E. Fox, for helping me with those final, ornery chapter titles I didn't know what to do with. I am further indebted to long-time reader and friend Katie Bruce for suggesting Debts of Fire as a tighter version of my original title concept, because naming is definitely not my superpower. (Additional shout out to Katie for coming up alongside me to help me plan Debts of Fire's release and launch the deluxe edition Kickstarter—so grateful to be working with you!)

I'm also so grateful to Lyssa Chiavari and the team at Snowy Wings Publishing for everything you've done to give this story a chance to fly, and for supporting so many authors. Thanks to Yasu Matsuoka for this utterly gorgeous cover art, and to my dear friend Virginia McClain (again!) for the beautiful typography, as well as her graphics wizardry for the deluxe edition Kickstarter campaign. A shout out to Kerstin Espinosa Rosero for these fabulous chapter header designs - I love them so much! And to Namra & Aqsa Tahir for the beautiful full-spread illustrations in the print editions. You all are amazing!

It takes a village to raise a child, and Hitomi (my disaster child extraordinaire) is no different. Thank you all so much!

My family, as always, has continued to be a fabulous support crew. Thanks to my two (no longer quite so young) daughters for making do when I had to take emergency writing retreats, or picked up yet another pizza for dinner. I am so amazed to see the wonderful young women you are growing up to be, and so grateful to be sharing this life with you. Gratitude also to my husband, my parents, and my brother and his beautiful family, for all your wonderful support along the way.

It bears mentioning again how grateful I am to the wonderful readers and reviewers who have kept Hitomi company on her adventures, and helped to share her story through reviews and conversations. Thank you for continuing to help this series find its home in readers' hearts.

Finally, I am grateful to God for all that He has given me, in my writing and in my life.

ABOUT THE AUTHOR

Intisar Khanani grew up a nomad and world traveler. Born in Wisconsin, USA, she has lived in five different states as well as in Jeddah on the coast of the Red Sea.

Intisar currently resides in Ohio, with her husband, two daughters, and two cats. In a previous life, she wrote grants and developed projects to address community health and infant mortality with the Cincinnati Health Department — which was as close as she could get to saving the world. Now she focuses her time on her two passions: raising her family and writing fantasy.

To keep up with what Intisar is working on next, join her monthly newsletter at booksbyintisar.com/newsletter. You can also follow Intisar for free on Patreon for sneak peeks, book recs, and more.

www.ingramcontent.com/pod-product-compliance
Lightning Source LLC
Chambersburg PA
CBHW051428190726
48289CB00001B/105